Facebook: **facebook.com/idwpublishing**
Twitter: **@idwpublishing**
YouTube: **youtube.com/idwpublishing**
Tumblr: **tumblr.idwpublishing.com**
Instagram: **instagram.com/idwpublishing**

Cover Artist
Jenn Woodall

Series Editor
Elizabeth Brei

Series Assistant Editor
Riley Farmer

Collection Editors
Alonzo Simon and
Zac Boone

Collection Designer
Jeff Powell

ISBN: 978-1-68405-760-3   24 23 22 21   1 2 3 4

SLEEPING BEAUTIES, VOLUME 1. MARCH 2021. FIRST PRINTING. COPYRIGHT © 2021 STEPHEN KING AND OWEN KING. The IDW logo is registered in the U.S. Patent and Trademark Office. IDW Publishing, a division of Idea and Design Works, LLC. Editorial offices: 2765 Truxtun Road, San Diego, CA 92106. Any similarities to persons living or dead are purely coincidental. With the exception of artwork used for review purposes, none of the contents of this publication may be reprinted without the permission of Idea and Design Works, LLC.

IDW Publishing does not read or accept unsolicited submissions of ideas, stories, or artwork. Printed in China.

Originally published as SLEEPING BEAUTIES issues #1–5.

Jerry Bennington, President
Nachie Marsham, Publisher
Cara Morrison, Chief Financial Officer
Matthew Ruzicka, Chief Accounting Officer
Rebekah Cahalin, EVP of Operations
John Barber, Editor-in-Chief
Justin Eisinger, Editorial Director, Graphic Novels & Collections

Scott Dunbier, Director, Special Projects
Blake Kobashigawa, VP of Sales
Anna Morrow, Sr Marketing Director
Tara McCrillis, Director of Design & Production
Mike Ford, Director of Operations
Shauna Monteforte, Sr Director of Manufacturing Operations

Ted Adams and Robbie Robbins, IDW Founders

Sleeping Beauties

BASED ON THE NOVEL BY *STEPHEN KING* AND *OWEN KING*

ADAPTED BY *RIO YOUERS*

ART BY *ALISON SAMPSON*

COLORS BY *TRIONA TREE FARRELL*

LETTERS BY *CHRISTA MIESNER*
AND *VALERIE LOPEZ*

AMHERST PUBLIC LIBRARY
221 SPRING ST.
AMHERST, OH 44001

ART BY ANNIE WU

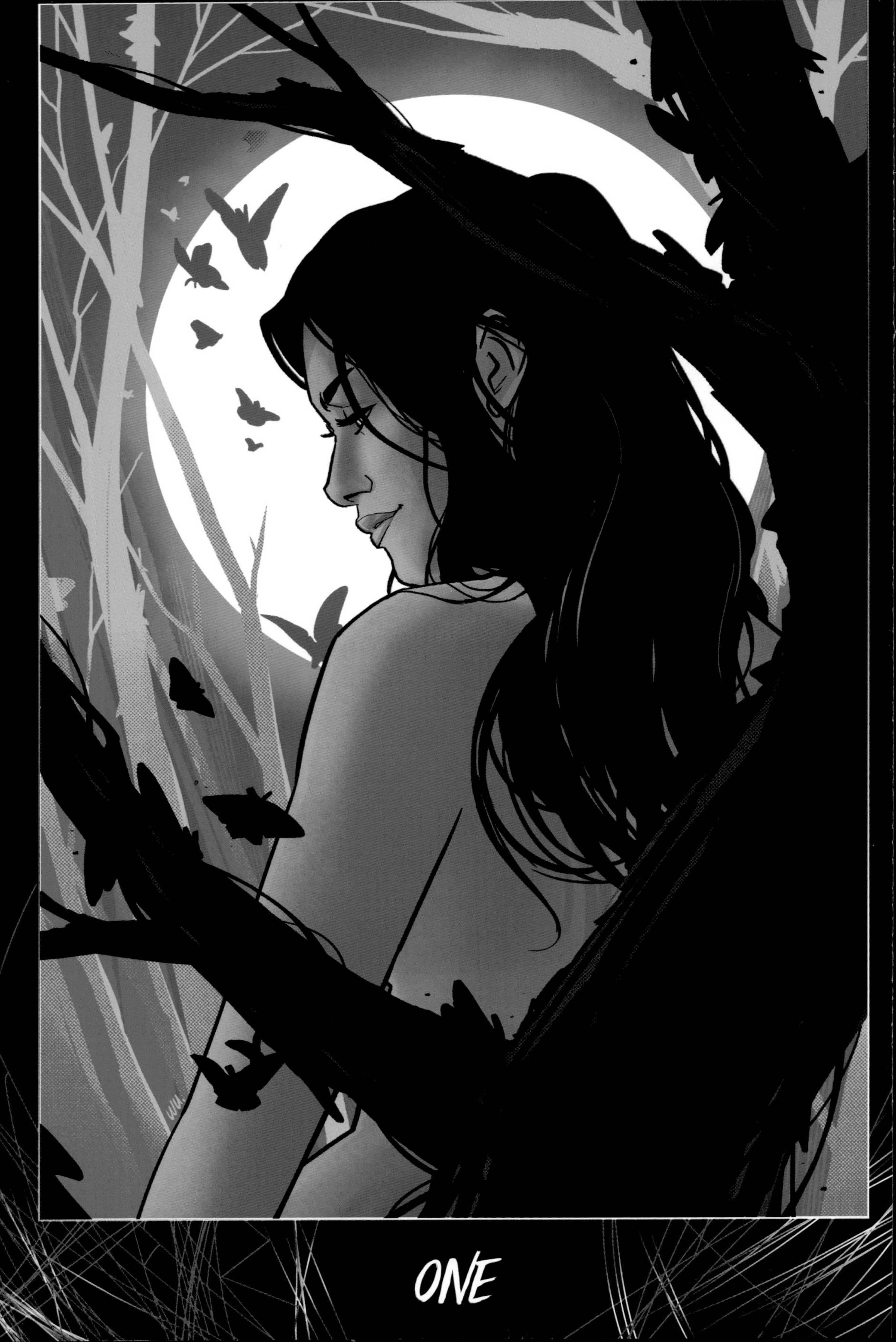

ONE

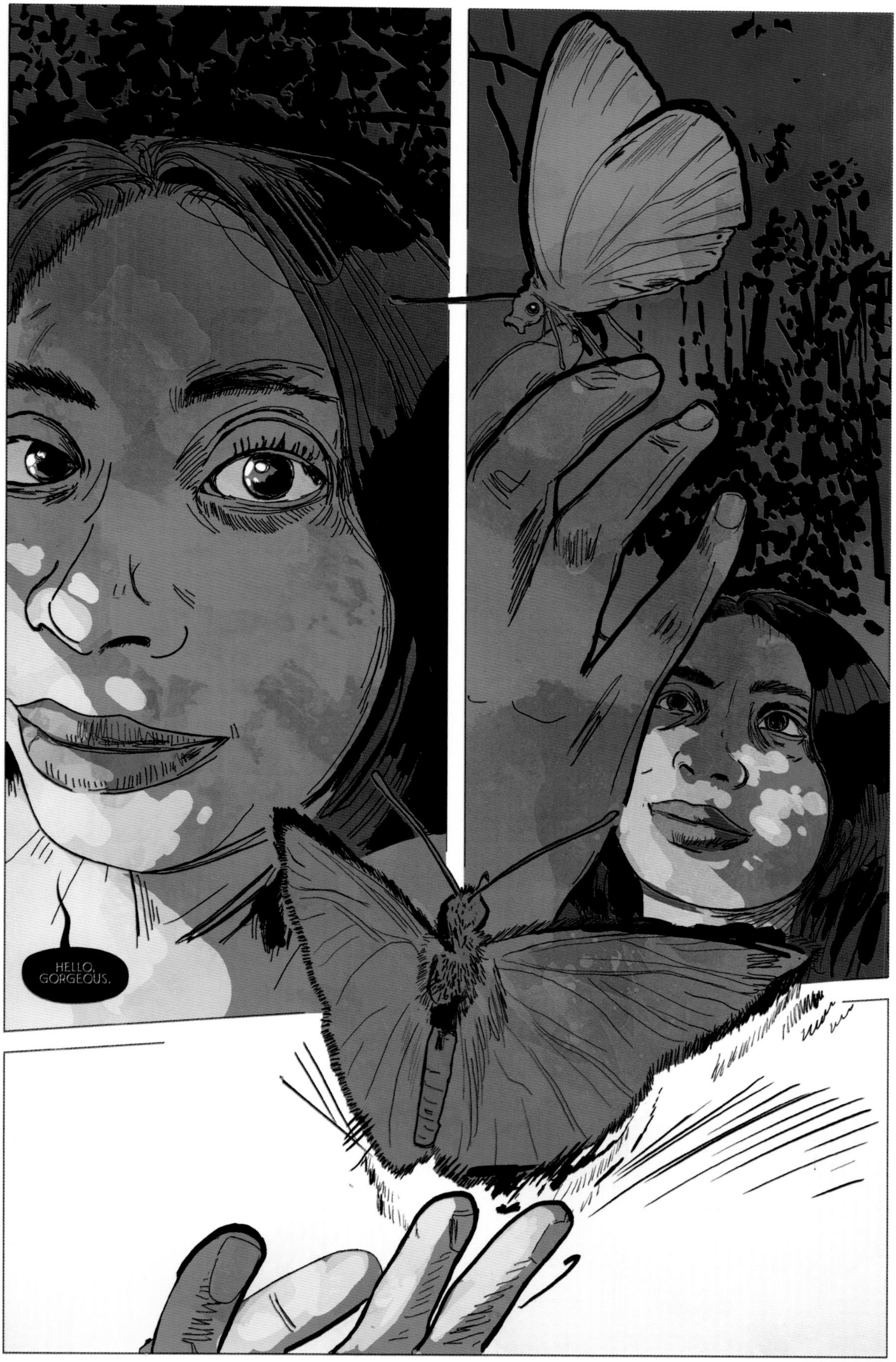
HELLO, GORGEOUS.

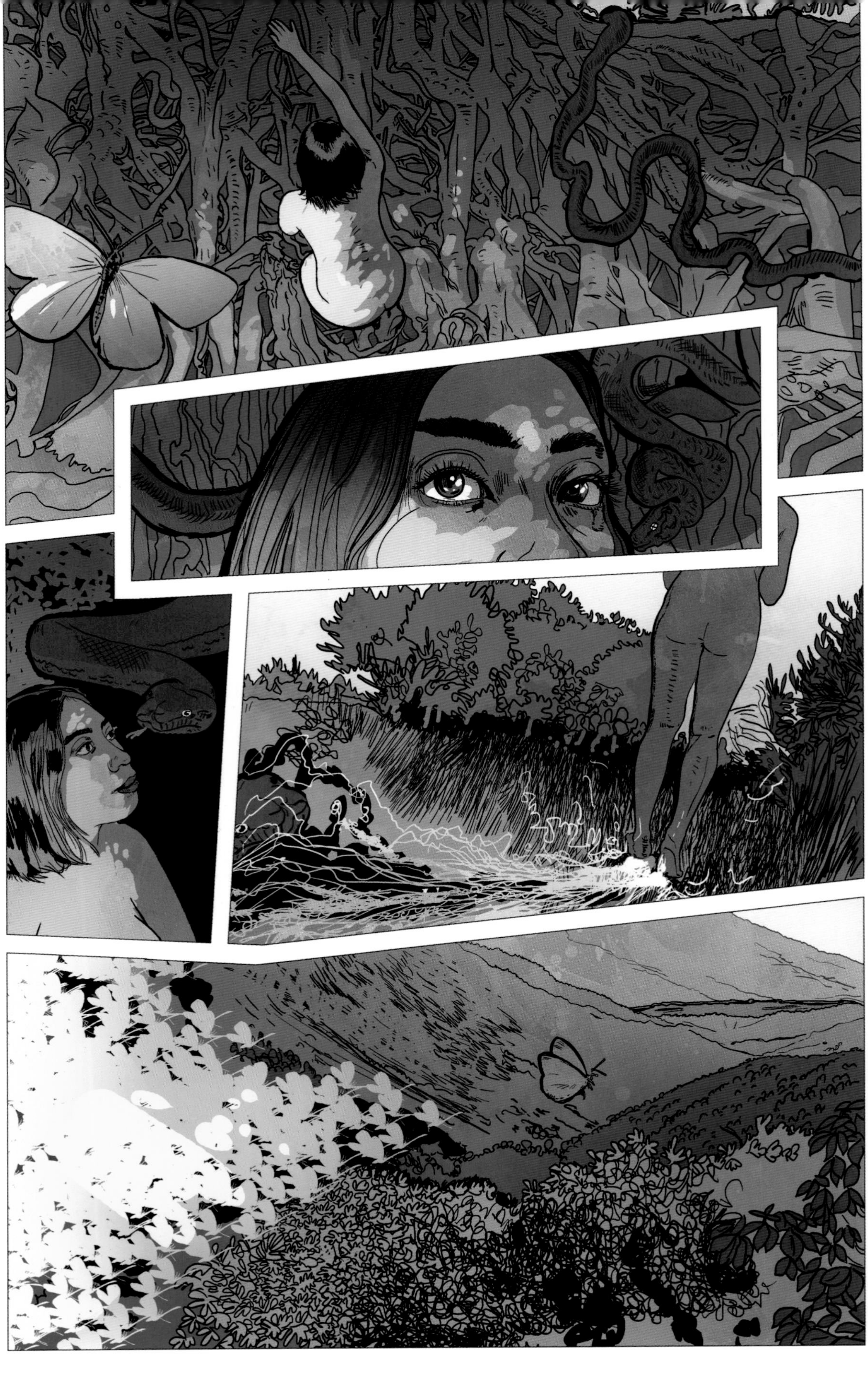

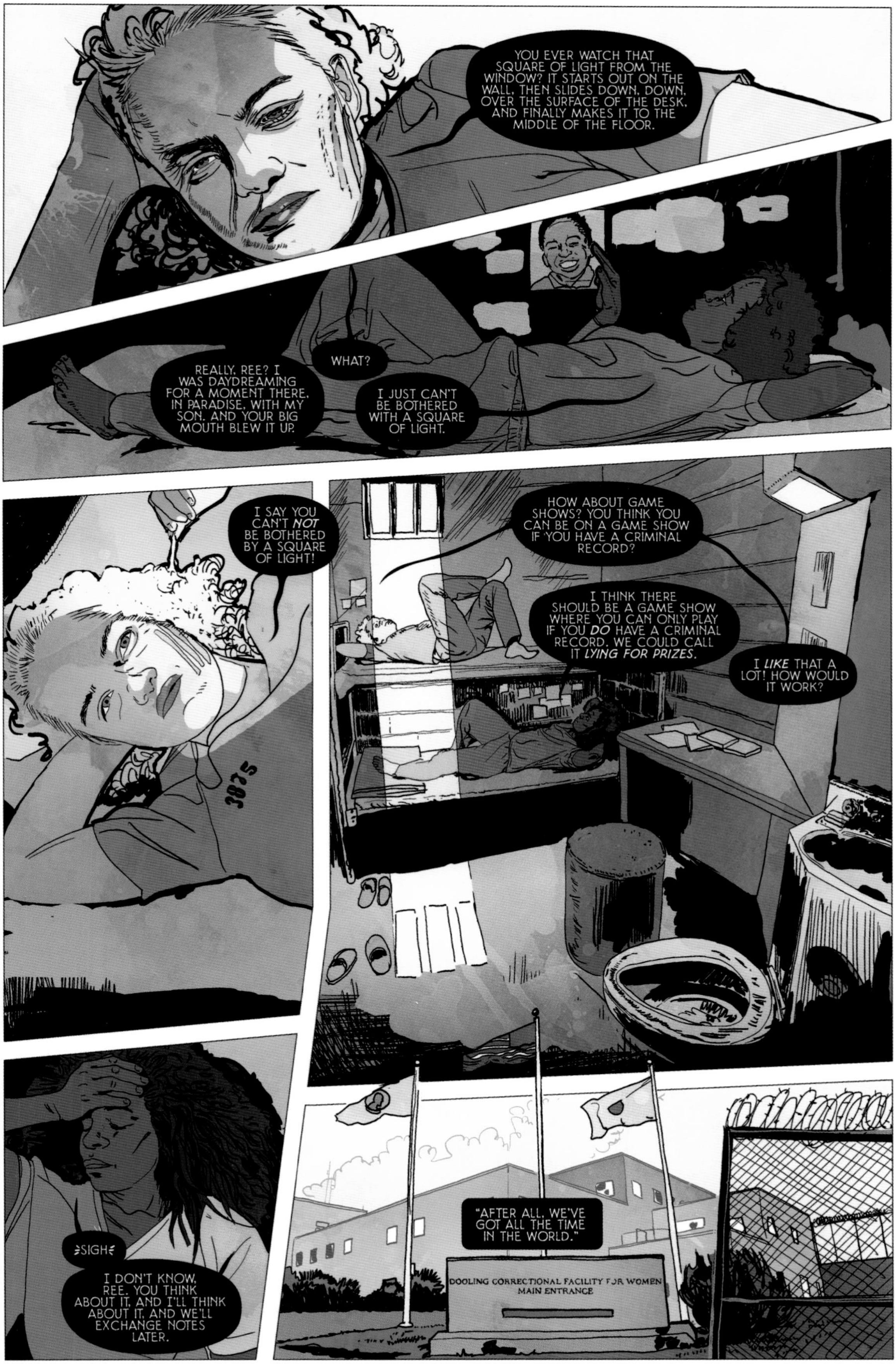
YOU EVER WATCH THAT SQUARE OF LIGHT FROM THE WINDOW? IT STARTS OUT ON THE WALL, THEN SLIDES DOWN, DOWN, OVER THE SURFACE OF THE DESK, AND FINALLY MAKES IT TO THE MIDDLE OF THE FLOOR.
WHAT?
REALLY, REE? I WAS DAYDREAMING FOR A MOMENT THERE, IN PARADISE, WITH MY SON. AND YOUR BIG MOUTH BLEW IT UP.
I JUST CAN'T BE BOTHERED WITH A SQUARE OF LIGHT.
I SAY YOU CAN'T *NOT* BE BOTHERED BY A SQUARE OF LIGHT!
3875
HOW ABOUT GAME SHOWS? YOU THINK YOU CAN BE ON A GAME SHOW IF YOU HAVE A CRIMINAL RECORD?
I THINK THERE SHOULD BE A GAME SHOW WHERE YOU CAN ONLY PLAY IF YOU *DO* HAVE A CRIMINAL RECORD. WE COULD CALL IT *LYING FOR PRIZES.*
I *LIKE* THAT A LOT! HOW WOULD IT WORK?
SIGH
I DON'T KNOW, REE. YOU THINK ABOUT IT, AND I'LL THINK ABOUT IT, AND WE'LL EXCHANGE NOTES LATER.
"AFTER ALL, WE'VE GOT ALL THE TIME IN THE WORLD."
DOOLING CORRECTIONAL FACILITY FOR WOMEN
MAIN ENTRANCE

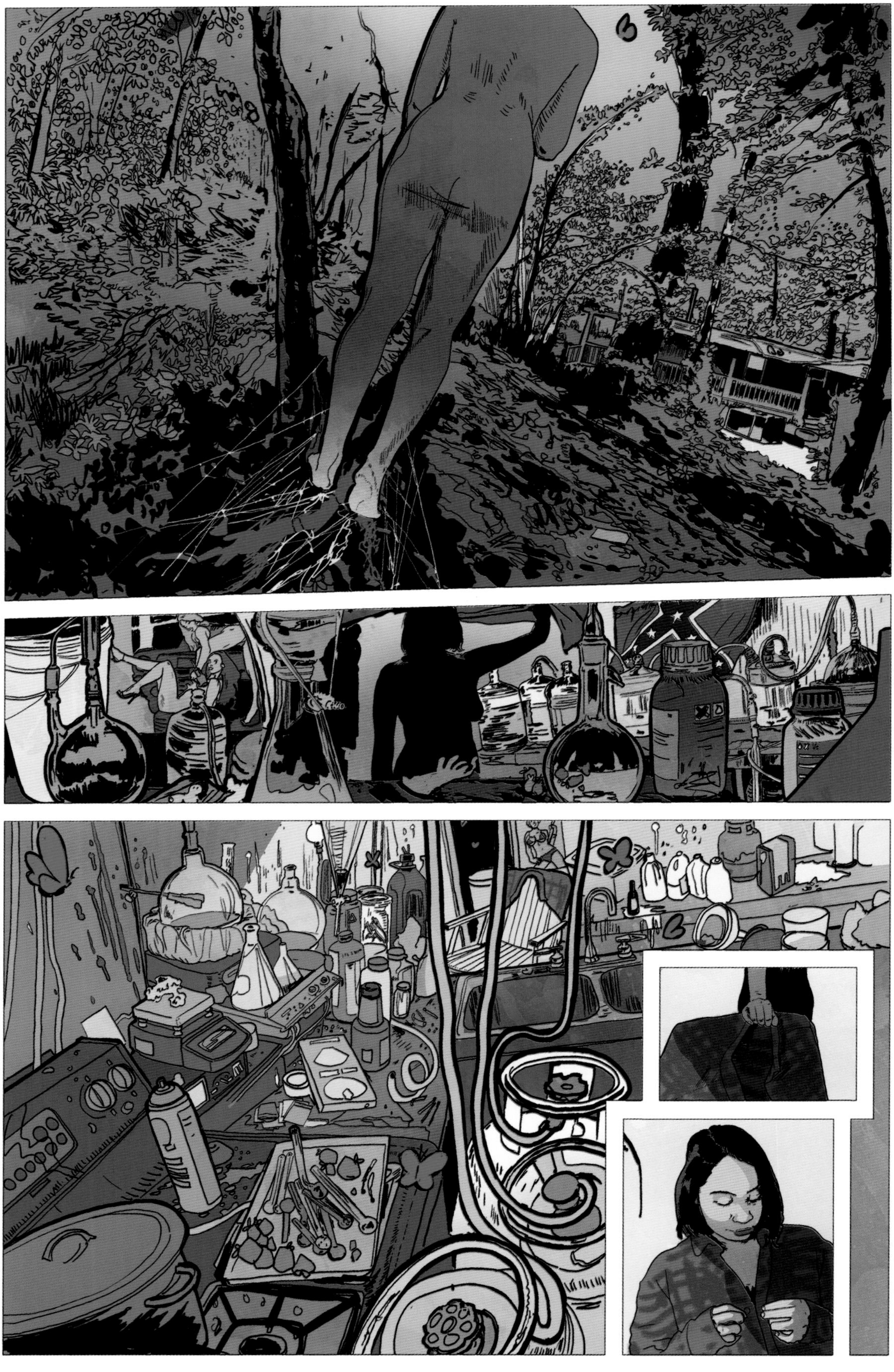

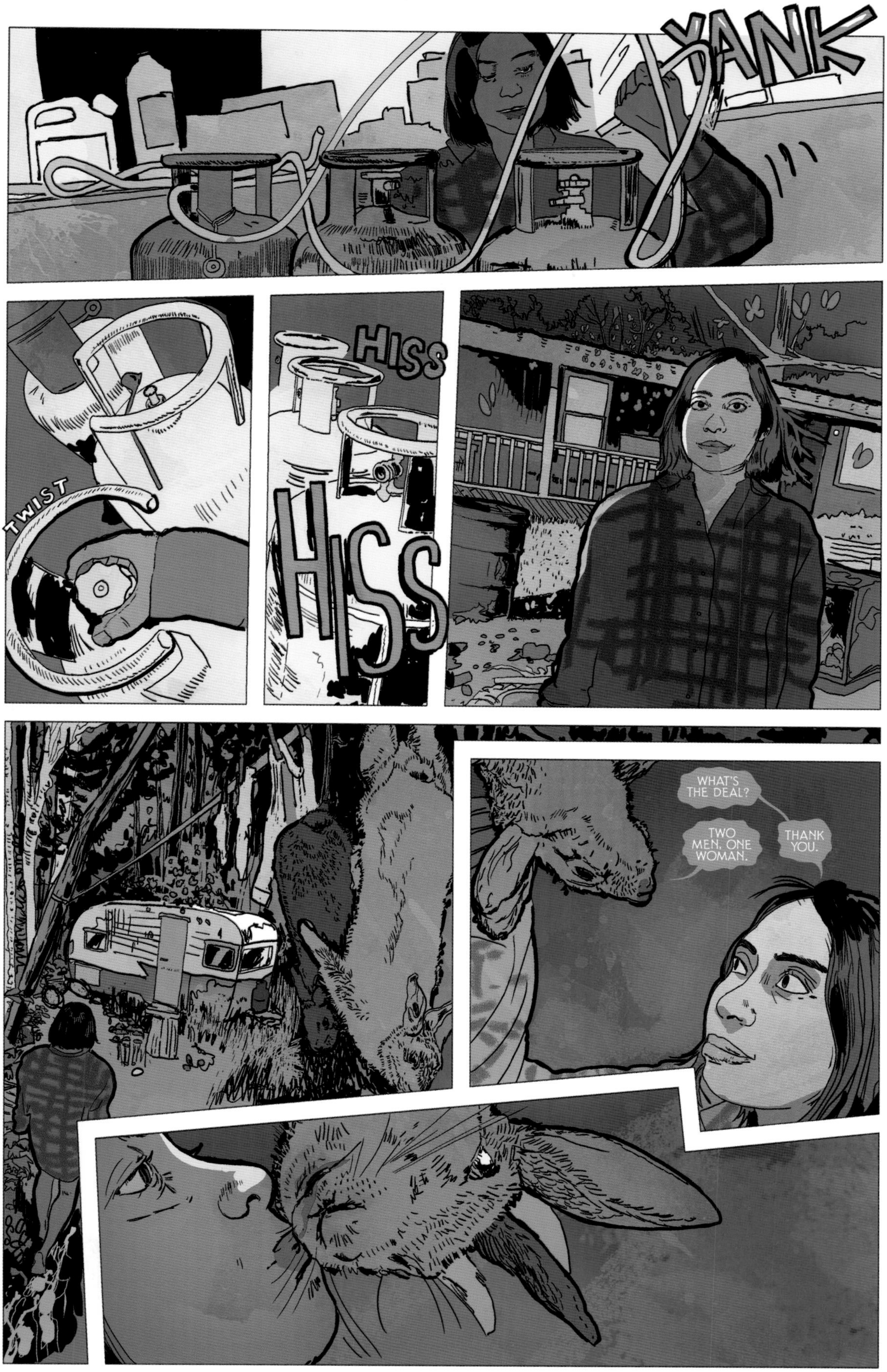
YANK
TWIST
HISS
HISS
WHAT'S THE DEAL?
TWO MEN, ONE WOMAN.
THANK YOU.

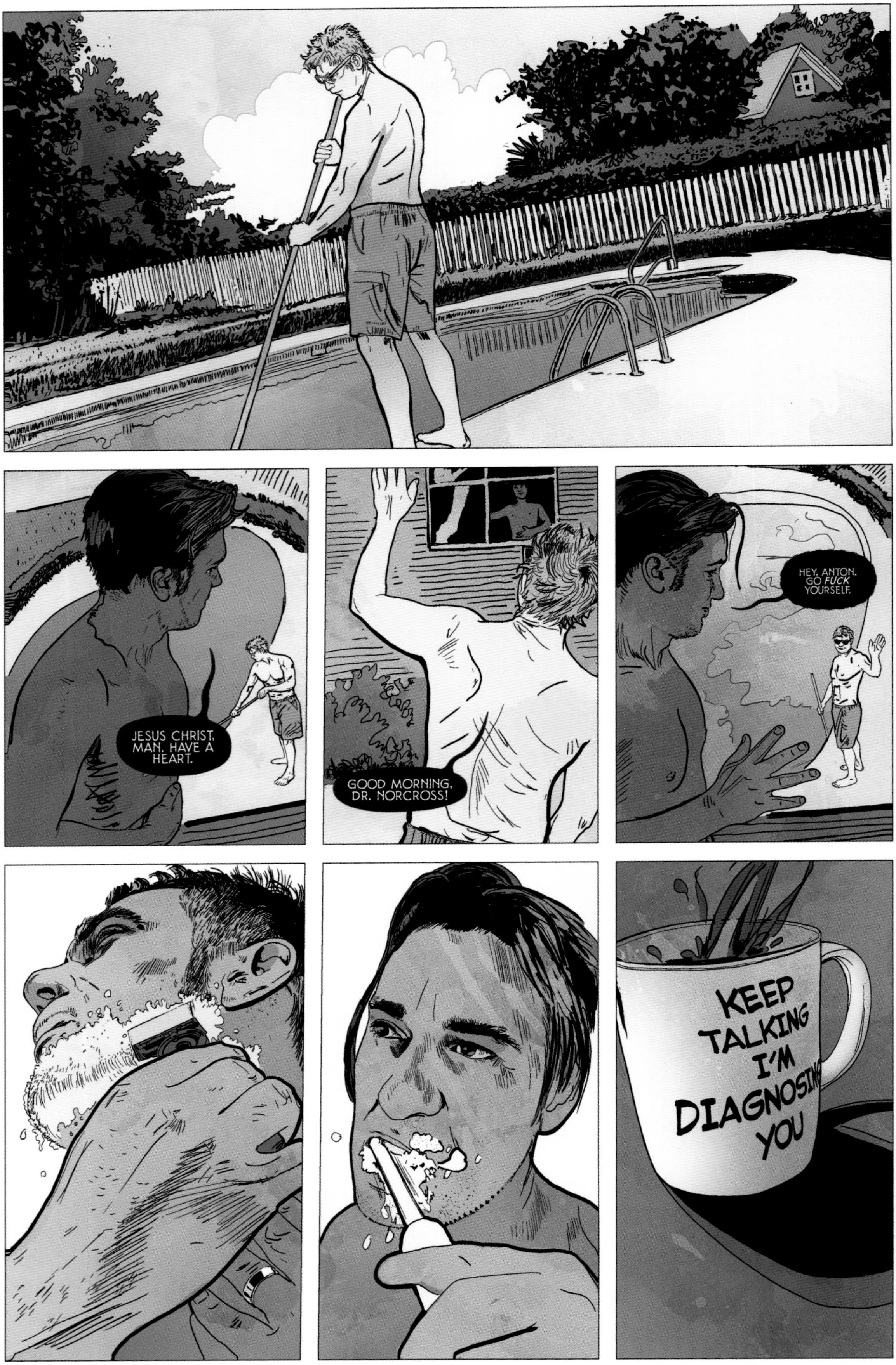
JESUS CHRIST, MAN. HAVE A HEART.
GOOD MORNING, DR. NORCROSS!
HEY, ANTON. GO *FUCK* YOURSELF.
KEEP TALKING I'M DIAGNOSING YOU

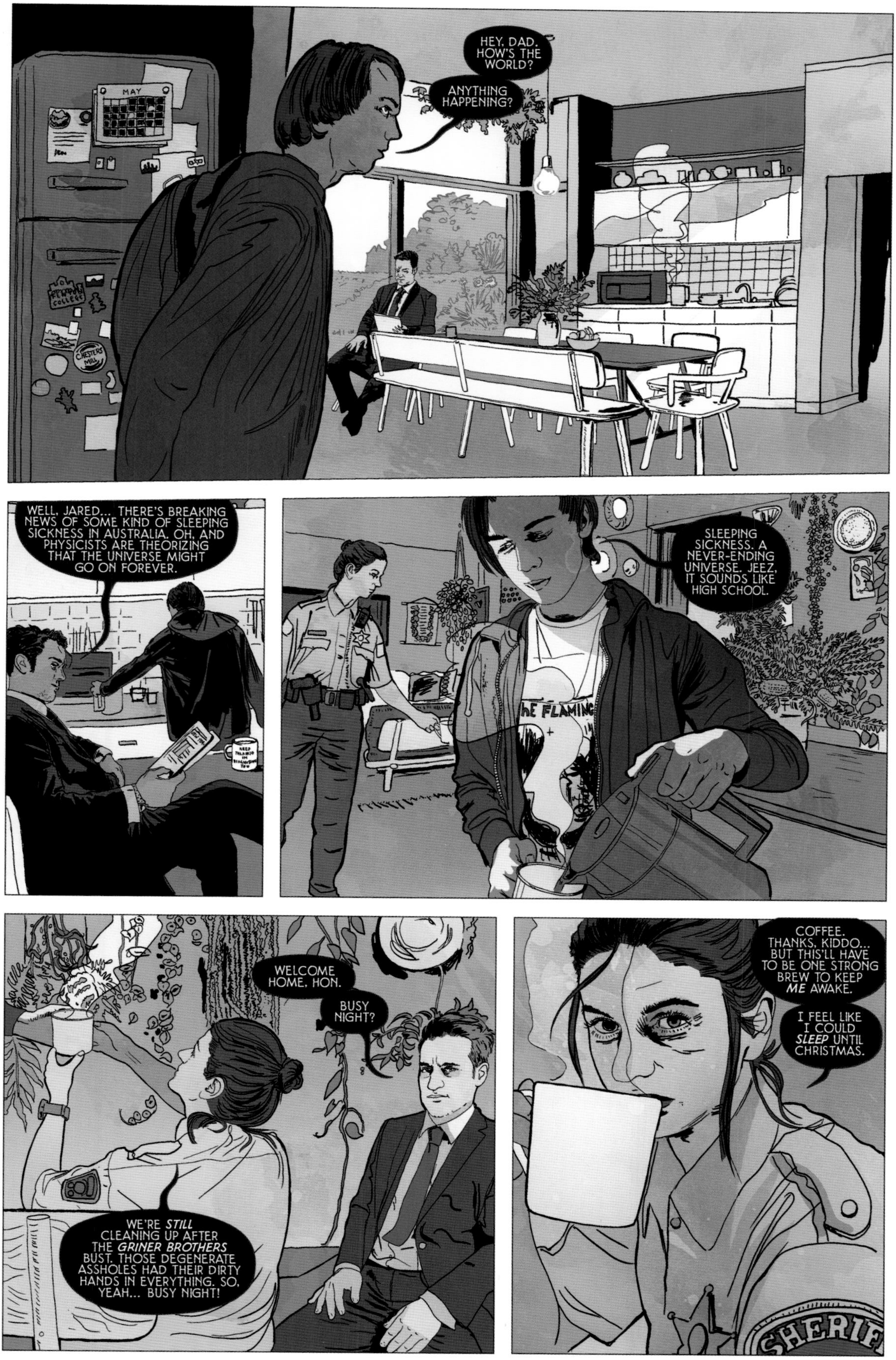
HEY, DAD. HOW'S THE WORLD?
ANYTHING HAPPENING?
WELL, JARED... THERE'S BREAKING NEWS OF SOME KIND OF SLEEPING SICKNESS IN AUSTRALIA. OH, AND PHYSICISTS ARE THEORIZING THAT THE UNIVERSE MIGHT GO ON FOREVER.
SLEEPING SICKNESS. A NEVER-ENDING UNIVERSE. JEEZ, IT SOUNDS LIKE HIGH SCHOOL.
WELCOME HOME, HON.
BUSY NIGHT?
WE'RE *STILL* CLEANING UP AFTER THE *GRINER BROTHERS* BUST. THOSE DEGENERATE ASSHOLES HAD THEIR DIRTY HANDS IN EVERYTHING. SO, YEAH... BUSY NIGHT!
COFFEE. THANKS, KIDDO... BUT THIS'LL HAVE TO BE ONE STRONG BREW TO KEEP *ME* AWAKE.
I FEEL LIKE I COULD *SLEEP* UNTIL CHRISTMAS.

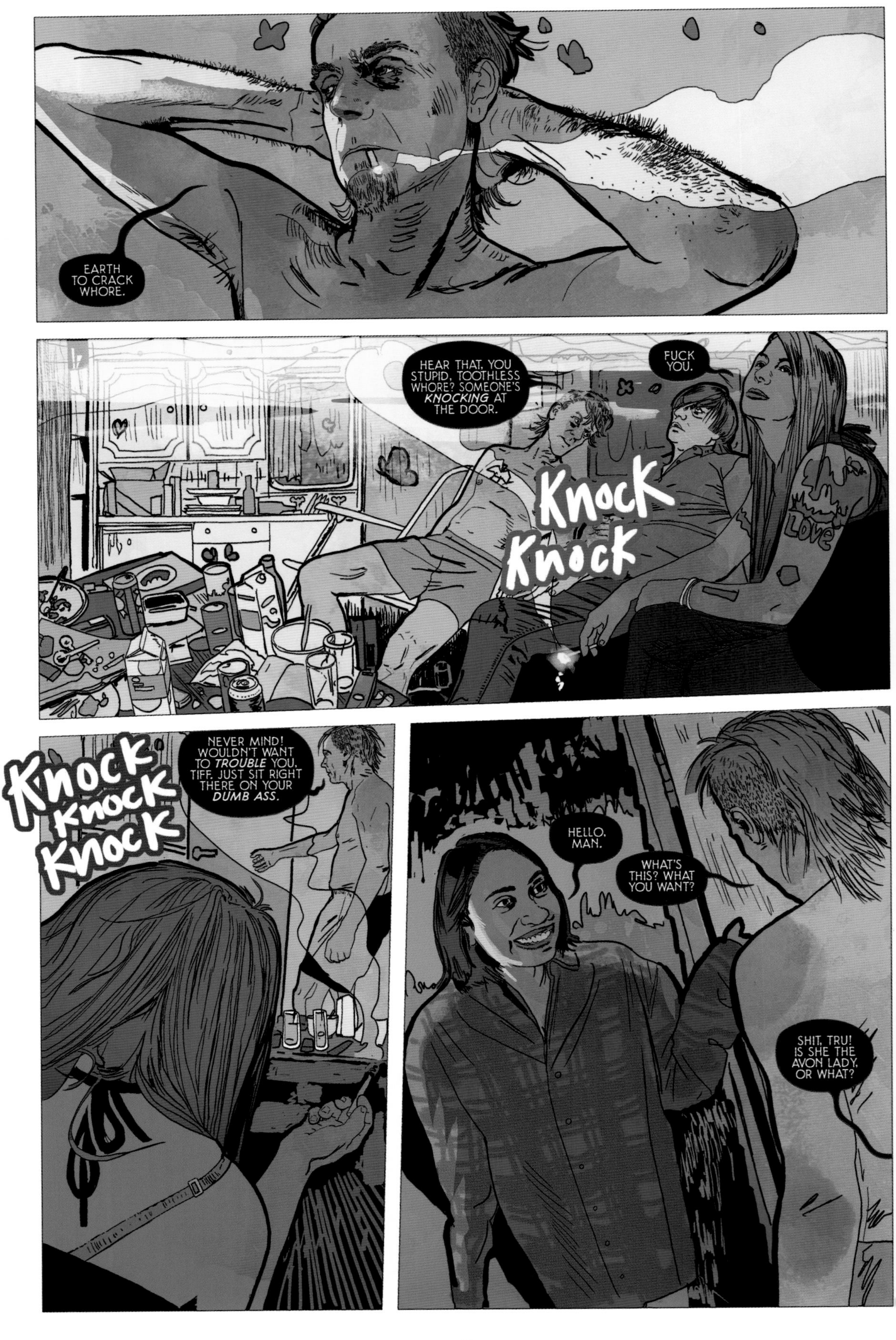
EARTH TO CRACK WHORE.
HEAR THAT, YOU STUPID, TOOTHLESS WHORE? SOMEONE'S *KNOCKING* AT THE DOOR.
FUCK YOU.
Knock Knock
LOVE
Knock knock Knock
NEVER MIND! WOULDN'T WANT TO *TROUBLE* YOU, TIFF. JUST SIT RIGHT THERE ON YOUR *DUMB ASS.*
HELLO, MAN.
WHAT'S THIS? WHAT YOU WANT?
SHIT, TRU! IS SHE THE AVON LADY, OR WHAT?

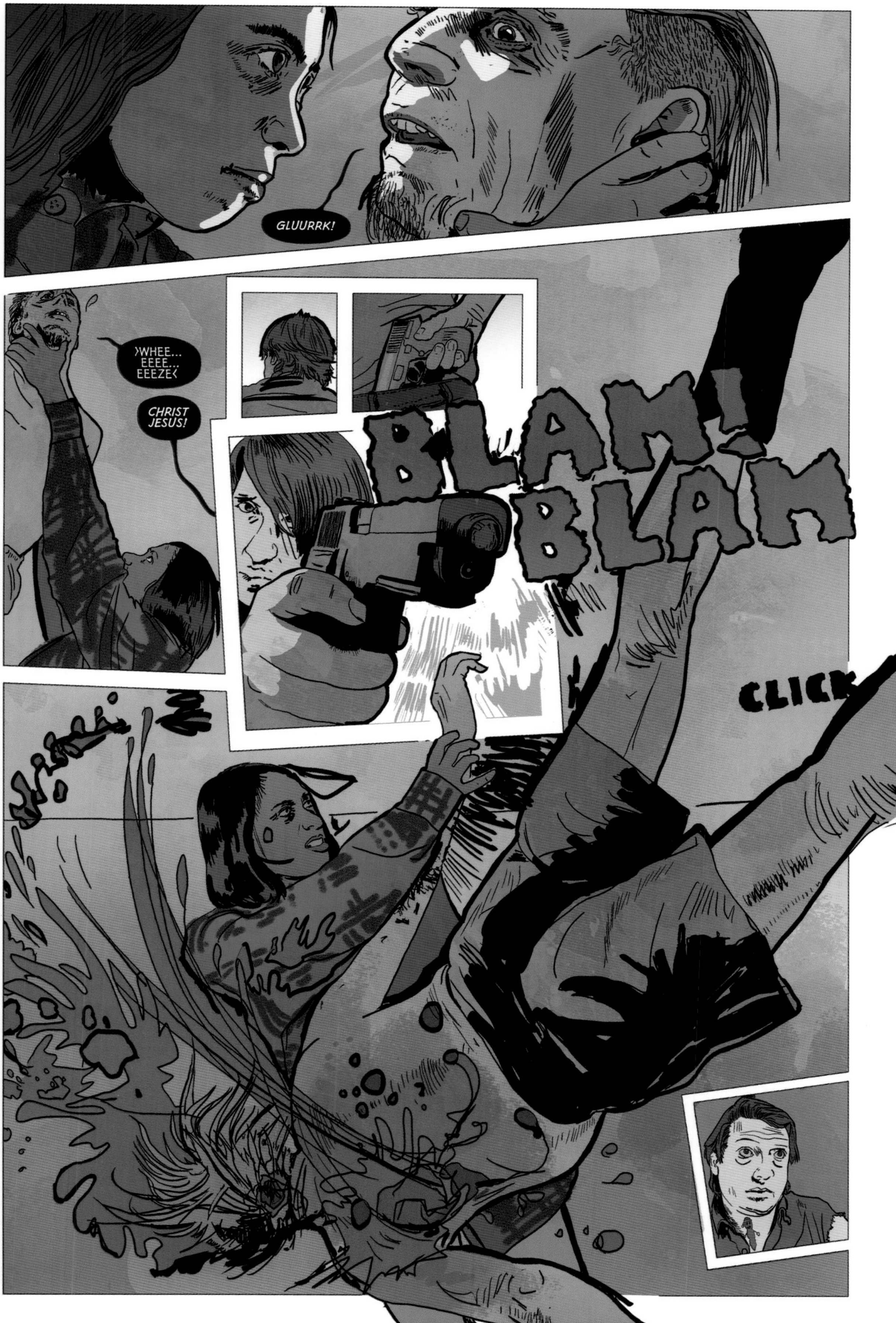
GLUURRK!
›WHEE... EEEE... EEEZE‹
CHRIST JESUS!
BLAM! BLAM
CLICK

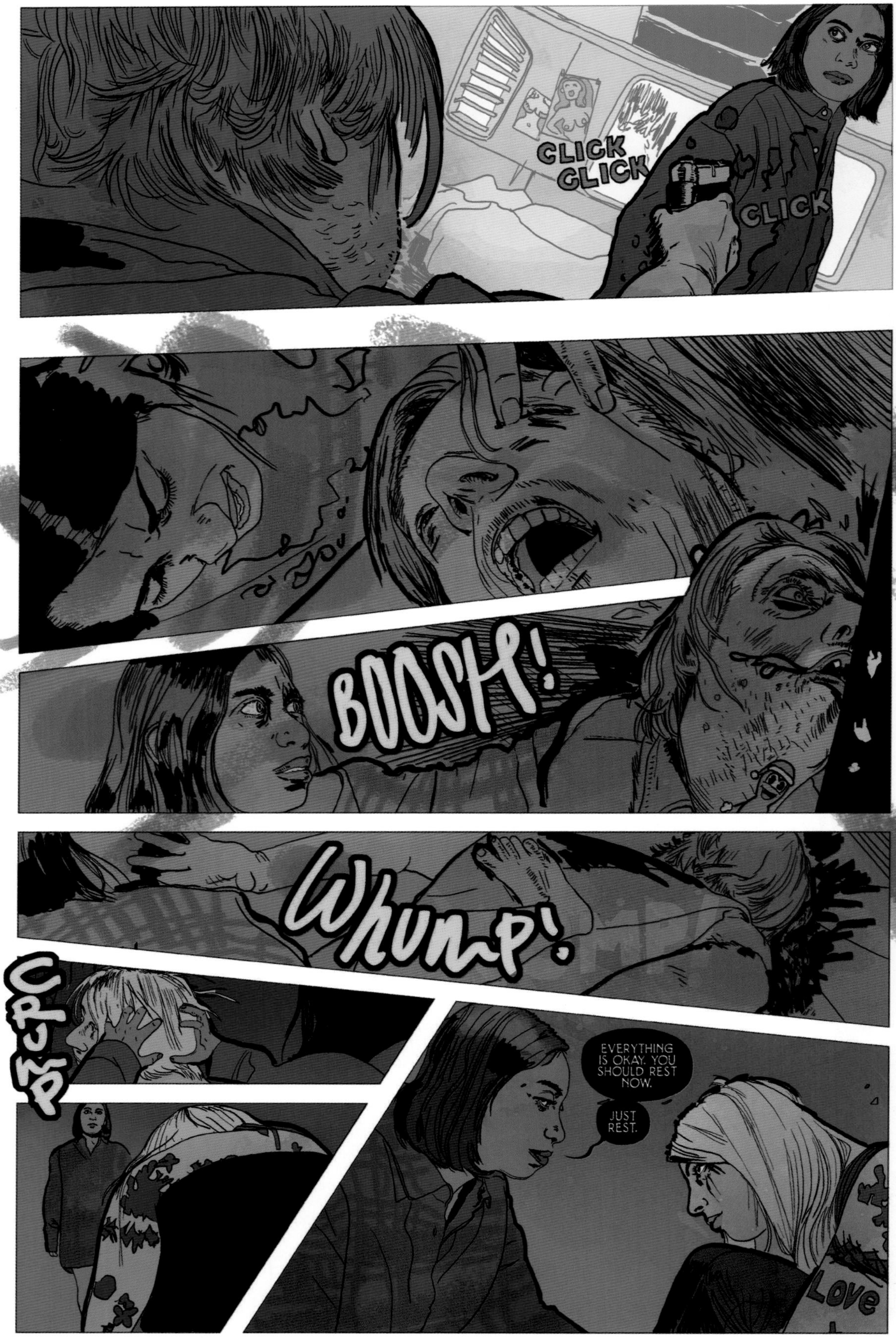
CLICK
CLICK
CLICK
BOOSH!
Whump!
EVERYTHING IS OKAY. YOU SHOULD REST NOW.
JUST REST.
Love

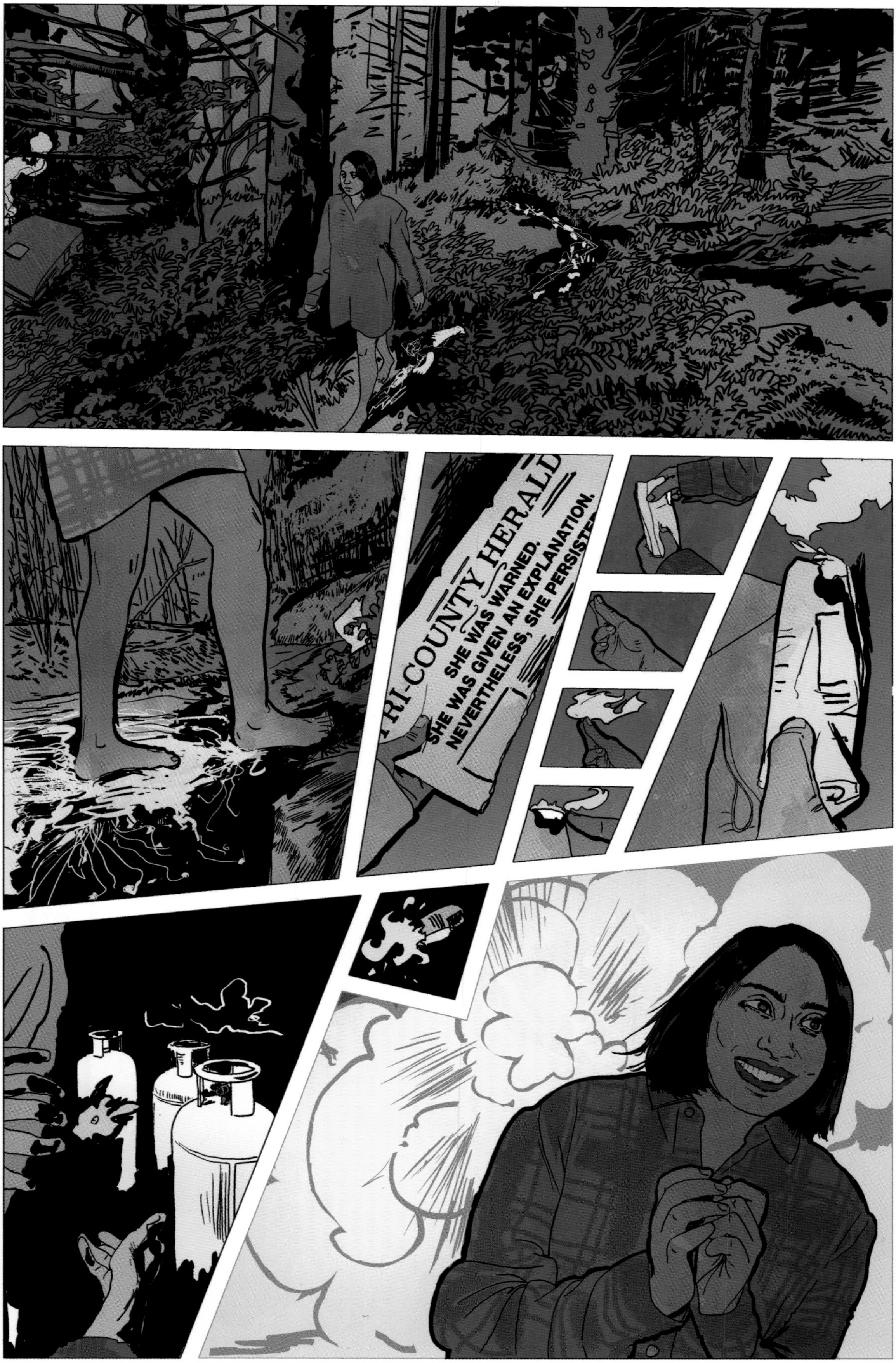
TRI-COUNTY HERALD
SHE WAS WARNED.
SHE WAS GIVEN AN EXPLANATION.
NEVERTHELESS, SHE PERSISTED.

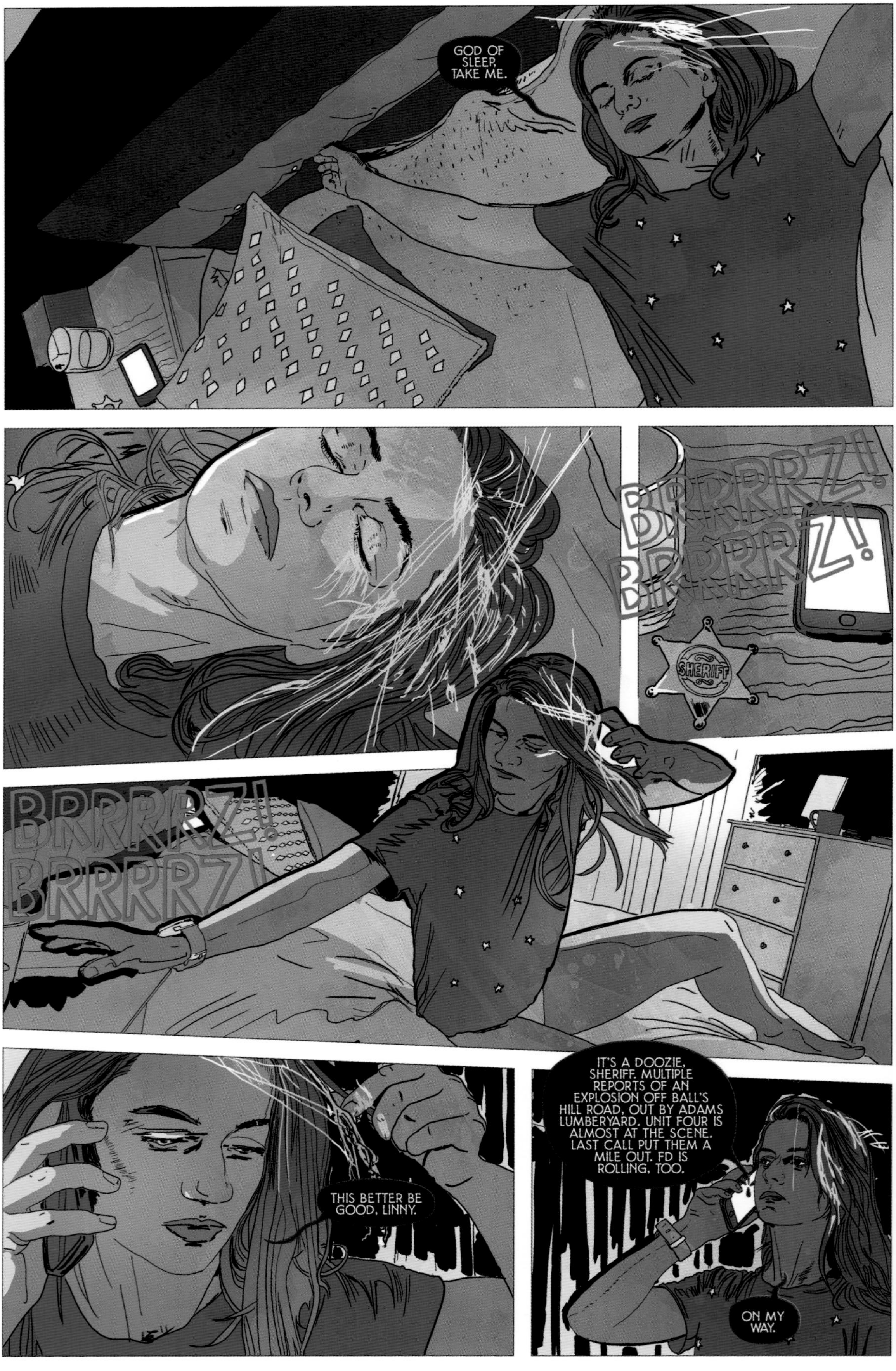
GOD OF SLEEP, TAKE ME.
BRRRRZ! BRRRRZ!
SHERIFF
BRRRRZ! BRRRRZ!
THIS BETTER BE GOOD, LINNY.
IT'S A DOOZIE, SHERIFF. MULTIPLE REPORTS OF AN EXPLOSION OFF BALL'S HILL ROAD, OUT BY ADAMS LUMBERYARD. UNIT FOUR IS ALMOST AT THE SCENE. LAST CALL PUT THEM A MILE OUT. FD IS ROLLING, TOO.
ON MY WAY.

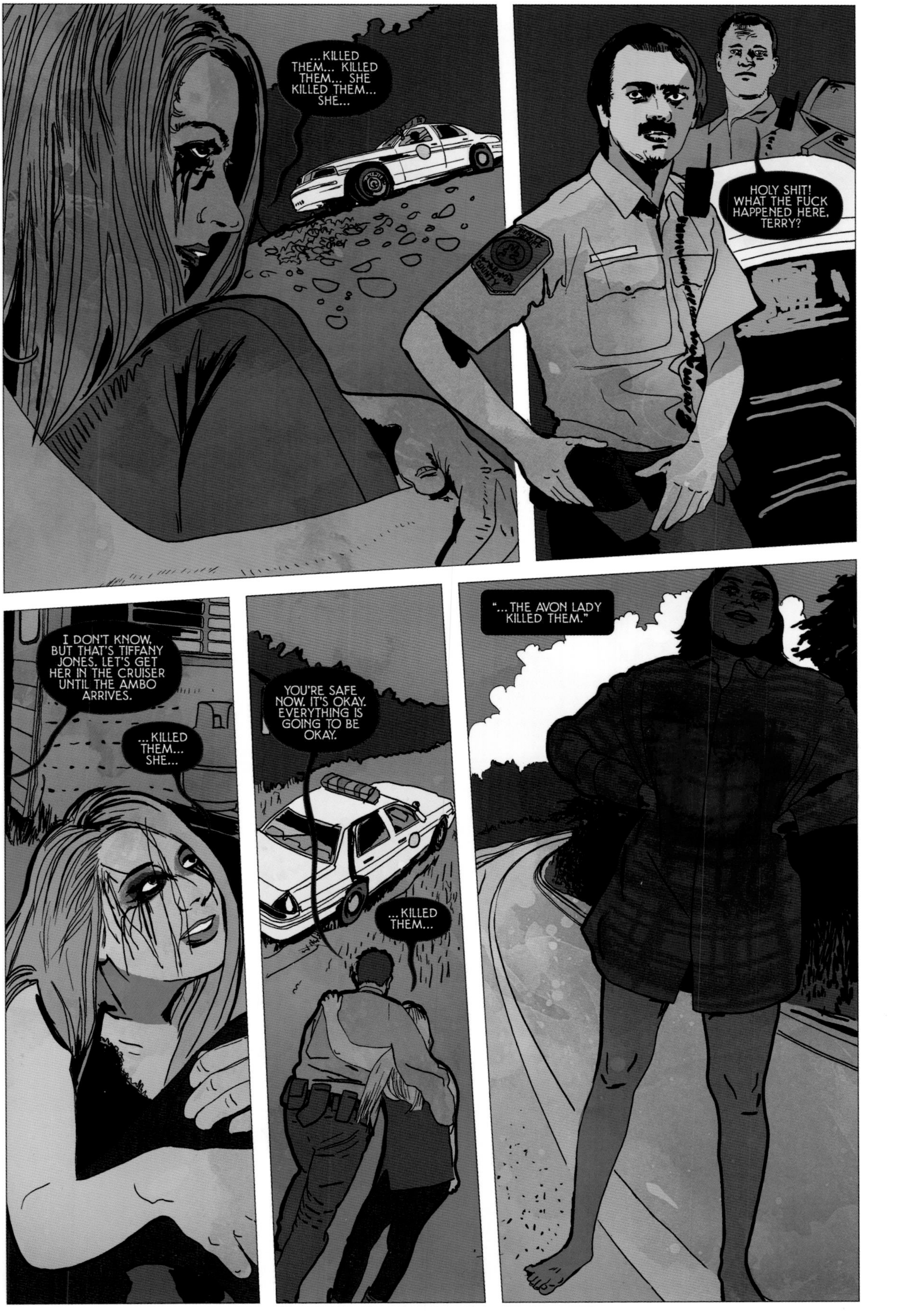
...KILLED THEM... KILLED THEM... SHE KILLED THEM... SHE...
HOLY SHIT! WHAT THE FUCK HAPPENED HERE, TERRY?
I DON'T KNOW. BUT THAT'S TIFFANY JONES. LET'S GET HER IN THE CRUISER UNTIL THE AMBO ARRIVES.
...KILLED THEM... SHE...
YOU'RE SAFE NOW. IT'S OKAY. EVERYTHING IS GOING TO BE OKAY.
...KILLED THEM...
"...THE AVON LADY KILLED THEM."

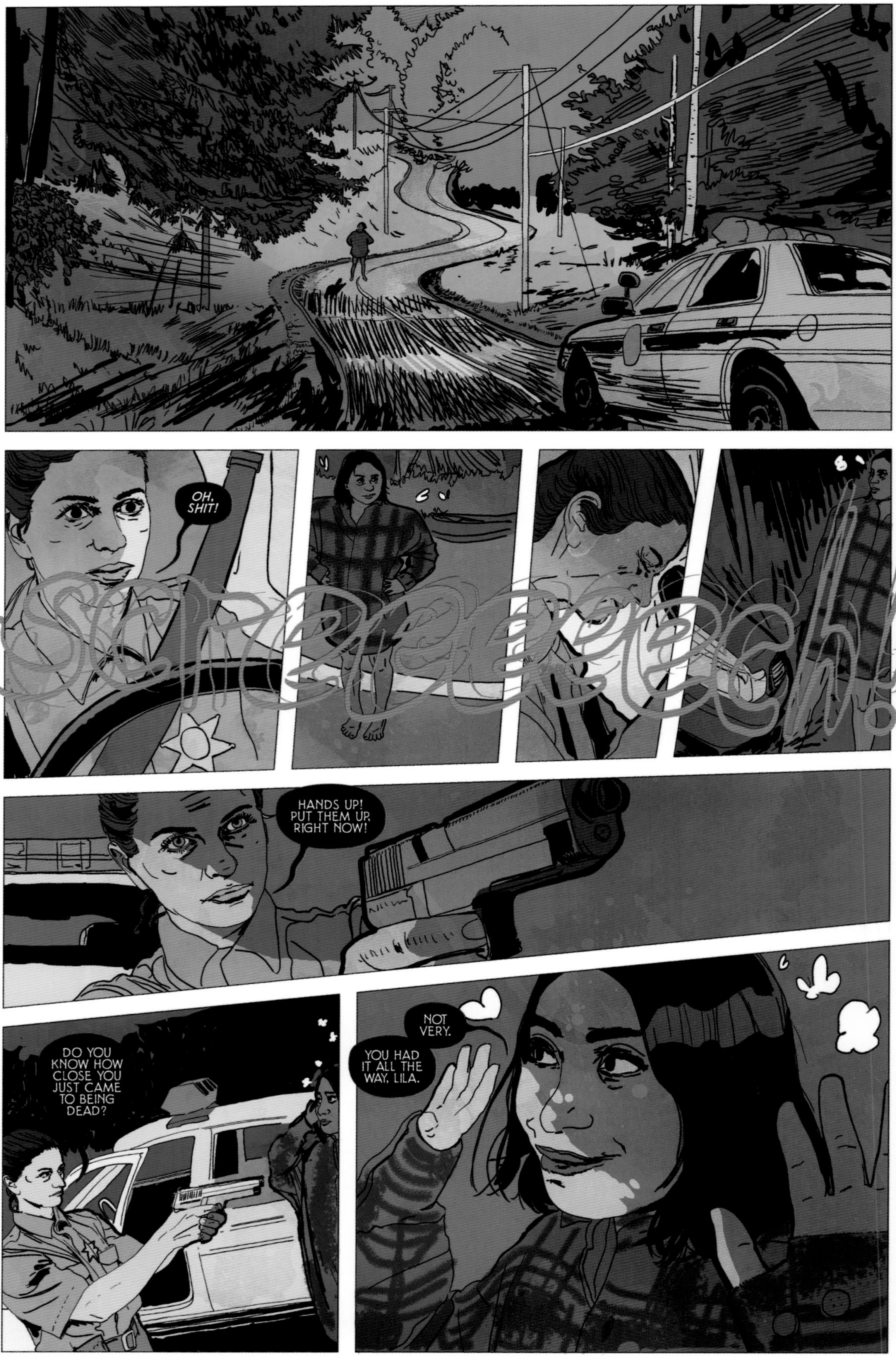
OH, SHIT!
Screeeeeech!
HANDS UP! PUT THEM UP, RIGHT NOW!
DO YOU KNOW HOW CLOSE YOU JUST CAME TO BEING DEAD?
NOT VERY.
YOU HAD IT ALL THE WAY, LILA.

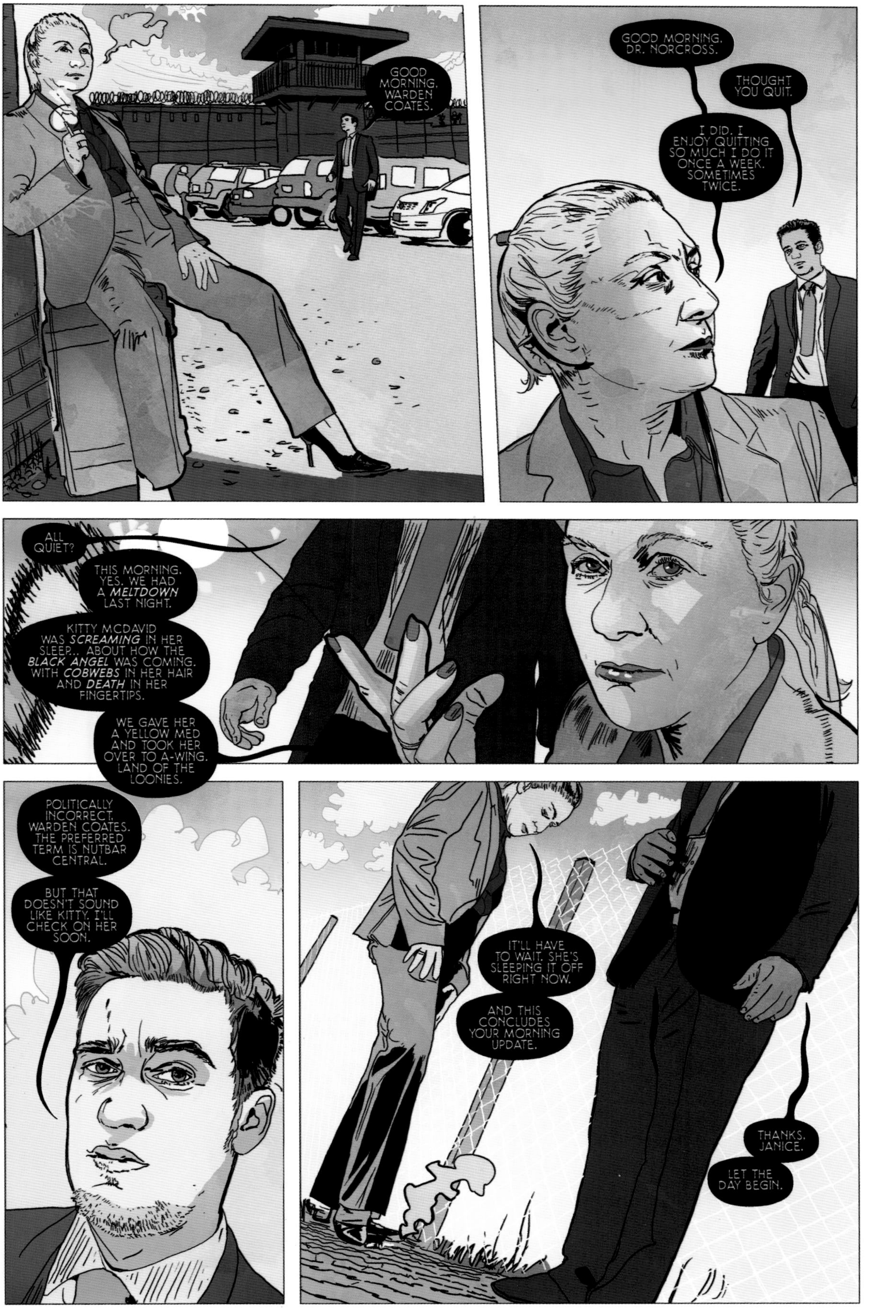
GOOD MORNING, WARDEN COATES.
GOOD MORNING, DR. NORCROSS.
THOUGHT YOU QUIT.
I DID. I ENJOY QUITTING SO MUCH I DO IT ONCE A WEEK. SOMETIMES TWICE.
ALL QUIET?
THIS MORNING, YES. WE HAD A MELTDOWN LAST NIGHT.
KITTY MCDAVID WAS SCREAMING IN HER SLEEP... ABOUT HOW THE BLACK ANGEL WAS COMING. WITH COBWEBS IN HER HAIR AND DEATH IN HER FINGERTIPS.
WE GAVE HER A YELLOW MED AND TOOK HER OVER TO A-WING. LAND OF THE LOONIES.
POLITICALLY INCORRECT, WARDEN COATES. THE PREFERRED TERM IS NUTBAR CENTRAL.
BUT THAT DOESN'T SOUND LIKE KITTY. I'LL CHECK ON HER SOON.
IT'LL HAVE TO WAIT. SHE'S SLEEPING IT OFF RIGHT NOW.
AND THIS CONCLUDES YOUR MORNING UPDATE.
THANKS, JANICE.
LET THE DAY BEGIN.

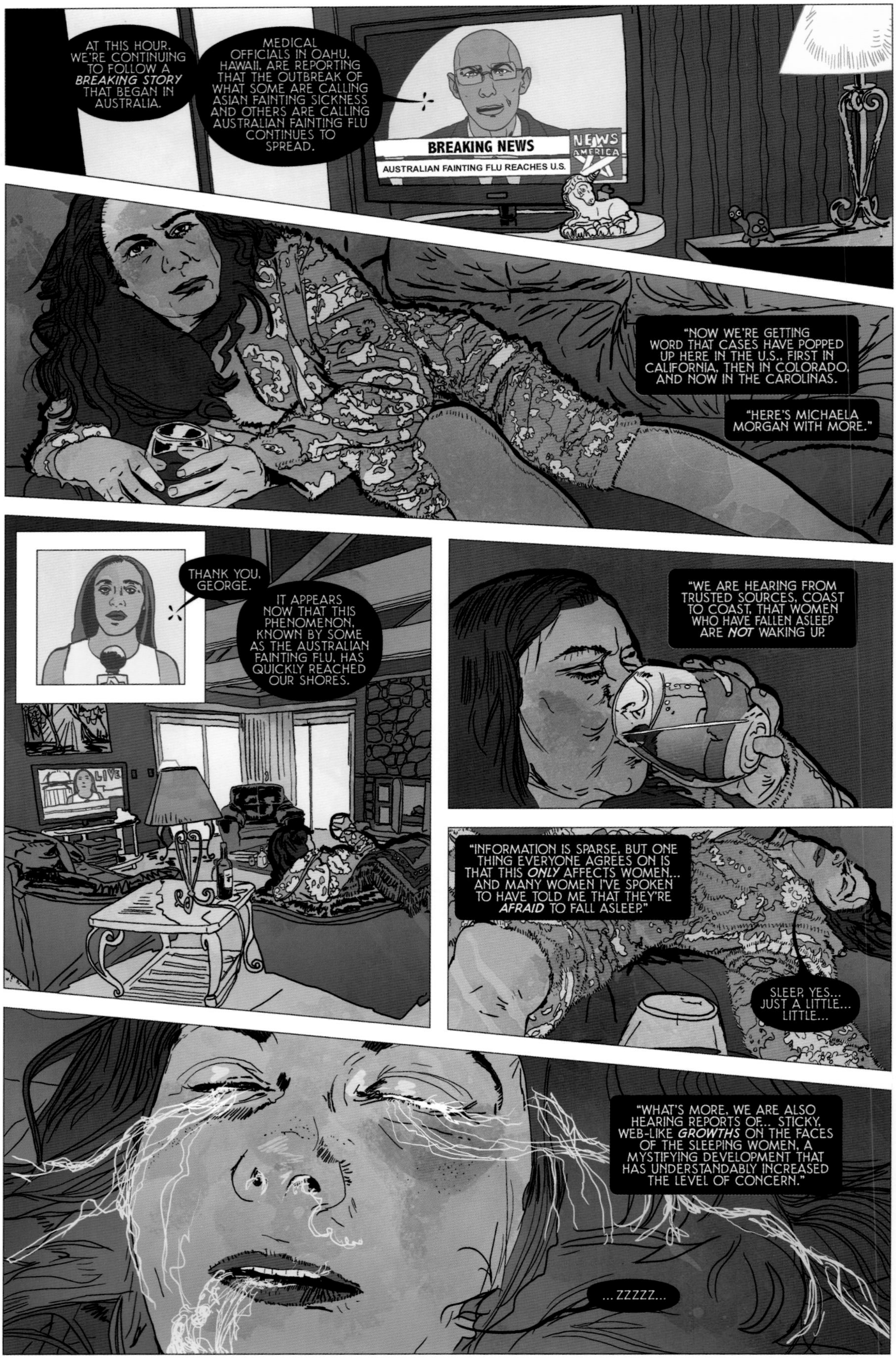

AT THIS HOUR, WE'RE CONTINUING TO FOLLOW A *BREAKING STORY* THAT BEGAN IN AUSTRALIA.
MEDICAL OFFICIALS IN OAHU, HAWAII, ARE REPORTING THAT THE OUTBREAK OF WHAT SOME ARE CALLING ASIAN FAINTING SICKNESS AND OTHERS ARE CALLING AUSTRALIAN FAINTING FLU CONTINUES TO SPREAD.
BREAKING NEWS
AUSTRALIAN FAINTING FLU REACHES U.S.
NEWS AMERICA
"NOW WE'RE GETTING WORD THAT CASES HAVE POPPED UP HERE IN THE U.S., FIRST IN CALIFORNIA, THEN IN COLORADO, AND NOW IN THE CAROLINAS.
"HERE'S MICHAELA MORGAN WITH MORE."
THANK YOU, GEORGE.
IT APPEARS NOW THAT THIS PHENOMENON, KNOWN BY SOME AS THE AUSTRALIAN FAINTING FLU, HAS QUICKLY REACHED OUR SHORES.
LIVE
"WE ARE HEARING FROM TRUSTED SOURCES, COAST TO COAST, THAT WOMEN WHO HAVE FALLEN ASLEEP ARE *NOT* WAKING UP.
"INFORMATION IS SPARSE, BUT ONE THING EVERYONE AGREES ON IS THAT THIS *ONLY* AFFECTS WOMEN... AND MANY WOMEN I'VE SPOKEN TO HAVE TOLD ME THAT THEY'RE *AFRAID* TO FALL ASLEEP."
SLEEP, YES... JUST A LITTLE... LITTLE...
"WHAT'S MORE, WE ARE ALSO HEARING REPORTS OF... STICKY, WEB-LIKE *GROWTHS* ON THE FACES OF THE SLEEPING WOMEN, A MYSTIFYING DEVELOPMENT THAT HAS UNDERSTANDABLY INCREASED THE LEVEL OF CONCERN."
...ZZZZZ...

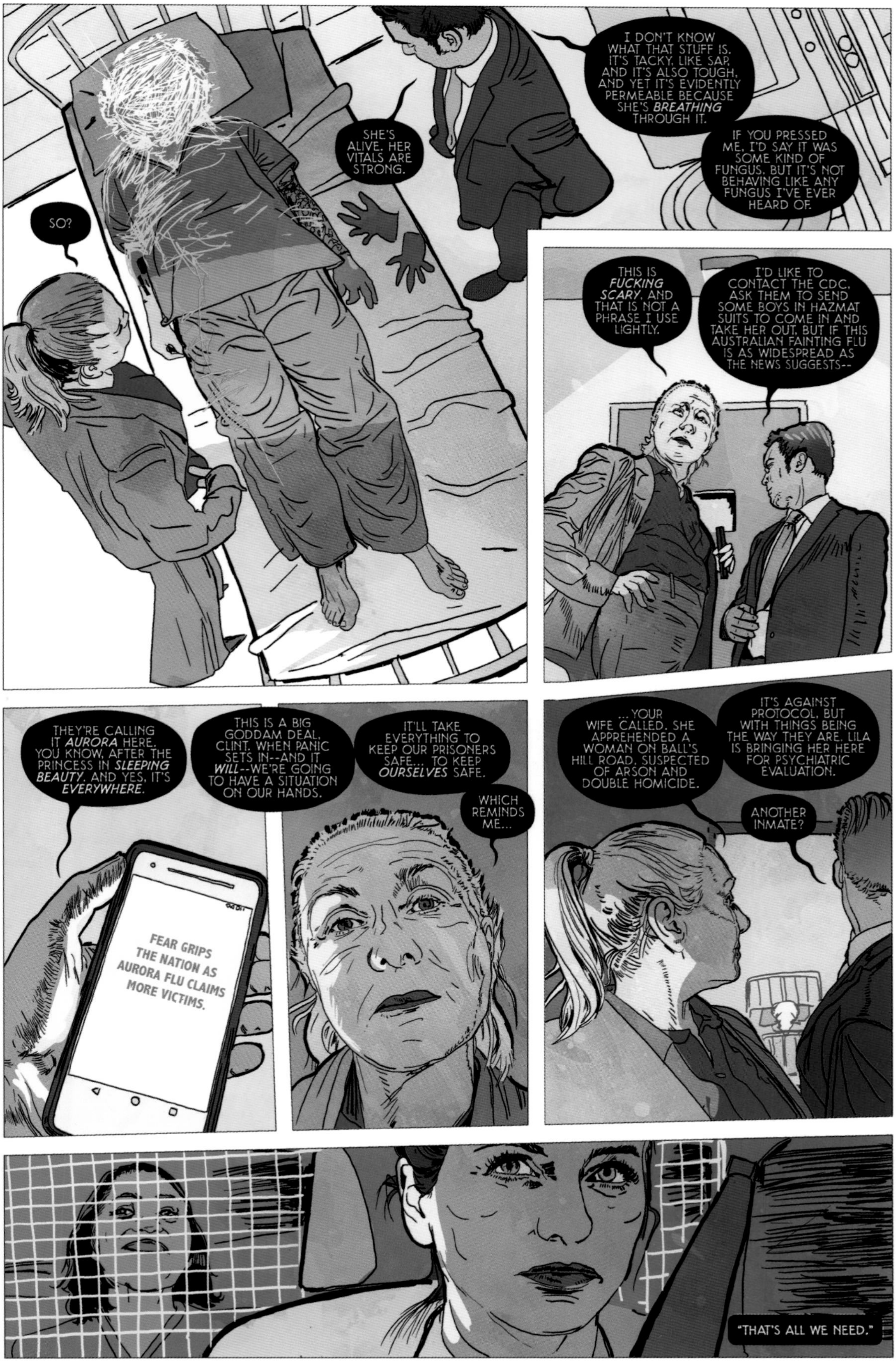
SO?
SHE'S ALIVE. HER VITALS ARE STRONG.
I DON'T KNOW WHAT THAT STUFF IS. IT'S TACKY, LIKE SAP, AND IT'S ALSO TOUGH, AND YET IT'S EVIDENTLY PERMEABLE BECAUSE SHE'S *BREATHING* THROUGH IT.
IF YOU PRESSED ME, I'D SAY IT WAS SOME KIND OF FUNGUS. BUT IT'S NOT BEHAVING LIKE ANY FUNGUS I'VE EVER HEARD OF.
THIS IS *FUCKING SCARY*, AND THAT IS NOT A PHRASE I USE LIGHTLY.
I'D LIKE TO CONTACT THE CDC, ASK THEM TO SEND SOME BOYS IN HAZMAT SUITS TO COME IN AND TAKE HER OUT. BUT IF THIS AUSTRALIAN FAINTING FLU IS AS WIDESPREAD AS THE NEWS SUGGESTS--
THEY'RE CALLING IT *AURORA* HERE. YOU KNOW, AFTER THE PRINCESS IN *SLEEPING BEAUTY*. AND YES, IT'S *EVERYWHERE*.
FEAR GRIPS THE NATION AS AURORA FLU CLAIMS MORE VICTIMS.
THIS IS A BIG GODDAM DEAL, CLINT. WHEN PANIC SETS IN--AND IT *WILL*--WE'RE GOING TO HAVE A SITUATION ON OUR HANDS.
IT'LL TAKE EVERYTHING TO KEEP OUR PRISONERS SAFE... TO KEEP *OURSELVES* SAFE.
WHICH REMINDS ME...
...YOUR WIFE CALLED. SHE APPREHENDED A WOMAN ON BALL'S HILL ROAD, SUSPECTED OF ARSON AND DOUBLE HOMICIDE.
IT'S AGAINST PROTOCOL, BUT WITH THINGS BEING THE WAY THEY ARE, LILA IS BRINGING HER HERE FOR PSYCHIATRIC EVALUATION.
ANOTHER INMATE?
"THAT'S ALL WE NEED."

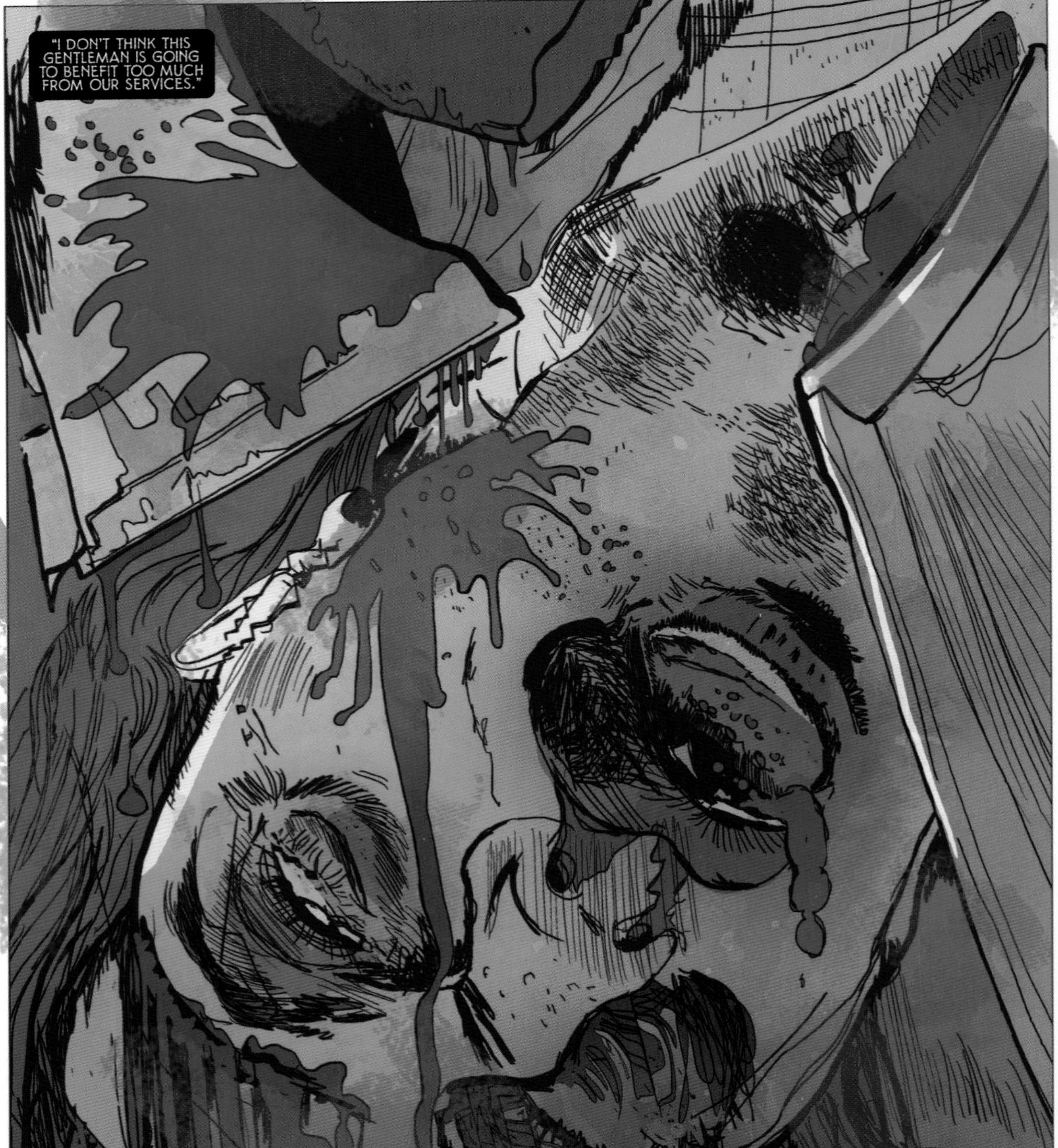
"I DON'T THINK THIS GENTLEMAN IS GOING TO BENEFIT TOO MUCH FROM OUR SERVICES."

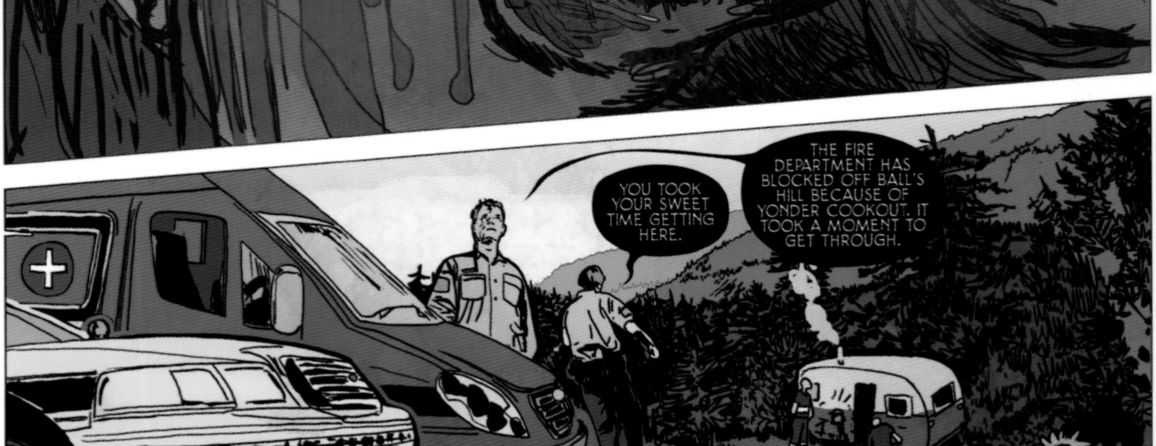
YOU TOOK YOUR SWEET TIME GETTING HERE.
THE FIRE DEPARTMENT HAS BLOCKED OFF BALL'S HILL BECAUSE OF YONDER COOKOUT. IT TOOK A MOMENT TO GET THROUGH.

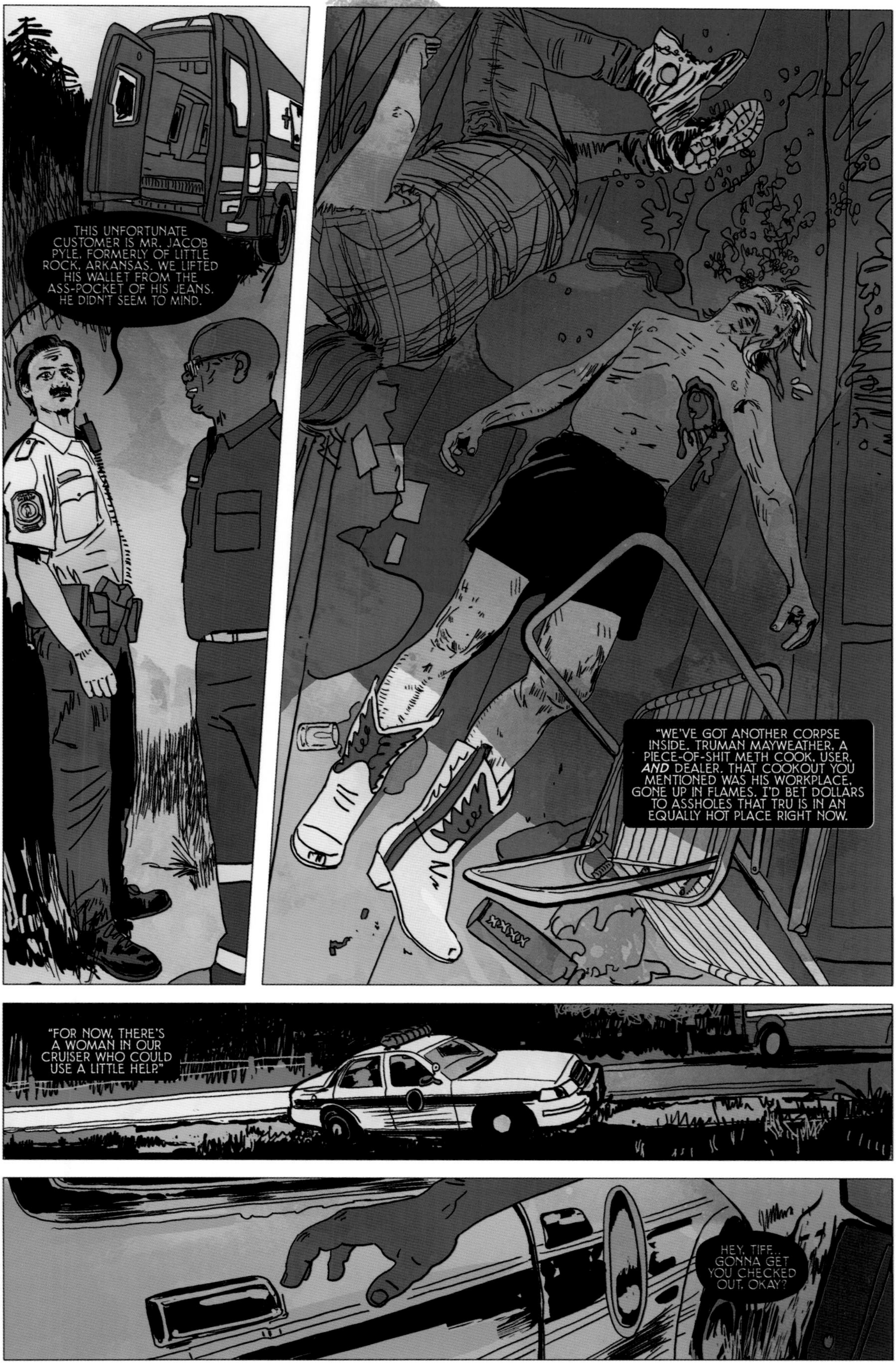
THIS UNFORTUNATE CUSTOMER IS MR. JACOB PYLE, FORMERLY OF LITTLE ROCK, ARKANSAS. WE LIFTED HIS WALLET FROM THE ASS-POCKET OF HIS JEANS. HE DIDN'T SEEM TO MIND.
"WE'VE GOT ANOTHER CORPSE INSIDE. TRUMAN MAYWEATHER, A PIECE-OF-SHIT METH COOK, USER, AND DEALER. THAT COOKOUT YOU MENTIONED WAS HIS WORKPLACE, GONE UP IN FLAMES. I'D BET DOLLARS TO ASSHOLES THAT TRU IS IN AN EQUALLY HOT PLACE RIGHT NOW.
XXXX
"FOR NOW, THERE'S A WOMAN IN OUR CRUISER WHO COULD USE A LITTLE HELP."
HEY, TIFF... GONNA GET YOU CHECKED OUT, OKAY?

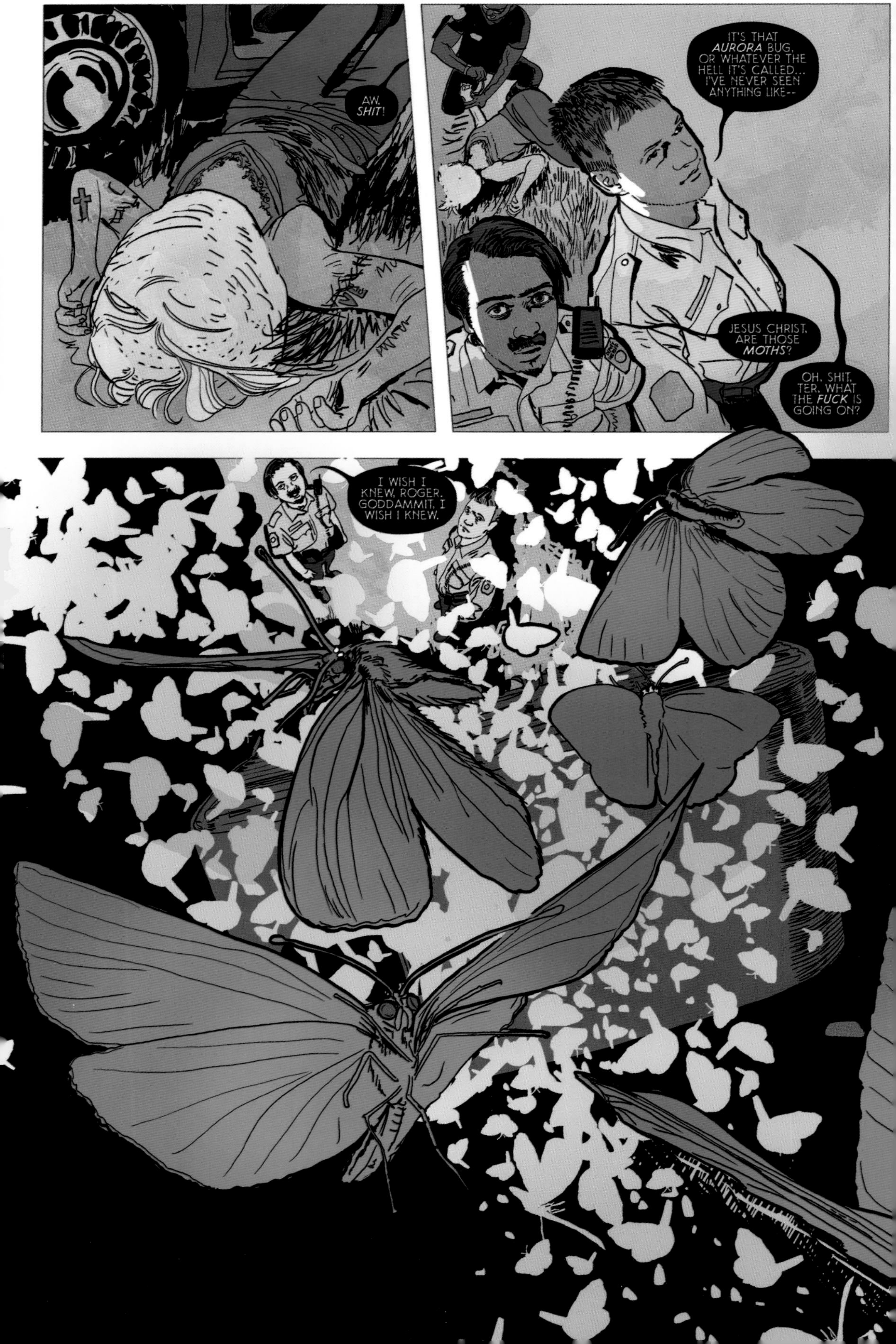
AW, *SHIT*!
IT'S THAT *AURORA* BUG, OR WHATEVER THE HELL IT'S CALLED... I'VE NEVER SEEN ANYTHING LIKE--
JESUS CHRIST, ARE THOSE *MOTHS*?
OH, SHIT, TER, WHAT THE *FUCK* IS GOING ON?
I WISH I KNEW, ROGER. GODDAMMIT, I WISH I KNEW.

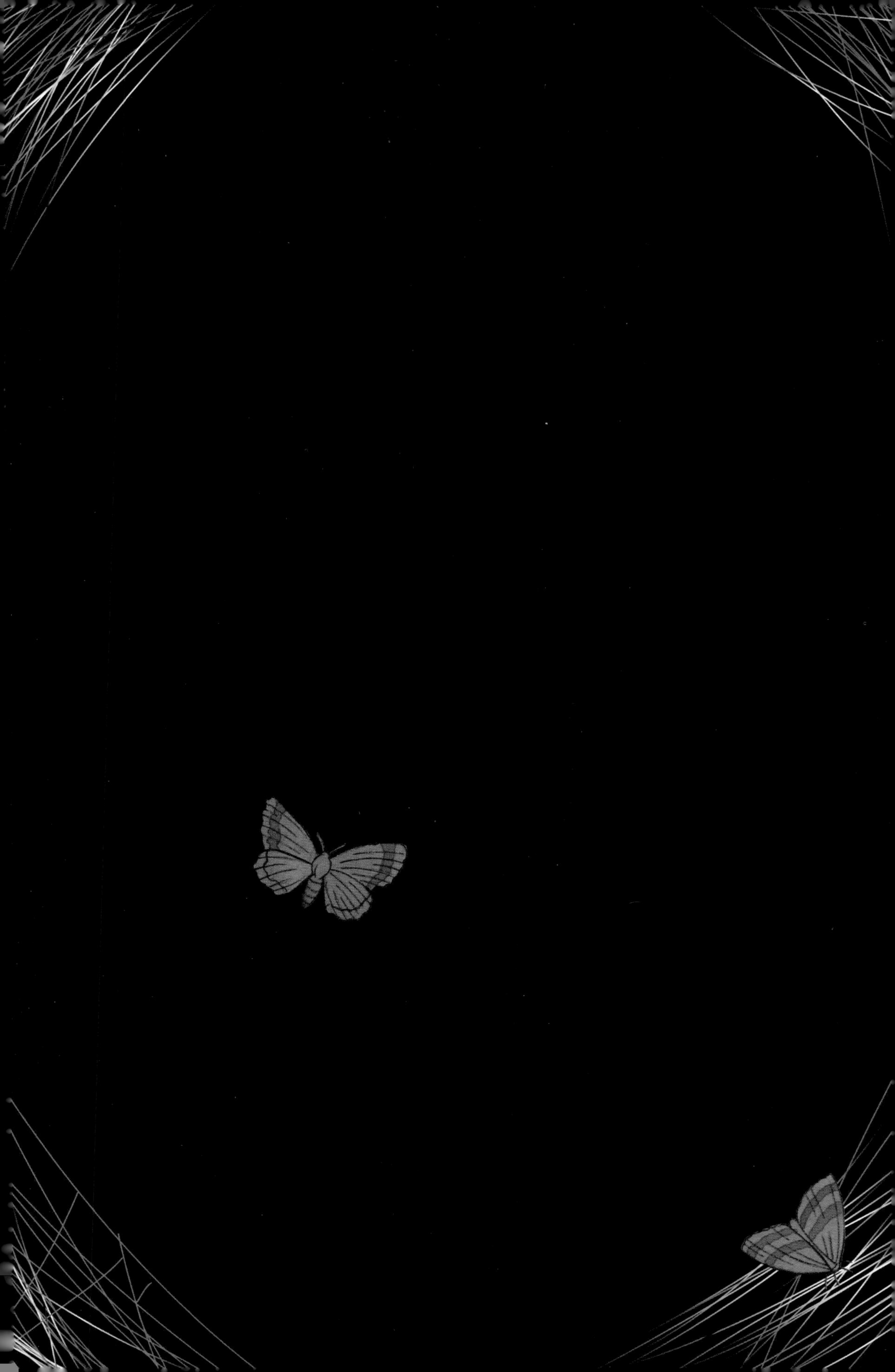

ART BY ANNIE WU

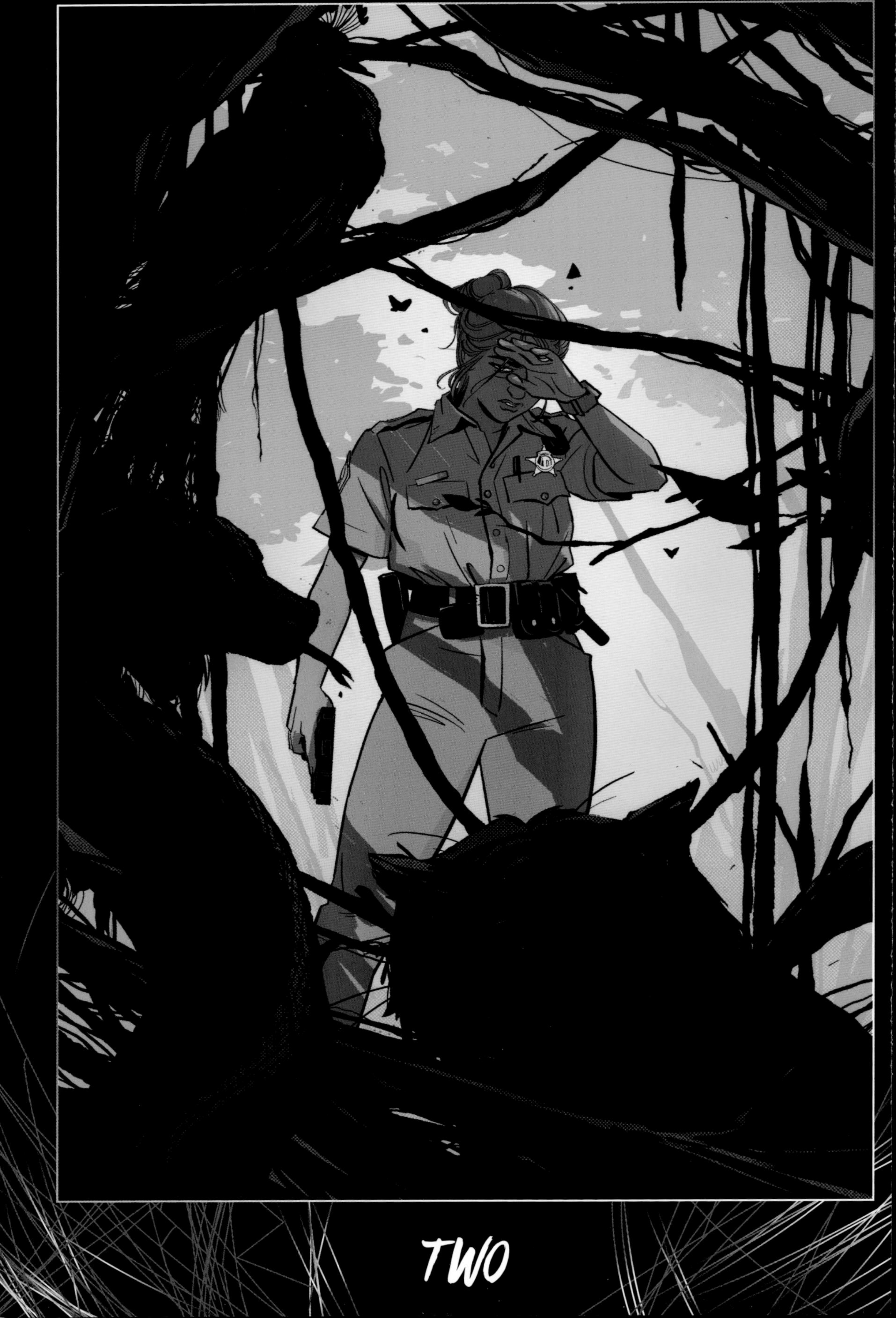

TWO

HEY, MOM. I'M HOME!

"CONTINUING NOW WITH AN **ALARMING** DEVELOPMENT IN THE AURORA EPIDEMIC. HERE'S MICHAELA MORGAN WITH MORE."

MOM?

THANK YOU, GEORGE.

I'M AFRAID ALARMING DOESN'T BEGIN TO DESCRIBE IT.

WITH THE HORRIFIC CELL PHONE FOOTAGE...

DES REPORTED WHEN WEBBING REMOVED

MOM? WHAT THE... JESUS CHRIST... **MOM?**

"... FROM AUSTRALIA AND THE WEST COAST HAVING BEEN RECENTLY AUTHENTICATED, WE ARE NOW HEARING FROM OFFICIAL SOURCES THAT REMOVING THE COCOON-LIKE COATING FROM SLEEPING WOMEN CAN ELICIT AN EXCEPTIONALLY VIOLENT REACTION.

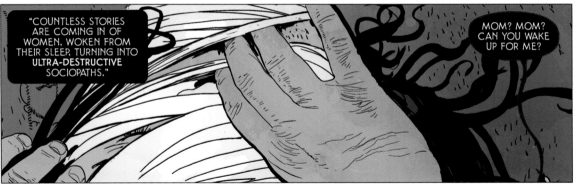

"COUNTLESS STORIES ARE COMING IN OF WOMEN, WOKEN FROM THEIR SLEEP, TURNING INTO **ULTRA-DESTRUCTIVE** SOCIOPATHS."

MOM? MOM? CAN YOU WAKE UP FOR ME?

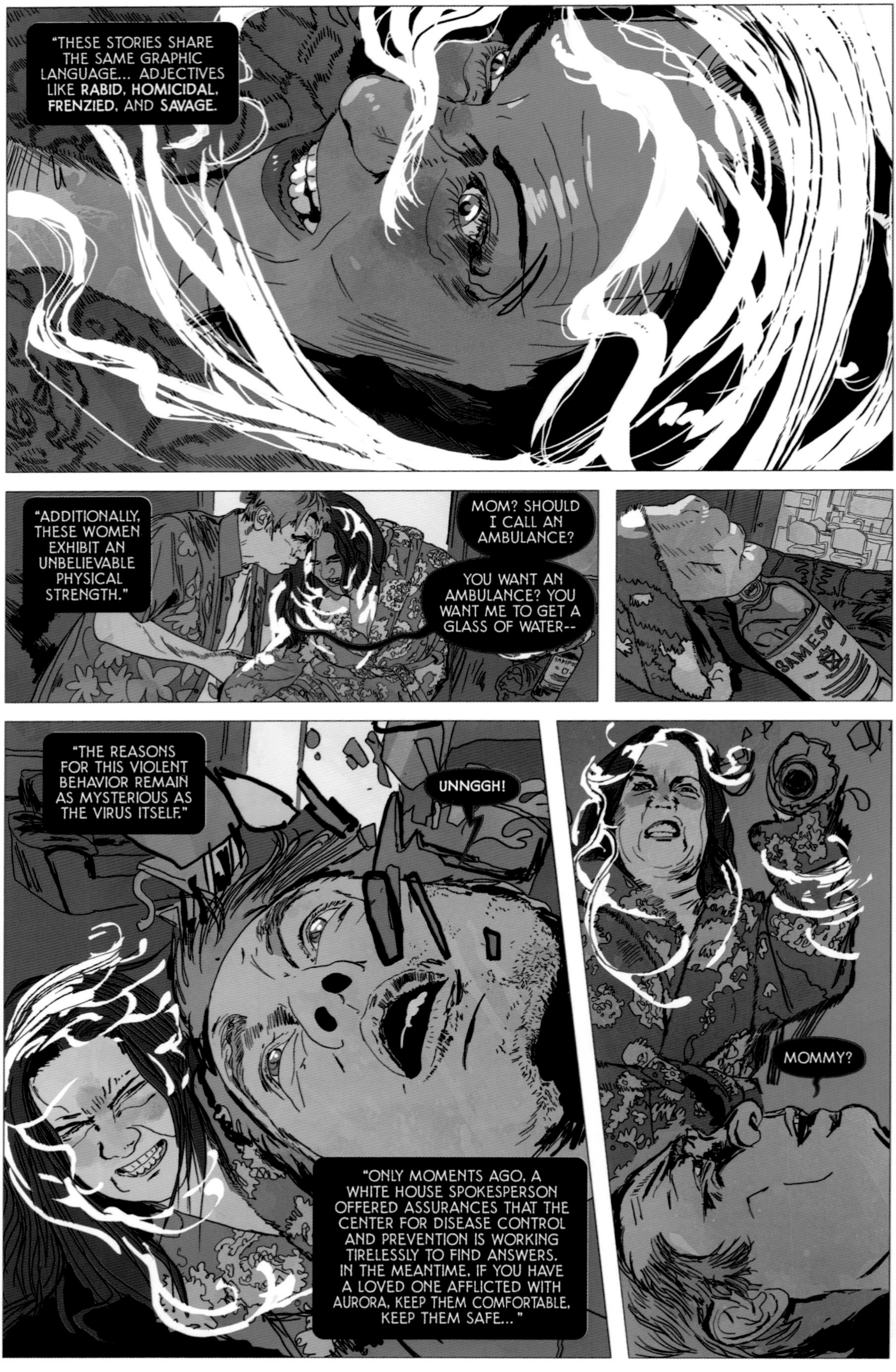
"THESE STORIES SHARE THE SAME GRAPHIC LANGUAGE... ADJECTIVES LIKE RABID, HOMICIDAL, FRENZIED, AND SAVAGE.
"ADDITIONALLY, THESE WOMEN EXHIBIT AN UNBELIEVABLE PHYSICAL STRENGTH."
MOM? SHOULD I CALL AN AMBULANCE?
YOU WANT AN AMBULANCE? YOU WANT ME TO GET A GLASS OF WATER--
"THE REASONS FOR THIS VIOLENT BEHAVIOR REMAIN AS MYSTERIOUS AS THE VIRUS ITSELF."
UNNGGH!
"ONLY MOMENTS AGO, A WHITE HOUSE SPOKESPERSON OFFERED ASSURANCES THAT THE CENTER FOR DISEASE CONTROL AND PREVENTION IS WORKING TIRELESSLY TO FIND ANSWERS. IN THE MEANTIME, IF YOU HAVE A LOVED ONE AFFLICTED WITH AURORA, KEEP THEM COMFORTABLE, KEEP THEM SAFE..."
MOMMY?

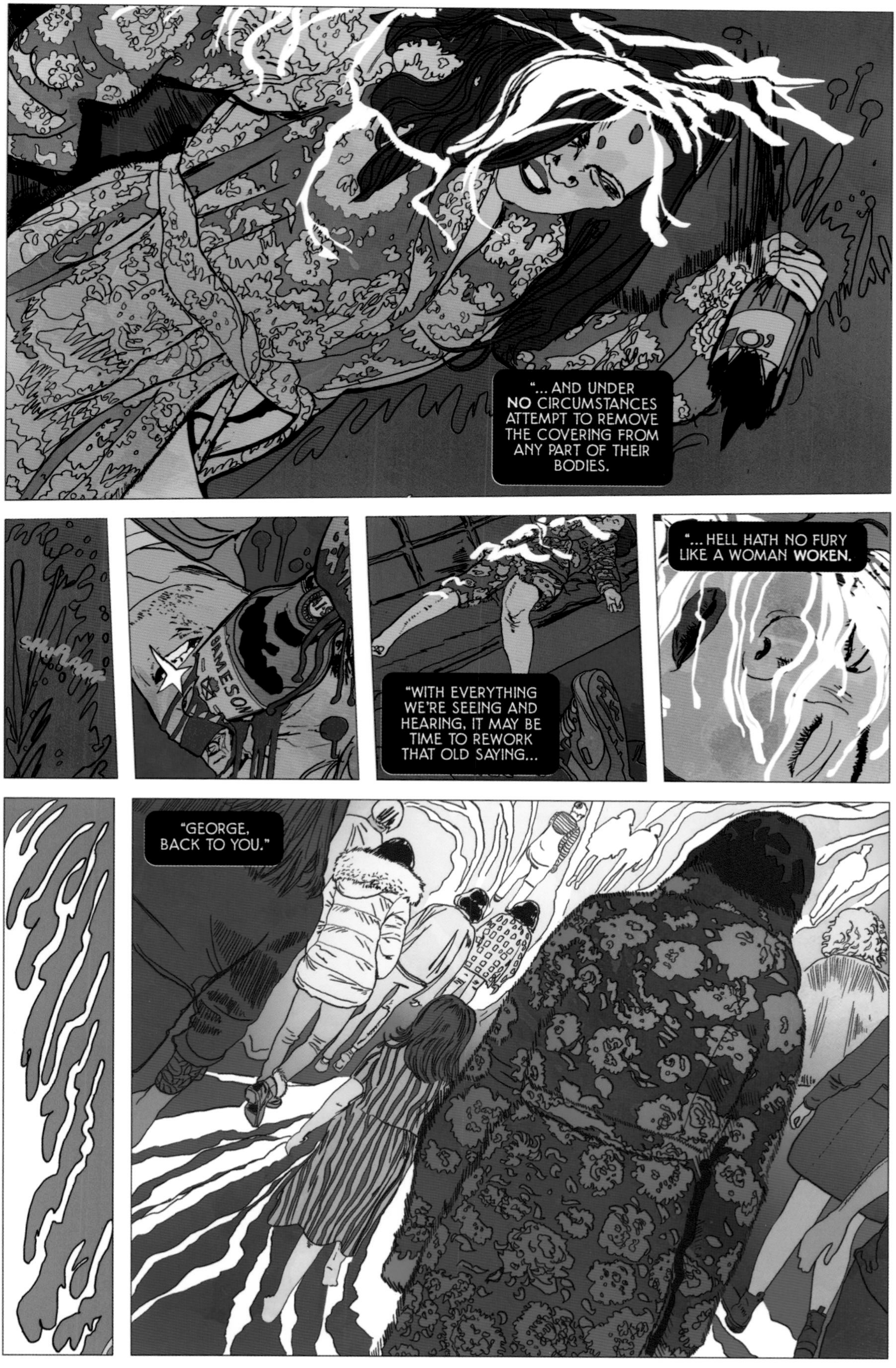
"... AND UNDER **NO** CIRCUMSTANCES ATTEMPT TO REMOVE THE COVERING FROM ANY PART OF THEIR BODIES.
"WITH EVERYTHING WE'RE SEEING AND HEARING, IT MAY BE TIME TO REWORK THAT OLD SAYING...
"... HELL HATH NO FURY LIKE A WOMAN **WOKEN.**
"GEORGE, BACK TO YOU."

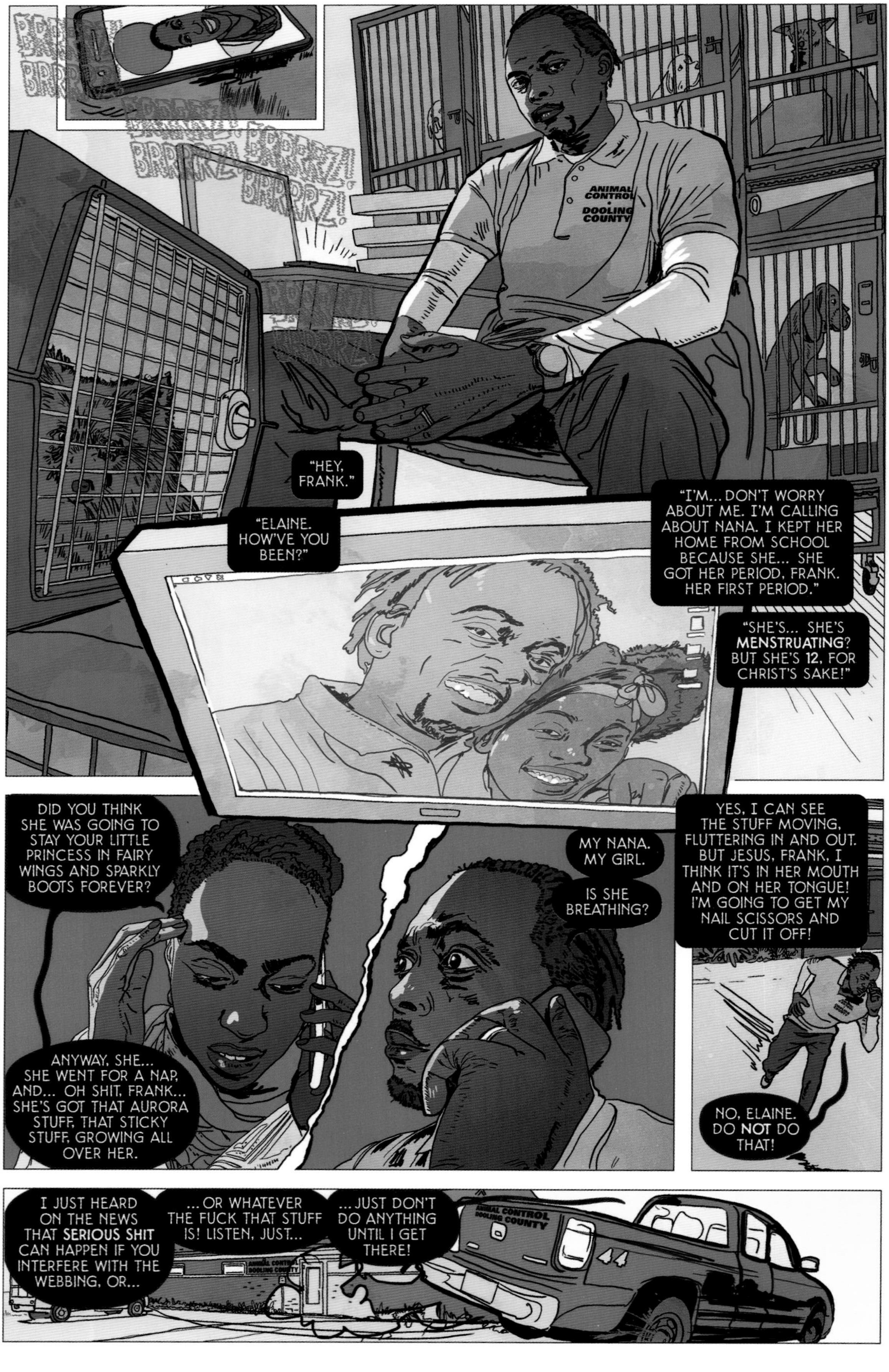

BRRRRZ! BRRRRZ! BRRRRZ! BRRRRZ! BRRRRZ!
ANIMAL CONTROL • DOOLING COUNTY
"HEY, FRANK."
"ELAINE. HOW'VE YOU BEEN?"
"I'M... DON'T WORRY ABOUT ME. I'M CALLING ABOUT NANA. I KEPT HER HOME FROM SCHOOL BECAUSE SHE... SHE GOT HER PERIOD, FRANK. HER FIRST PERIOD."
"SHE'S... SHE'S **MENSTRUATING**? BUT SHE'S **12**, FOR CHRIST'S SAKE!"
DID YOU THINK SHE WAS GOING TO STAY YOUR LITTLE PRINCESS IN FAIRY WINGS AND SPARKLY BOOTS FOREVER?
ANYWAY, SHE... SHE WENT FOR A NAP, AND... OH SHIT, FRANK... SHE'S GOT THAT AURORA STUFF, THAT STICKY STUFF, GROWING ALL OVER HER.
MY NANA. MY GIRL.
IS SHE BREATHING?
YES, I CAN SEE THE STUFF MOVING, FLUTTERING IN AND OUT. BUT JESUS, FRANK, I THINK IT'S IN HER MOUTH AND ON HER TONGUE! I'M GOING TO GET MY NAIL SCISSORS AND CUT IT OFF!
NO, ELAINE. DO **NOT** DO THAT!
I JUST HEARD ON THE NEWS THAT **SERIOUS SHIT** CAN HAPPEN IF YOU INTERFERE WITH THE WEBBING, OR...
...OR WHATEVER THE FUCK THAT STUFF IS! LISTEN, JUST...
...JUST DON'T DO ANYTHING UNTIL I GET THERE!
ANIMAL CONTROL DOOLING COUNTY
44

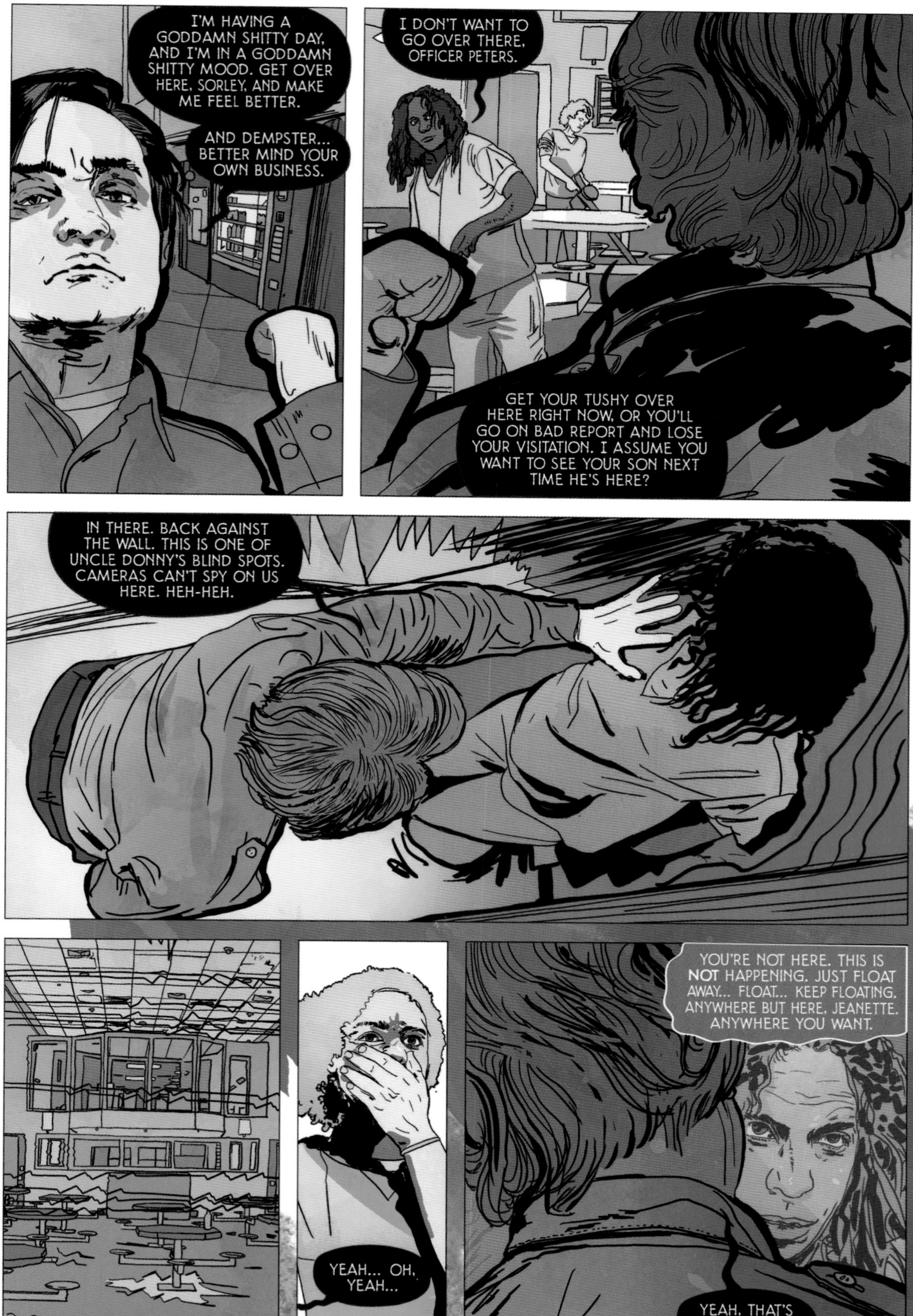
I'M HAVING A GODDAMN SHITTY DAY, AND I'M IN A GODDAMN SHITTY MOOD. GET OVER HERE, SORLEY, AND MAKE ME FEEL BETTER.
AND DEMPSTER... BETTER MIND YOUR OWN BUSINESS.
I DON'T WANT TO GO OVER THERE, OFFICER PETERS.
GET YOUR TUSHY OVER HERE RIGHT NOW, OR YOU'LL GO ON BAD REPORT AND LOSE YOUR VISITATION. I ASSUME YOU WANT TO SEE YOUR SON NEXT TIME HE'S HERE?
IN THERE. BACK AGAINST THE WALL. THIS IS ONE OF UNCLE DONNY'S BLIND SPOTS. CAMERAS CAN'T SPY ON US HERE. HEH-HEH.
YEAH... OH, YEAH...
YOU'RE NOT HERE. THIS IS NOT HAPPENING. JUST FLOAT AWAY... FLOAT... KEEP FLOATING. ANYWHERE BUT HERE, JEANETTE. ANYWHERE YOU WANT.
YEAH, THAT'S IT, GIRL... KEEP GOING...

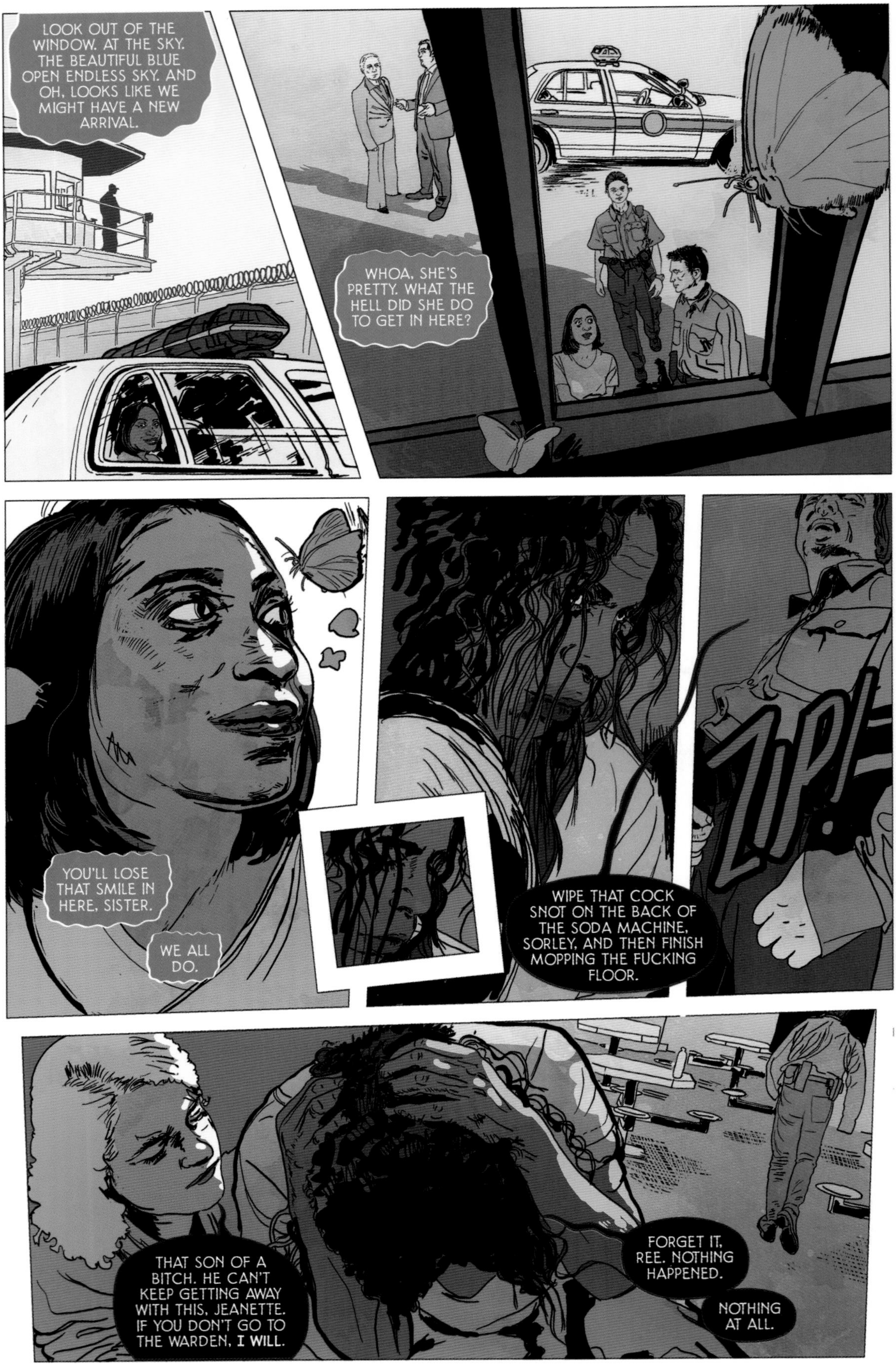

LOOK OUT OF THE WINDOW. AT THE SKY. THE BEAUTIFUL BLUE OPEN ENDLESS SKY. AND OH, LOOKS LIKE WE MIGHT HAVE A NEW ARRIVAL.
WHOA, SHE'S PRETTY. WHAT THE HELL DID SHE DO TO GET IN HERE?
YOU'LL LOSE THAT SMILE IN HERE, SISTER.
WE ALL DO.
WIPE THAT COCK SNOT ON THE BACK OF THE SODA MACHINE, SORLEY, AND THEN FINISH MOPPING THE FUCKING FLOOR.
ZIP!
THAT SON OF A BITCH. HE CAN'T KEEP GETTING AWAY WITH THIS, JEANETTE. IF YOU DON'T GO TO THE WARDEN, **I WILL.**
FORGET IT, REE. NOTHING HAPPENED.
NOTHING AT ALL.

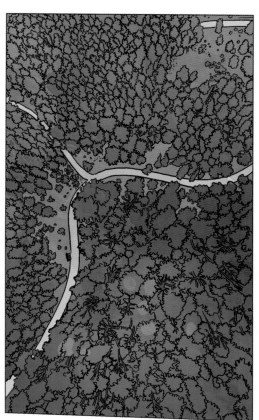

WAKEY-WAKEY, WILLY.

I WOULD HOPE ONE OF OUR LOYAL VOLUNTEERS KNOWS BETTER THAN TO FALL ASLEEP WITH A PIPE ON THE GO, ESPECIALLY CONSIDERING WE'VE HAD ONE BIG FIRE ALREADY TODAY.

I PUT FIRES OUT, SHERIFF. I DON'T START 'EM. BUT ANYWAY, I'M GLAD YOU'RE HERE.

COULD BE SOME CHEMICAL REACTION GOING ON BEYOND WHAT'S LEFT OF THAT SHED WE JUST HOSED DOWN. YOU MIGHT WANT TO HIKE UP THERE A QUARTER MILE OR SO AND TAKE A LOOK.

"LOOK IN THE TREES. ON THE GROUND. WHITE STUFF. ALL THICK AND STICKY. NEVER SEEN NOTHIN' LIKE IT, SHERIFF, AND I KNOW THESE WOODS A-COUNTRY FAIR."

WHAT THE HELL? THESE LOOK LIKE TRACKS ON THE GROUND... LIKE **FOOTPRINTS.**

SWEET JESUS...

33

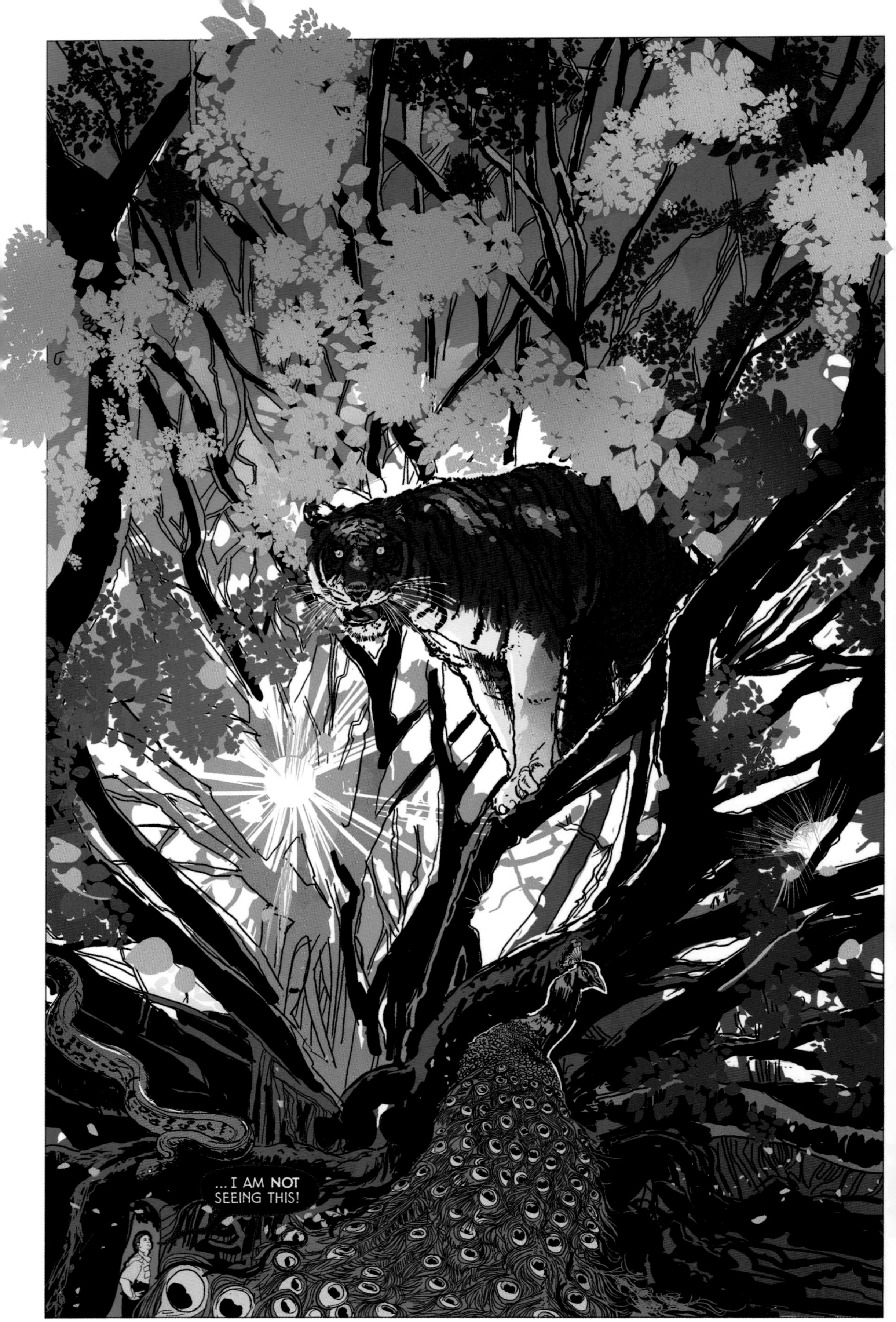
...I AM **NOT** SEEING THIS!

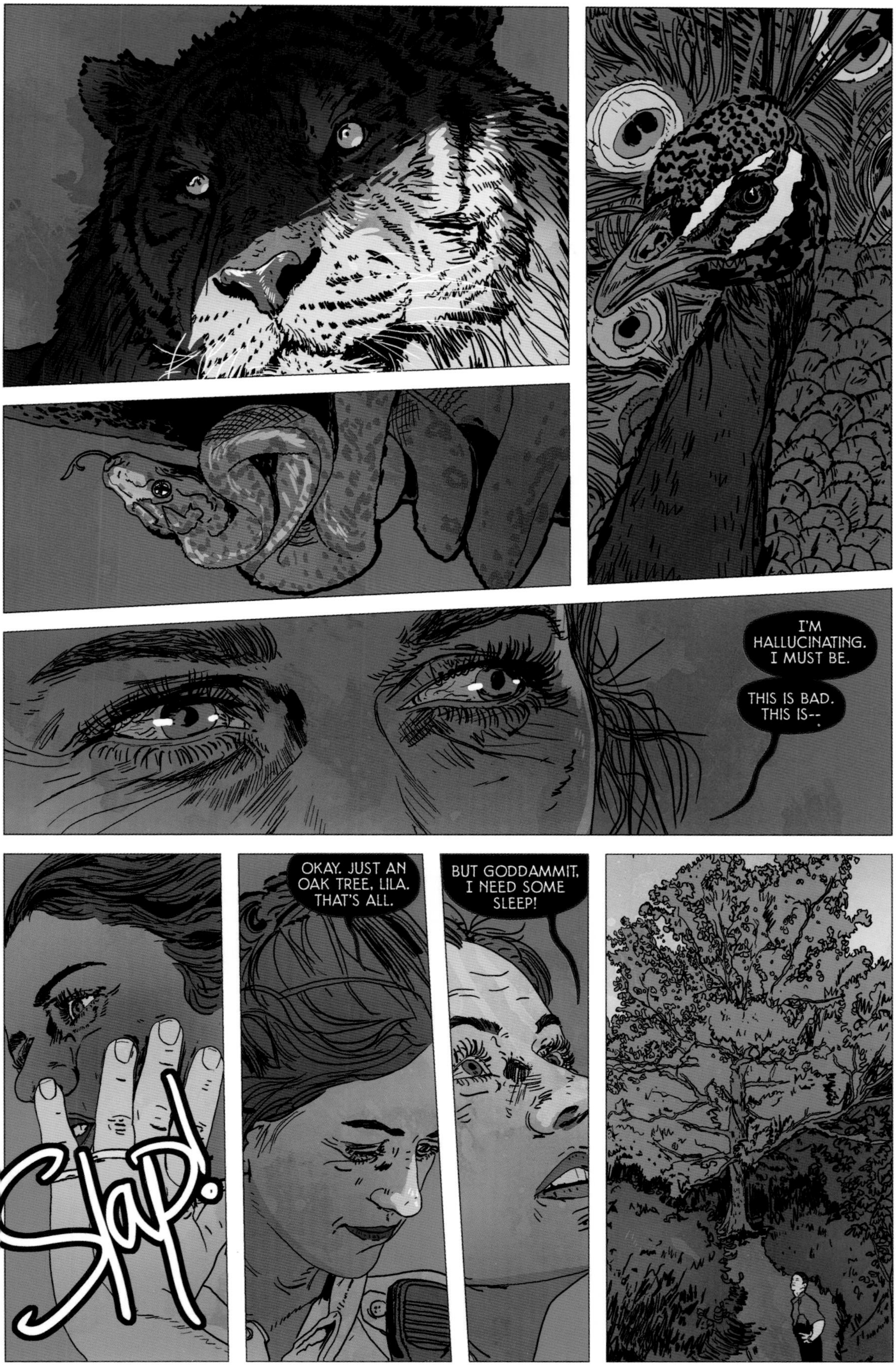
I'M HALLUCINATING. I MUST BE.
THIS IS BAD. THIS IS--
SLAP!
OKAY. JUST AN OAK TREE, LILA. THAT'S ALL.
BUT GODDAMMIT, I NEED SOME SLEEP!

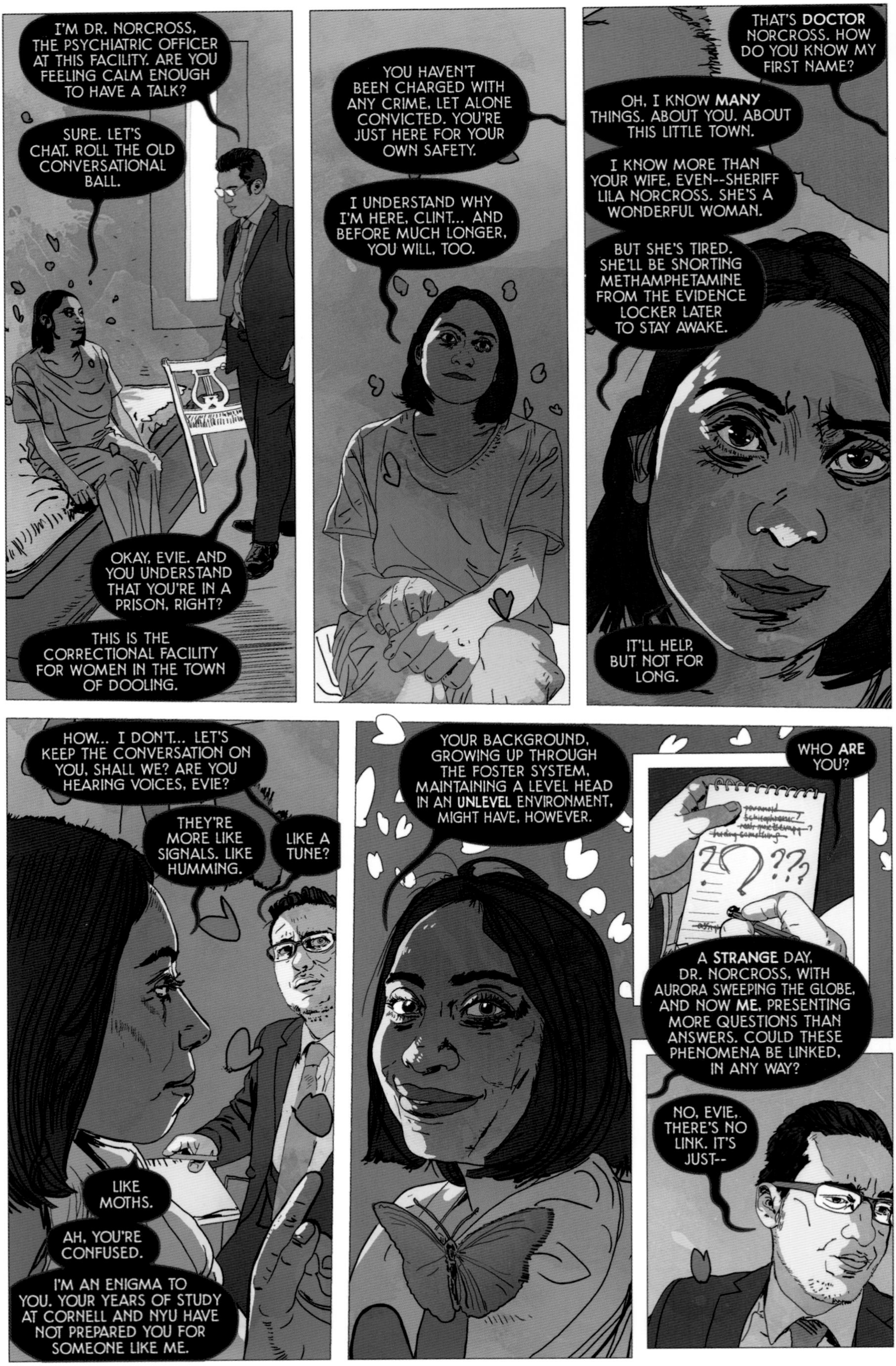

I'M DR. NORCROSS, THE PSYCHIATRIC OFFICER AT THIS FACILITY. ARE YOU FEELING CALM ENOUGH TO HAVE A TALK?
SURE. LET'S CHAT. ROLL THE OLD CONVERSATIONAL BALL.
OKAY, EVIE. AND YOU UNDERSTAND THAT YOU'RE IN A PRISON, RIGHT?
THIS IS THE CORRECTIONAL FACILITY FOR WOMEN IN THE TOWN OF DOOLING.
YOU HAVEN'T BEEN CHARGED WITH ANY CRIME, LET ALONE CONVICTED. YOU'RE JUST HERE FOR YOUR OWN SAFETY.
I UNDERSTAND WHY I'M HERE, CLINT... AND BEFORE MUCH LONGER, YOU WILL, TOO.
THAT'S **DOCTOR** NORCROSS. HOW DO YOU KNOW MY FIRST NAME?
OH, I KNOW **MANY** THINGS. ABOUT YOU. ABOUT THIS LITTLE TOWN.
I KNOW MORE THAN YOUR WIFE, EVEN--SHERIFF LILA NORCROSS. SHE'S A WONDERFUL WOMAN.
BUT SHE'S TIRED. SHE'LL BE SNORTING METHAMPHETAMINE FROM THE EVIDENCE LOCKER LATER TO STAY AWAKE.
IT'LL HELP, BUT NOT FOR LONG.
HOW... I DON'T... LET'S KEEP THE CONVERSATION ON YOU, SHALL WE? ARE YOU HEARING VOICES, EVIE?
THEY'RE MORE LIKE SIGNALS. LIKE HUMMING.
LIKE A TUNE?
LIKE MOTHS.
AH, YOU'RE CONFUSED.
I'M AN ENIGMA TO YOU. YOUR YEARS OF STUDY AT CORNELL AND NYU HAVE NOT PREPARED YOU FOR SOMEONE LIKE ME.
YOUR BACKGROUND, GROWING UP THROUGH THE FOSTER SYSTEM, MAINTAINING A LEVEL HEAD IN AN **UNLEVEL** ENVIRONMENT, MIGHT HAVE, HOWEVER.
WHO **ARE** YOU?
A **STRANGE** DAY, DR. NORCROSS, WITH AURORA SWEEPING THE GLOBE, AND NOW **ME**, PRESENTING MORE QUESTIONS THAN ANSWERS. COULD THESE PHENOMENA BE LINKED, IN ANY WAY?
NO, EVIE, THERE'S NO LINK. IT'S JUST--

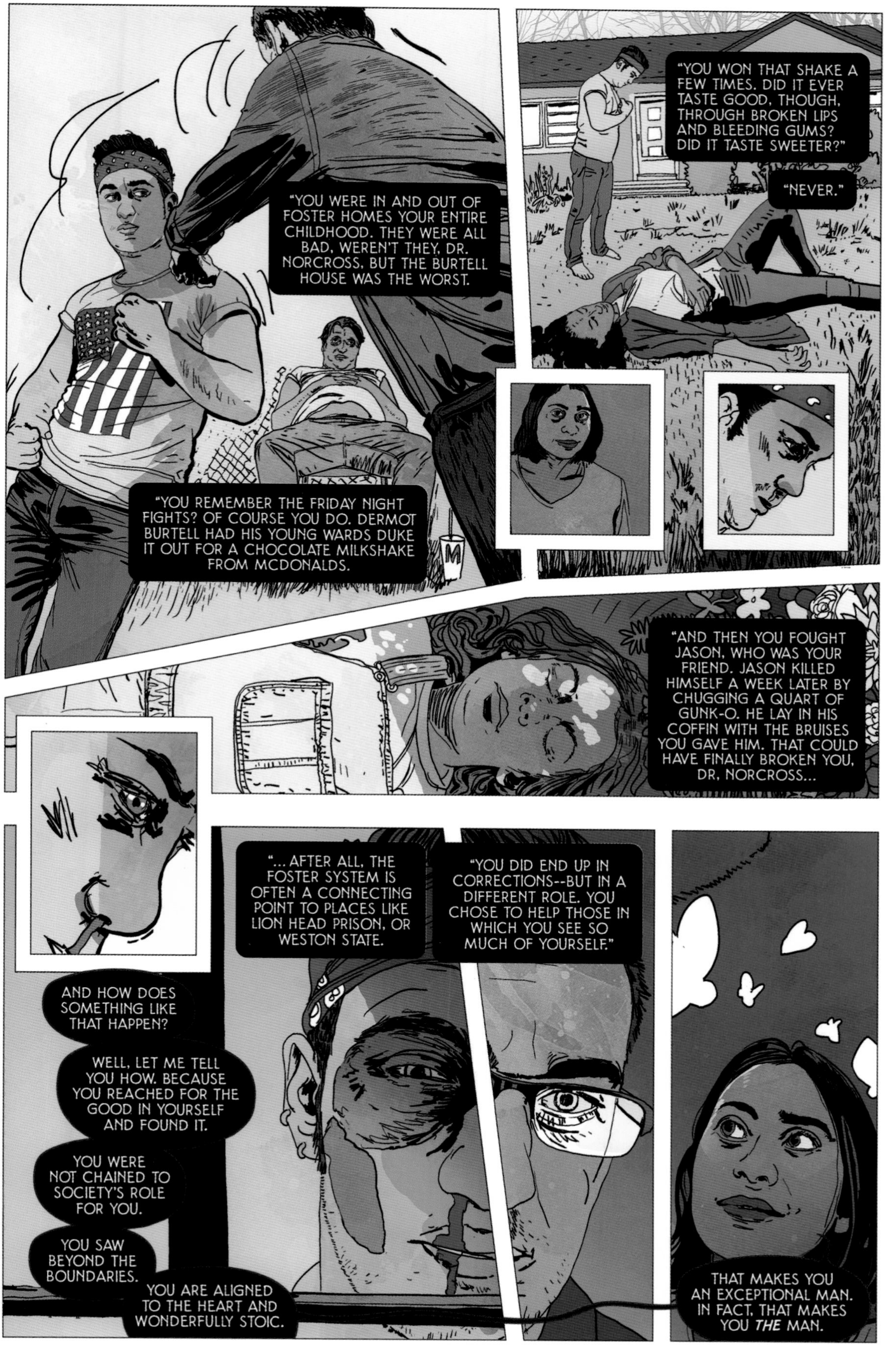

"YOU WERE IN AND OUT OF FOSTER HOMES YOUR ENTIRE CHILDHOOD. THEY WERE ALL BAD, WEREN'T THEY, DR. NORCROSS. BUT THE BURTELL HOUSE WAS THE WORST.
"YOU REMEMBER THE FRIDAY NIGHT FIGHTS? OF COURSE YOU DO. DERMOT BURTELL HAD HIS YOUNG WARDS DUKE IT OUT FOR A CHOCOLATE MILKSHAKE FROM MCDONALDS.
"YOU WON THAT SHAKE A FEW TIMES. DID IT EVER TASTE GOOD, THOUGH, THROUGH BROKEN LIPS AND BLEEDING GUMS? DID IT TASTE SWEETER?"
"NEVER."
"AND THEN YOU FOUGHT JASON, WHO WAS YOUR FRIEND. JASON KILLED HIMSELF A WEEK LATER BY CHUGGING A QUART OF GUNK-O. HE LAY IN HIS COFFIN WITH THE BRUISES YOU GAVE HIM. THAT COULD HAVE FINALLY BROKEN YOU, DR. NORCROSS...
"... AFTER ALL, THE FOSTER SYSTEM IS OFTEN A CONNECTING POINT TO PLACES LIKE LION HEAD PRISON, OR WESTON STATE.
"YOU DID END UP IN CORRECTIONS--BUT IN A DIFFERENT ROLE. YOU CHOSE TO HELP THOSE IN WHICH YOU SEE SO MUCH OF YOURSELF."
AND HOW DOES SOMETHING LIKE THAT HAPPEN?
WELL, LET ME TELL YOU HOW. BECAUSE YOU REACHED FOR THE GOOD IN YOURSELF AND FOUND IT.
YOU WERE NOT CHAINED TO SOCIETY'S ROLE FOR YOU.
YOU SAW BEYOND THE BOUNDARIES.
YOU ARE ALIGNED TO THE HEART AND WONDERFULLY STOIC.
THAT MAKES YOU AN EXCEPTIONAL MAN. IN FACT, THAT MAKES YOU *THE* MAN.

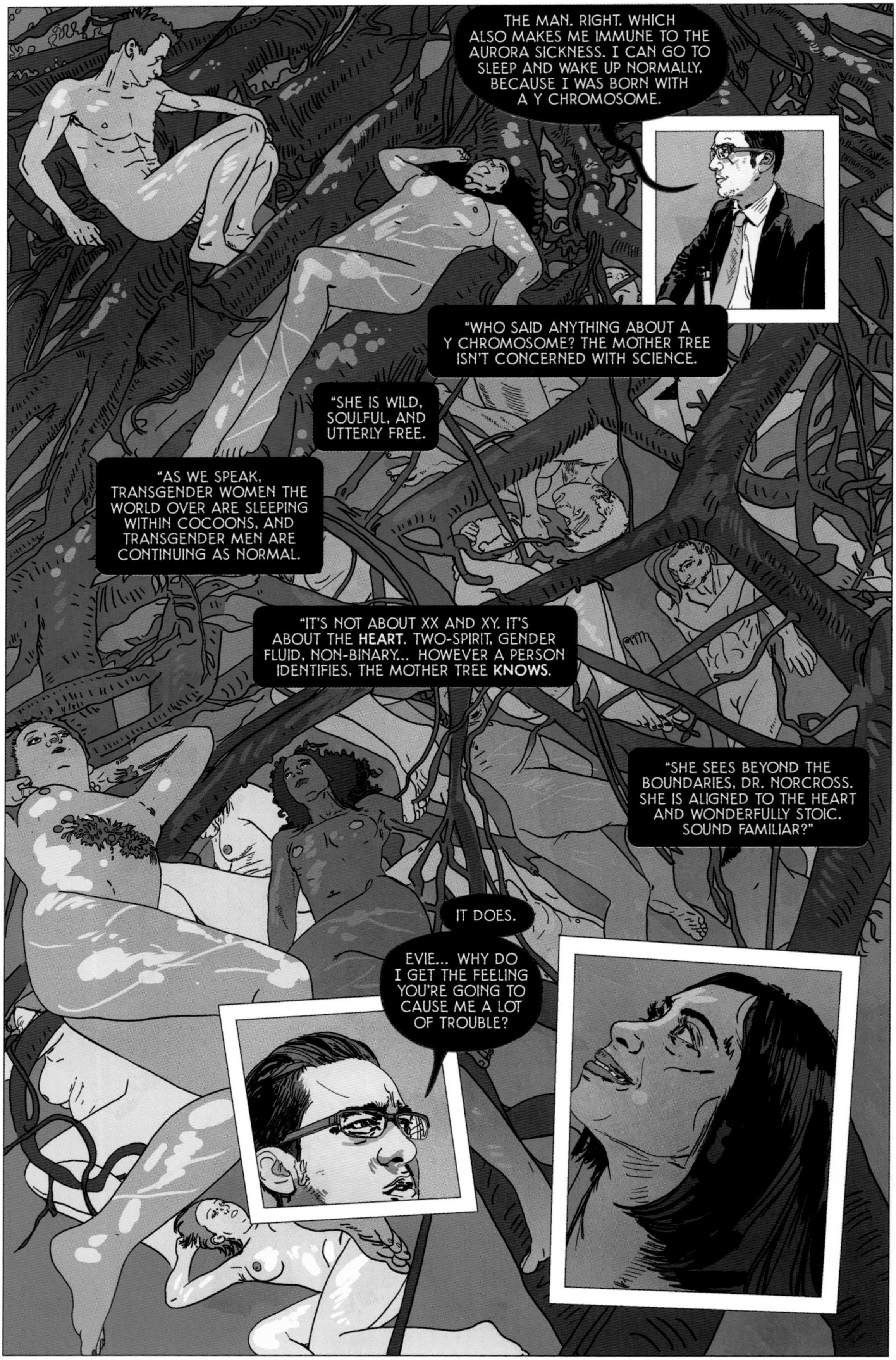
THE MAN. RIGHT. WHICH ALSO MAKES ME IMMUNE TO THE AURORA SICKNESS. I CAN GO TO SLEEP AND WAKE UP NORMALLY, BECAUSE I WAS BORN WITH A Y CHROMOSOME.
"WHO SAID ANYTHING ABOUT A Y CHROMOSOME? THE MOTHER TREE ISN'T CONCERNED WITH SCIENCE.
"SHE IS WILD, SOULFUL, AND UTTERLY FREE.
"AS WE SPEAK, TRANSGENDER WOMEN THE WORLD OVER ARE SLEEPING WITHIN COCOONS, AND TRANSGENDER MEN ARE CONTINUING AS NORMAL.
"IT'S NOT ABOUT XX AND XY. IT'S ABOUT THE **HEART**. TWO-SPIRIT, GENDER FLUID, NON-BINARY... HOWEVER A PERSON IDENTIFIES, THE MOTHER TREE **KNOWS**.
"SHE SEES BEYOND THE BOUNDARIES, DR. NORCROSS. SHE IS ALIGNED TO THE HEART AND WONDERFULLY STOIC. SOUND FAMILIAR?"
IT DOES.
EVIE... WHY DO I GET THE FEELING YOU'RE GOING TO CAUSE ME A LOT OF TROUBLE?

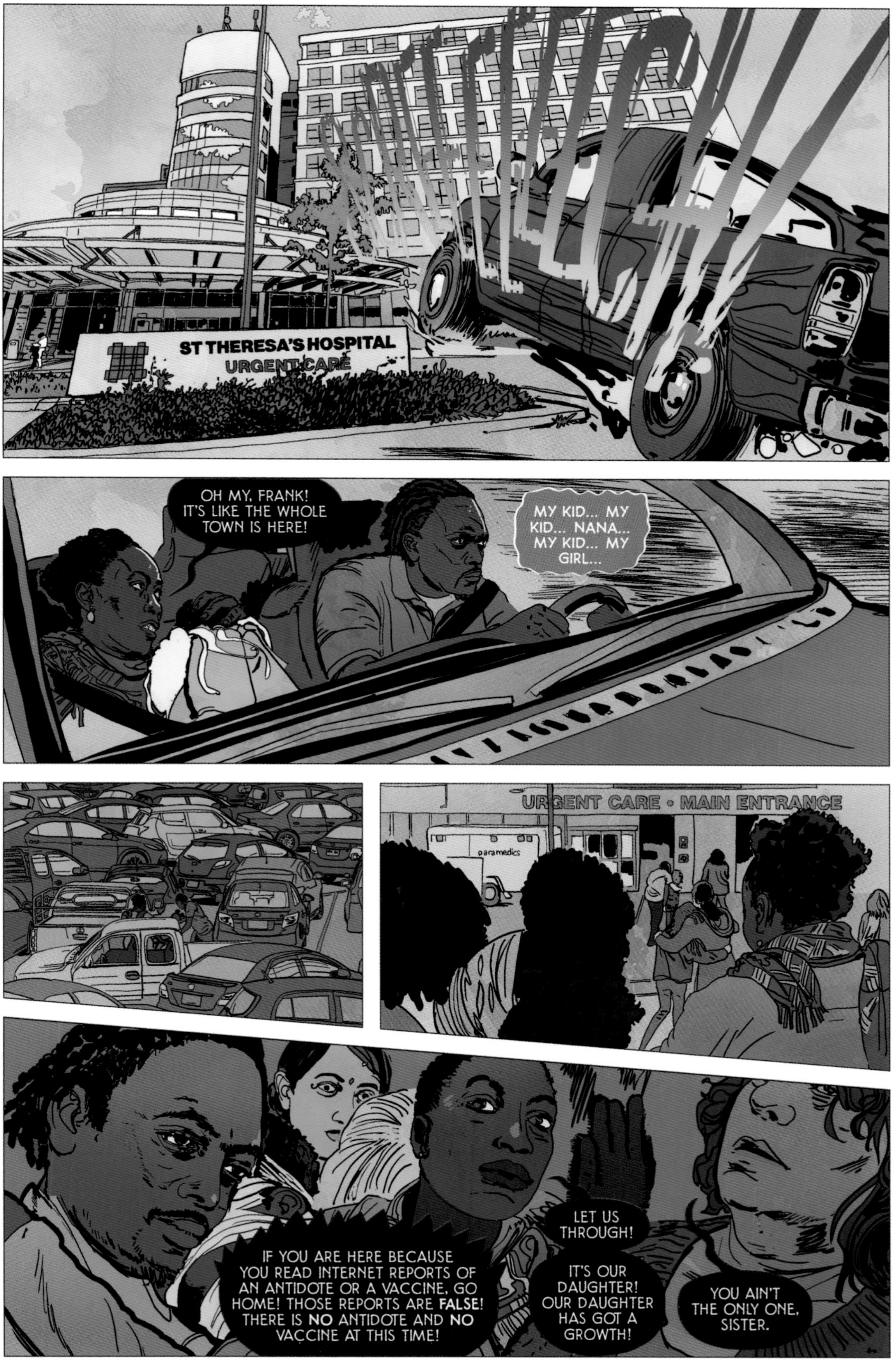
SCREEEECH
ST THERESA'S HOSPITAL
URGENT CARE
OH MY, FRANK! IT'S LIKE THE WHOLE TOWN IS HERE!
MY KID... MY KID... NANA... MY KID... MY GIRL...
URGENT CARE • MAIN ENTRANCE
paramedics
IF YOU ARE HERE BECAUSE YOU READ INTERNET REPORTS OF AN ANTIDOTE OR A VACCINE, GO HOME! THOSE REPORTS ARE **FALSE**! THERE IS **NO** ANTIDOTE AND **NO** VACCINE AT THIS TIME!
LET US THROUGH!
IT'S OUR DAUGHTER! OUR DAUGHTER HAS GOT A GROWTH!
YOU AIN'T THE ONLY ONE, SISTER.

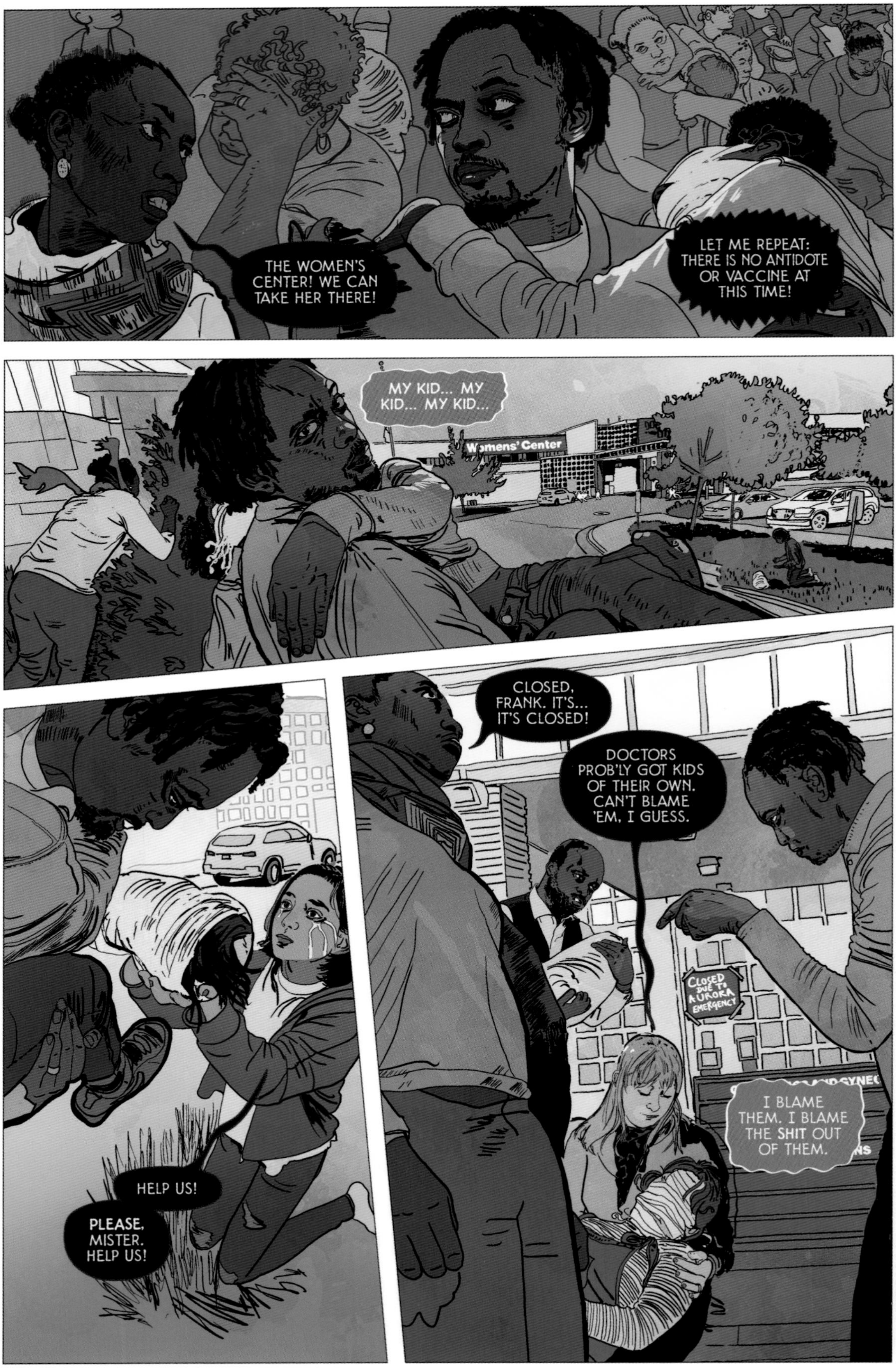
THE WOMEN'S CENTER! WE CAN TAKE HER THERE!
LET ME REPEAT: THERE IS NO ANTIDOTE OR VACCINE AT THIS TIME!
MY KID... MY KID... MY KID...
Womens' Center
HELP US!
PLEASE, MISTER. HELP US!
CLOSED, FRANK. IT'S... IT'S CLOSED!
DOCTORS PROB'LY GOT KIDS OF THEIR OWN. CAN'T BLAME 'EM, I GUESS.
CLOSED DUE TO AURORA EMERGENCY
I BLAME THEM. I BLAME THE **SHIT** OUT OF THEM.

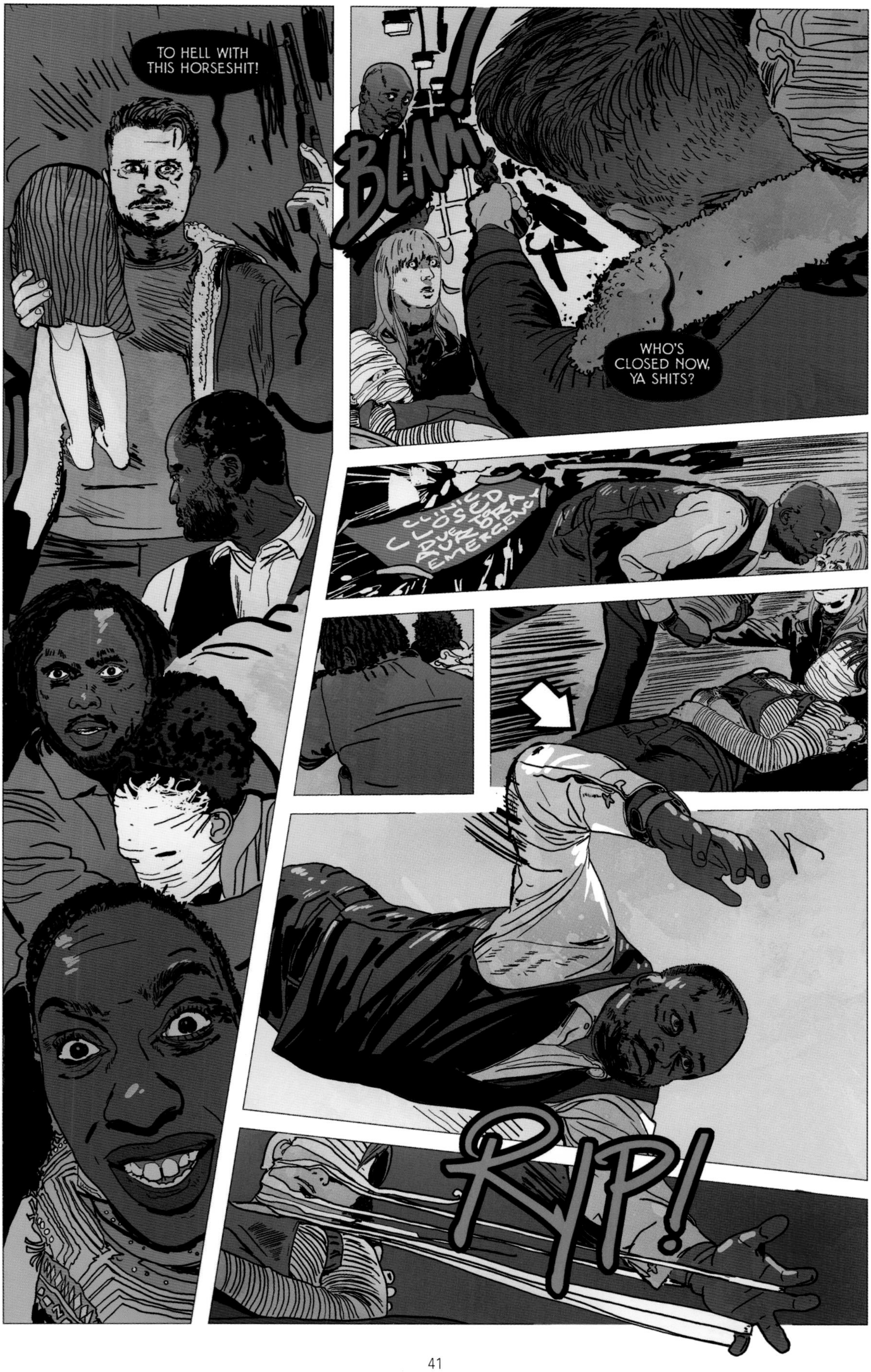
TO HELL WITH THIS HORSESHIT!
BLAM!
WHO'S CLOSED NOW, YA SHITS?
RIP!

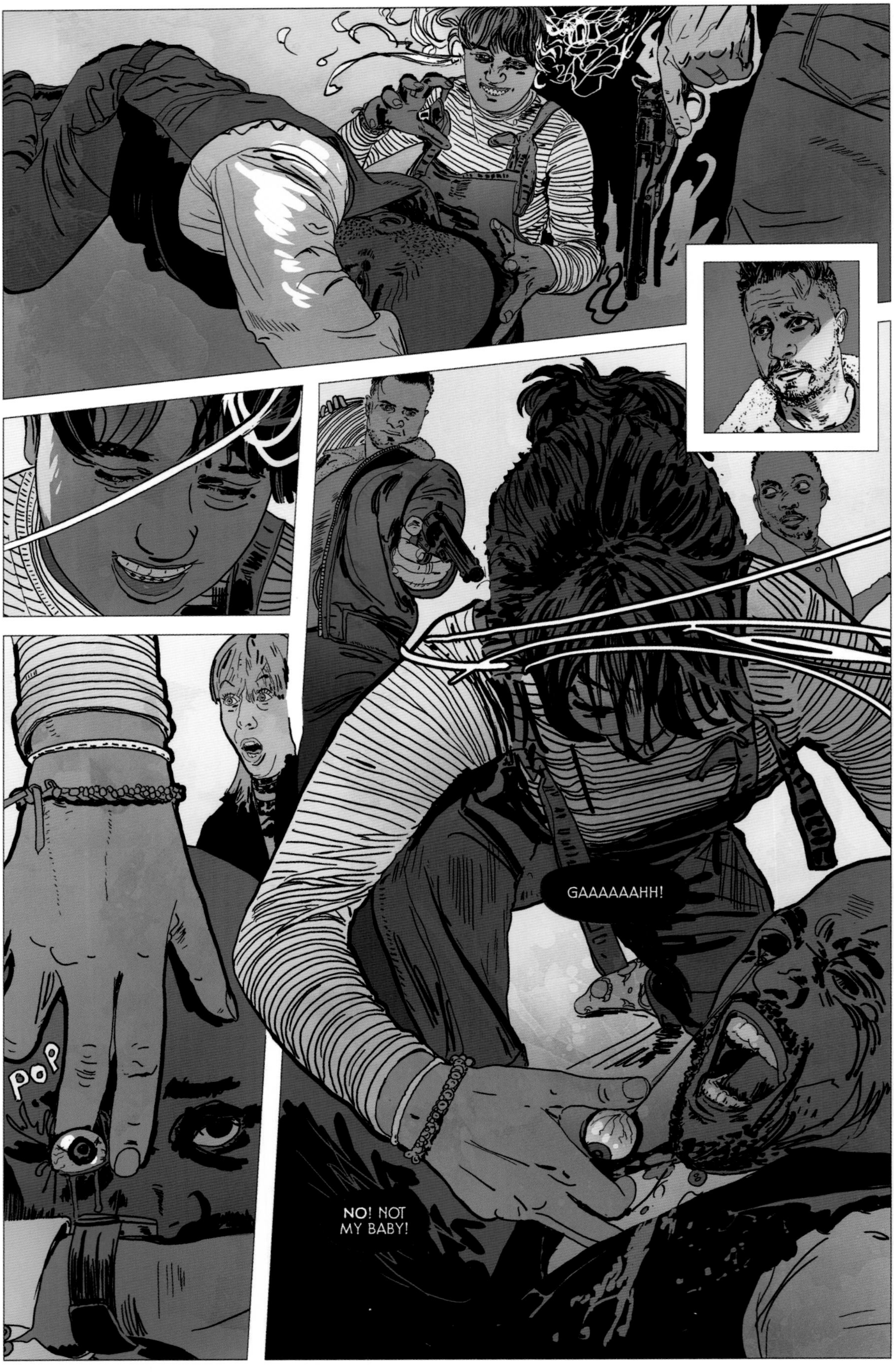

GAAAAAAHH!
POP
NO! NOT
MY BABY!

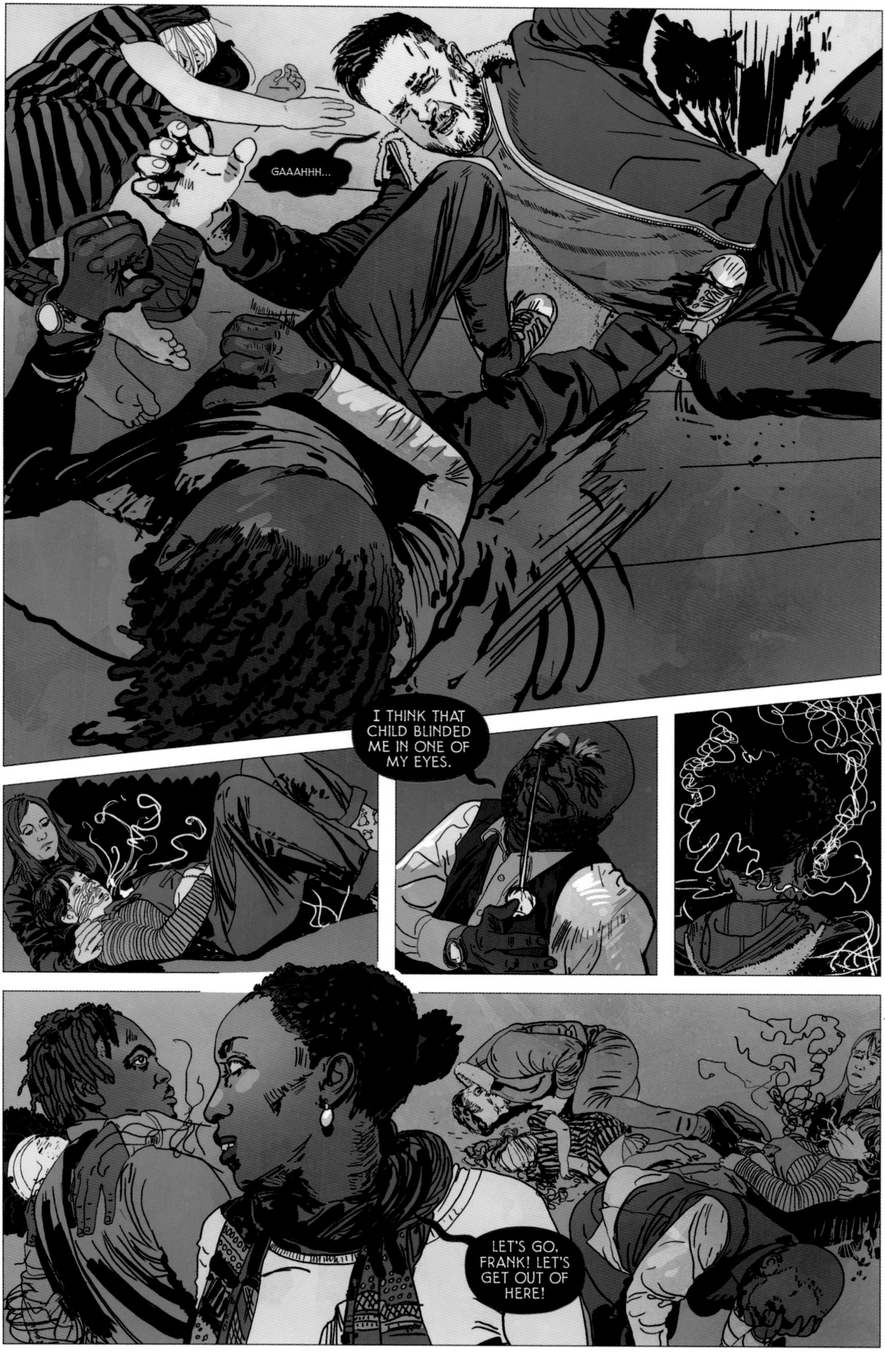
GAAAHHH...
I THINK THAT CHILD BLINDED ME IN ONE OF MY EYES.
LET'S GO, FRANK! LET'S GET OUT OF HERE!

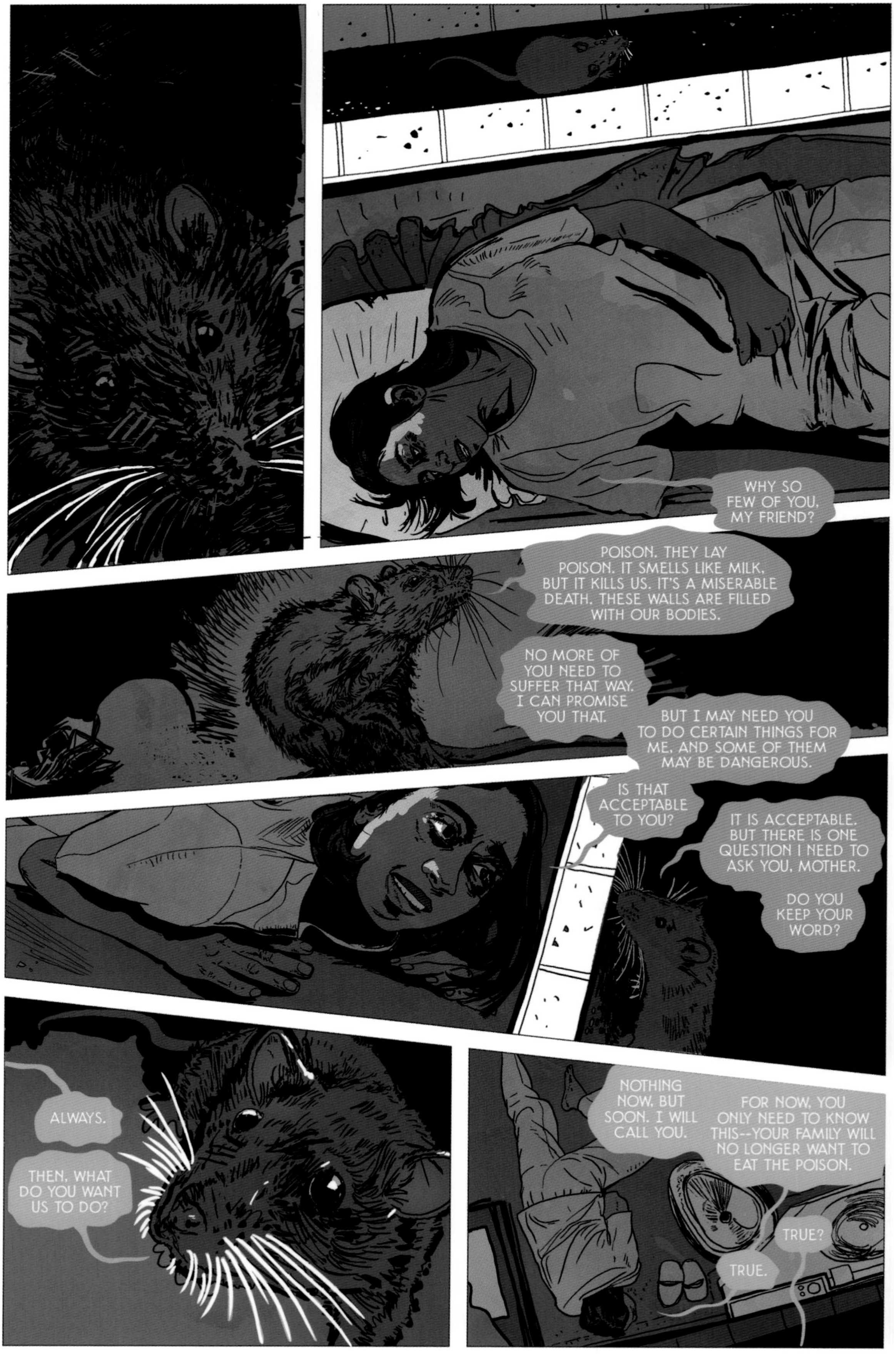
WHY SO FEW OF YOU, MY FRIEND?
POISON. THEY LAY POISON. IT SMELLS LIKE MILK, BUT IT KILLS US. IT'S A MISERABLE DEATH. THESE WALLS ARE FILLED WITH OUR BODIES.
NO MORE OF YOU NEED TO SUFFER THAT WAY. I CAN PROMISE YOU THAT.
BUT I MAY NEED YOU TO DO CERTAIN THINGS FOR ME, AND SOME OF THEM MAY BE DANGEROUS.
IS THAT ACCEPTABLE TO YOU?
IT IS ACCEPTABLE. BUT THERE IS ONE QUESTION I NEED TO ASK YOU, MOTHER.
DO YOU KEEP YOUR WORD?
ALWAYS.
THEN, WHAT DO YOU WANT US TO DO?
NOTHING NOW, BUT SOON. I WILL CALL YOU.
FOR NOW, YOU ONLY NEED TO KNOW THIS--YOUR FAMILY WILL NO LONGER WANT TO EAT THE POISON.
TRUE?
TRUE.

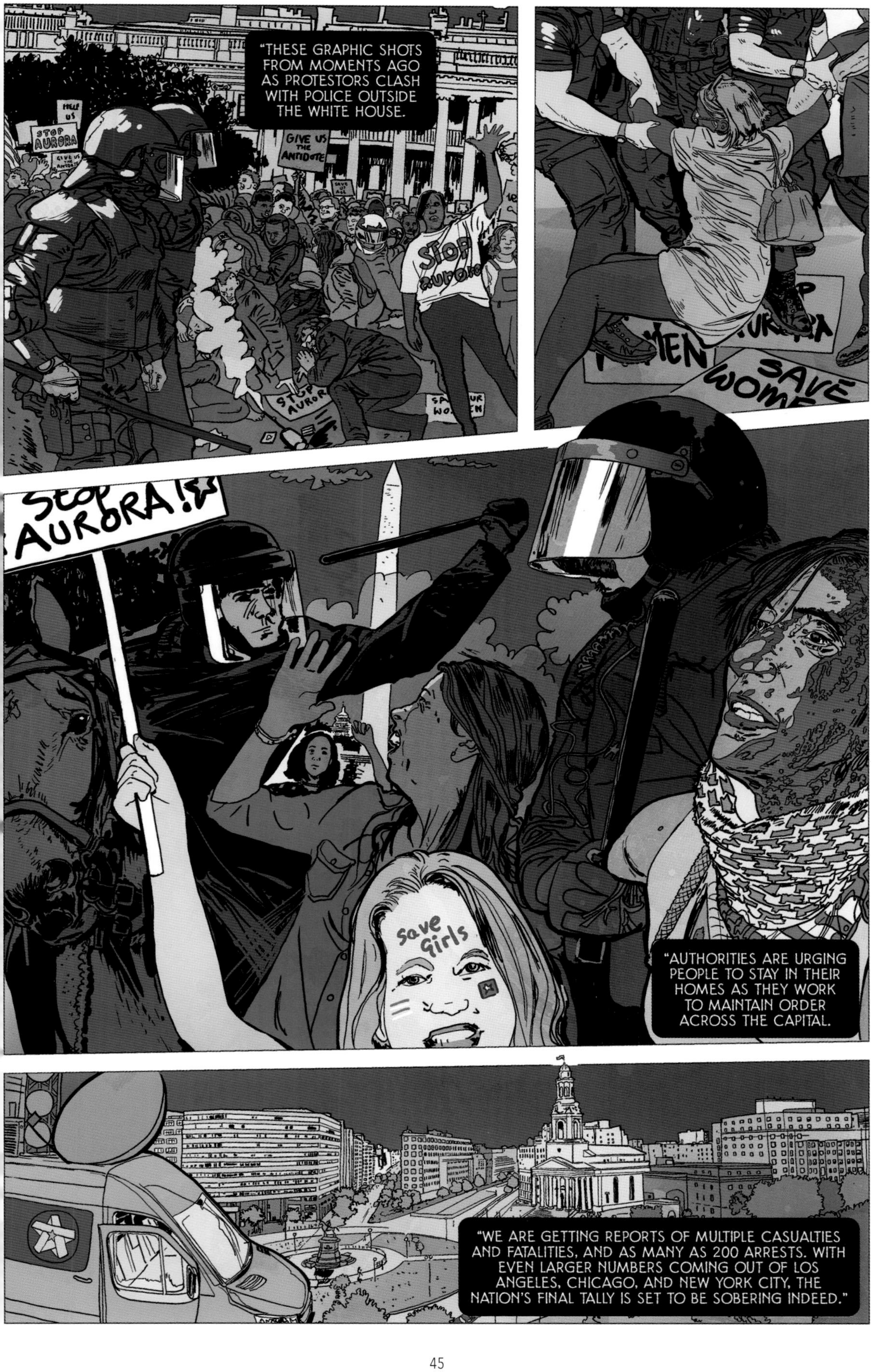

"THESE GRAPHIC SHOTS FROM MOMENTS AGO AS PROTESTORS CLASH WITH POLICE OUTSIDE THE WHITE HOUSE.
STOP AURORA
GIVE US THE ANTIDOTE
STOP AURORA
SAVE WOMEN
Stop AURORA!
save Girls
"AUTHORITIES ARE URGING PEOPLE TO STAY IN THEIR HOMES AS THEY WORK TO MAINTAIN ORDER ACROSS THE CAPITAL.
"WE ARE GETTING REPORTS OF MULTIPLE CASUALTIES AND FATALITIES, AND AS MANY AS 200 ARRESTS. WITH EVEN LARGER NUMBERS COMING OUT OF LOS ANGELES, CHICAGO, AND NEW YORK CITY, THE NATION'S FINAL TALLY IS SET TO BE SOBERING INDEED."

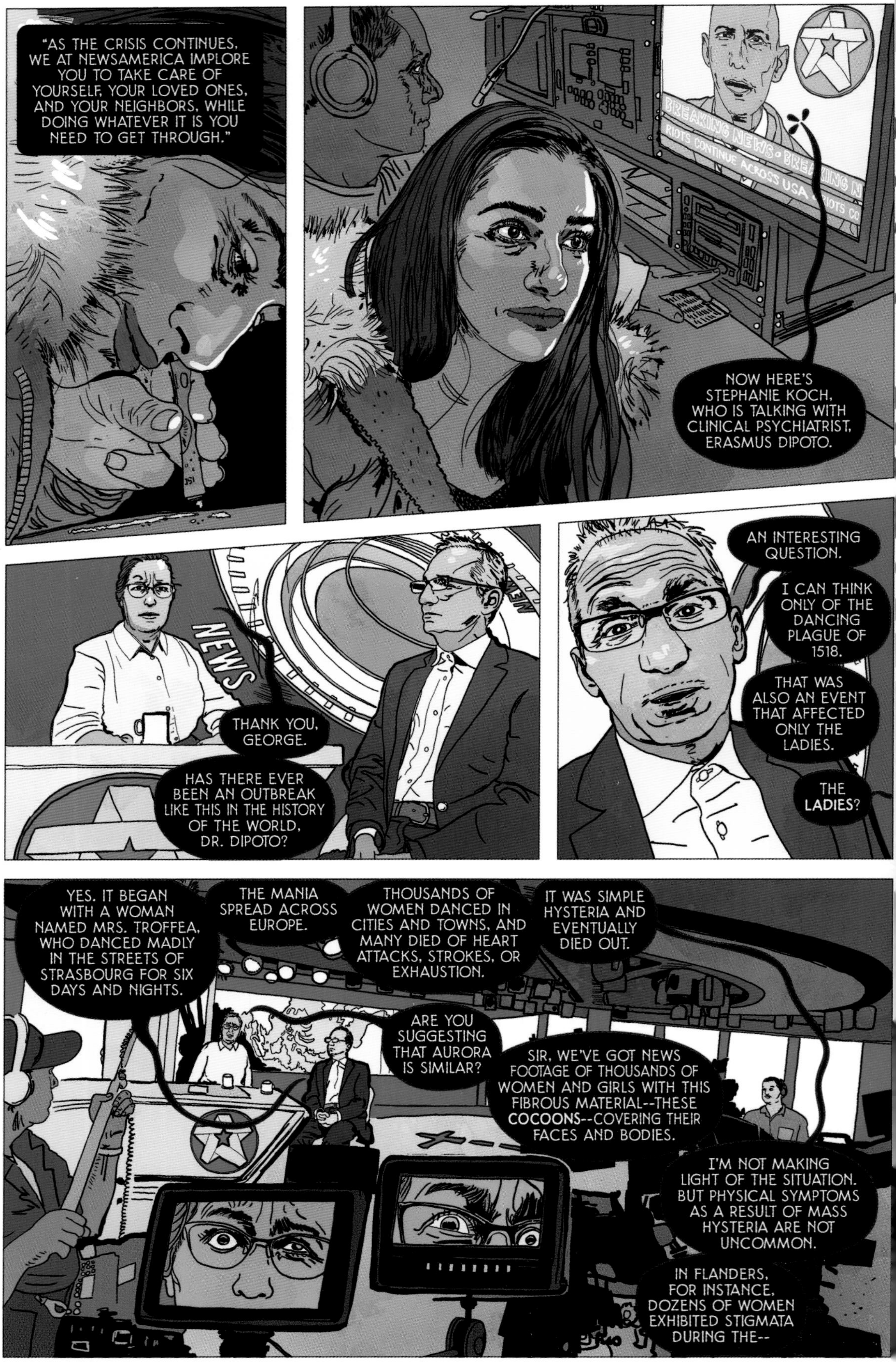
"AS THE CRISIS CONTINUES, WE AT NEWSAMERICA IMPLORE YOU TO TAKE CARE OF YOURSELF, YOUR LOVED ONES, AND YOUR NEIGHBORS, WHILE DOING WHATEVER IT IS YOU NEED TO GET THROUGH."
BREAKING NEWS
RIOTS CONTINUE ACROSS USA
NOW HERE'S STEPHANIE KOCH, WHO IS TALKING WITH CLINICAL PSYCHIATRIST, ERASMUS DIPOTO.
NEWS
THANK YOU, GEORGE.
HAS THERE EVER BEEN AN OUTBREAK LIKE THIS IN THE HISTORY OF THE WORLD, DR. DIPOTO?
AN INTERESTING QUESTION.
I CAN THINK ONLY OF THE DANCING PLAGUE OF 1518.
THAT WAS ALSO AN EVENT THAT AFFECTED ONLY THE LADIES.
THE **LADIES**?
YES. IT BEGAN WITH A WOMAN NAMED MRS. TROFFEA, WHO DANCED MADLY IN THE STREETS OF STRASBOURG FOR SIX DAYS AND NIGHTS.
THE MANIA SPREAD ACROSS EUROPE.
THOUSANDS OF WOMEN DANCED IN CITIES AND TOWNS, AND MANY DIED OF HEART ATTACKS, STROKES, OR EXHAUSTION.
IT WAS SIMPLE HYSTERIA AND EVENTUALLY DIED OUT.
ARE YOU SUGGESTING THAT AURORA IS SIMILAR?
SIR, WE'VE GOT NEWS FOOTAGE OF THOUSANDS OF WOMEN AND GIRLS WITH THIS FIBROUS MATERIAL--THESE **COCOONS**--COVERING THEIR FACES AND BODIES.
I'M NOT MAKING LIGHT OF THE SITUATION. BUT PHYSICAL SYMPTOMS AS A RESULT OF MASS HYSTERIA ARE NOT UNCOMMON.
IN FLANDERS, FOR INSTANCE, DOZENS OF WOMEN EXHIBITED STIGMATA DURING THE--

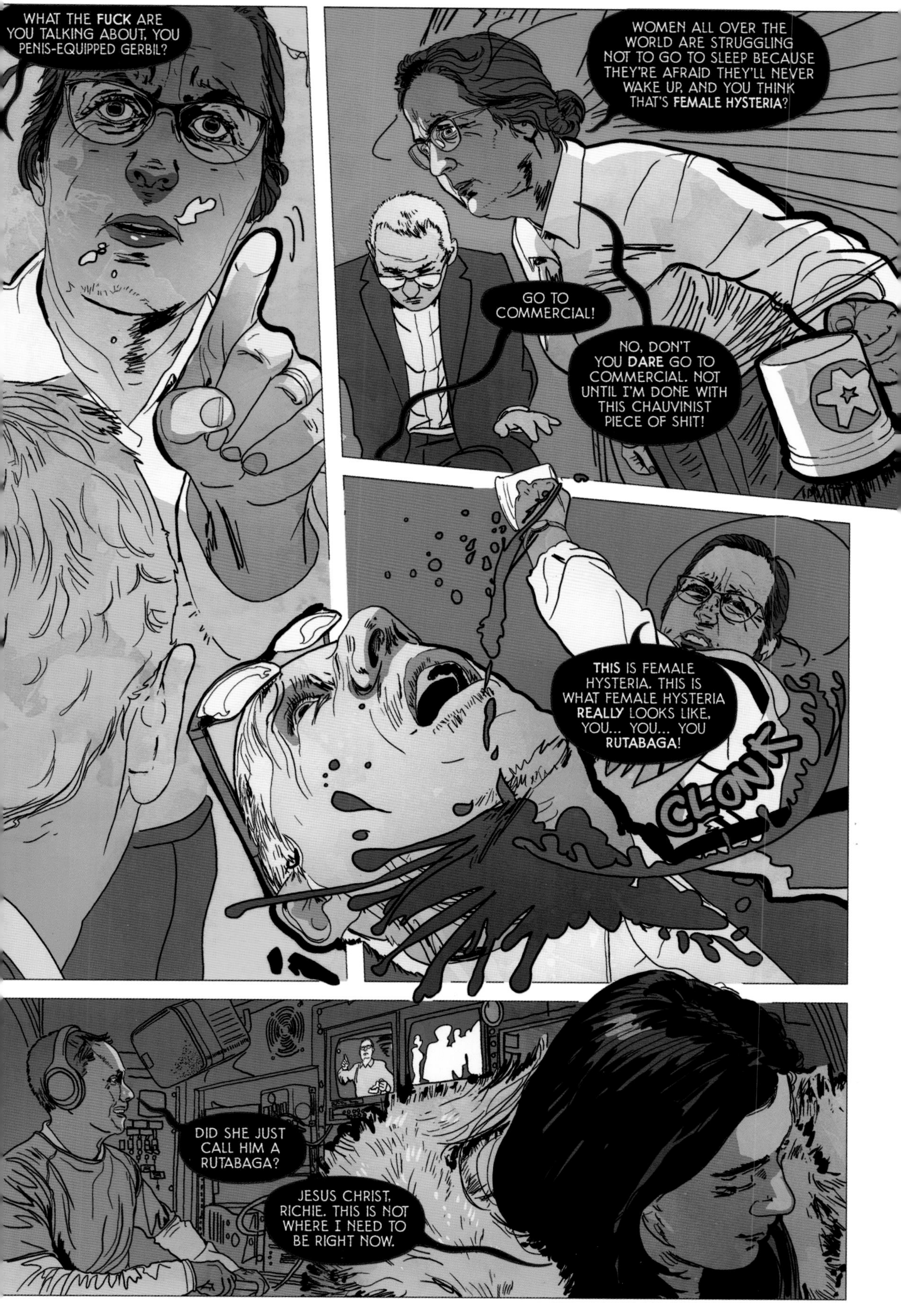
WHAT THE **FUCK** ARE YOU TALKING ABOUT, YOU PENIS-EQUIPPED GERBIL?
WOMEN ALL OVER THE WORLD ARE STRUGGLING NOT TO GO TO SLEEP BECAUSE THEY'RE AFRAID THEY'LL NEVER WAKE UP, AND YOU THINK THAT'S **FEMALE HYSTERIA**?
GO TO COMMERCIAL!
NO, DON'T YOU **DARE** GO TO COMMERCIAL. NOT UNTIL I'M DONE WITH THIS CHAUVINIST PIECE OF SHIT!
THIS IS FEMALE HYSTERIA. THIS IS WHAT FEMALE HYSTERIA **REALLY** LOOKS LIKE. YOU... YOU... YOU **RUTABAGA**!
CLONK
DID SHE JUST CALL HIM A RUTABAGA?
JESUS CHRIST, RICHIE. THIS IS NOT WHERE I NEED TO BE RIGHT NOW.

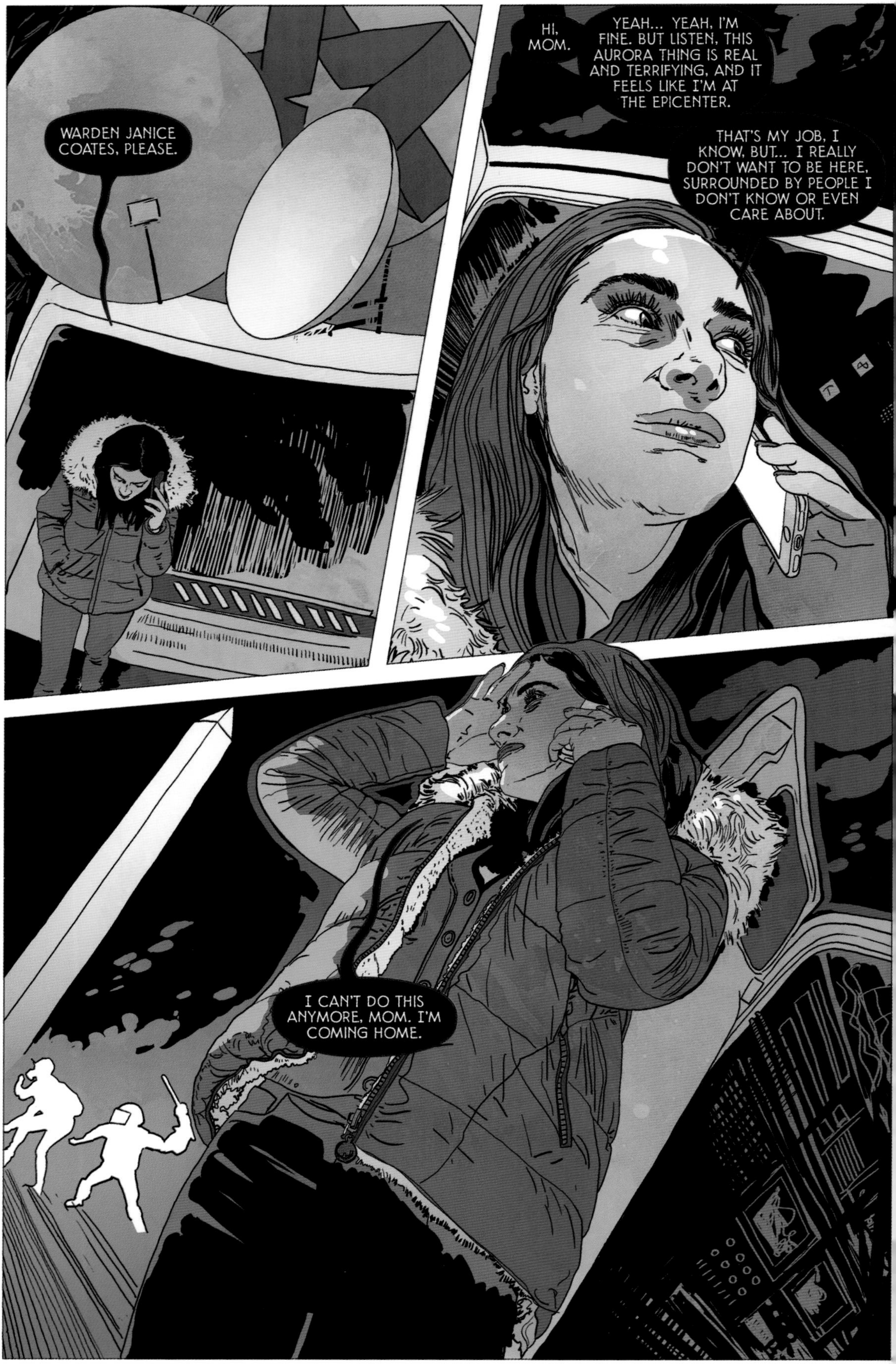
WARDEN JANICE COATES, PLEASE.
HI, MOM.
YEAH... YEAH, I'M FINE. BUT LISTEN, THIS AURORA THING IS REAL AND TERRIFYING, AND IT FEELS LIKE I'M AT THE EPICENTER.
THAT'S MY JOB, I KNOW, BUT... I REALLY DON'T WANT TO BE HERE, SURROUNDED BY PEOPLE I DON'T KNOW OR EVEN CARE ABOUT.
I CAN'T DO THIS ANYMORE, MOM. I'M COMING HOME.

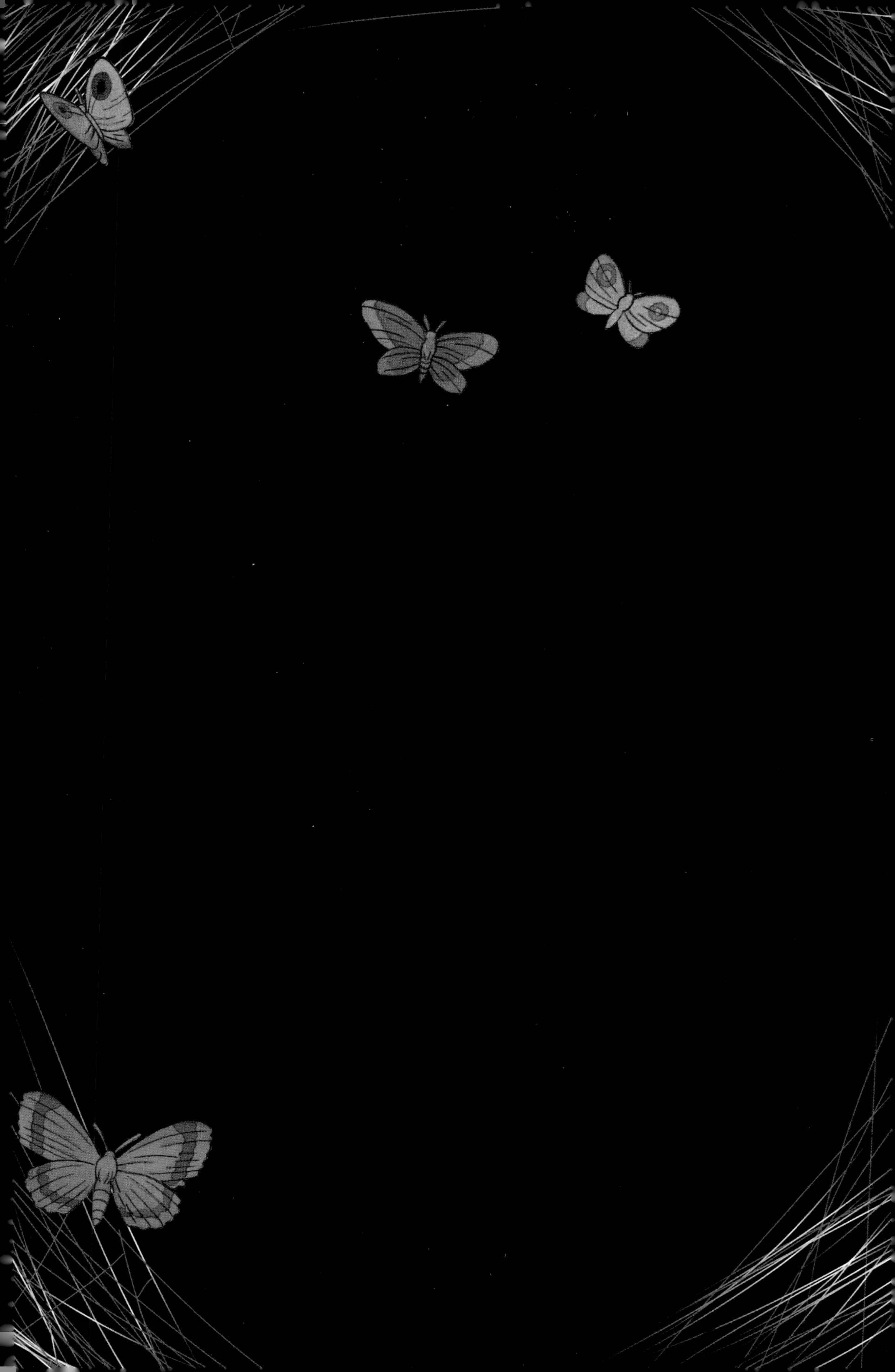

ART BY ANNIE WU

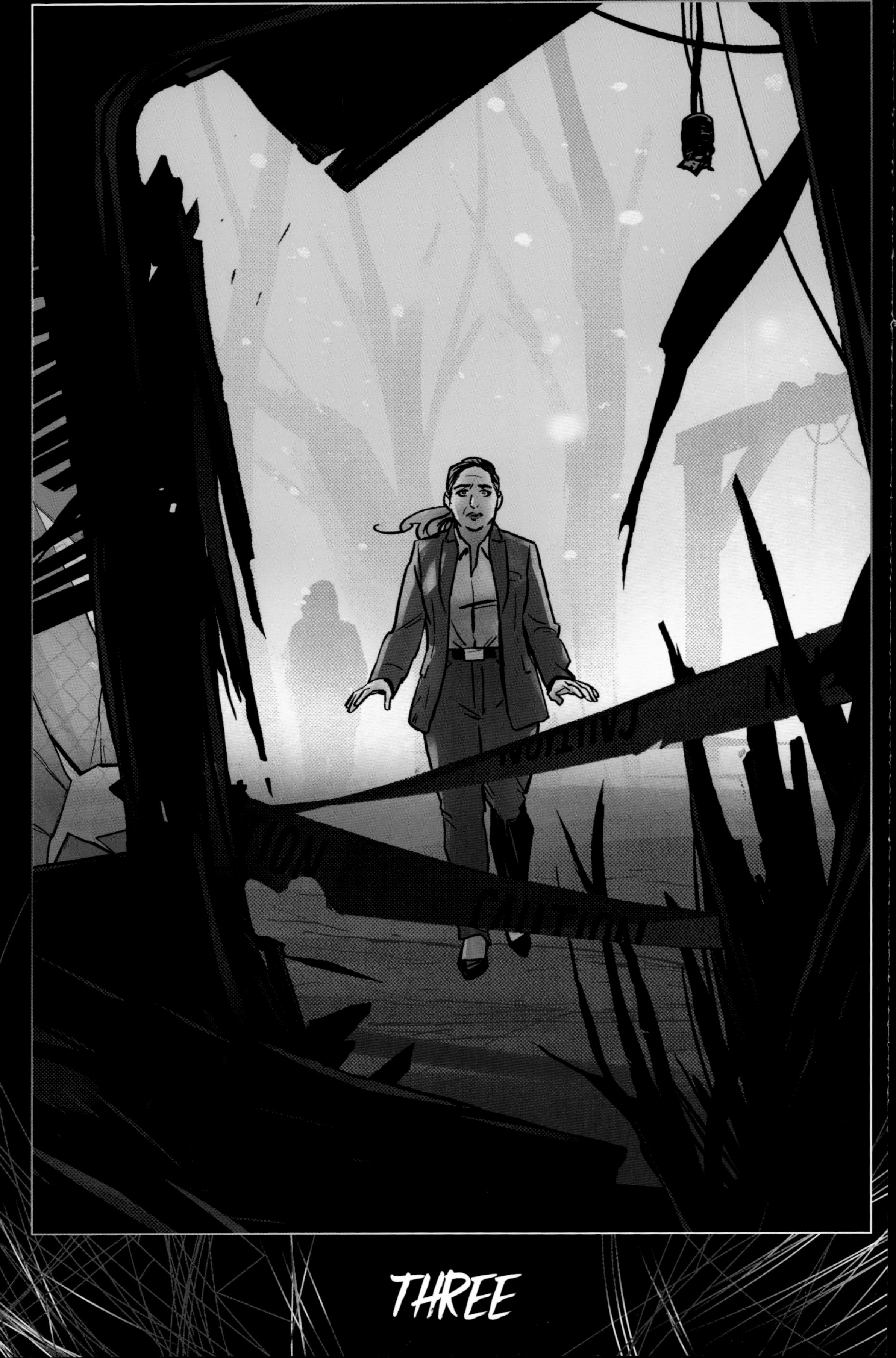

THREE

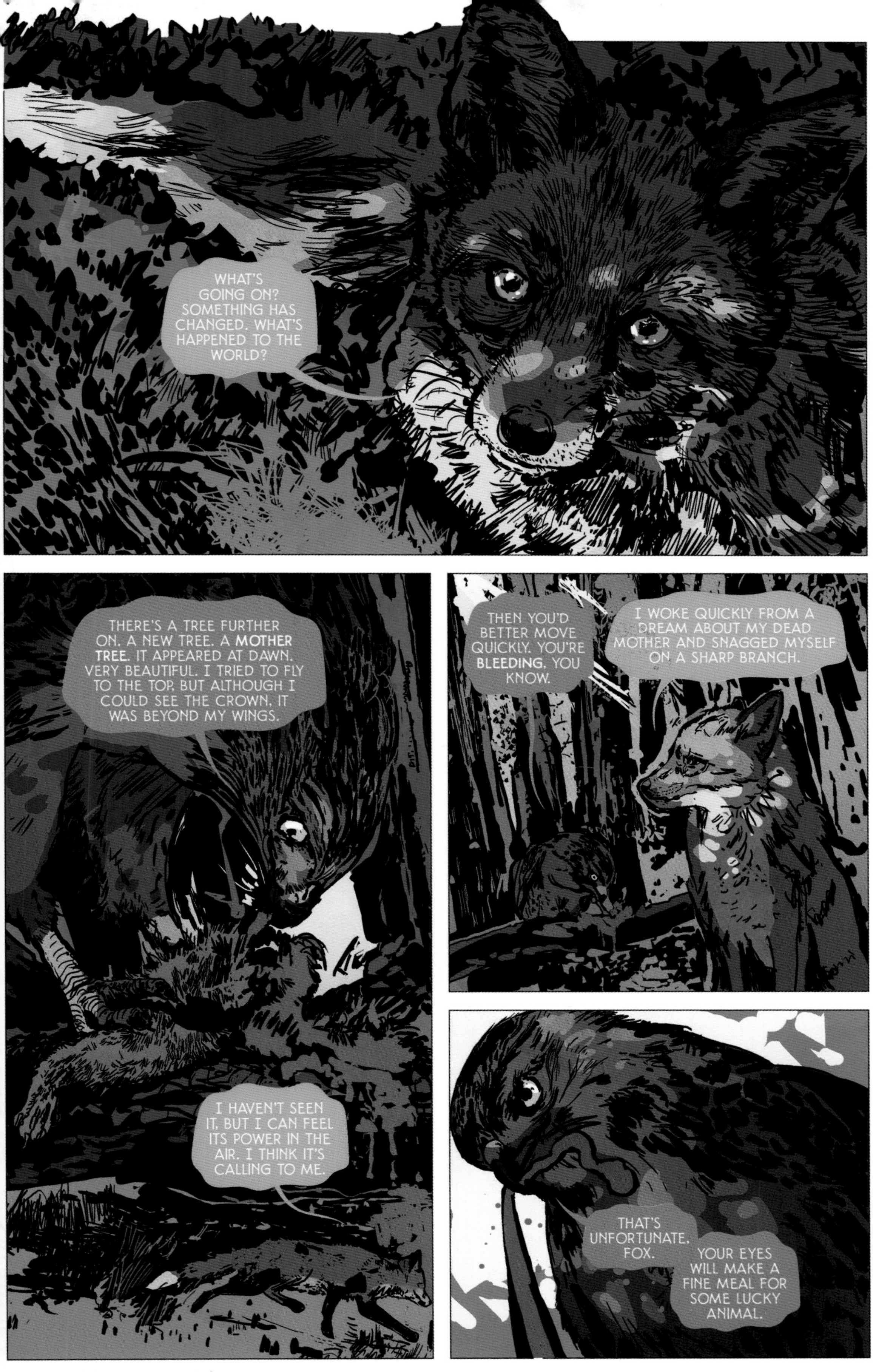
WHAT'S GOING ON? SOMETHING HAS CHANGED. WHAT'S HAPPENED TO THE WORLD?
THERE'S A TREE FURTHER ON. A NEW TREE. A MOTHER TREE. IT APPEARED AT DAWN. VERY BEAUTIFUL. I TRIED TO FLY TO THE TOP, BUT ALTHOUGH I COULD SEE THE CROWN, IT WAS BEYOND MY WINGS.
I HAVEN'T SEEN IT, BUT I CAN FEEL ITS POWER IN THE AIR. I THINK IT'S CALLING TO ME.
THEN YOU'D BETTER MOVE QUICKLY. YOU'RE BLEEDING, YOU KNOW.
I WOKE QUICKLY FROM A DREAM ABOUT MY DEAD MOTHER AND SNAGGED MYSELF ON A SHARP BRANCH.
THAT'S UNFORTUNATE, FOX.
YOUR EYES WILL MAKE A FINE MEAL FOR SOME LUCKY ANIMAL.

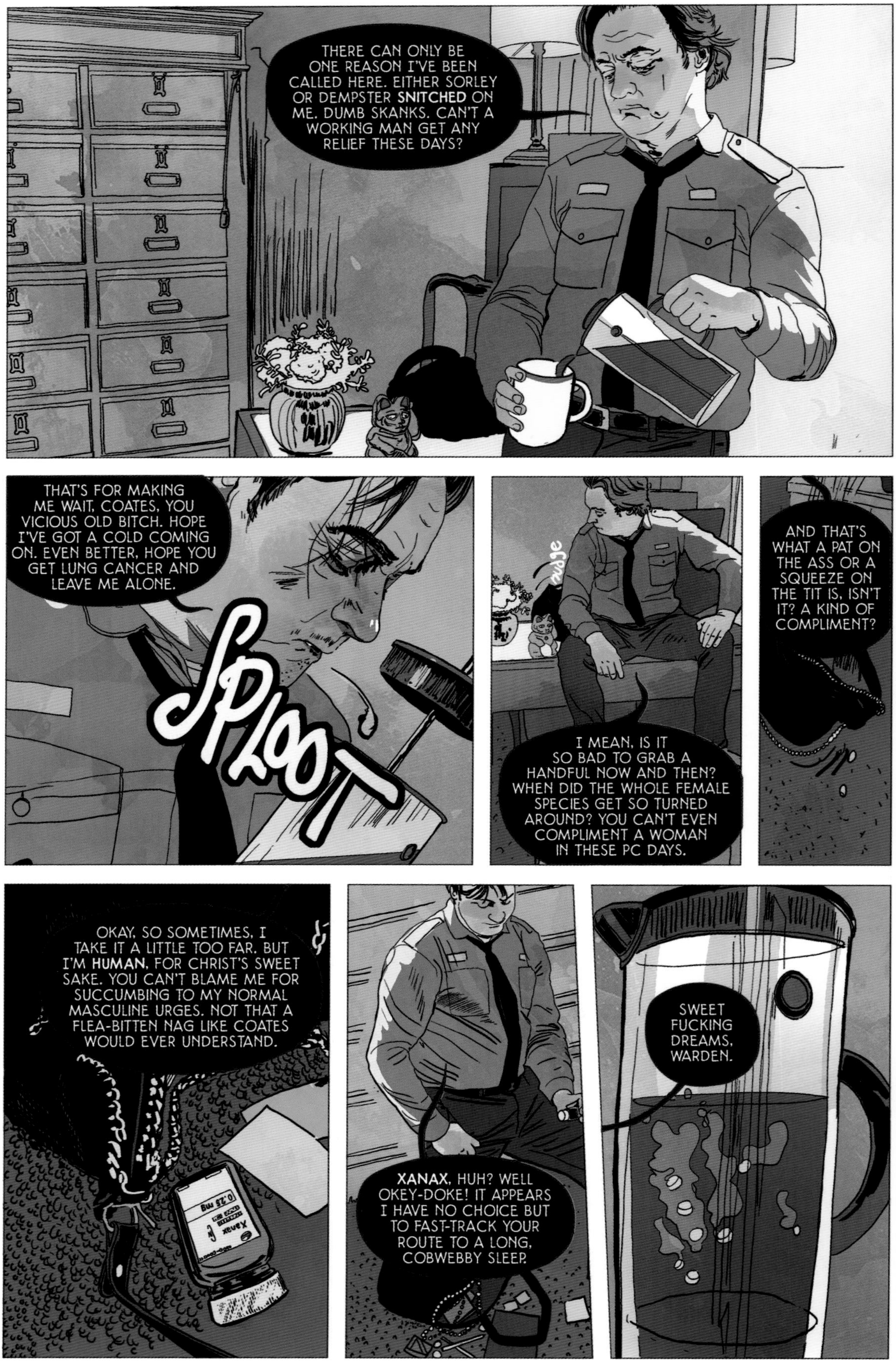
THERE CAN ONLY BE ONE REASON I'VE BEEN CALLED HERE. EITHER SORLEY OR DEMPSTER **SNITCHED** ON ME. DUMB SKANKS. CAN'T A WORKING MAN GET ANY RELIEF THESE DAYS?
THAT'S FOR MAKING ME WAIT, COATES, YOU VICIOUS OLD BITCH. HOPE I'VE GOT A COLD COMING ON. EVEN BETTER, HOPE YOU GET LUNG CANCER AND LEAVE ME ALONE.
SPLOOT
I MEAN, IS IT SO BAD TO GRAB A HANDFUL NOW AND THEN? WHEN DID THE WHOLE FEMALE SPECIES GET SO TURNED AROUND? YOU CAN'T EVEN COMPLIMENT A WOMAN IN THESE PC DAYS.
AND THAT'S WHAT A PAT ON THE ASS OR A SQUEEZE ON THE TIT IS, ISN'T IT? A KIND OF COMPLIMENT?
OKAY, SO SOMETIMES, I TAKE IT A LITTLE TOO FAR. BUT I'M **HUMAN**, FOR CHRIST'S SWEET SAKE. YOU CAN'T BLAME ME FOR SUCCUMBING TO MY NORMAL MASCULINE URGES. NOT THAT A FLEA-BITTEN NAG LIKE COATES WOULD EVER UNDERSTAND.
XANAX, HUH? WELL OKEY-DOKE! IT APPEARS I HAVE NO CHOICE BUT TO FAST-TRACK YOUR ROUTE TO A LONG, COBWEBBY SLEEP.
SWEET FUCKING DREAMS, WARDEN.

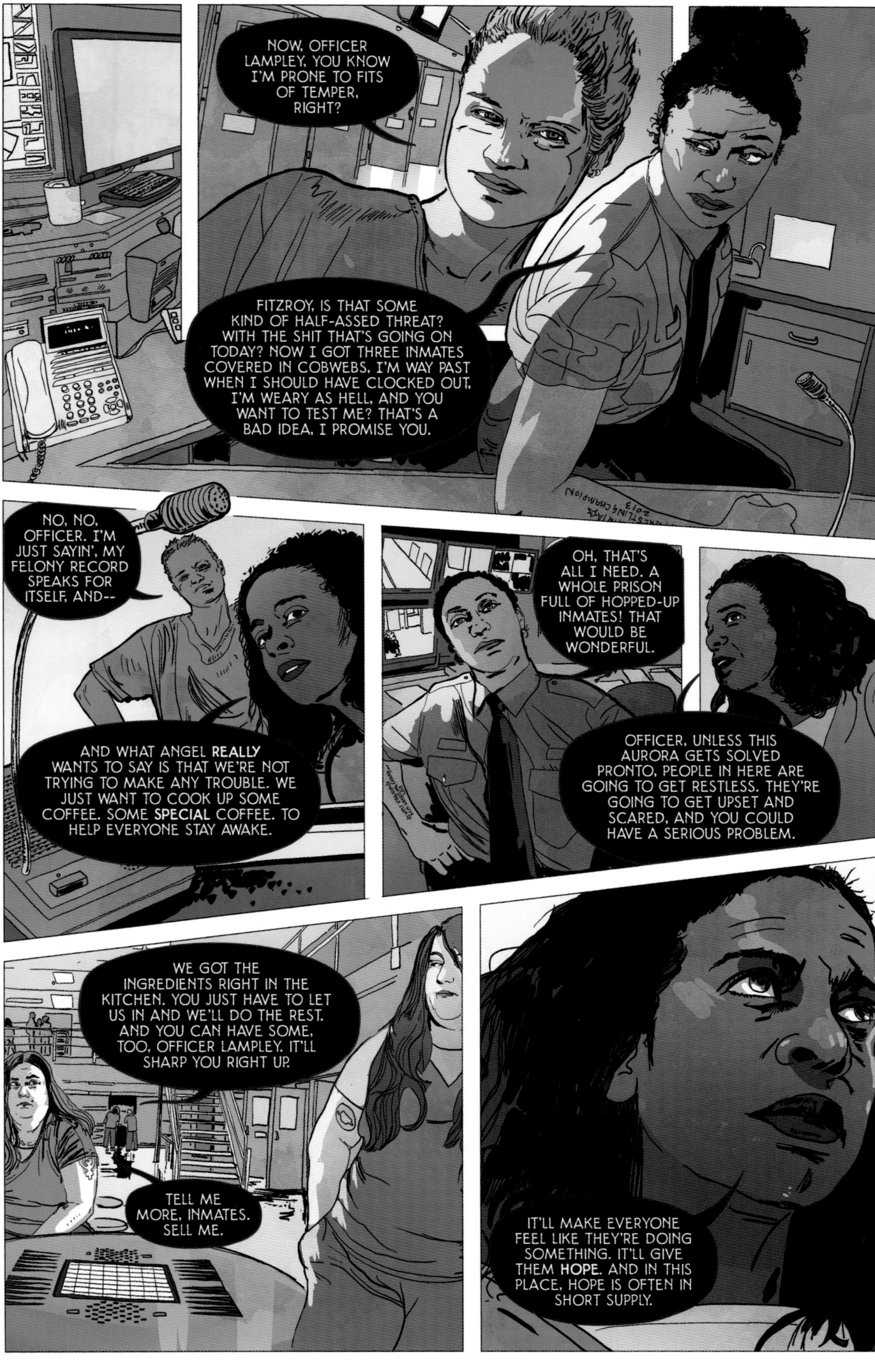
NOW, OFFICER LAMPLEY, YOU KNOW I'M PRONE TO FITS OF TEMPER, RIGHT?
FITZROY, IS THAT SOME KIND OF HALF-ASSED THREAT? WITH THE SHIT THAT'S GOING ON TODAY? NOW I GOT THREE INMATES COVERED IN COBWEBS, I'M WAY PAST WHEN I SHOULD HAVE CLOCKED OUT, I'M WEARY AS HELL, AND YOU WANT TO TEST ME? THAT'S A BAD IDEA, I PROMISE YOU.
NO, NO, OFFICER. I'M JUST SAYIN', MY FELONY RECORD SPEAKS FOR ITSELF, AND--
AND WHAT ANGEL **REALLY** WANTS TO SAY IS THAT WE'RE NOT TRYING TO MAKE ANY TROUBLE. WE JUST WANT TO COOK UP SOME COFFEE. SOME **SPECIAL** COFFEE. TO HELP EVERYONE STAY AWAKE.
OH, THAT'S ALL I NEED. A WHOLE PRISON FULL OF HOPPED-UP INMATES! THAT WOULD BE WONDERFUL.
OFFICER, UNLESS THIS AURORA GETS SOLVED PRONTO, PEOPLE IN HERE ARE GOING TO GET RESTLESS. THEY'RE GOING TO GET UPSET AND SCARED, AND YOU COULD HAVE A SERIOUS PROBLEM.
WE GOT THE INGREDIENTS RIGHT IN THE KITCHEN. YOU JUST HAVE TO LET US IN AND WE'LL DO THE REST. AND YOU CAN HAVE SOME, TOO, OFFICER LAMPLEY. IT'LL SHARP YOU RIGHT UP.
TELL ME MORE, INMATES. SELL ME.
IT'LL MAKE EVERYONE FEEL LIKE THEY'RE DOING SOMETHING. IT'LL GIVE THEM **HOPE**. AND IN THIS PLACE, HOPE IS OFTEN IN SHORT SUPPLY.

YOU'RE TAKING THIS RATHER WELL.

I'M JUST ENJOYING THINKING ABOUT HOW MY LAWYER IS GOING TO MAKE ME A MILLIONAIRE OFF THIS WRONGFUL FIRING.

YOU GOT NO PROOF, SEE?

I'M GOING TO ROLL YOU UP IN COURT.

YOU OKAY? I SEE YOU STANDING THERE AND MAKING FISTS. YOU NEED TO PINCH A LOAF OR SOMETHING, DOC.

FUCK YOU.

YOU'RE A SCUMBAG, AND YOU'RE LUCKY WE CAN'T DEAL WITH YOU TO THE EXTENT YOU DESERVE RIGHT NOW. BECAUSE, YOU SEE, WE **DO** HAVE PROOF.

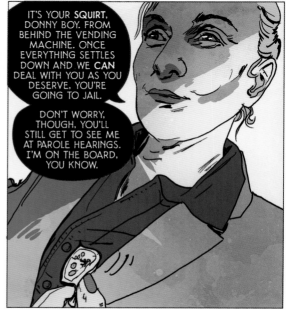

IT'S YOUR **SQUIRT**, DONNY BOY. FROM BEHIND THE VENDING MACHINE. ONCE EVERYTHING SETTLES DOWN AND WE **CAN** DEAL WITH YOU AS YOU DESERVE, YOU'RE GOING TO JAIL.

DON'T WORRY, THOUGH, YOU'LL STILL GET TO SEE ME AT PAROLE HEARINGS. I'M ON THE BOARD, YOU KNOW.

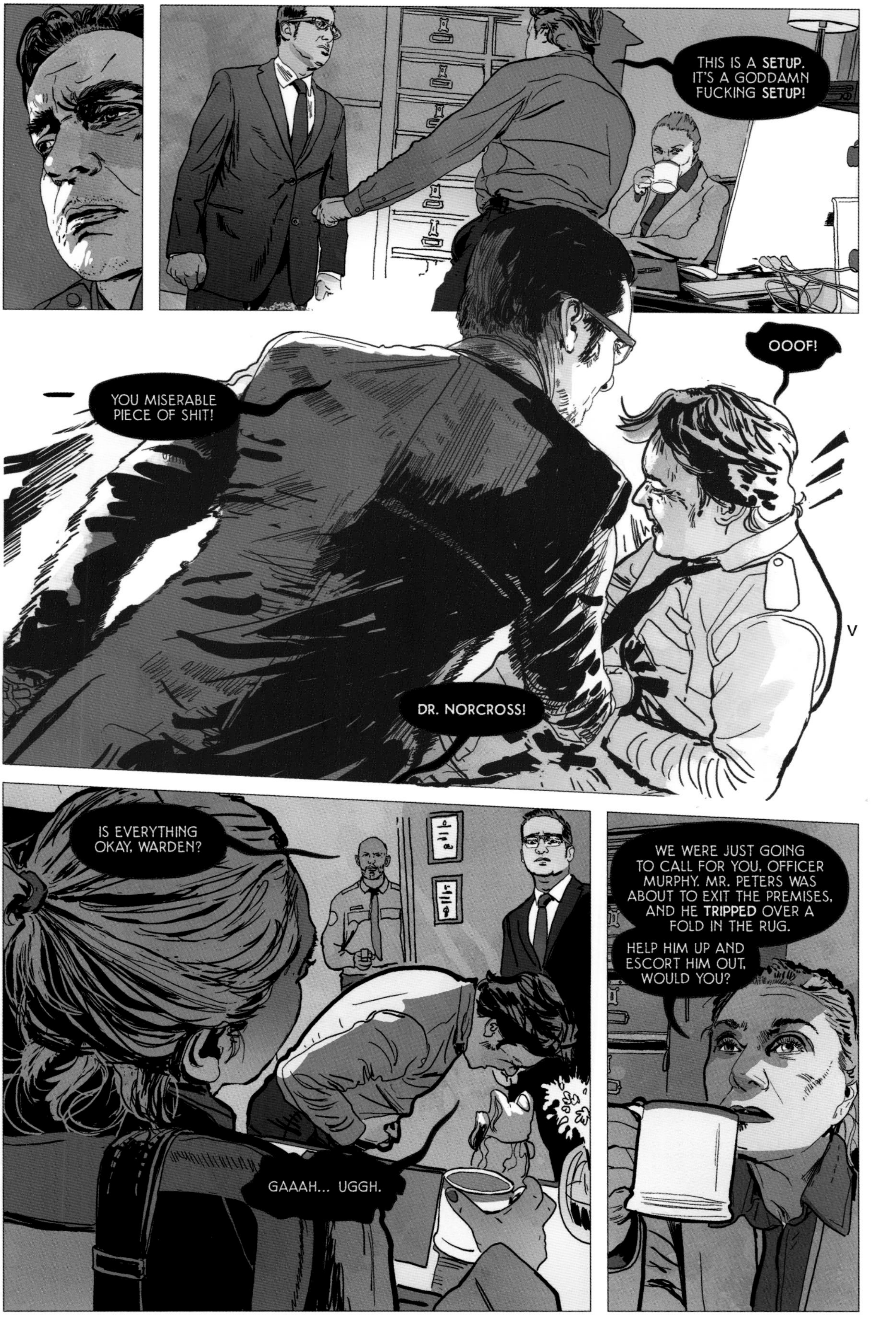
THIS IS A SETUP. IT'S A GODDAMN FUCKING SETUP!
YOU MISERABLE PIECE OF SHIT!
OOOF!
DR. NORCROSS!
IS EVERYTHING OKAY, WARDEN?
GAAAH... UGGH.
WE WERE JUST GOING TO CALL FOR YOU, OFFICER MURPHY. MR. PETERS WAS ABOUT TO EXIT THE PREMISES, AND HE TRIPPED OVER A FOLD IN THE RUG.
HELP HIM UP AND ESCORT HIM OUT, WOULD YOU?

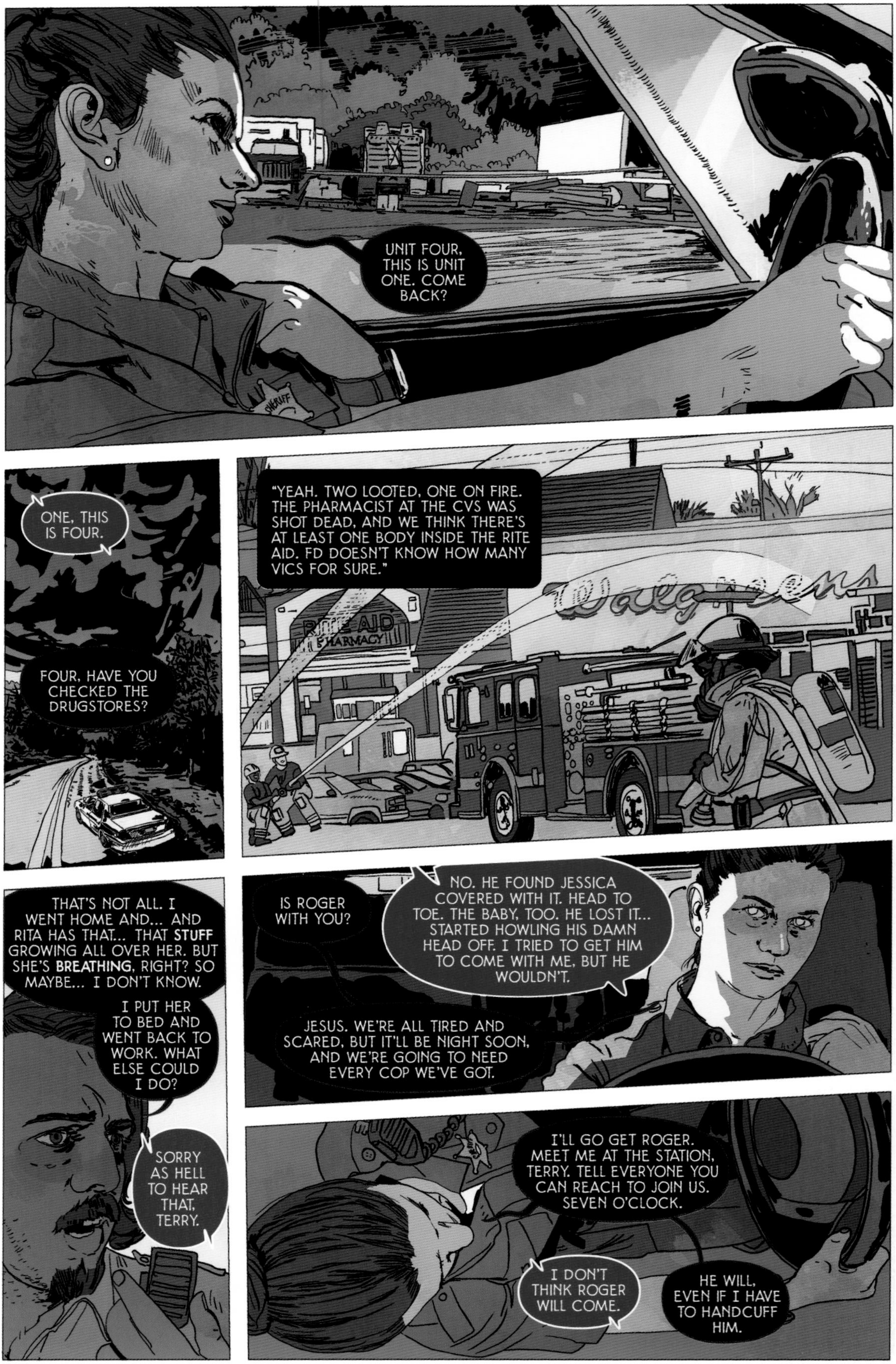
UNIT FOUR, THIS IS UNIT ONE. COME BACK?
SHERIFF
ONE, THIS IS FOUR.
FOUR, HAVE YOU CHECKED THE DRUGSTORES?
"YEAH. TWO LOOTED, ONE ON FIRE. THE PHARMACIST AT THE CVS WAS SHOT DEAD, AND WE THINK THERE'S AT LEAST ONE BODY INSIDE THE RITE AID. FD DOESN'T KNOW HOW MANY VICS FOR SURE."
Walgreens
RITE AID PHARMACY
THAT'S NOT ALL. I WENT HOME AND... AND RITA HAS THAT... THAT **STUFF** GROWING ALL OVER HER. BUT SHE'S **BREATHING**, RIGHT? SO MAYBE... I DON'T KNOW.
I PUT HER TO BED AND WENT BACK TO WORK. WHAT ELSE COULD I DO?
SORRY AS HELL TO HEAR THAT, TERRY.
IS ROGER WITH YOU?
NO. HE FOUND JESSICA COVERED WITH IT. HEAD TO TOE. THE BABY, TOO. HE LOST IT... STARTED HOWLING HIS DAMN HEAD OFF. I TRIED TO GET HIM TO COME WITH ME, BUT HE WOULDN'T.
JESUS. WE'RE ALL TIRED AND SCARED, BUT IT'LL BE NIGHT SOON, AND WE'RE GOING TO NEED EVERY COP WE'VE GOT.
I'LL GO GET ROGER. MEET ME AT THE STATION, TERRY. TELL EVERYONE YOU CAN REACH TO JOIN US. SEVEN O'CLOCK.
I DON'T THINK ROGER WILL COME.
HE WILL, EVEN IF I HAVE TO HANDCUFF HIM.

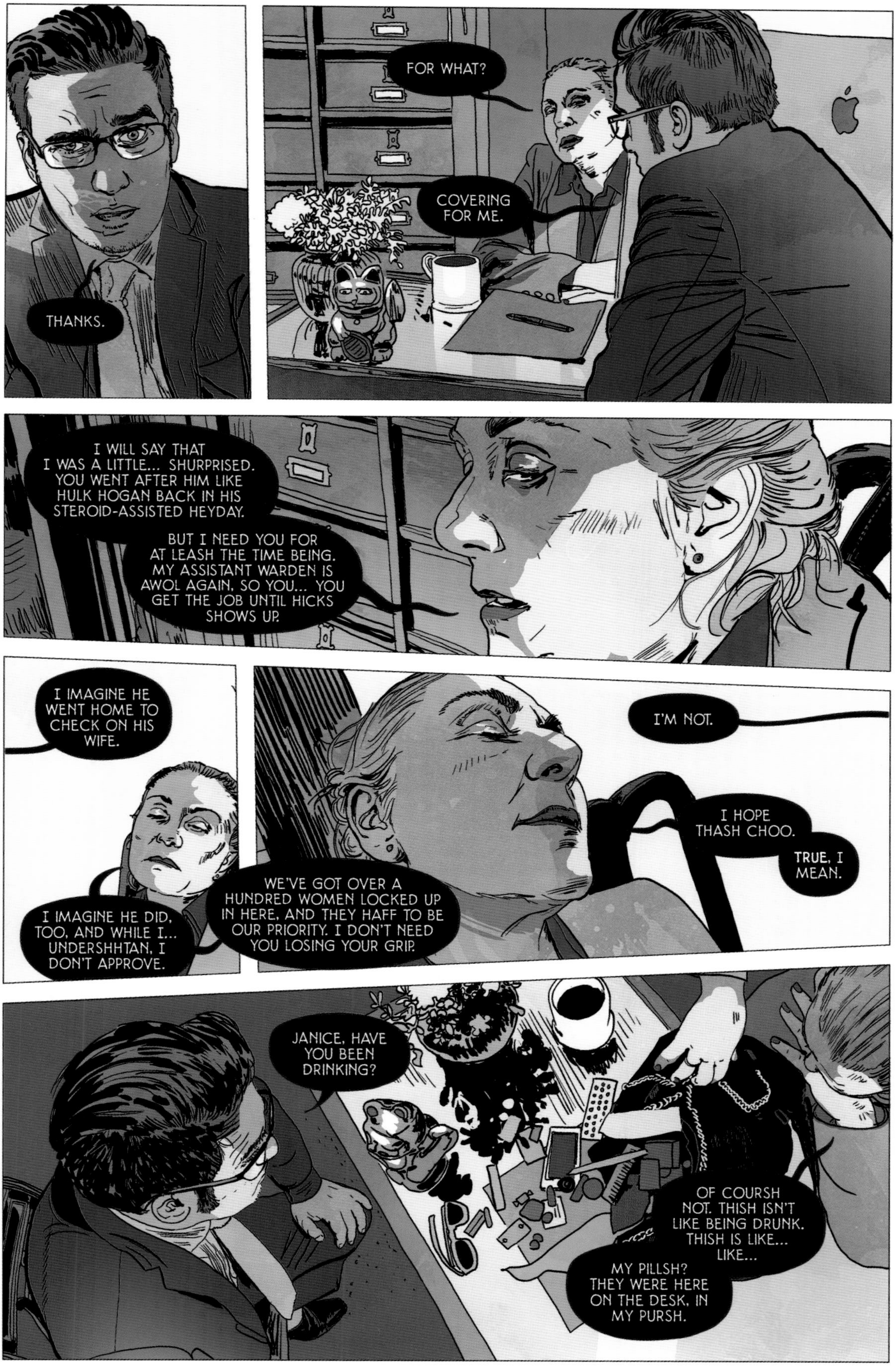
THANKS.
FOR WHAT?
COVERING FOR ME.
I WILL SAY THAT I WAS A LITTLE... SHURPRISED. YOU WENT AFTER HIM LIKE HULK HOGAN BACK IN HIS STEROID-ASSISTED HEYDAY.
BUT I NEED YOU FOR AT LEASH THE TIME BEING. MY ASSISTANT WARDEN IS AWOL AGAIN, SO YOU... YOU GET THE JOB UNTIL HICKS SHOWS UP.
I IMAGINE HE WENT HOME TO CHECK ON HIS WIFE.
I IMAGINE HE DID, TOO, AND WHILE I... UNDERSHHTAN, I DON'T APPROVE.
WE'VE GOT OVER A HUNDRED WOMEN LOCKED UP IN HERE, AND THEY HAFF TO BE OUR PRIORITY. I DON'T NEED YOU LOSING YOUR GRIP.
I'M NOT.
I HOPE THASH CHOO.
TRUE, I MEAN.
JANICE, HAVE YOU BEEN DRINKING?
OF COURSH NOT. THISH ISN'T LIKE BEING DRUNK. THISH IS LIKE... LIKE...
MY PILLSH? THEY WERE HERE ON THE DESK, IN MY PURSH.

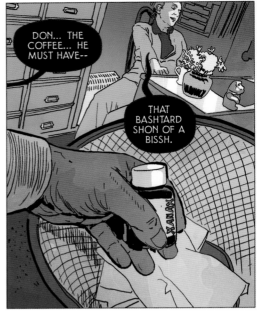

WHAT PILLS? WHAT ARE YOU TAKING?

ZHAN... ZHAN... AH, **FUCK.**

GOIN' BYE-BYE, DOC. GOIN' SHLEEP.

DON... THE COFFEE... HE MUST HAVE--

THAT BASHTARD SHON OF A BISSH.

...TELL MICKEY... TELL MICKEY I LOVE HER.

YOU'RE IN CHARGE NOW, DOC. AT LEAST... UNTIL HICKS COMESH BACK. YOU... KEEP THEM SHAFE UNTIL THEY ALL GO TO SHEEP... KEEP THEM...

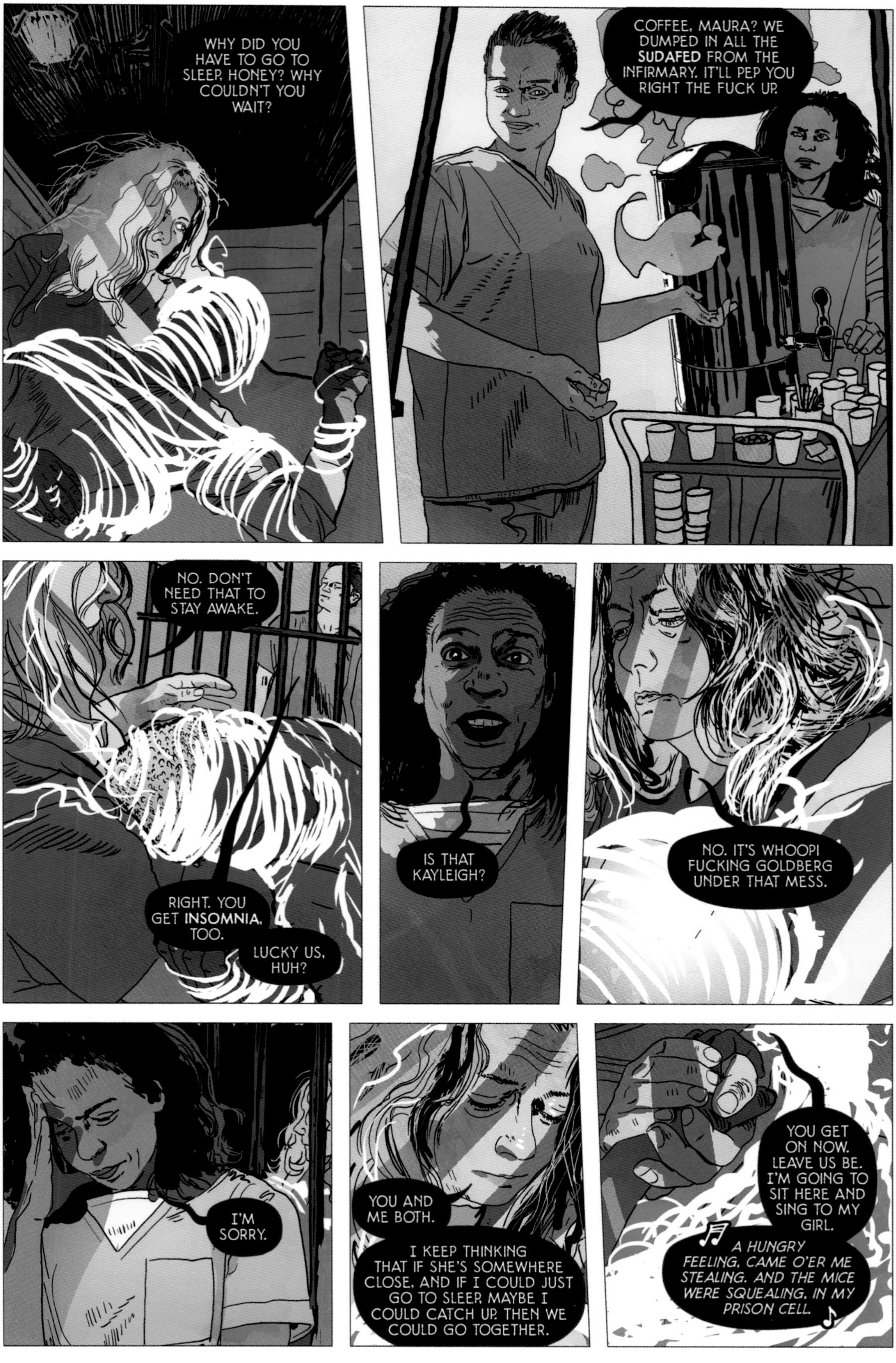
WHY DID YOU HAVE TO GO TO SLEEP, HONEY? WHY COULDN'T YOU WAIT?
COFFEE, MAURA? WE DUMPED IN ALL THE **SUDAFED** FROM THE INFIRMARY. IT'LL PEP YOU RIGHT THE FUCK UP.
NO. DON'T NEED THAT TO STAY AWAKE.
RIGHT. YOU GET **INSOMNIA**, TOO.
LUCKY US, HUH?
IS THAT KAYLEIGH?
NO. IT'S WHOOPI FUCKING GOLDBERG UNDER THAT MESS.
I'M SORRY.
YOU AND ME BOTH.
I KEEP THINKING THAT IF SHE'S SOMEWHERE CLOSE, AND IF I COULD JUST GO TO SLEEP, MAYBE I COULD CATCH UP. THEN WE COULD GO TOGETHER.
YOU GET ON NOW. LEAVE US BE. I'M GOING TO SIT HERE AND SING TO MY GIRL.
♬ *A HUNGRY FEELING, CAME O'ER ME STEALING, AND THE MICE WERE SQUEALING, IN MY PRISON CELL.* ♪

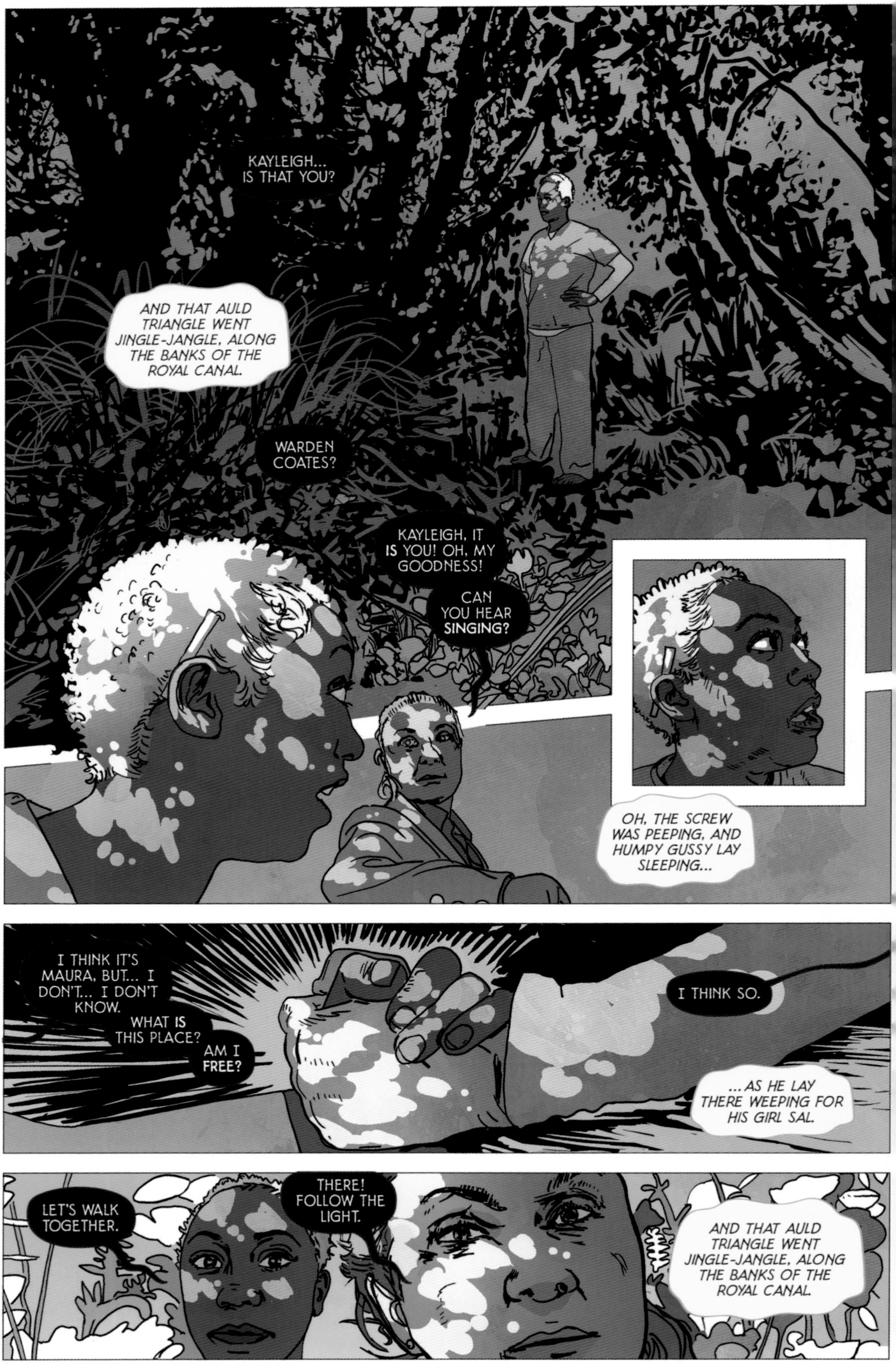
KAYLEIGH... IS THAT YOU?
AND THAT AULD TRIANGLE WENT JINGLE-JANGLE, ALONG THE BANKS OF THE ROYAL CANAL.
WARDEN COATES?
KAYLEIGH, IT **IS** YOU! OH, MY GOODNESS!
CAN YOU HEAR **SINGING?**
OH, THE SCREW WAS PEEPING, AND HUMPY GUSSY LAY SLEEPING...
I THINK IT'S MAURA, BUT... I DON'T... I DON'T KNOW.
WHAT **IS** THIS PLACE?
AM I **FREE?**
I THINK SO.
...AS HE LAY THERE WEEPING FOR HIS GIRL SAL.
LET'S WALK TOGETHER.
THERE! FOLLOW THE LIGHT.
AND THAT AULD TRIANGLE WENT JINGLE-JANGLE, ALONG THE BANKS OF THE ROYAL CANAL.

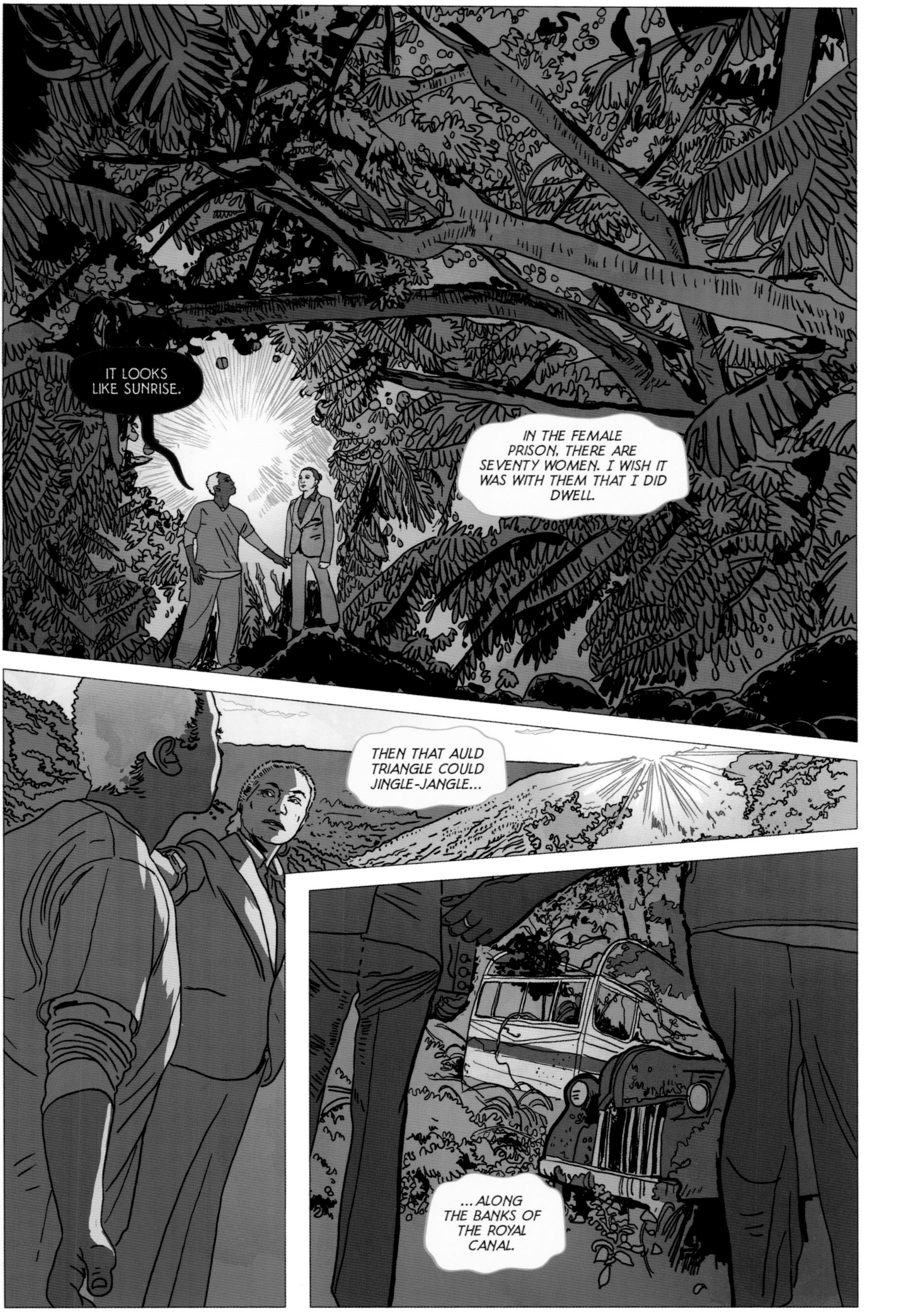
IT LOOKS LIKE SUNRISE.
IN THE FEMALE PRISON, THERE ARE SEVENTY WOMEN. I WISH IT WAS WITH THEM THAT I DID DWELL.
THEN THAT AULD TRIANGLE COULD JINGLE-JANGLE...
...ALONG THE BANKS OF THE ROYAL CANAL.

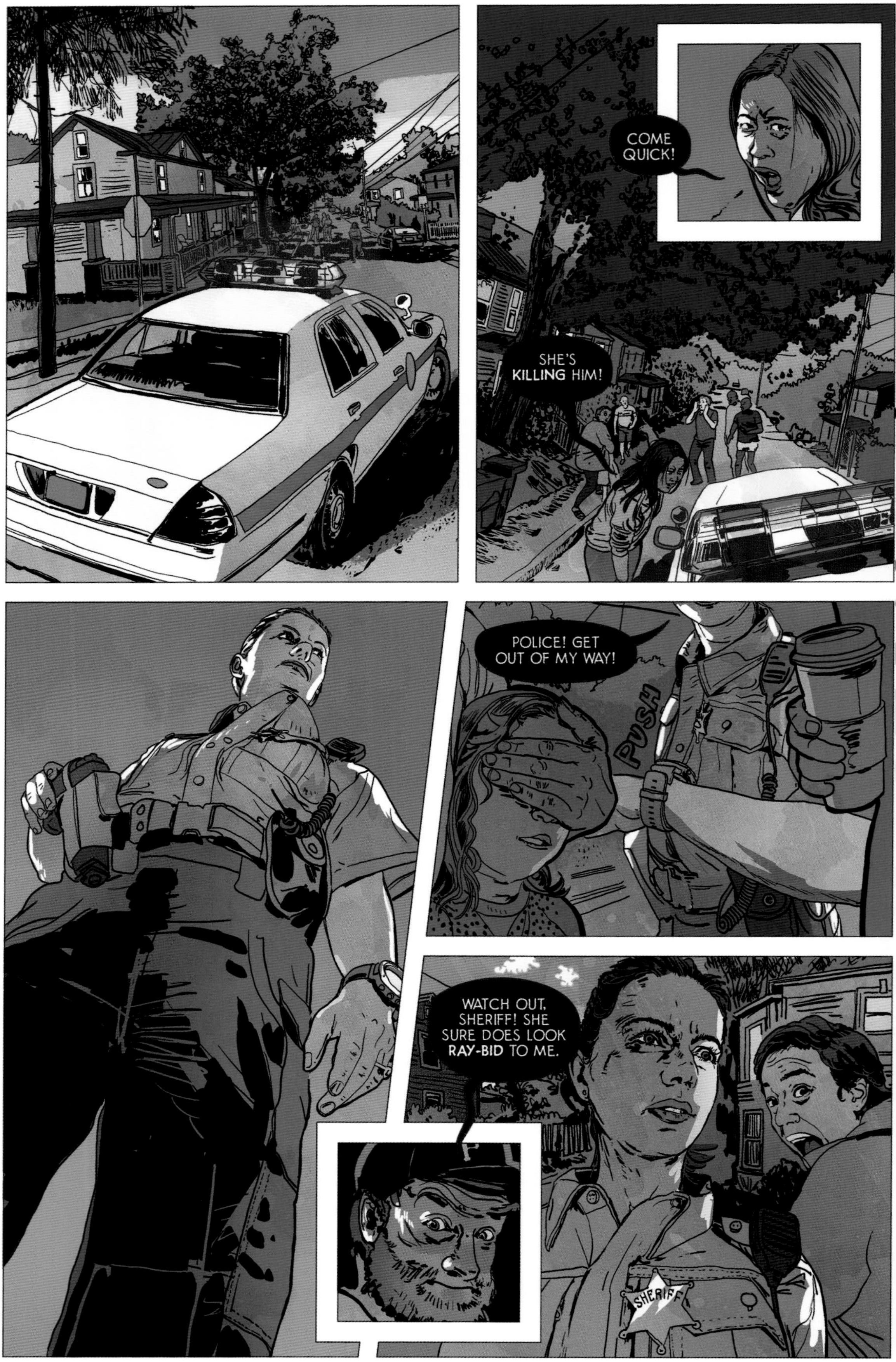
COME QUICK!
SHE'S KILLING HIM!
POLICE! GET OUT OF MY WAY!
PUSH
WATCH OUT, SHERIFF! SHE SURE DOES LOOK RAY-BID TO ME.
SHERIFF

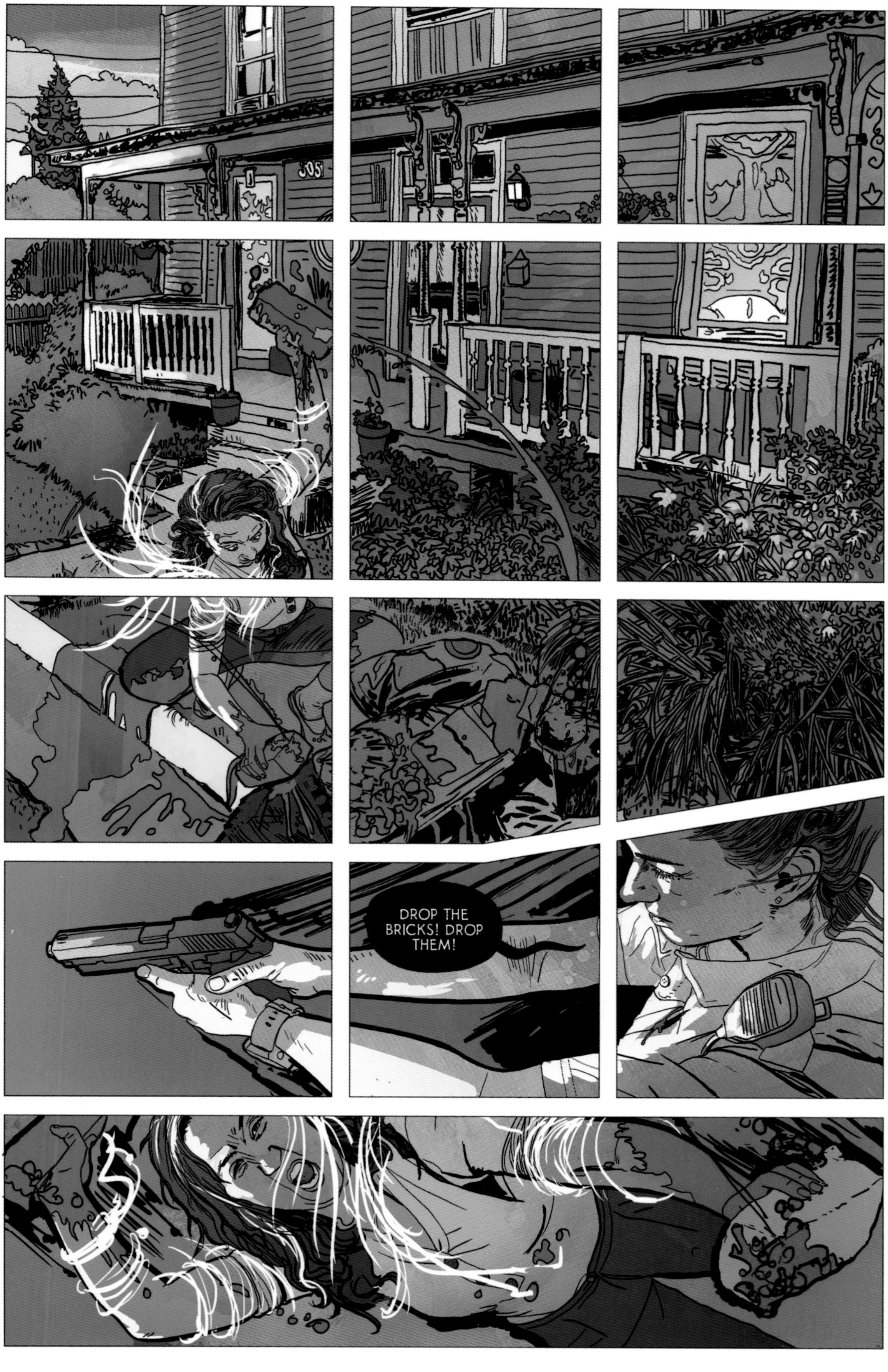
DROP THE BRICKS! DROP THEM!

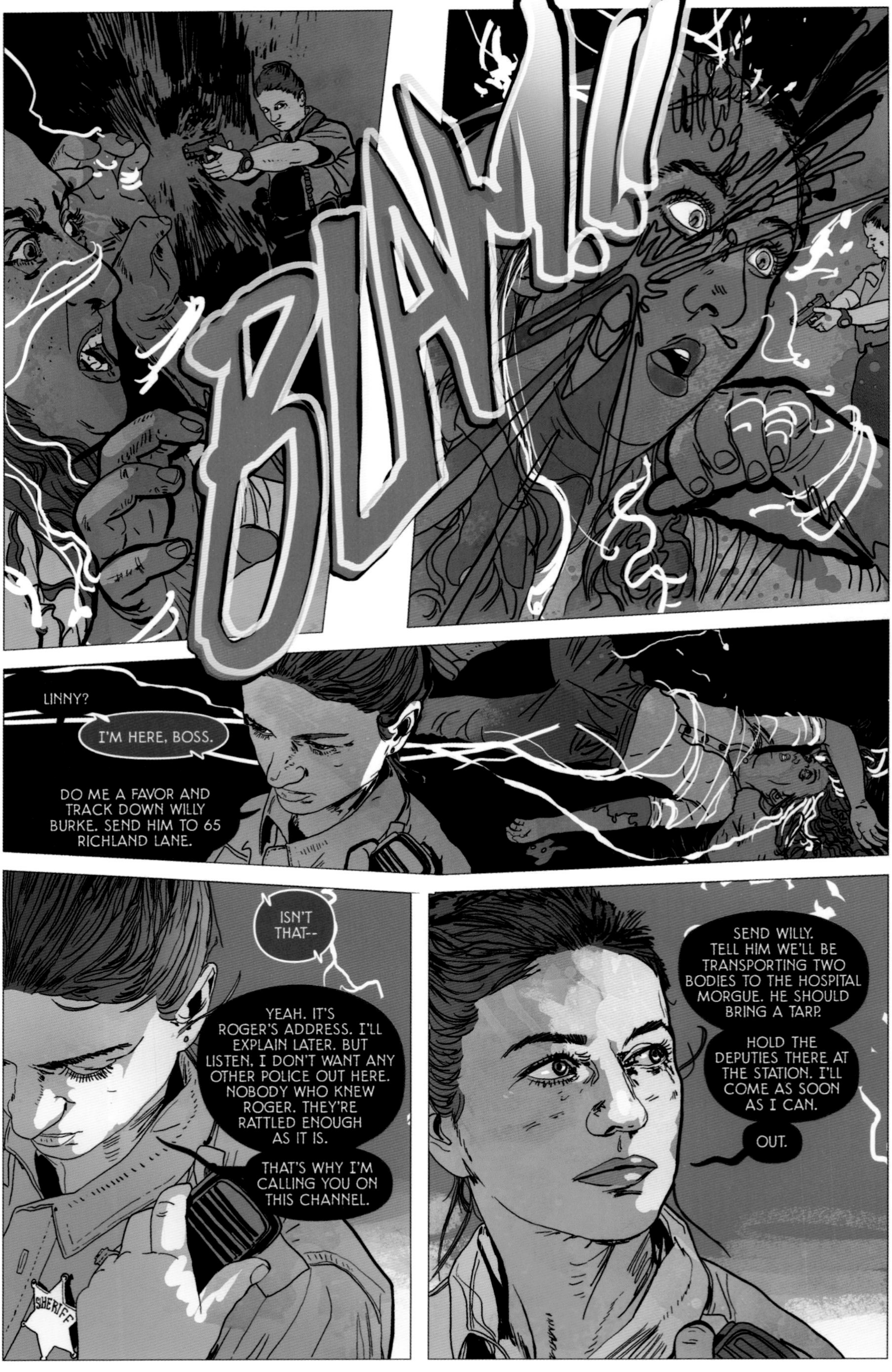
BLAM!!
LINNY?
I'M HERE, BOSS.
DO ME A FAVOR AND TRACK DOWN WILLY BURKE. SEND HIM TO 65 RICHLAND LANE.
ISN'T THAT--
YEAH. IT'S ROGER'S ADDRESS. I'LL EXPLAIN LATER. BUT LISTEN. I DON'T WANT ANY OTHER POLICE OUT HERE. NOBODY WHO KNEW ROGER. THEY'RE RATTLED ENOUGH AS IT IS.
THAT'S WHY I'M CALLING YOU ON THIS CHANNEL.
SHERIFF
SEND WILLY. TELL HIM WE'LL BE TRANSPORTING TWO BODIES TO THE HOSPITAL MORGUE. HE SHOULD BRING A TARP.
HOLD THE DEPUTIES THERE AT THE STATION. I'LL COME AS SOON AS I CAN.
OUT.

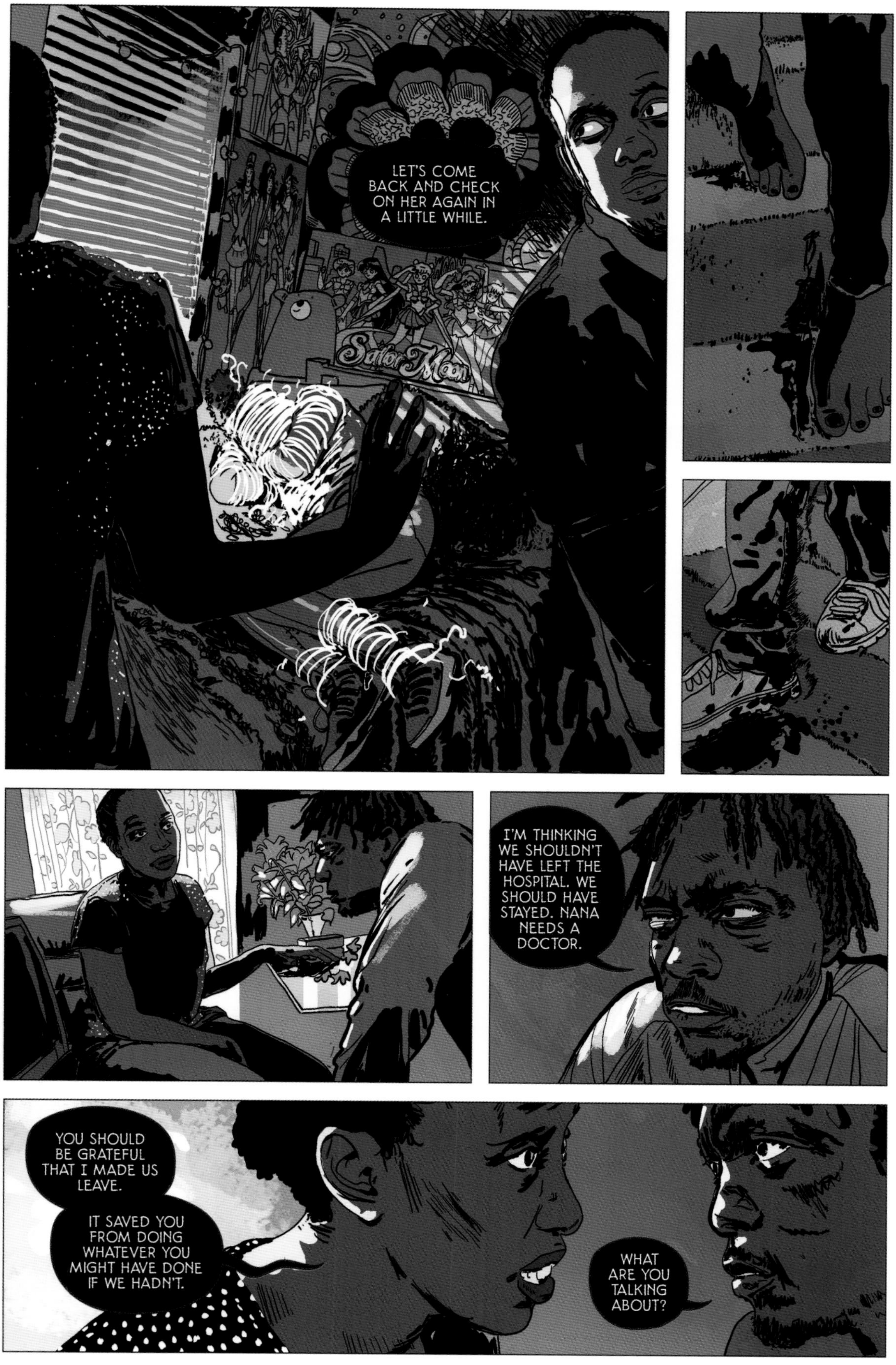
LET'S COME BACK AND CHECK ON HER AGAIN IN A LITTLE WHILE.
Sailor Moon
I'M THINKING WE SHOULDN'T HAVE LEFT THE HOSPITAL. WE SHOULD HAVE STAYED. NANA NEEDS A DOCTOR.
YOU SHOULD BE GRATEFUL THAT I MADE US LEAVE.
IT SAVED YOU FROM DOING WHATEVER YOU MIGHT HAVE DONE IF WE HADN'T.
WHAT ARE YOU TALKING ABOUT?

"TWO WORDS... FRITZ MESHAUM."

"ELAINE, FRITZ MESHAUM IS A TWO-BIT GUN DEALER AND HABITUAL **ABUSER**. I NEVER SAW WHAT HE **DID** TO HIS WIFE, BUT I DID SEE WHAT HE **DID** TO HIS DOG. AND I MADE THE DIRTY SON OF A BITCH PAY."

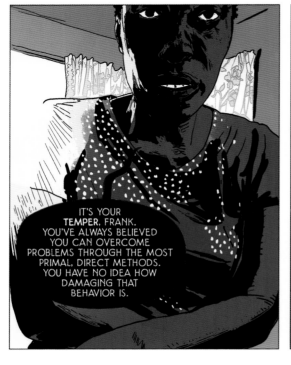

IT'S YOUR **TEMPER**, FRANK. YOU'VE ALWAYS BELIEVED YOU CAN OVERCOME PROBLEMS THROUGH THE MOST PRIMAL, DIRECT METHODS. YOU HAVE NO IDEA HOW DAMAGING THAT BEHAVIOR IS.

BUT YOU'RE NOT ALONE. THE WORLD IS FULL OF MEN LIKE YOU. IMPETUOUS, ANGRY, THOUGHTLESS MEN. JUST TURN ON THE TV OR CHECK YOUR SOCIAL MEDIA...

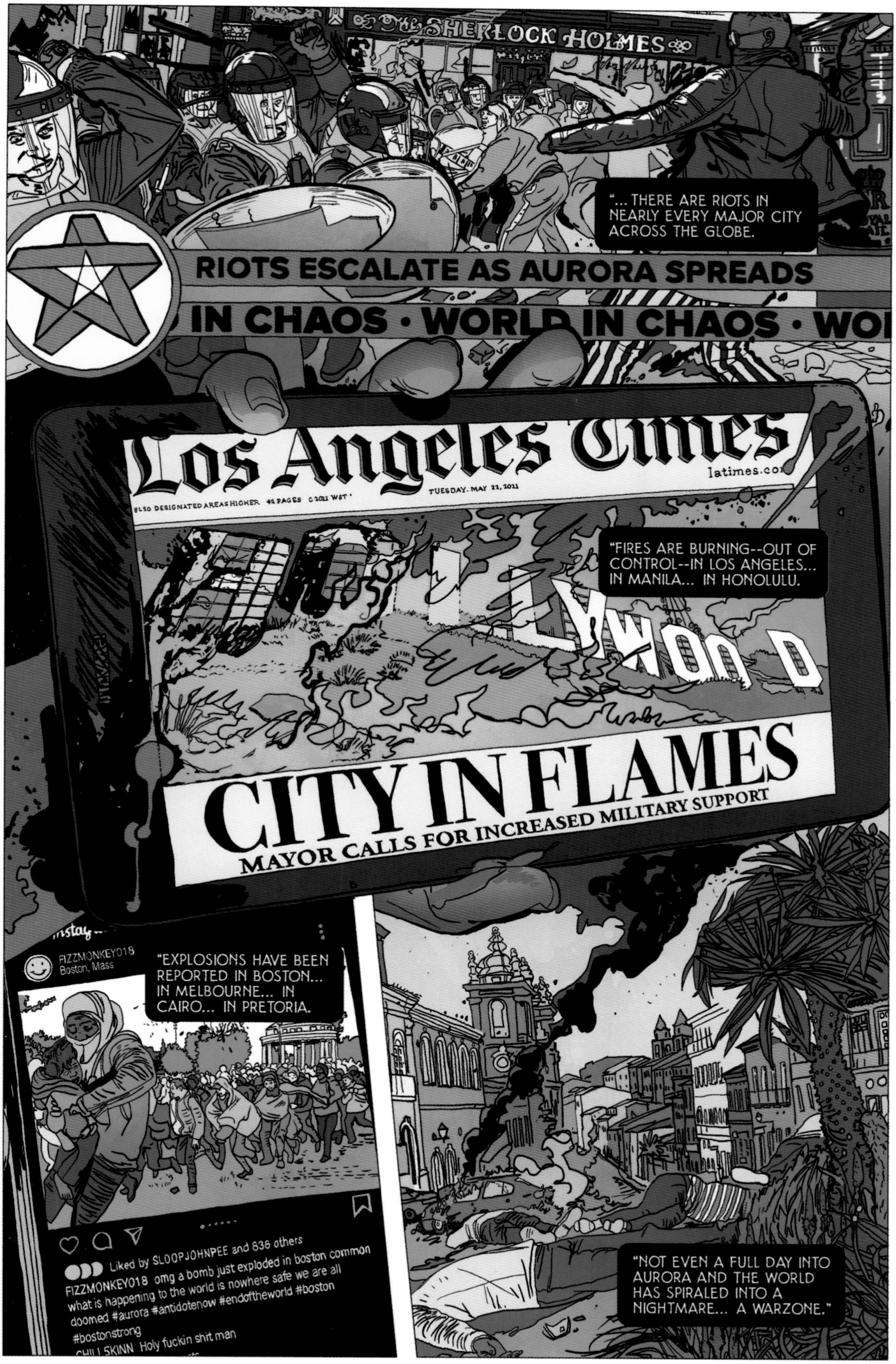
SHERLOCK HOLMES
"... THERE ARE RIOTS IN NEARLY EVERY MAJOR CITY ACROSS THE GLOBE.
RIOTS ESCALATE AS AURORA SPREADS
D IN CHAOS • WORLD IN CHAOS • WO
Los Angeles Times
latimes.com
8L50 DESIGNATED AREAS HIGHER 42 PAGES ©2021 WST
TUESDAY, MAY 22, 2021
"FIRES ARE BURNING--OUT OF CONTROL--IN LOS ANGELES... IN MANILA... IN HONOLULU.
CITY IN FLAMES
MAYOR CALLS FOR INCREASED MILITARY SUPPORT
FIZZMONKEY018
Boston, Mass
"EXPLOSIONS HAVE BEEN REPORTED IN BOSTON... IN MELBOURNE... IN CAIRO... IN PRETORIA.
Liked by SLOOPJOHNPEE and 836 others
FIZZMONKEY018 omg a bomb just exploded in boston common what is happening to the world is nowhere safe we are all doomed #aurora #antidotenow #endoftheworld #boston #bostonstrong
CHILL5KINN Holy fuckin shit man
"NOT EVEN A FULL DAY INTO AURORA AND THE WORLD HAS SPIRALED INTO A NIGHTMARE... A WARZONE."

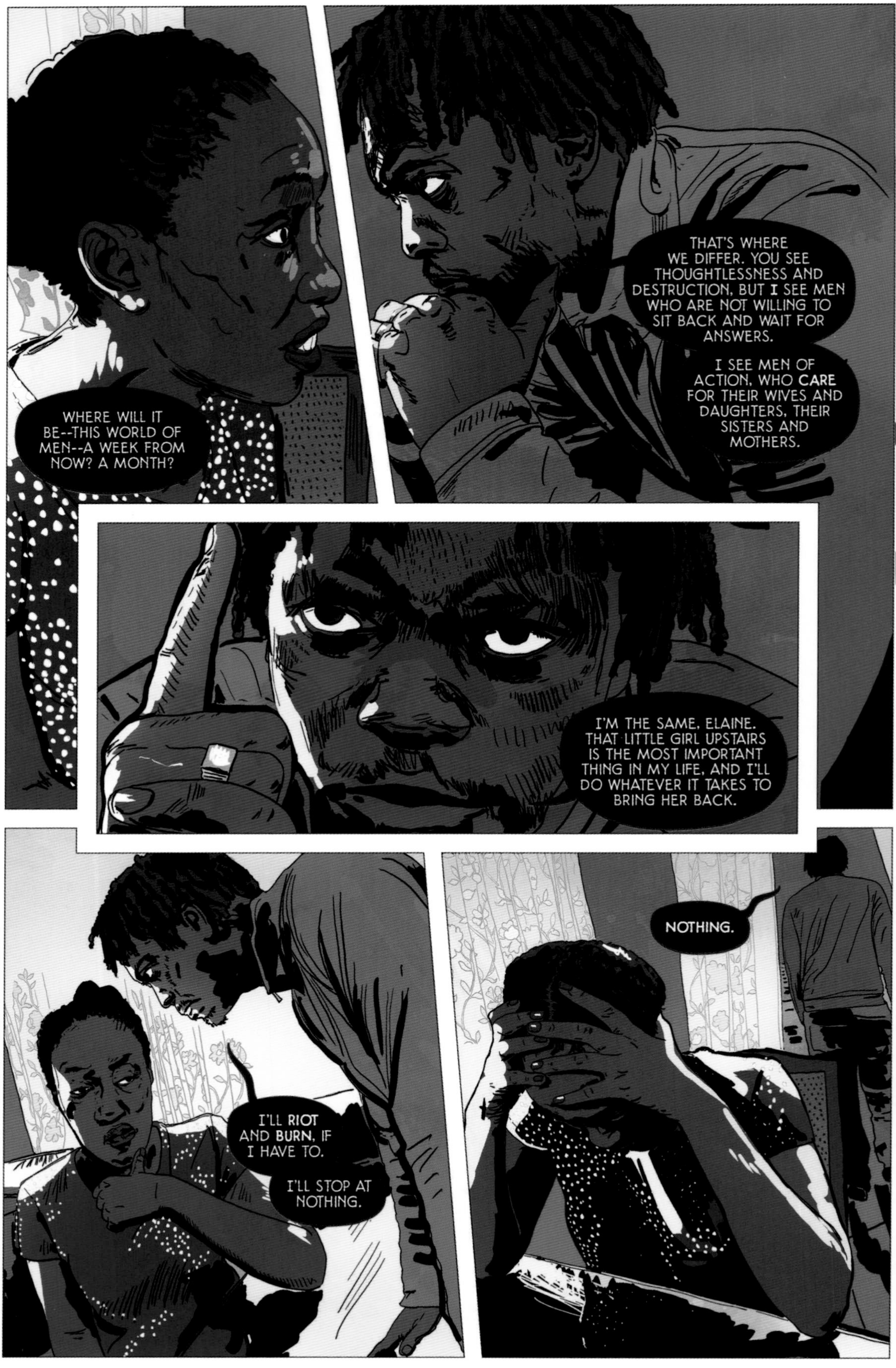
WHERE WILL IT BE--THIS WORLD OF MEN--A WEEK FROM NOW? A MONTH?
THAT'S WHERE WE DIFFER. YOU SEE THOUGHTLESSNESS AND DESTRUCTION, BUT I SEE MEN WHO ARE NOT WILLING TO SIT BACK AND WAIT FOR ANSWERS.
I SEE MEN OF ACTION, WHO CARE FOR THEIR WIVES AND DAUGHTERS, THEIR SISTERS AND MOTHERS.
I'M THE SAME, ELAINE. THAT LITTLE GIRL UPSTAIRS IS THE MOST IMPORTANT THING IN MY LIFE, AND I'LL DO WHATEVER IT TAKES TO BRING HER BACK.
I'LL RIOT AND BURN, IF I HAVE TO.
I'LL STOP AT NOTHING.
NOTHING.

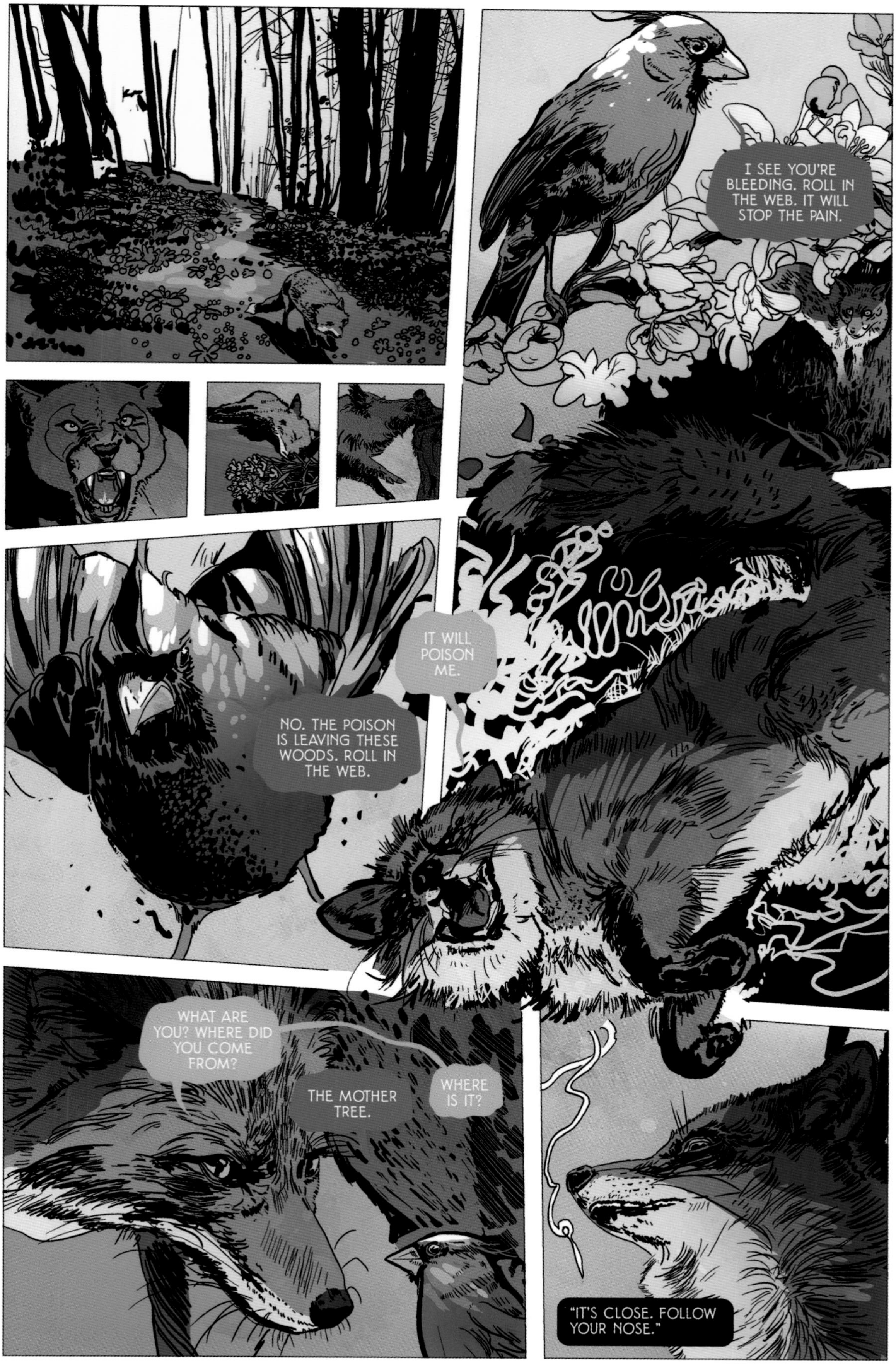
I SEE YOU'RE BLEEDING. ROLL IN THE WEB. IT WILL STOP THE PAIN.
IT WILL POISON ME.
NO. THE POISON IS LEAVING THESE WOODS. ROLL IN THE WEB.
WHAT ARE YOU? WHERE DID YOU COME FROM?
THE MOTHER TREE.
WHERE IS IT?
"IT'S CLOSE. FOLLOW YOUR NOSE."

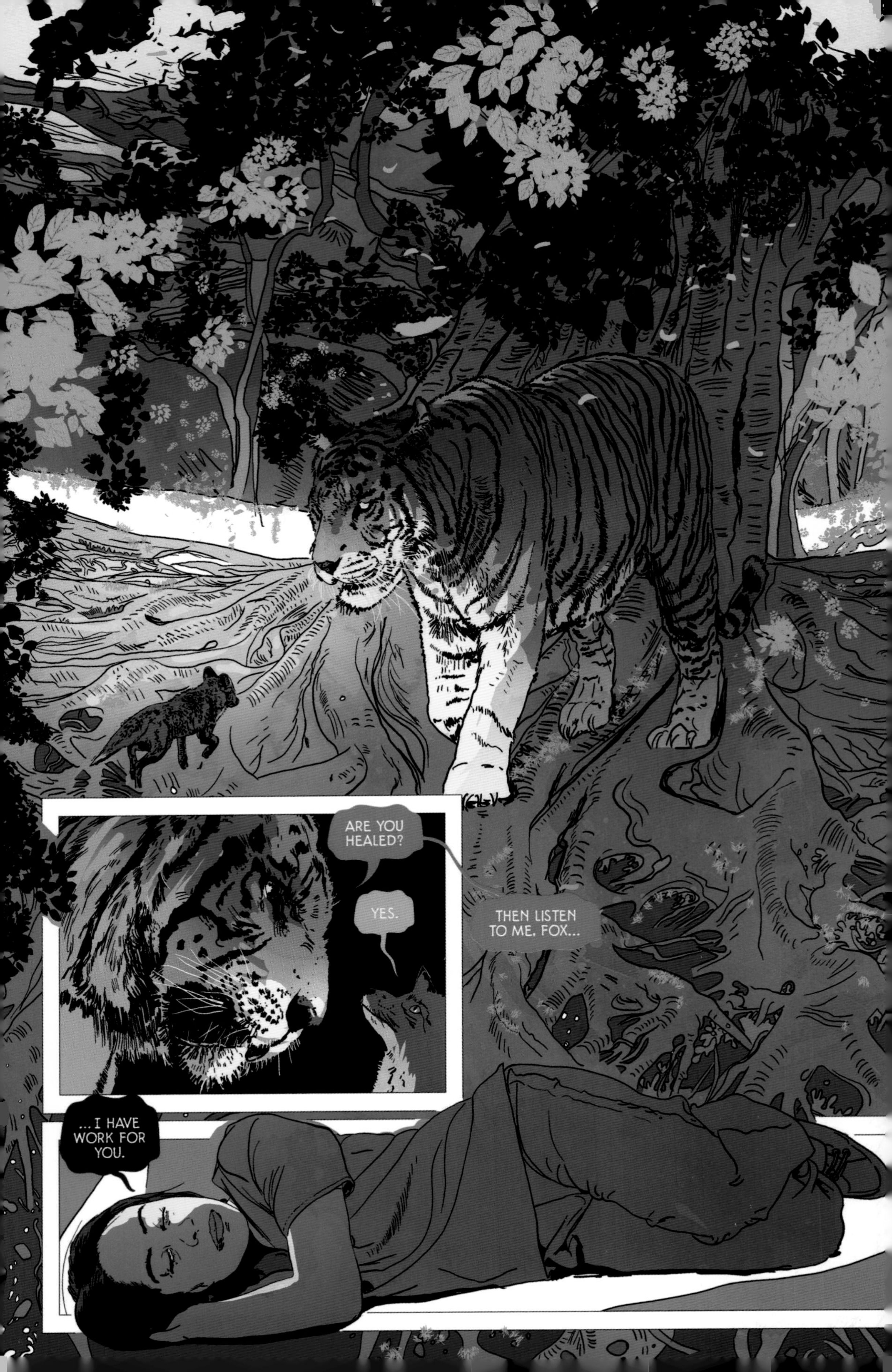
ARE YOU HEALED?
YES.
THEN LISTEN TO ME, FOX...
...I HAVE WORK FOR YOU.

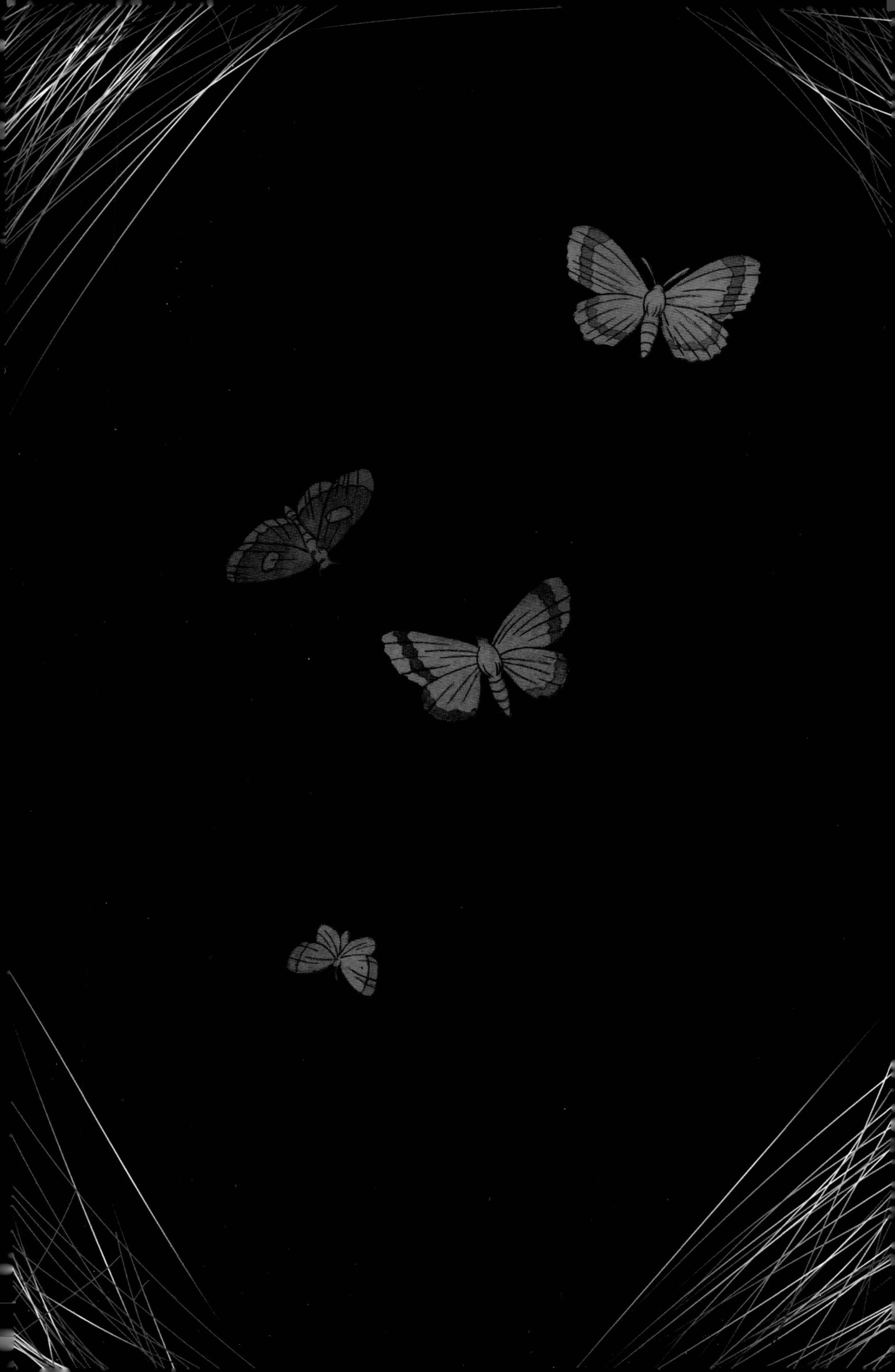

ART BY ANNIE WU

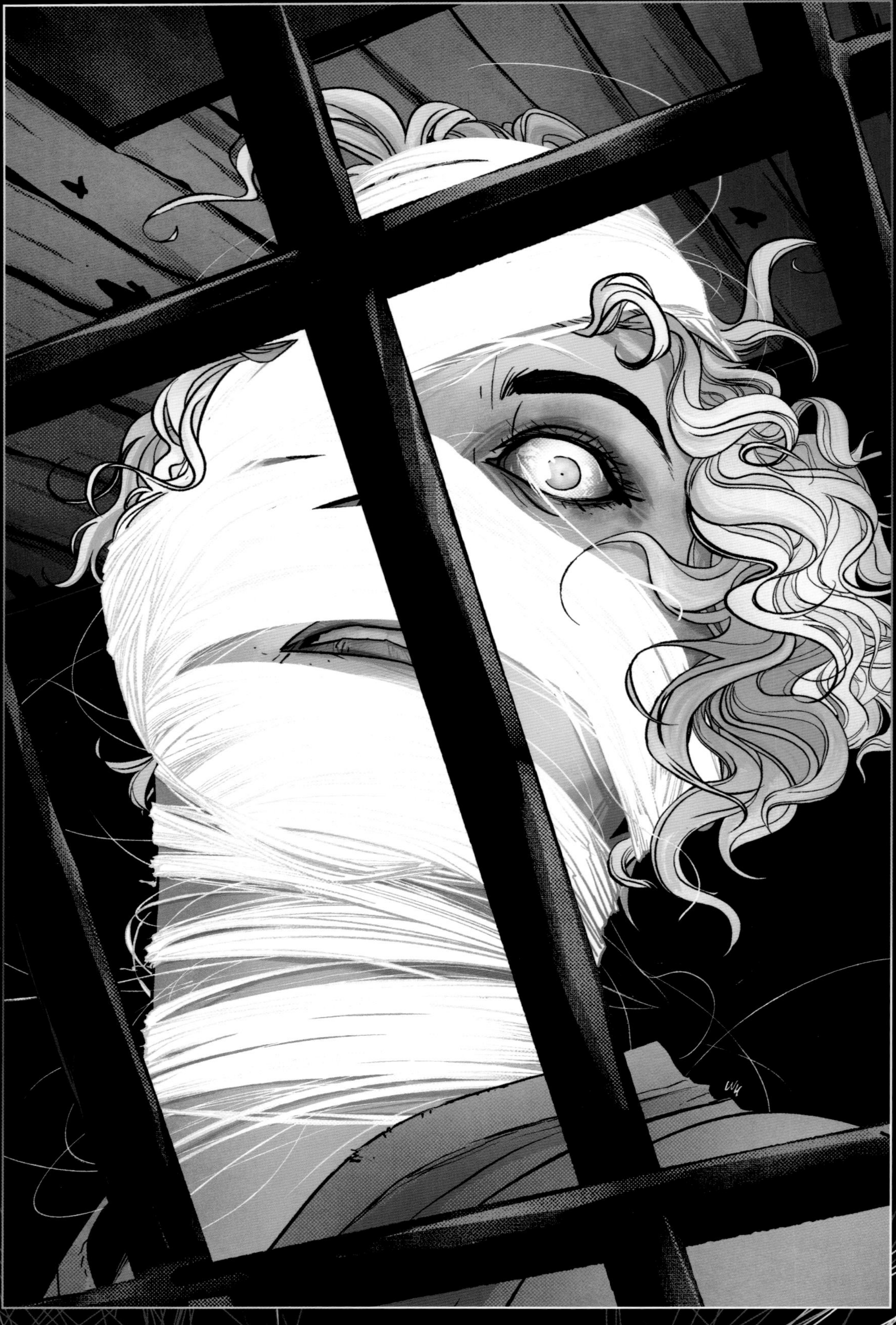

FOUR

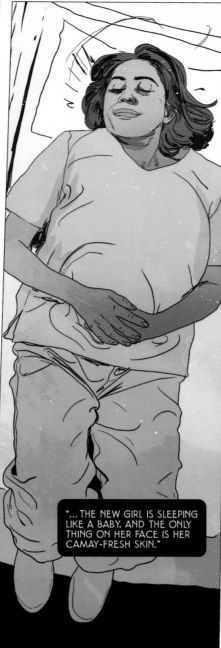

SHE'S NOT NECESSARILY ASLEEP BECAUSE HER EYES ARE SHUT.

LISTEN, DOC, I'VE BEEN DOING THIS JOB A LOT LONGER THAN YOU'VE BEEN DOING YOURS. I KNOW WHEN THEY'RE AWAKE AND I KNOW WHEN THEY'RE ASLEEP.

THAT ONE IS ASLEEP AND HAS BEEN FOR AT LEAST 45 MINUTES.

WE'VE GOT AT LEAST 15 WOMEN SLEEPING INSIDE THAT WEBBING CRAP. THAT SHIT SPINS OUT OF THEM AS SOON AS THEY FALL ASLEEP. *EXCEPT...*

"...THE NEW GIRL IS SLEEPING LIKE A BABY, AND THE ONLY THING ON HER FACE IS HER CAMAY-FRESH SKIN."

I NEED TO GO HOME, CHECK IN WITH LILA AND JARED. BUT... THIS *DEVELOPMENT* CAN'T LEAVE THE PRISON. EVIE IS CLEARLY DIFFERENT FROM OTHER WOMEN. SHE *KNOWS* THINGS, SHE... I MEAN, JUST *LOOK* AT HER.

IF THIS GETS OUT, IT COULD CAUSE A RIOT. DO YOU UNDERSTAND?

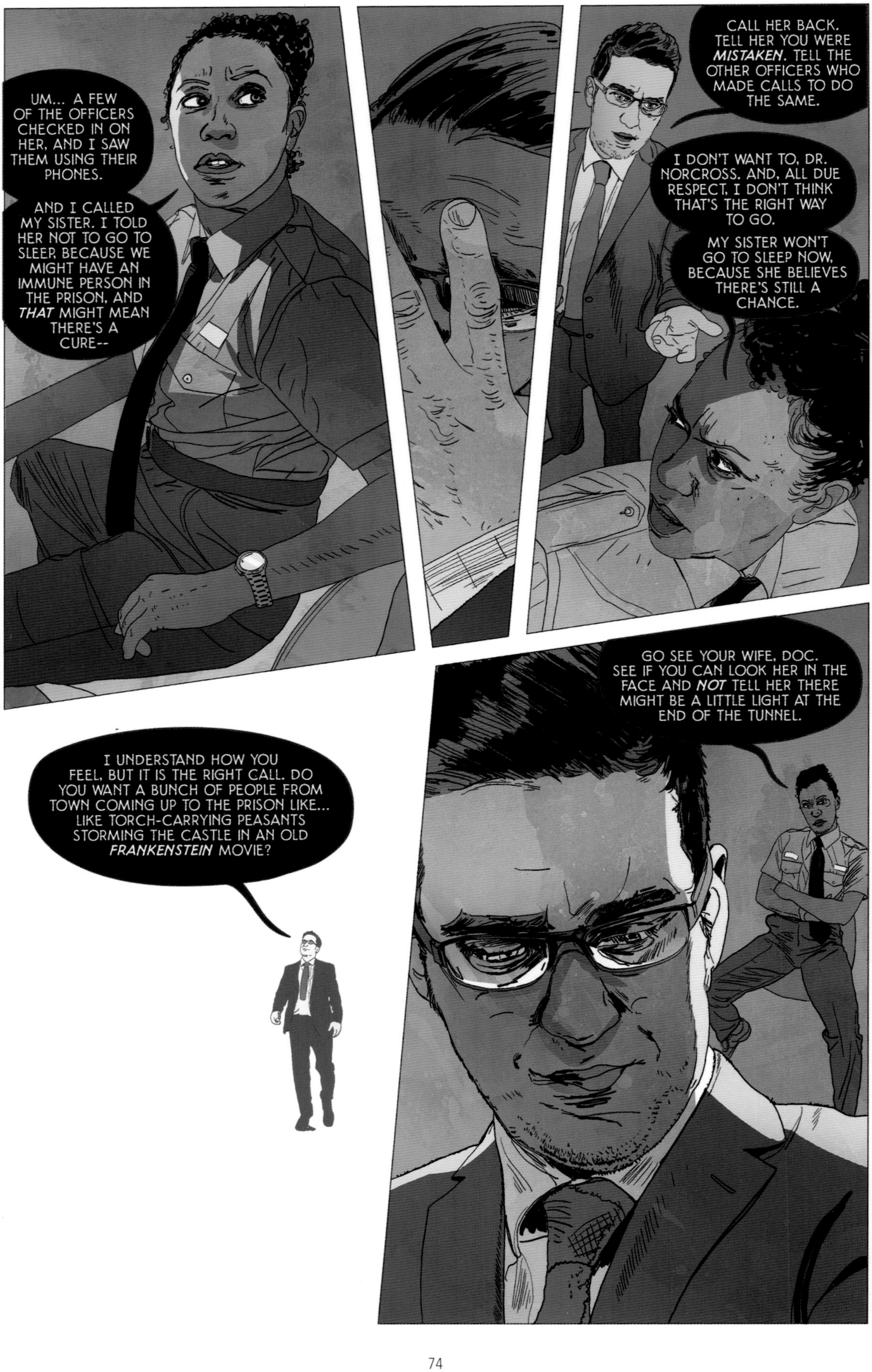
UM... A FEW OF THE OFFICERS CHECKED IN ON HER, AND I SAW THEM USING THEIR PHONES.
AND I CALLED MY SISTER. I TOLD HER NOT TO GO TO SLEEP, BECAUSE WE MIGHT HAVE AN IMMUNE PERSON IN THE PRISON, AND *THAT* MIGHT MEAN THERE'S A CURE--
CALL HER BACK. TELL HER YOU WERE *MISTAKEN*. TELL THE OTHER OFFICERS WHO MADE CALLS TO DO THE SAME.
I DON'T WANT TO, DR. NORCROSS. AND, ALL DUE RESPECT, I DON'T THINK THAT'S THE RIGHT WAY TO GO.
MY SISTER WON'T GO TO SLEEP NOW, BECAUSE SHE BELIEVES THERE'S STILL A CHANCE.
I UNDERSTAND HOW YOU FEEL, BUT IT IS THE RIGHT CALL. DO YOU WANT A BUNCH OF PEOPLE FROM TOWN COMING UP TO THE PRISON LIKE... LIKE TORCH-CARRYING PEASANTS STORMING THE CASTLE IN AN OLD *FRANKENSTEIN* MOVIE?
GO SEE YOUR WIFE, DOC. SEE IF YOU CAN LOOK HER IN THE FACE AND *NOT* TELL HER THERE MIGHT BE A LITTLE LIGHT AT THE END OF THE TUNNEL.

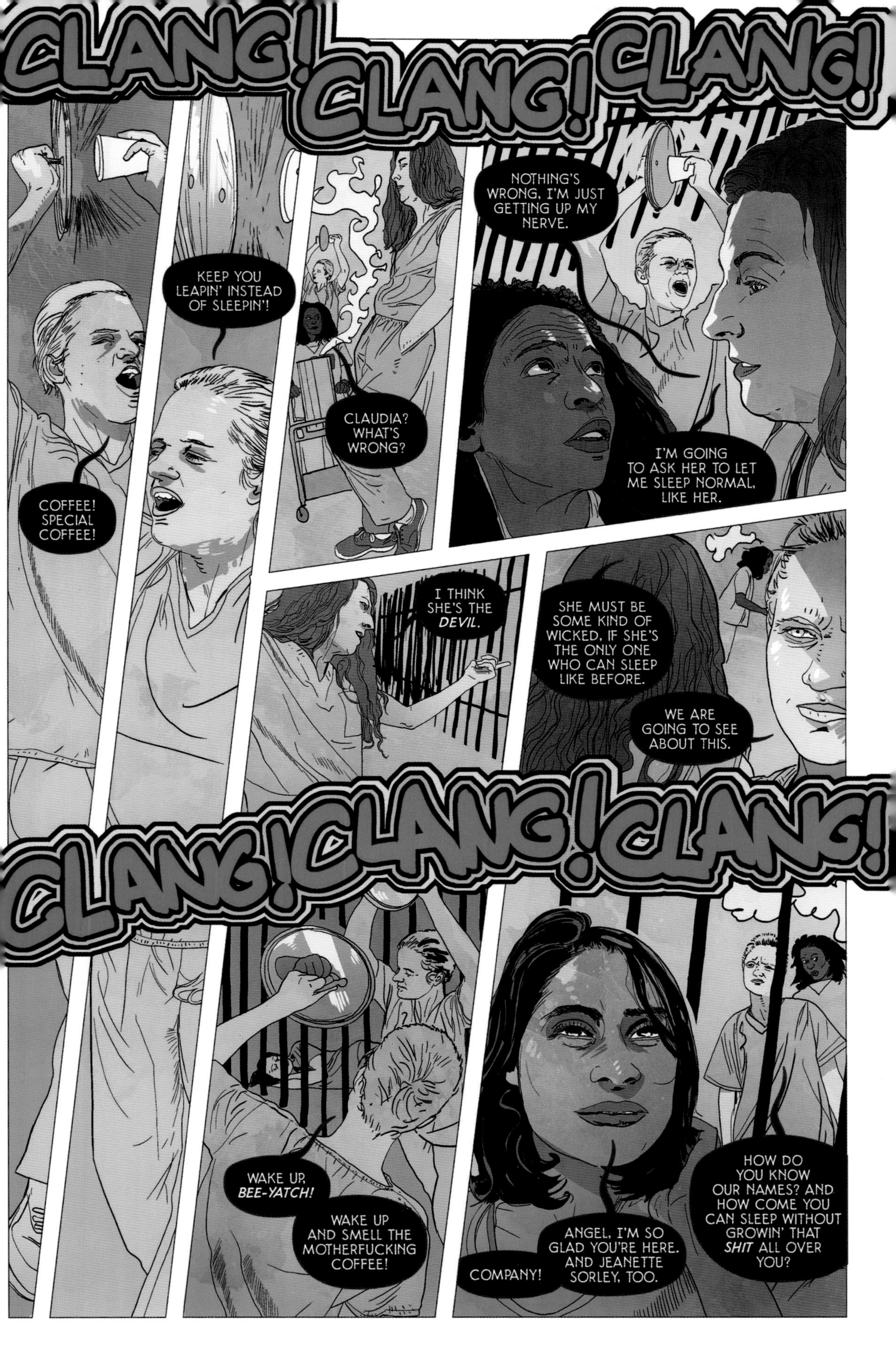
CLANG! CLANG! CLANG!
KEEP YOU LEAPIN' INSTEAD OF SLEEPIN'!
COFFEE! SPECIAL COFFEE!
CLAUDIA? WHAT'S WRONG?
NOTHING'S WRONG, I'M JUST GETTING UP MY NERVE.
I'M GOING TO ASK HER TO LET ME SLEEP NORMAL, LIKE HER.
I THINK SHE'S THE *DEVIL*.
SHE MUST BE SOME KIND OF WICKED, IF SHE'S THE ONLY ONE WHO CAN SLEEP LIKE BEFORE.
WE ARE GOING TO SEE ABOUT THIS.
CLANG! CLANG! CLANG!
WAKE UP, *BEE-YATCH!*
WAKE UP AND SMELL THE MOTHERFUCKING COFFEE!
COMPANY!
ANGEL, I'M SO GLAD YOU'RE HERE. AND JEANETTE SORLEY, TOO.
HOW DO YOU KNOW OUR NAMES? AND HOW COME YOU CAN SLEEP WITHOUT GROWIN' THAT *SHIT* ALL OVER YOU?

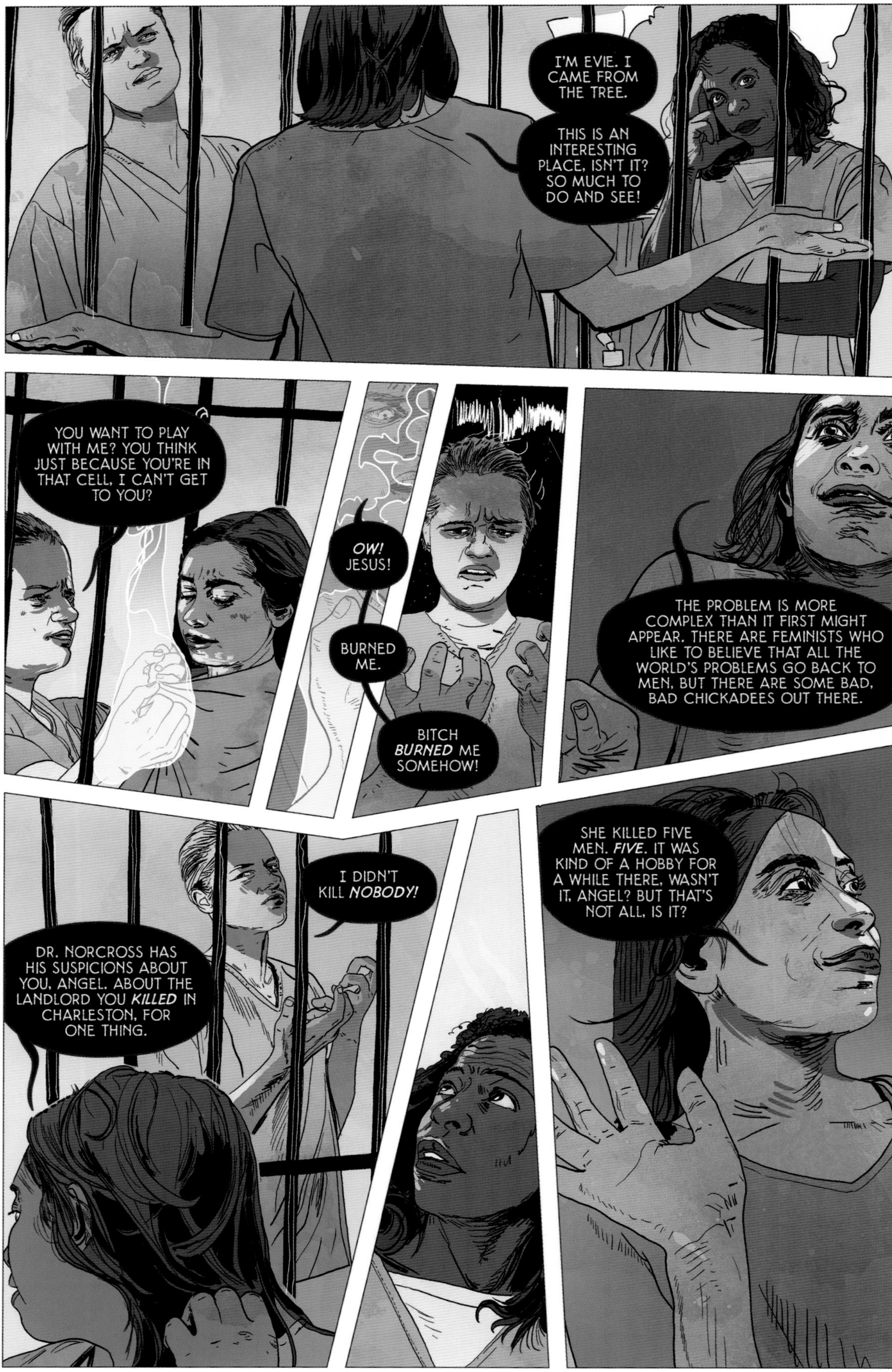
I'M EVIE. I CAME FROM THE TREE.
THIS IS AN INTERESTING PLACE, ISN'T IT? SO MUCH TO DO AND SEE!
YOU WANT TO PLAY WITH ME? YOU THINK JUST BECAUSE YOU'RE IN THAT CELL, I CAN'T GET TO YOU?
OW! JESUS!
BURNED ME.
BITCH BURNED ME SOMEHOW!
THE PROBLEM IS MORE COMPLEX THAN IT FIRST MIGHT APPEAR. THERE ARE FEMINISTS WHO LIKE TO BELIEVE THAT ALL THE WORLD'S PROBLEMS GO BACK TO MEN, BUT THERE ARE SOME BAD, BAD CHICKADEES OUT THERE.
DR. NORCROSS HAS HIS SUSPICIONS ABOUT YOU, ANGEL. ABOUT THE LANDLORD YOU KILLED IN CHARLESTON, FOR ONE THING.
I DIDN'T KILL NOBODY!
SHE KILLED FIVE MEN. FIVE. IT WAS KIND OF A HOBBY FOR A WHILE THERE, WASN'T IT, ANGEL? BUT THAT'S NOT ALL, IS IT?

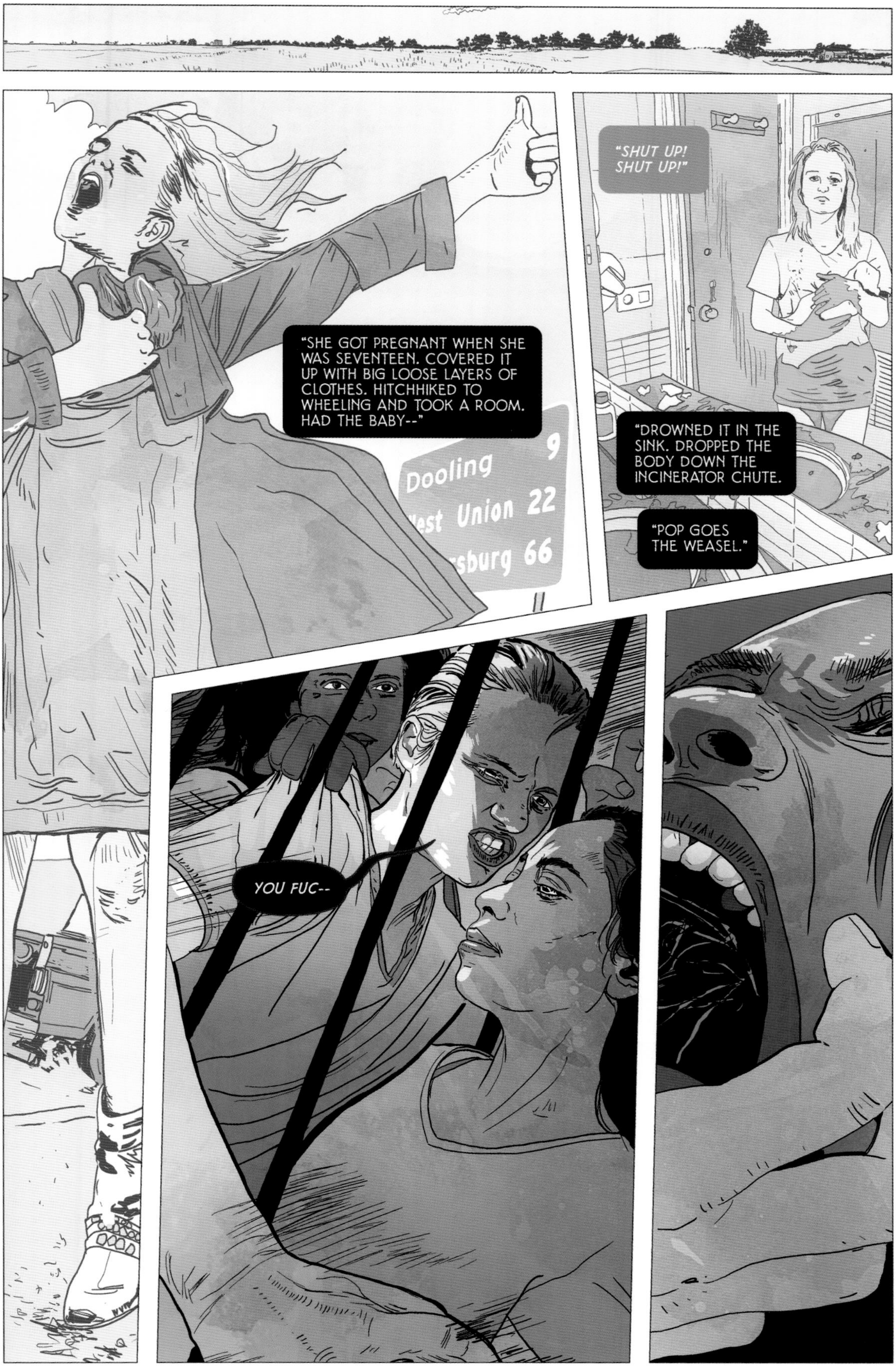

"SHE GOT PREGNANT WHEN SHE WAS SEVENTEEN. COVERED IT UP WITH BIG LOOSE LAYERS OF CLOTHES. HITCHHIKED TO WHEELING AND TOOK A ROOM. HAD THE BABY--"
Dooling 9
West Union 22
rsburg 66
"SHUT UP! SHUT UP!"
"DROWNED IT IN THE SINK. DROPPED THE BODY DOWN THE INCINERATOR CHUTE.
"POP GOES THE WEASEL."
YOU FUC--

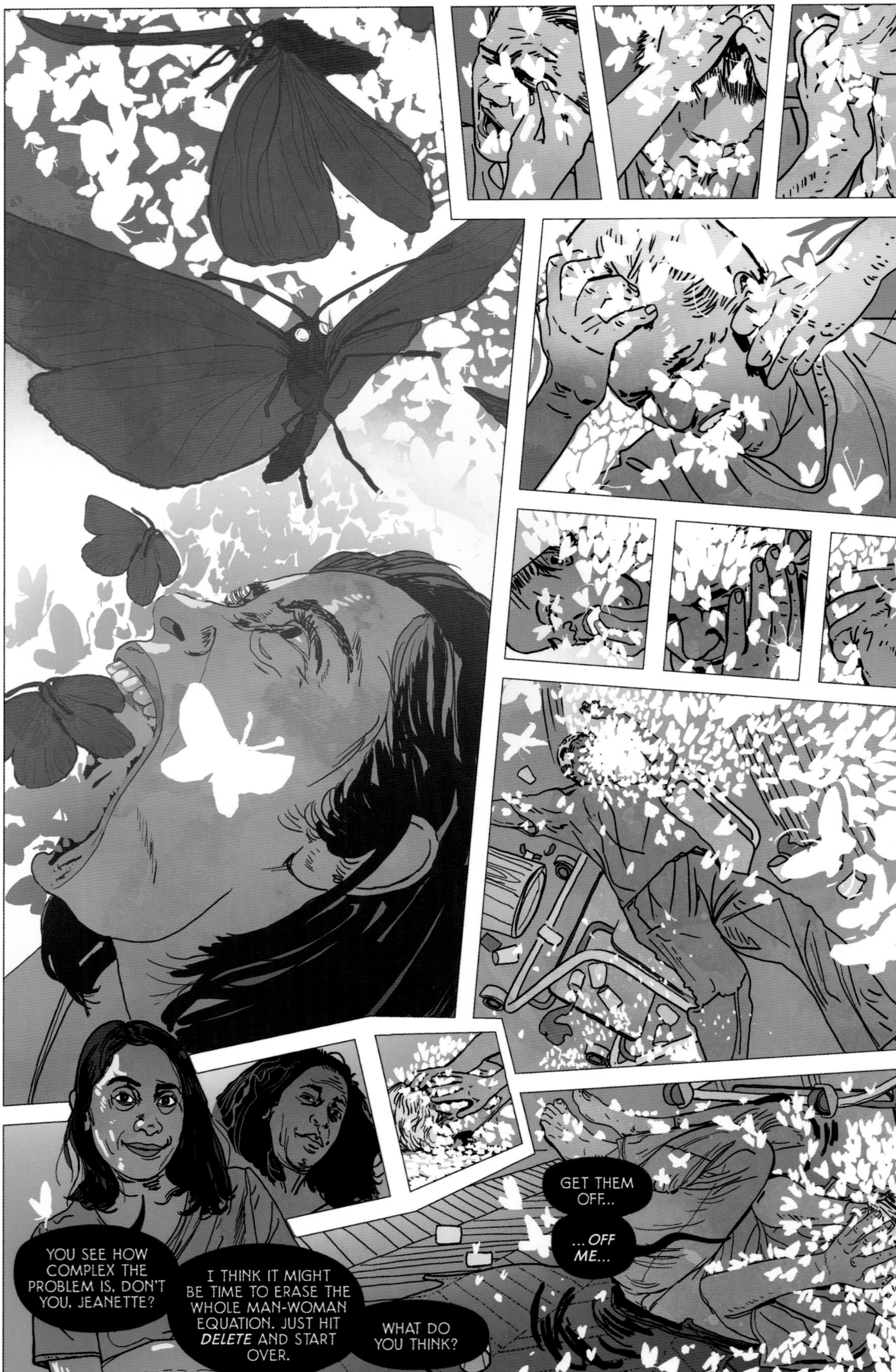
GET THEM OFF...
...OFF ME...
YOU SEE HOW COMPLEX THE PROBLEM IS, DON'T YOU, JEANETTE?
I THINK IT MIGHT BE TIME TO ERASE THE WHOLE MAN-WOMAN EQUATION. JUST HIT *DELETE* AND START OVER.
WHAT DO YOU THINK?

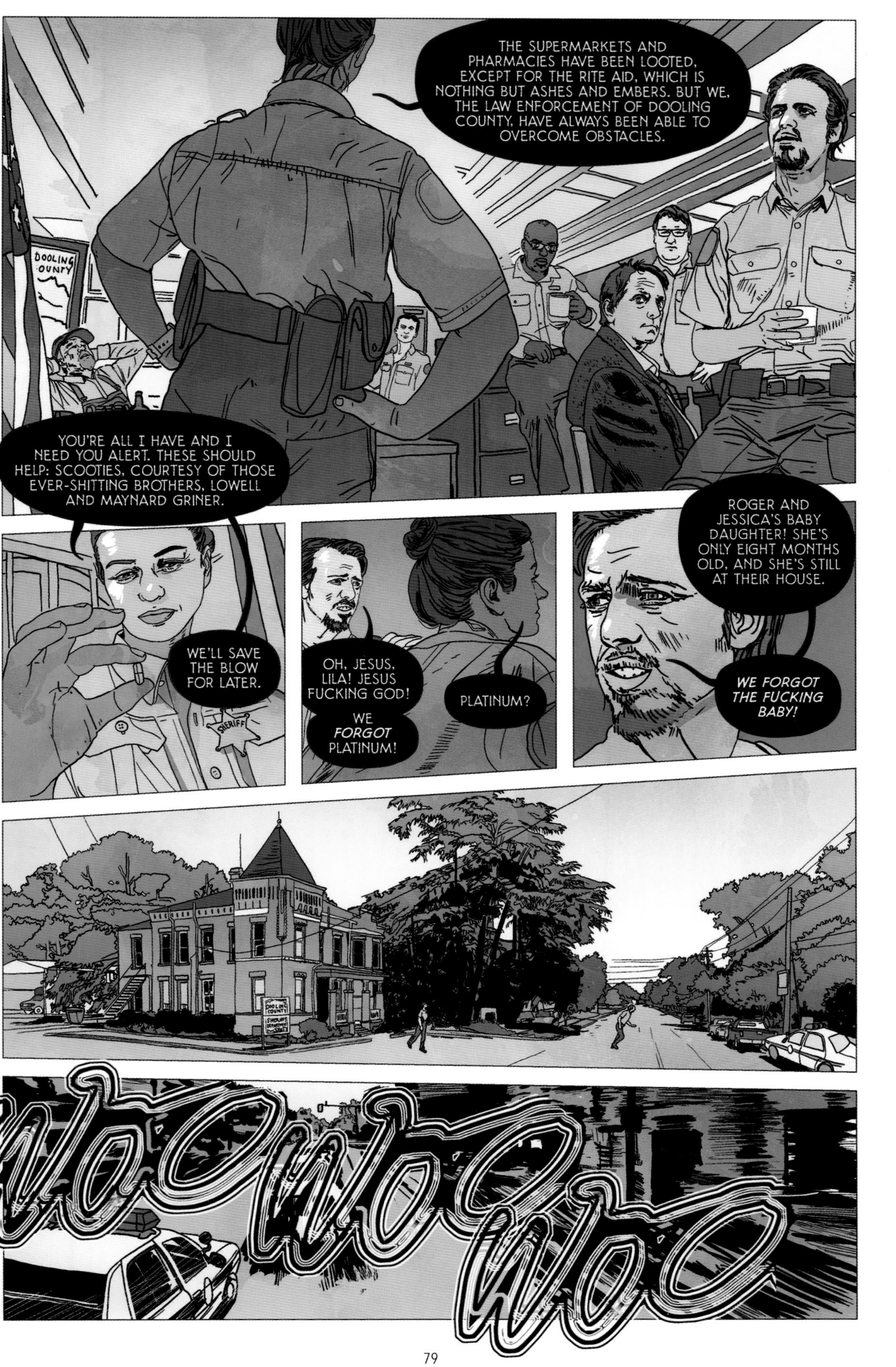
THE SUPERMARKETS AND PHARMACIES HAVE BEEN LOOTED, EXCEPT FOR THE RITE AID, WHICH IS NOTHING BUT ASHES AND EMBERS. BUT WE, THE LAW ENFORCEMENT OF DOOLING COUNTY, HAVE ALWAYS BEEN ABLE TO OVERCOME OBSTACLES.
DOOLING COUNTY
YOU'RE ALL I HAVE AND I NEED YOU ALERT. THESE SHOULD HELP: SCOOTIES, COURTESY OF THOSE EVER-SHITTING BROTHERS, LOWELL AND MAYNARD GRINER.
WE'LL SAVE THE BLOW FOR LATER.
SHERIFF
OH, JESUS, LILA! JESUS FUCKING GOD!
WE *FORGOT* PLATINUM!
PLATINUM?
ROGER AND JESSICA'S BABY DAUGHTER! SHE'S ONLY EIGHT MONTHS OLD, AND SHE'S STILL AT THEIR HOUSE.
WE FORGOT THE FUCKING BABY!
DOOLING COUNTY
WOOWOOWOO

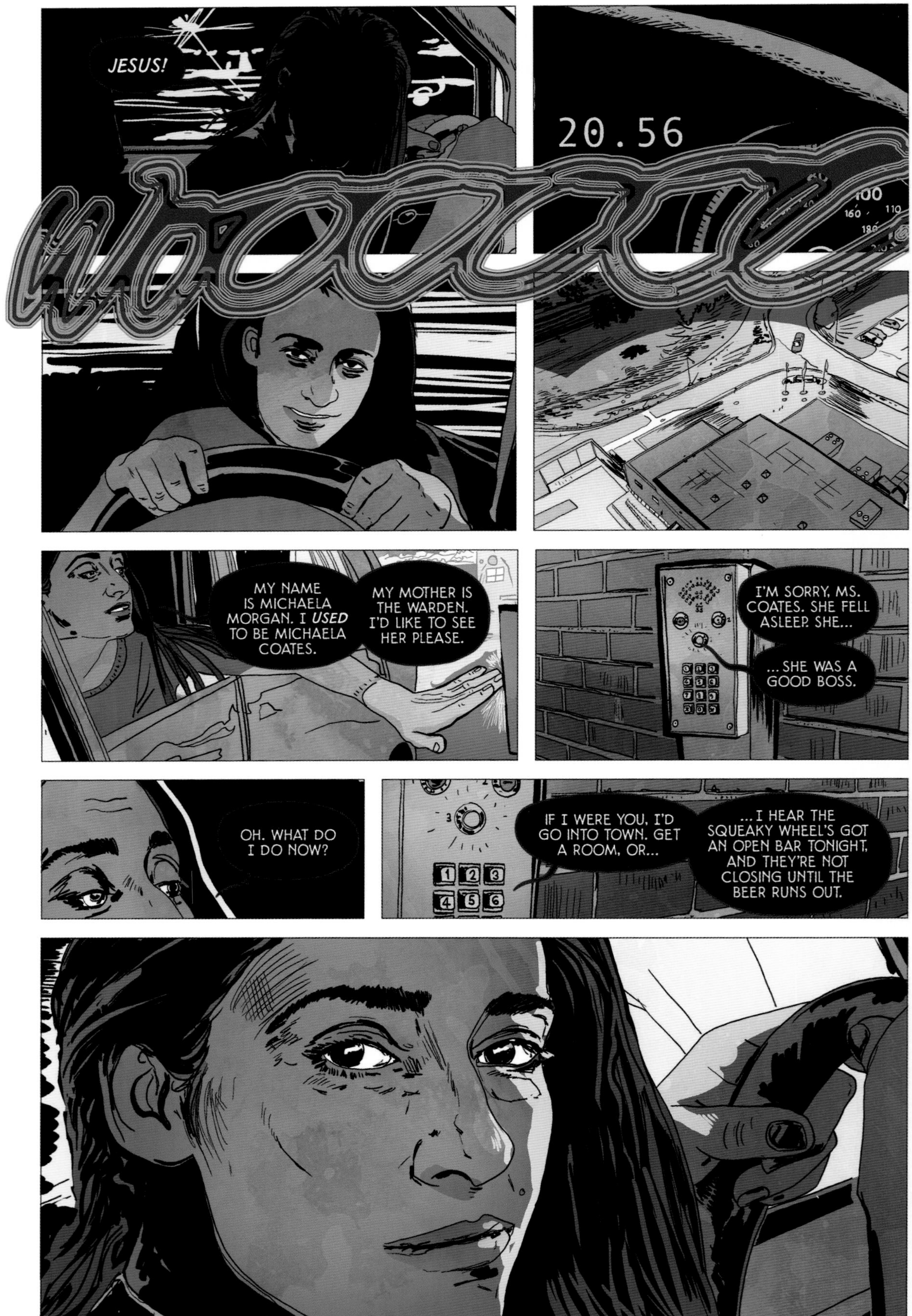
JESUS!
20.56
MY NAME IS MICHAELA MORGAN. I *USED* TO BE MICHAELA COATES.
MY MOTHER IS THE WARDEN. I'D LIKE TO SEE HER PLEASE.
I'M SORRY, MS. COATES. SHE FELL ASLEEP. SHE...
...SHE WAS A GOOD BOSS.
OH. WHAT DO I DO NOW?
IF I WERE YOU, I'D GO INTO TOWN. GET A ROOM, OR...
...I HEAR THE SQUEAKY WHEEL'S GOT AN OPEN BAR TONIGHT, AND THEY'RE NOT CLOSING UNTIL THE BEER RUNS OUT.

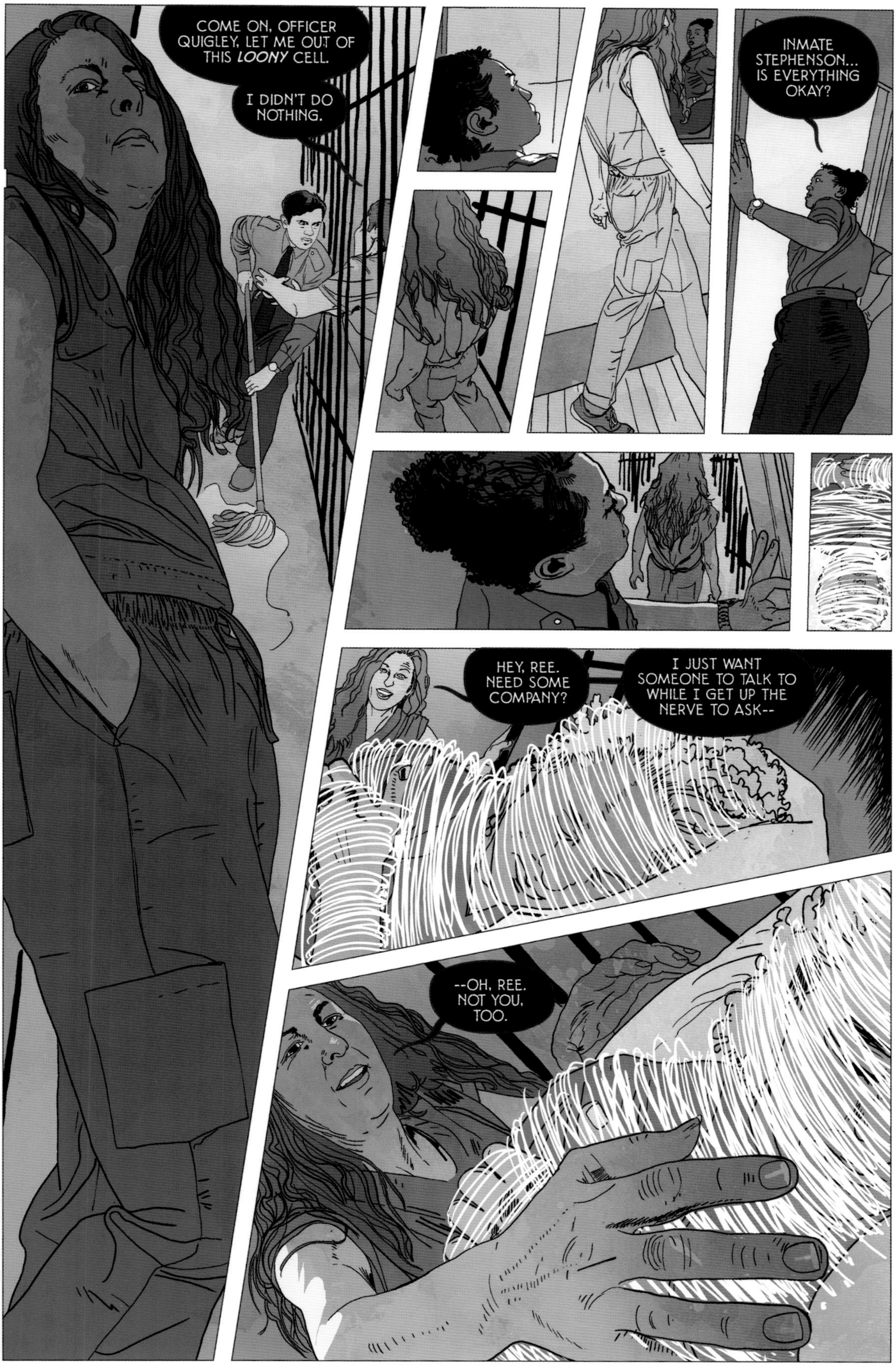
COME ON, OFFICER QUIGLEY, LET ME OUT OF THIS LOONY CELL.
I DIDN'T DO NOTHING.
INMATE STEPHENSON... IS EVERYTHING OKAY?
HEY, REE. NEED SOME COMPANY?
I JUST WANT SOMEONE TO TALK TO WHILE I GET UP THE NERVE TO ASK--
--OH, REE. NOT YOU, TOO.

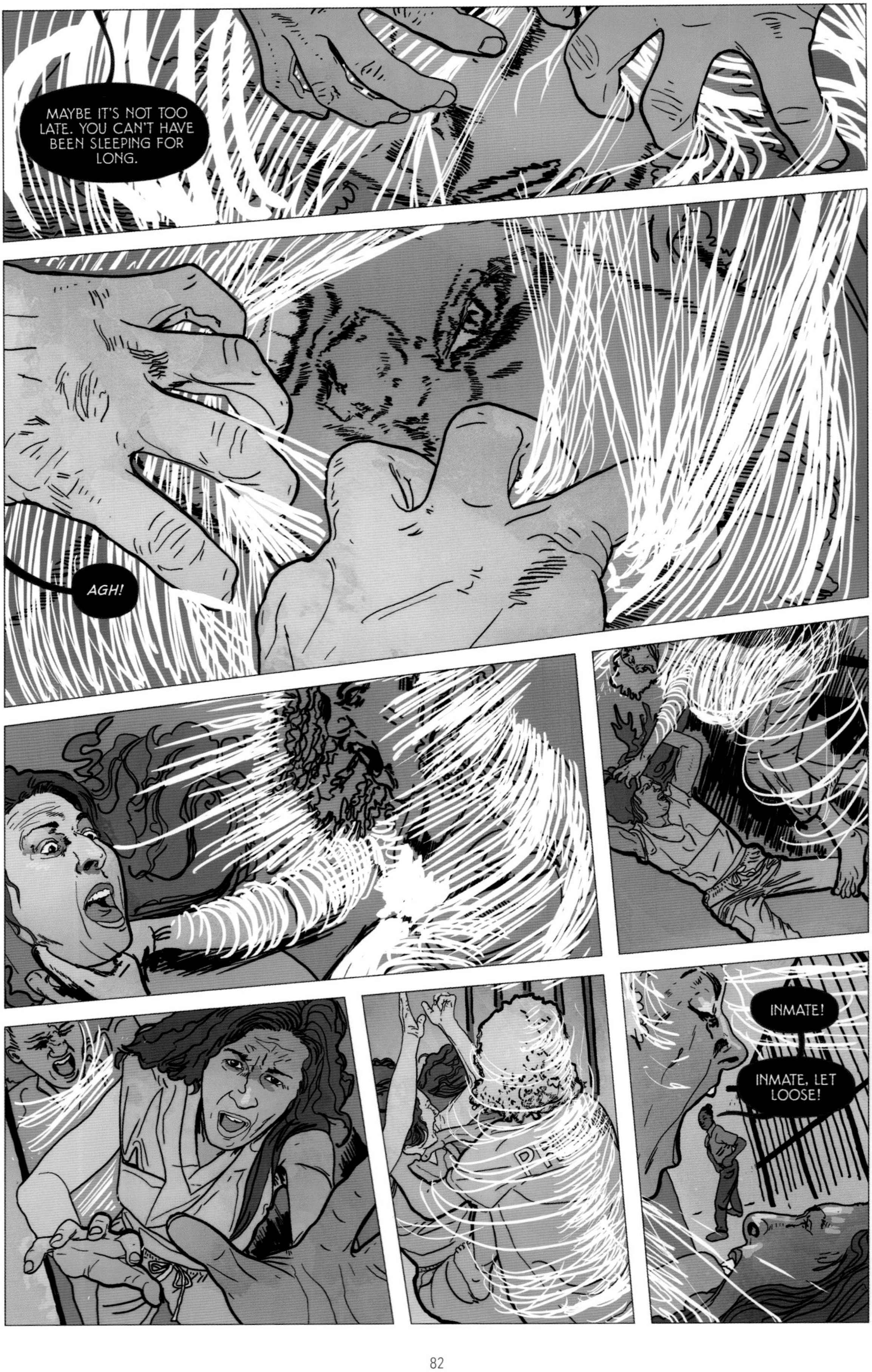
MAYBE IT'S NOT TOO LATE. YOU CAN'T HAVE BEEN SLEEPING FOR LONG.
AGH!
INMATE!
INMATE, LET LOOSE!

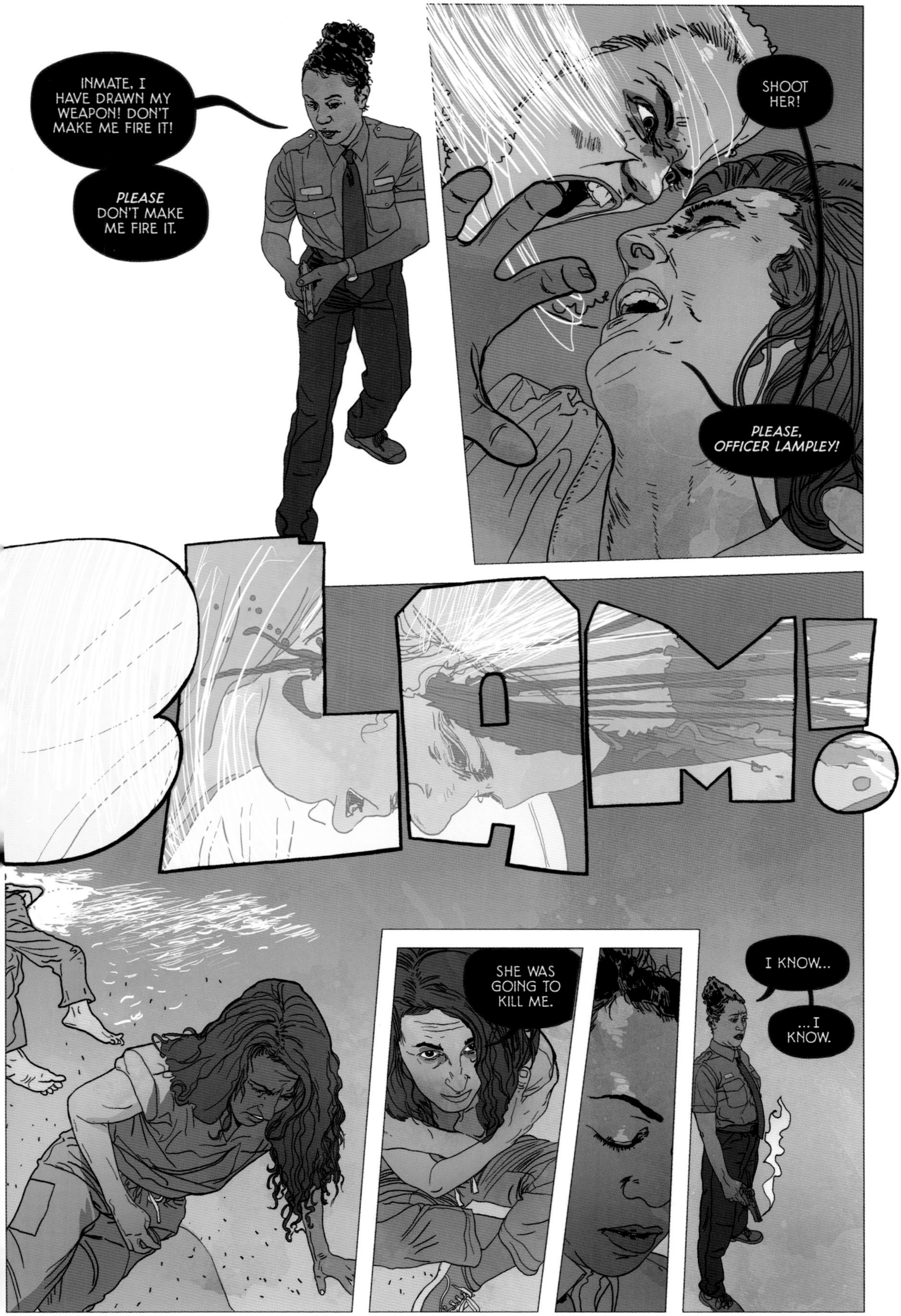
INMATE, I HAVE DRAWN MY WEAPON! DON'T MAKE ME FIRE IT!
PLEASE DON'T MAKE ME FIRE IT.
SHOOT HER!
PLEASE, OFFICER LAMPLEY!
BLAM!
SHE WAS GOING TO KILL ME.
I KNOW...
...I KNOW.

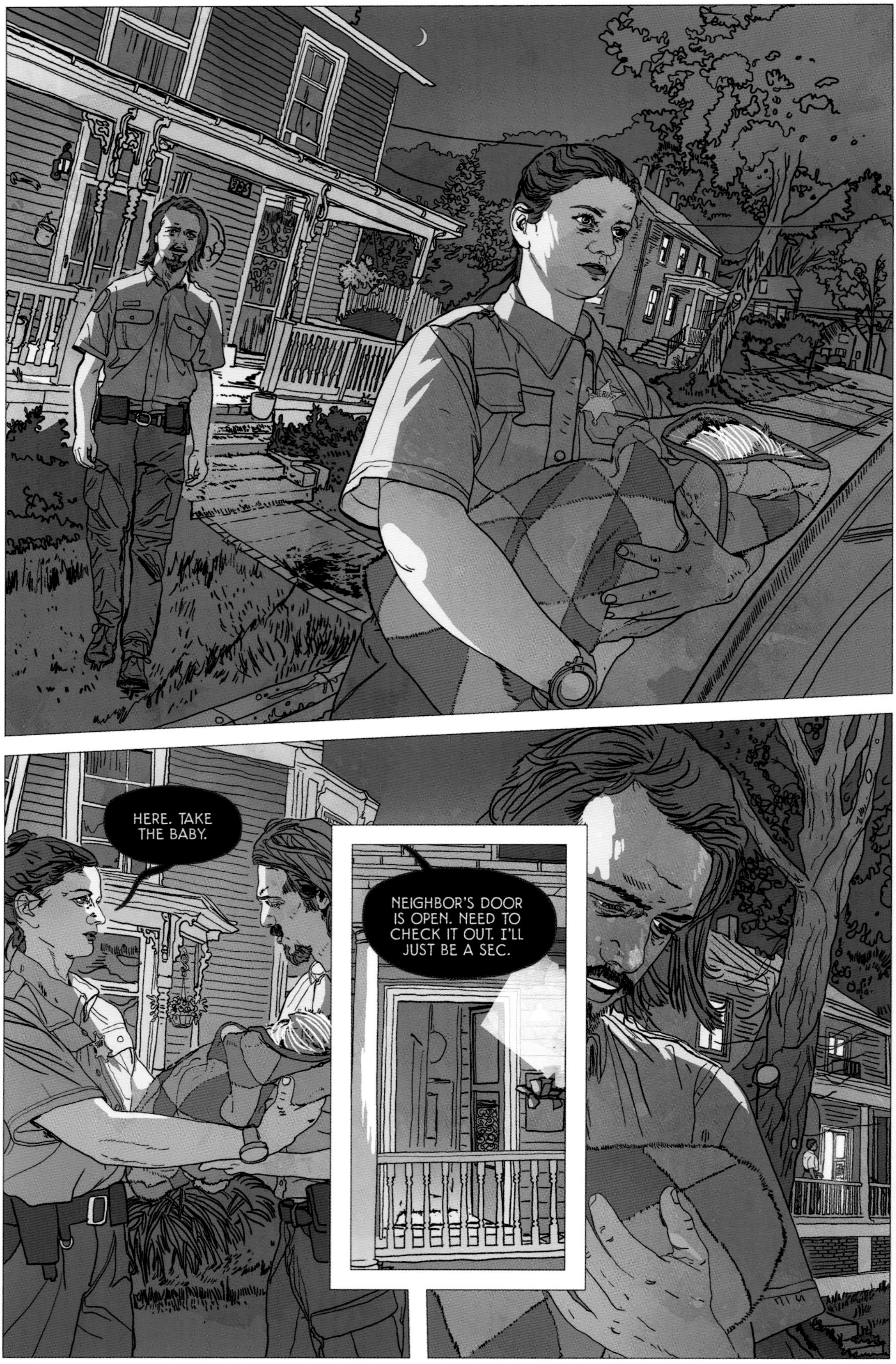
HERE. TAKE THE BABY.
NEIGHBOR'S DOOR IS OPEN. NEED TO CHECK IT OUT. I'LL JUST BE A SEC.

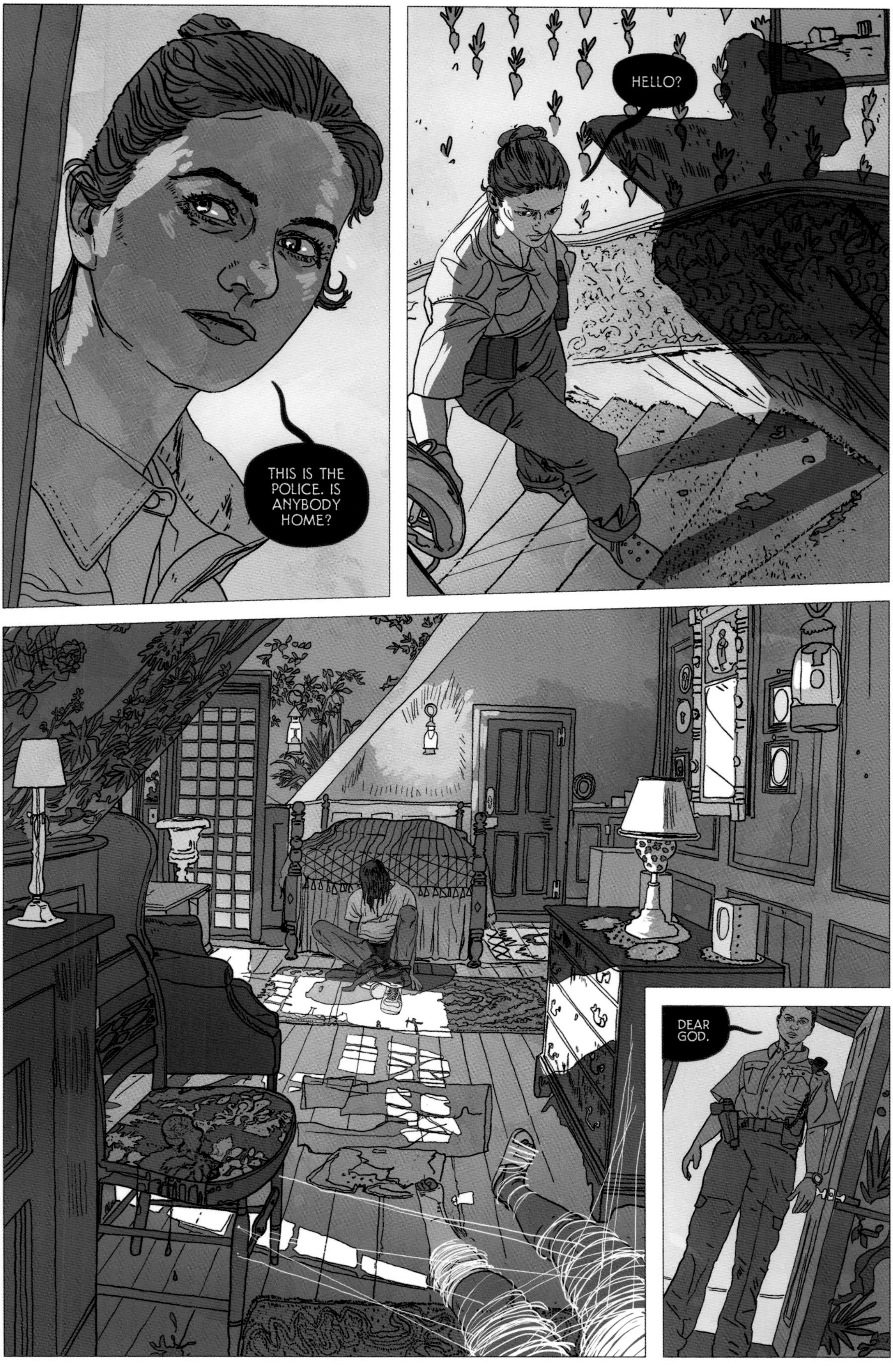

THIS IS THE POLICE. IS ANYBODY HOME?
HELLO?
DEAR GOD.

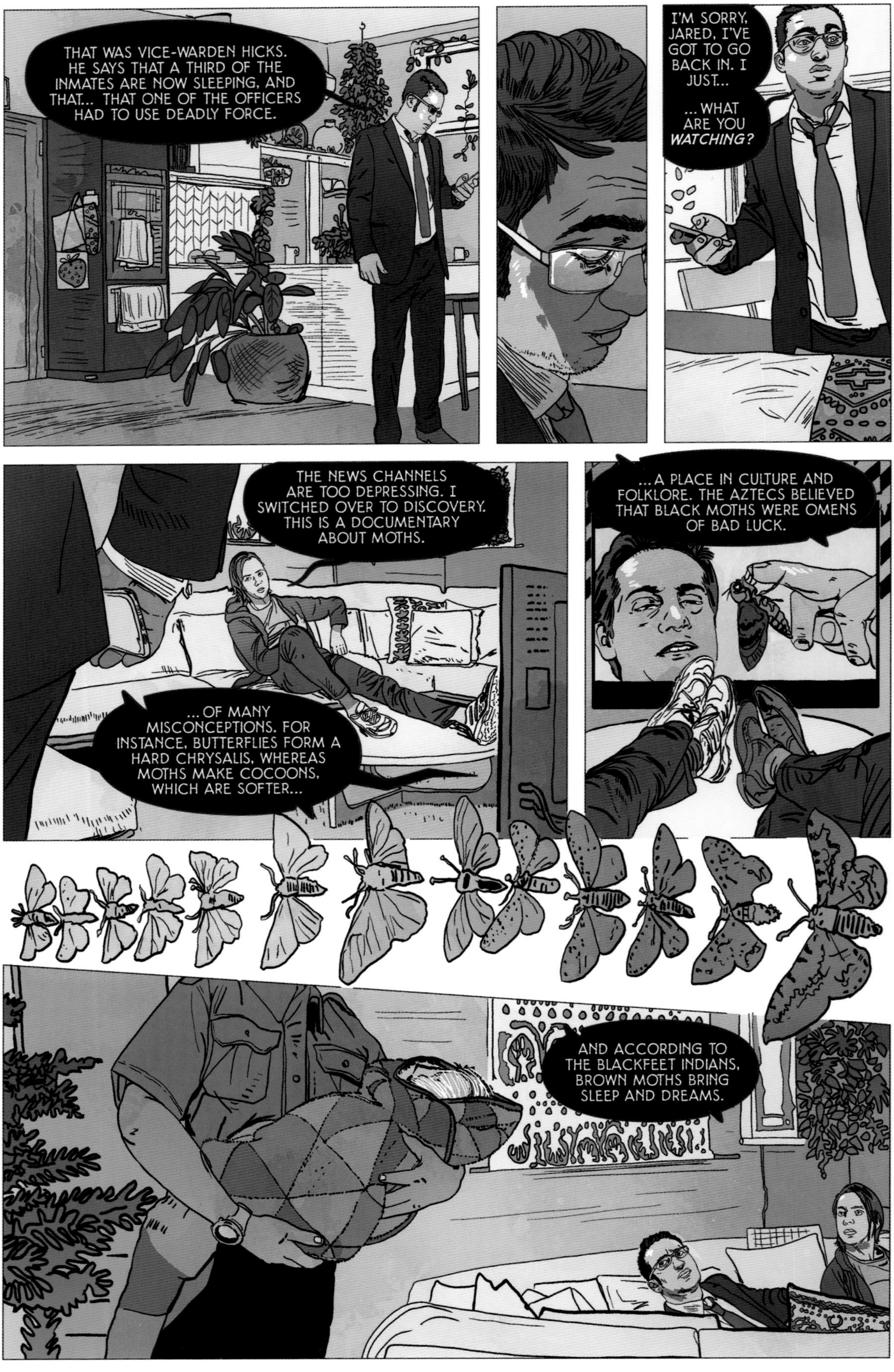
THAT WAS VICE-WARDEN HICKS. HE SAYS THAT A THIRD OF THE INMATES ARE NOW SLEEPING, AND THAT... THAT ONE OF THE OFFICERS HAD TO USE DEADLY FORCE.
I'M SORRY, JARED, I'VE GOT TO GO BACK IN. I JUST...
...WHAT ARE YOU *WATCHING?*
THE NEWS CHANNELS ARE TOO DEPRESSING. I SWITCHED OVER TO DISCOVERY. THIS IS A DOCUMENTARY ABOUT MOTHS.
...OF MANY MISCONCEPTIONS. FOR INSTANCE, BUTTERFLIES FORM A HARD CHRYSALIS, WHEREAS MOTHS MAKE COCOONS, WHICH ARE SOFTER...
...A PLACE IN CULTURE AND FOLKLORE. THE AZTECS BELIEVED THAT BLACK MOTHS WERE OMENS OF BAD LUCK.
AND ACCORDING TO THE BLACKFEET INDIANS, BROWN MOTHS BRING SLEEP AND DREAMS.

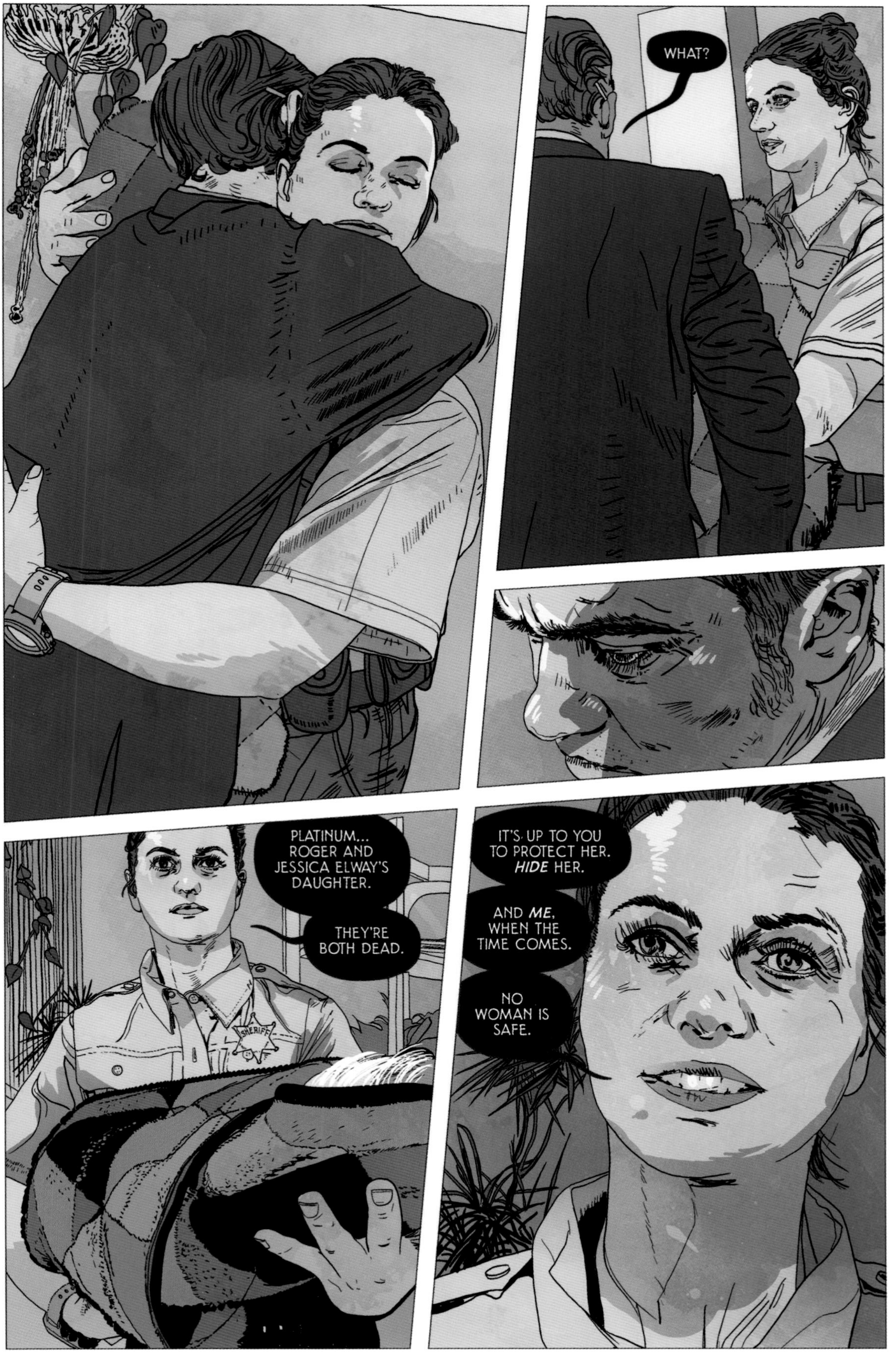

WHAT?
PLATINUM... ROGER AND JESSICA ELWAY'S DAUGHTER.
THEY'RE BOTH DEAD.
IT'S UP TO YOU TO PROTECT HER. *HIDE* HER.
AND *ME*, WHEN THE TIME COMES.
NO WOMAN IS SAFE.

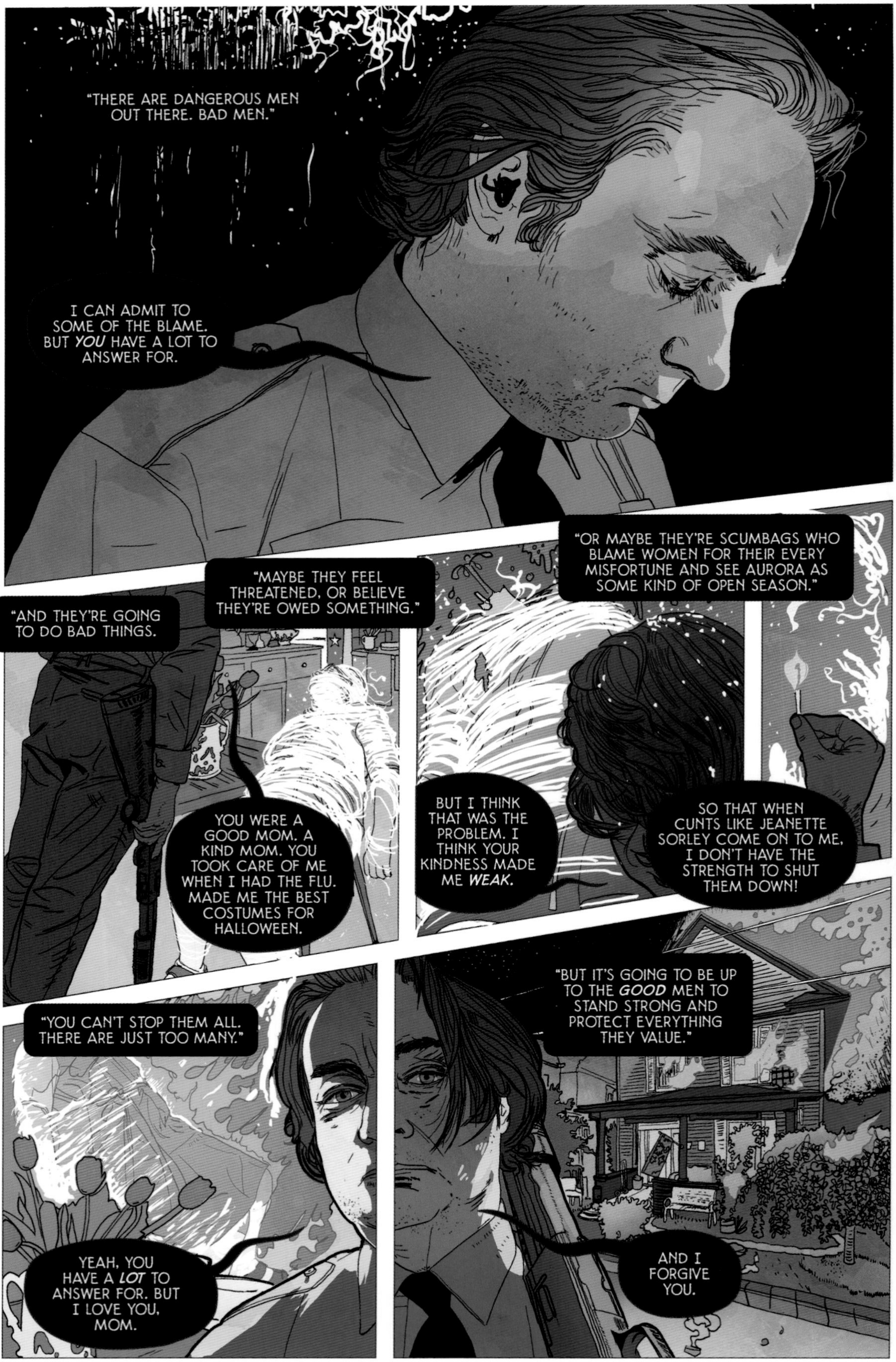
"THERE ARE DANGEROUS MEN OUT THERE. BAD MEN."
I CAN ADMIT TO SOME OF THE BLAME. BUT *YOU* HAVE A LOT TO ANSWER FOR.
"AND THEY'RE GOING TO DO BAD THINGS.
"MAYBE THEY FEEL THREATENED, OR BELIEVE THEY'RE OWED SOMETHING."
YOU WERE A GOOD MOM. A KIND MOM. YOU TOOK CARE OF ME WHEN I HAD THE FLU. MADE ME THE BEST COSTUMES FOR HALLOWEEN.
"OR MAYBE THEY'RE SCUMBAGS WHO BLAME WOMEN FOR THEIR EVERY MISFORTUNE AND SEE AURORA AS SOME KIND OF OPEN SEASON."
BUT I THINK THAT WAS THE PROBLEM. I THINK YOUR KINDNESS MADE ME *WEAK.*
SO THAT WHEN CUNTS LIKE JEANETTE SORLEY COME ON TO ME, I DON'T HAVE THE STRENGTH TO SHUT THEM DOWN!
"YOU CAN'T STOP THEM ALL. THERE ARE JUST TOO MANY."
YEAH, YOU HAVE A *LOT* TO ANSWER FOR. BUT I LOVE YOU, MOM.
"BUT IT'S GOING TO BE UP TO THE *GOOD* MEN TO STAND STRONG AND PROTECT EVERYTHING THEY VALUE."
AND I FORGIVE YOU.

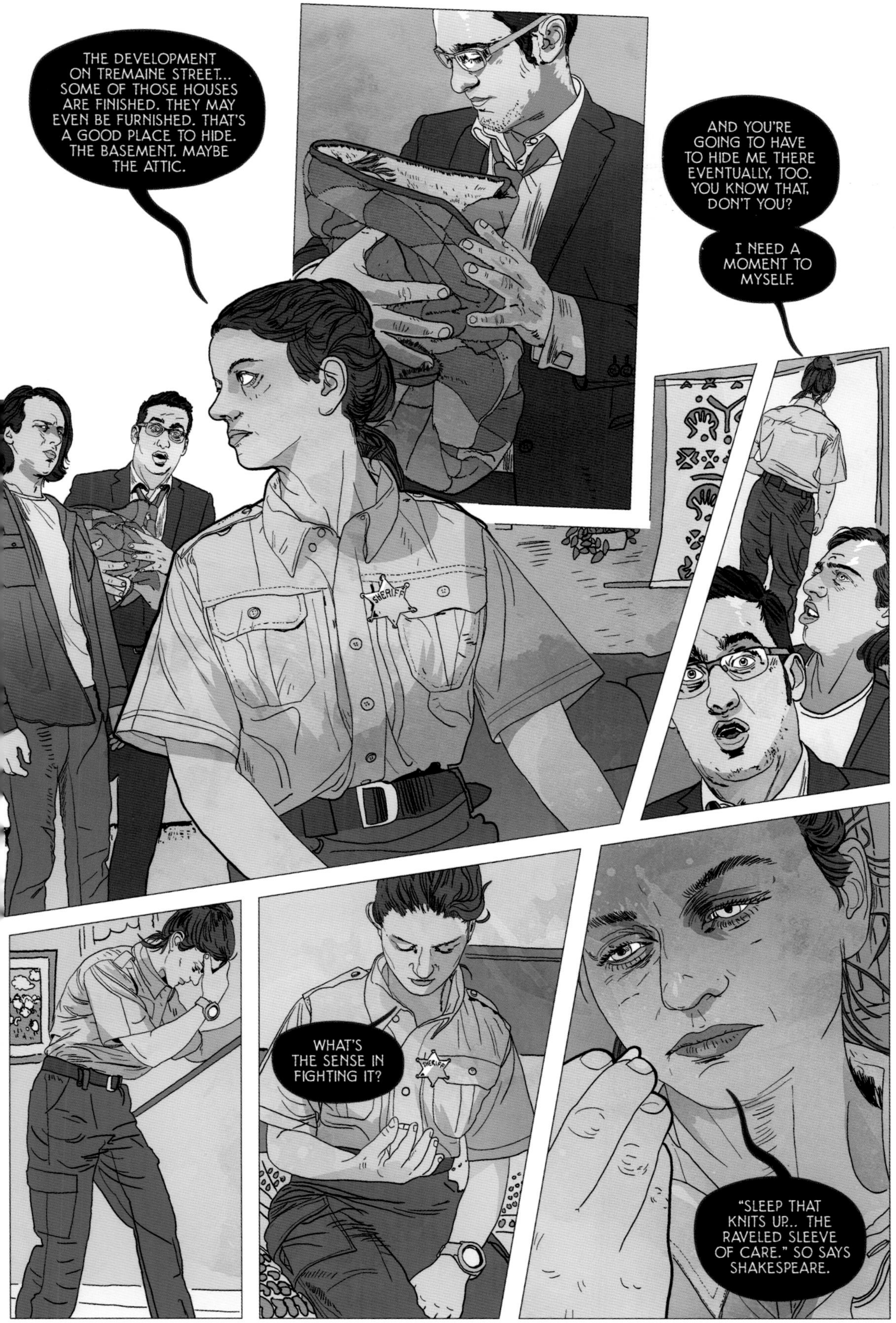
THE DEVELOPMENT ON TREMAINE STREET... SOME OF THOSE HOUSES ARE FINISHED. THEY MAY EVEN BE FURNISHED. THAT'S A GOOD PLACE TO HIDE. THE BASEMENT. MAYBE THE ATTIC.
AND YOU'RE GOING TO HAVE TO HIDE ME THERE EVENTUALLY, TOO. YOU KNOW THAT, DON'T YOU?
I NEED A MOMENT TO MYSELF.
SHERIFF
WHAT'S THE SENSE IN FIGHTING IT?
SHERIFF
"SLEEP THAT KNITS UP... THE RAVELED SLEEVE OF CARE." SO SAYS SHAKESPEARE.

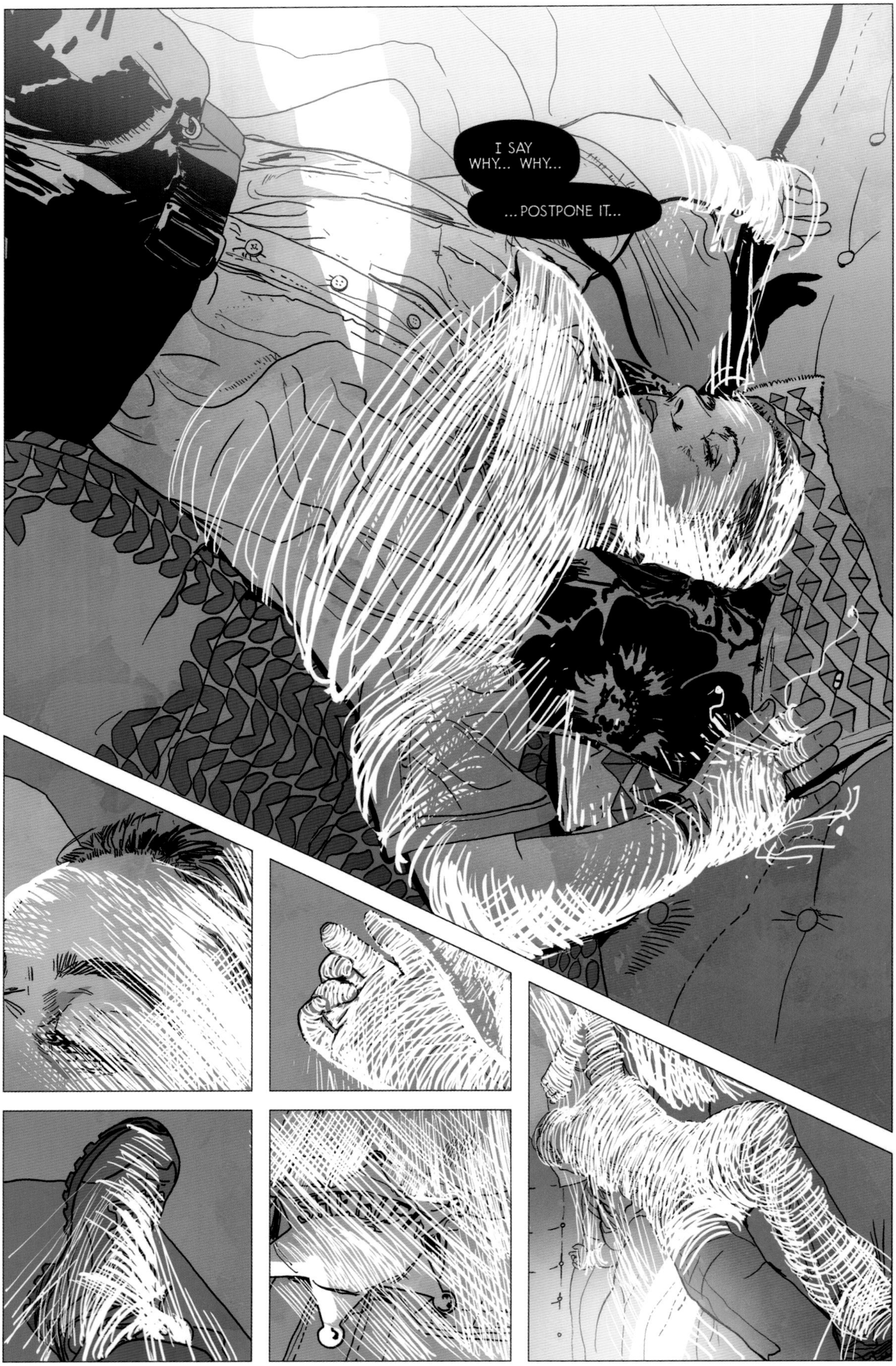
I SAY
WHY... WHY...
...POSTPONE IT...

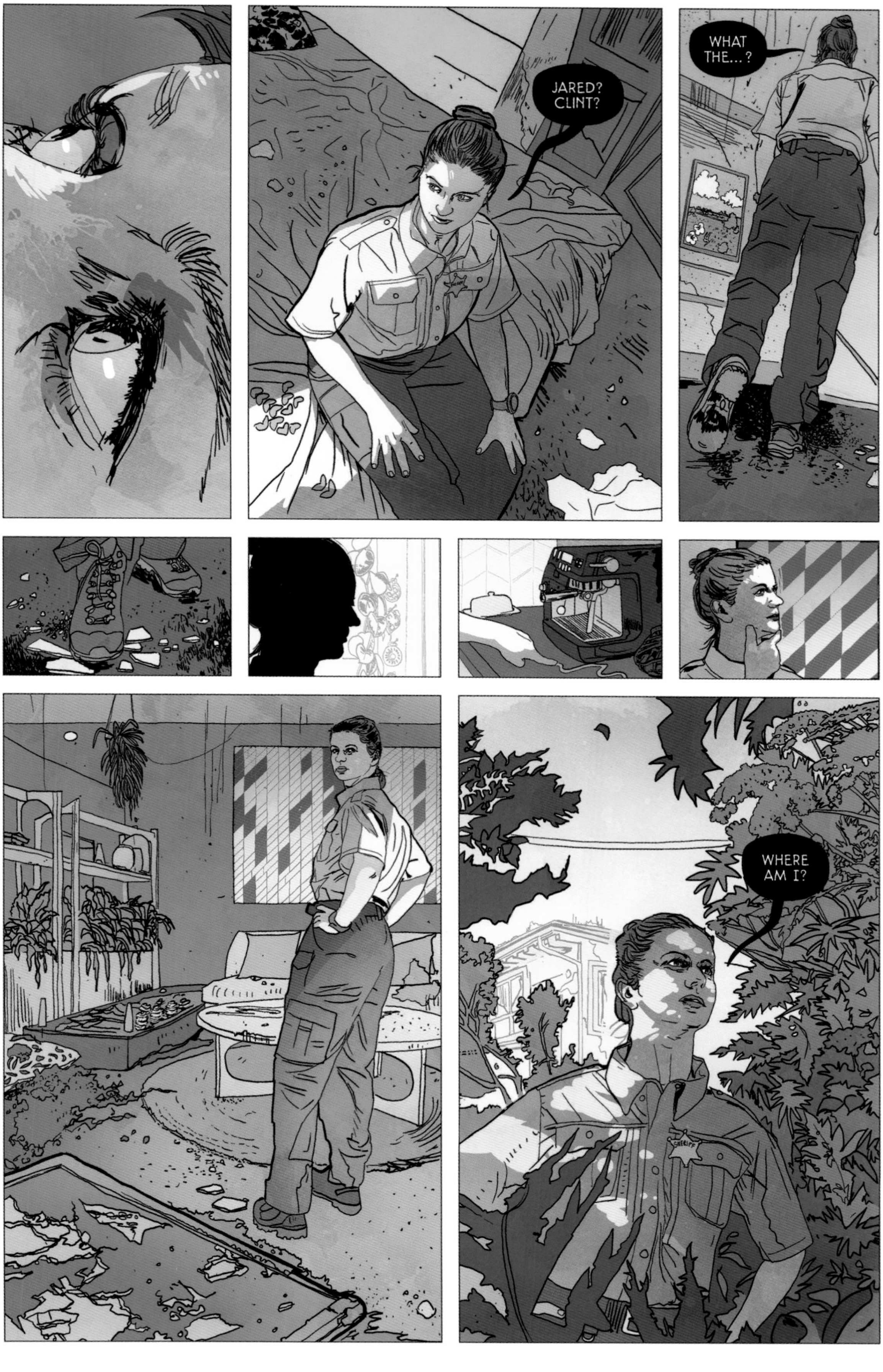
JARED? CLINT?
WHAT THE...?
WHERE AM I?

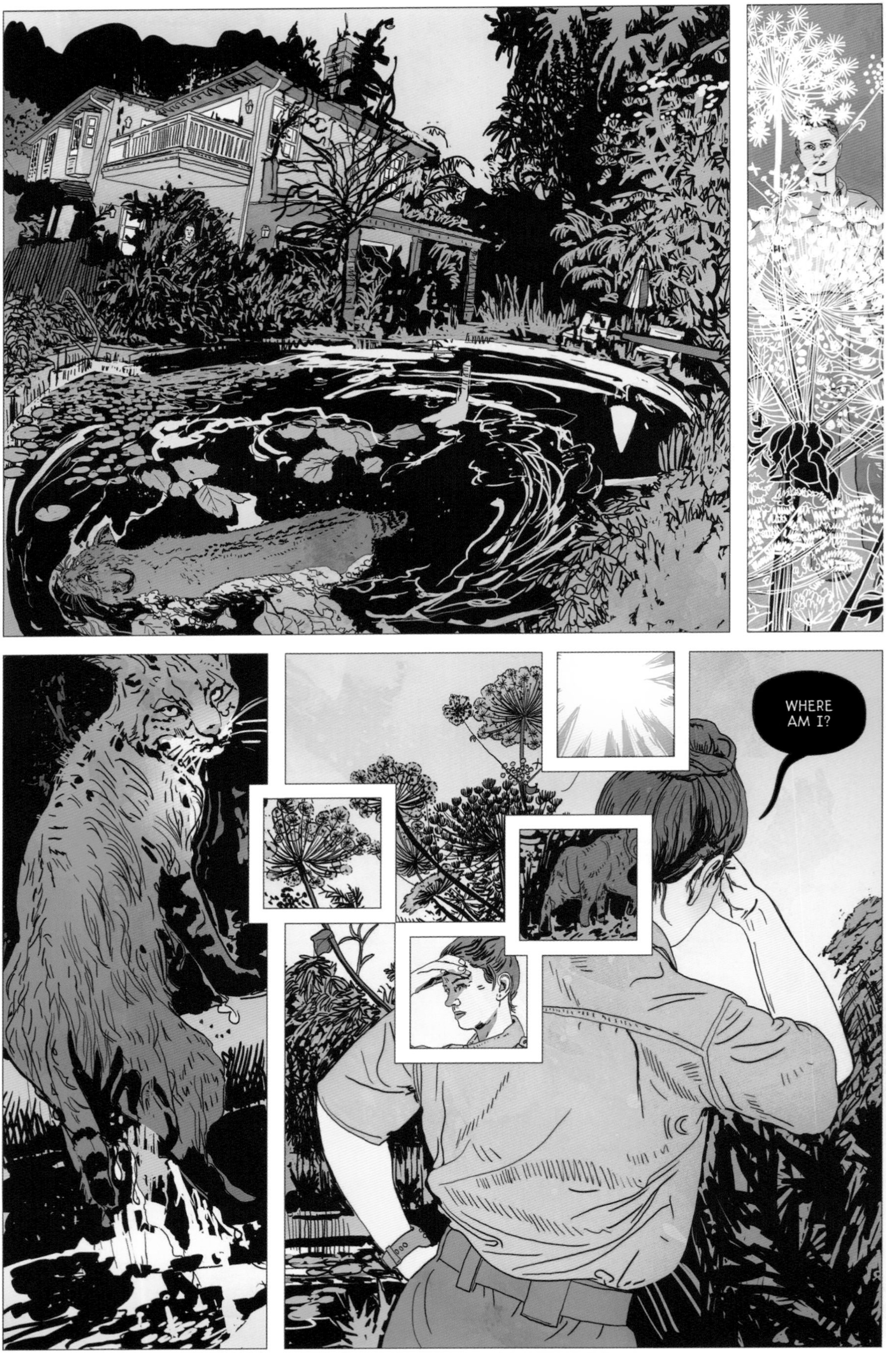
WHERE AM I?

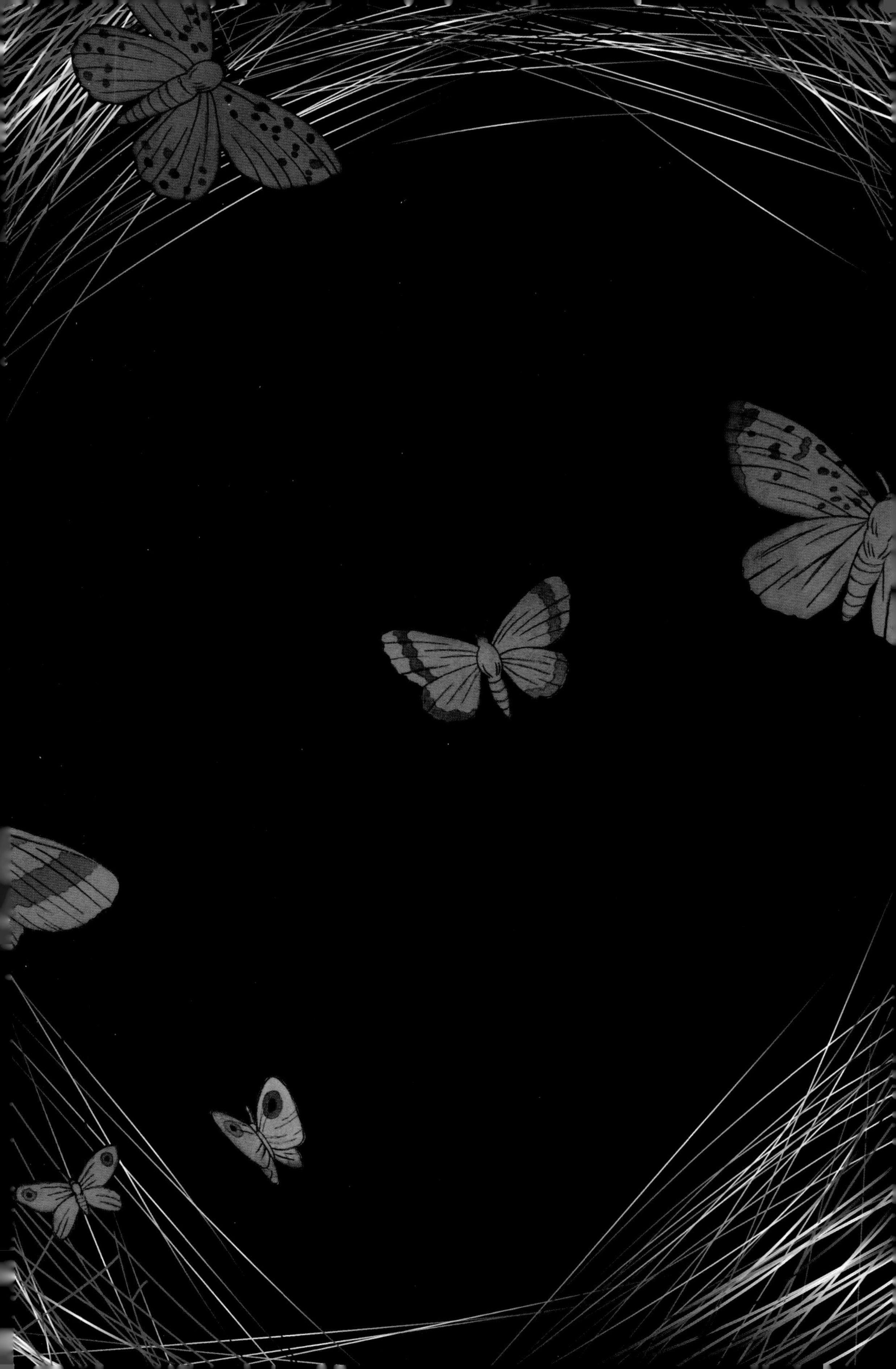

ART BY ANNIE WU

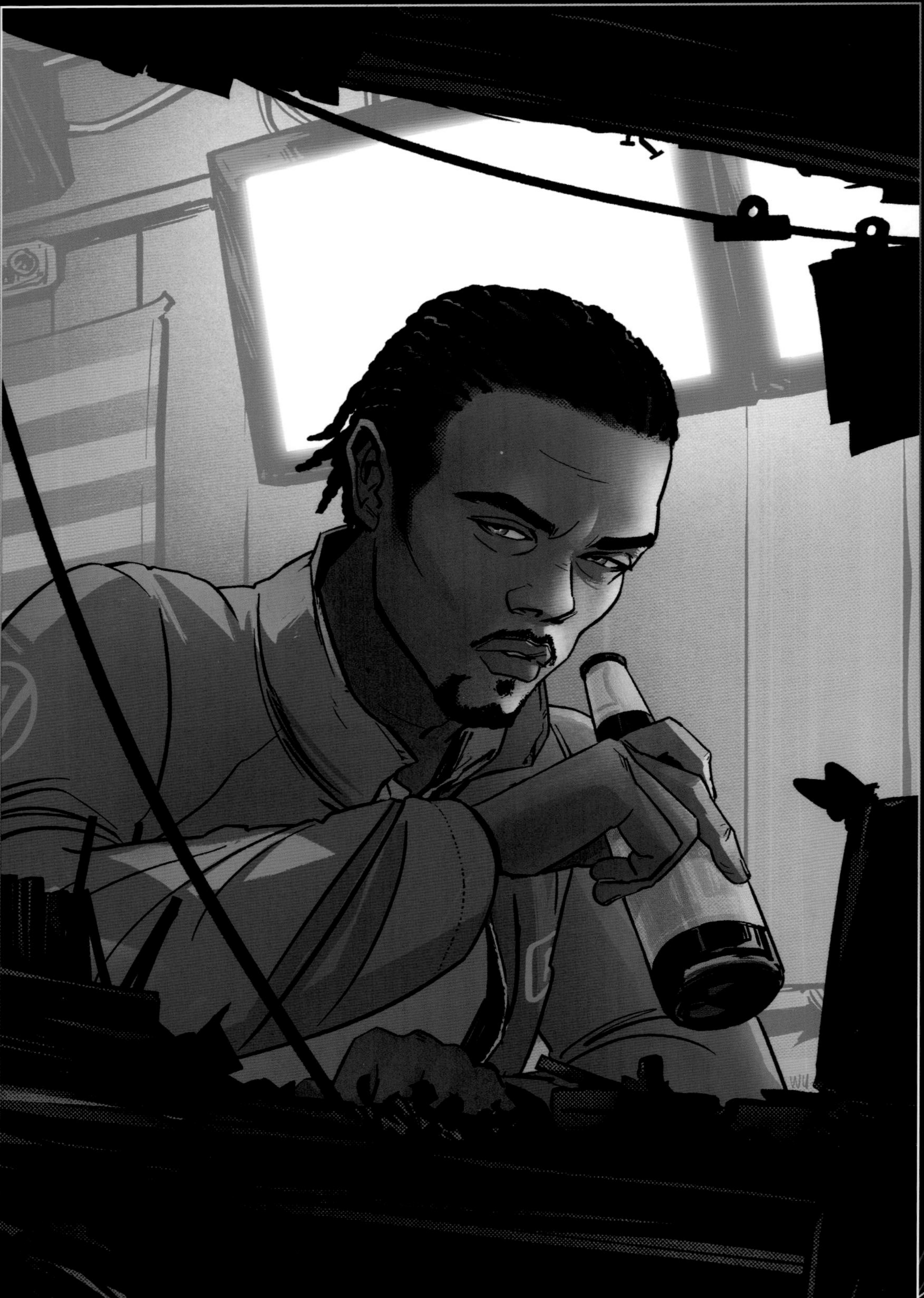
WU

FIVE

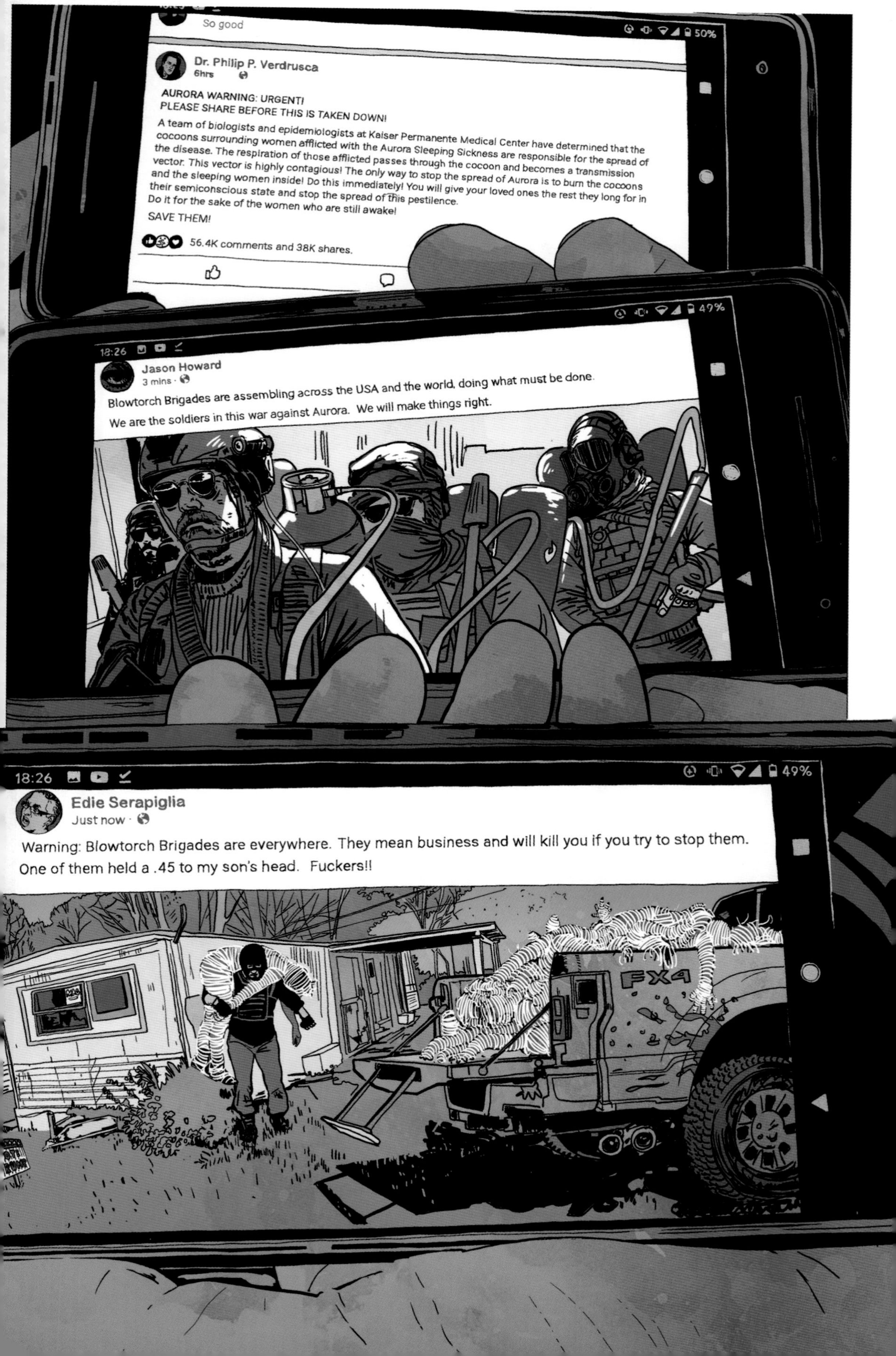
So good
50%
Dr. Philip P. Verdrusca
6hrs
AURORA WARNING: URGENT!
PLEASE SHARE BEFORE THIS IS TAKEN DOWN!
A team of biologists and epidemiologists at Kaiser Permanente Medical Center have determined that the cocoons surrounding women afflicted with the Aurora Sleeping Sickness are responsible for the spread of the disease. The respiration of those afflicted passes through the cocoon and becomes a transmission vector. This vector is highly contagious! The only way to stop the spread of Aurora is to burn the cocoons and the sleeping women inside! Do this immediately! You will give your loved ones the rest they long for in their semiconscious state and stop the spread of this pestilence.
Do it for the sake of the women who are still awake!
SAVE THEM!
56.4K comments and 38K shares.
18:26
49%
Jason Howard
3 mins ·
Blowtorch Brigades are assembling across the USA and the world, doing what must be done.
We are the soldiers in this war against Aurora. We will make things right.
18:26
49%
Edie Serapiglia
Just now ·
Warning: Blowtorch Brigades are everywhere. They mean business and will kill you if you try to stop them.
One of them held a .45 to my son's head. Fuckers!!
FX4

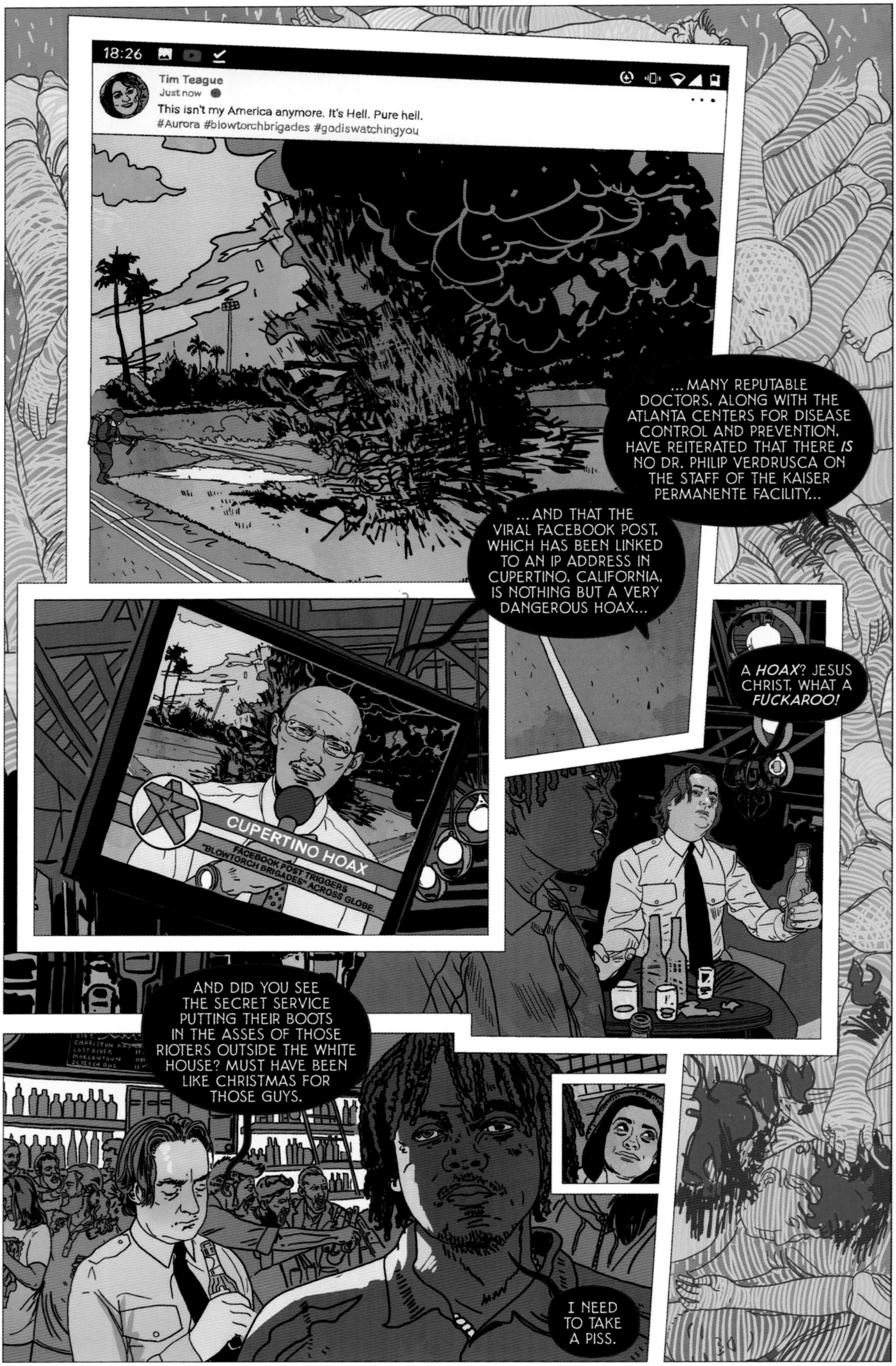
18:26
Tim Teague
Just now
This isn't my America anymore. It's Hell. Pure hell.
#Aurora #blowtorchbrigades #godiswatchingyou
...MANY REPUTABLE DOCTORS, ALONG WITH THE ATLANTA CENTERS FOR DISEASE CONTROL AND PREVENTION, HAVE REITERATED THAT THERE *IS* NO DR. PHILIP VERDRUSCA ON THE STAFF OF THE KAISER PERMANENTE FACILITY...
...AND THAT THE VIRAL FACEBOOK POST, WHICH HAS BEEN LINKED TO AN IP ADDRESS IN CUPERTINO, CALIFORNIA, IS NOTHING BUT A VERY DANGEROUS HOAX...
CUPERTINO HOAX
FACEBOOK POST TRIGGERS "BLOWTORCH BRIGADES" ACROSS GLOBE.
A *HOAX*? JESUS CHRIST, WHAT A *FUCKAROO!*
AND DID YOU SEE THE SECRET SERVICE PUTTING THEIR BOOTS IN THE ASSES OF THOSE RIOTERS OUTSIDE THE WHITE HOUSE? MUST HAVE BEEN LIKE CHRISTMAS FOR THOSE GUYS.
I NEED TO TAKE A PISS.

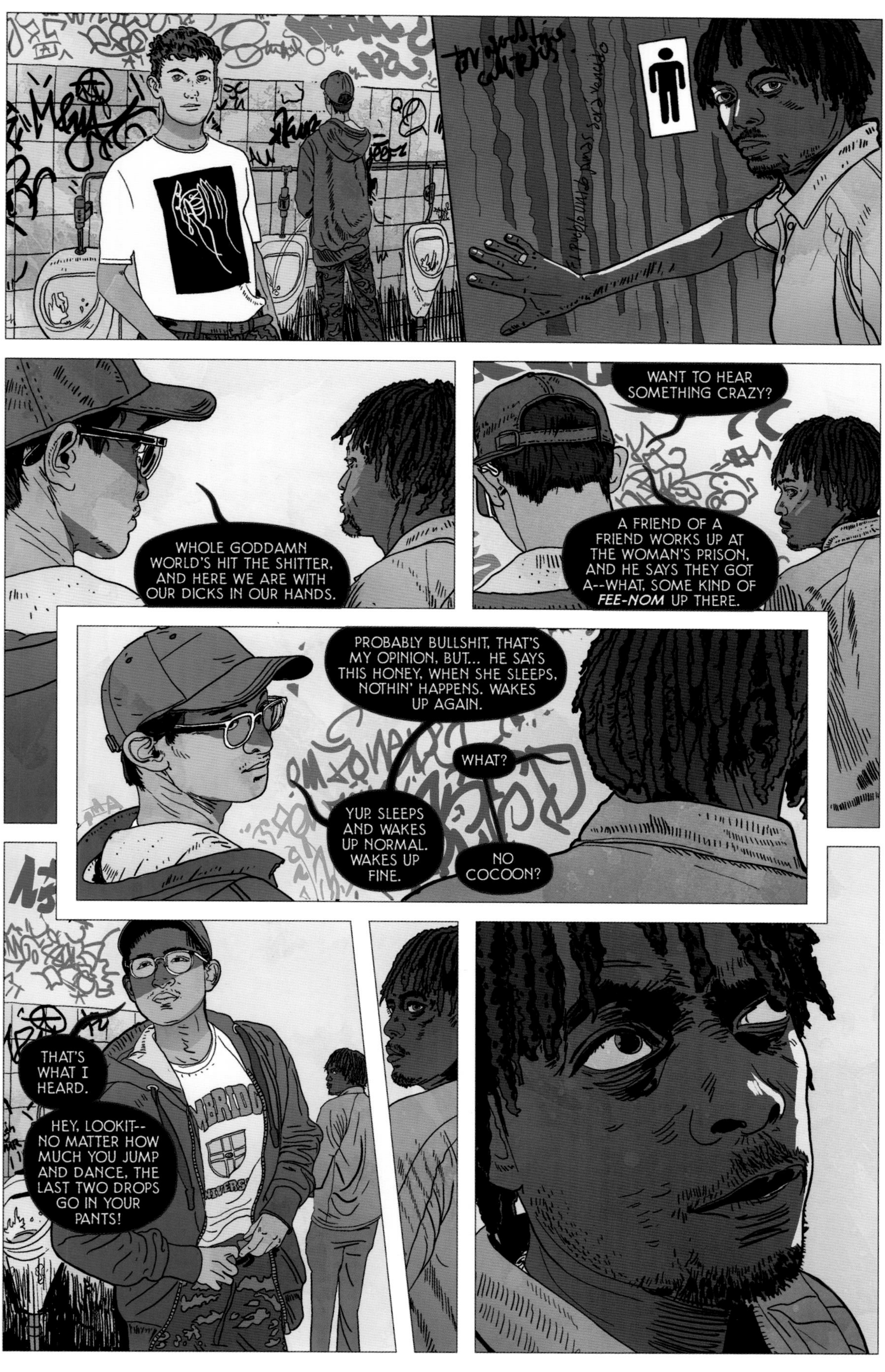
WHOLE GODDAMN WORLD'S HIT THE SHITTER, AND HERE WE ARE WITH OUR DICKS IN OUR HANDS.
WANT TO HEAR SOMETHING CRAZY?
A FRIEND OF A FRIEND WORKS UP AT THE WOMAN'S PRISON, AND HE SAYS THEY GOT A--WHAT, SOME KIND OF *FEE-NOM* UP THERE.
PROBABLY BULLSHIT, THAT'S MY OPINION, BUT... HE SAYS THIS HONEY, WHEN SHE SLEEPS, NOTHIN' HAPPENS. WAKES UP AGAIN.
WHAT?
YUP. SLEEPS AND WAKES UP NORMAL. WAKES UP FINE.
NO COCOON?
THAT'S WHAT I HEARD.
HEY, LOOKIT-- NO MATTER HOW MUCH YOU JUMP AND DANCE, THE LAST TWO DROPS GO IN YOUR PANTS!

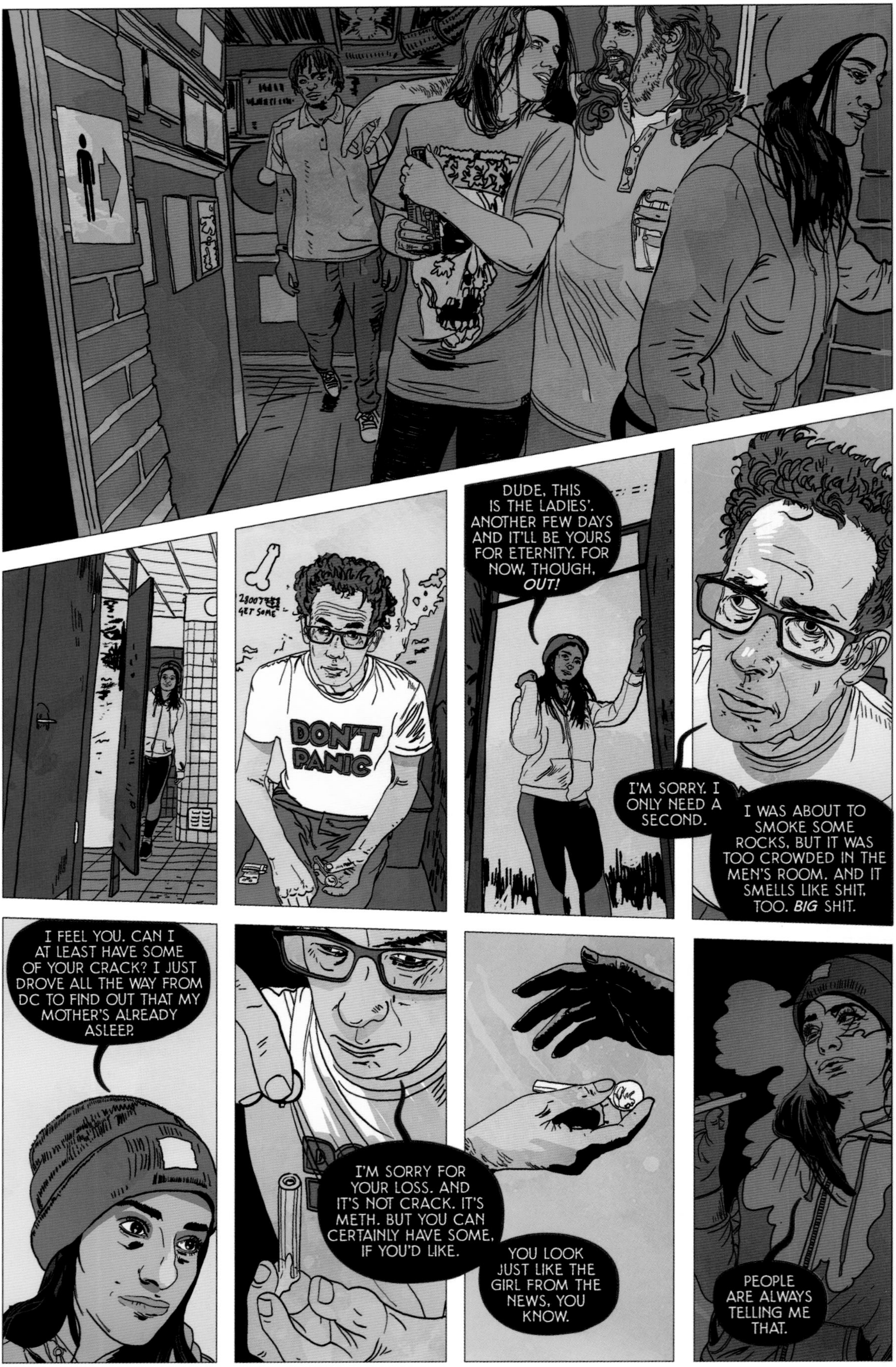
GET SOME
DUDE, THIS IS THE LADIES'. ANOTHER FEW DAYS AND IT'LL BE YOURS FOR ETERNITY. FOR NOW, THOUGH, *OUT!*
I'M SORRY. I ONLY NEED A SECOND.
I WAS ABOUT TO SMOKE SOME ROCKS, BUT IT WAS TOO CROWDED IN THE MEN'S ROOM. AND IT SMELLS LIKE SHIT, TOO. *BIG* SHIT.
I FEEL YOU. CAN I AT LEAST HAVE SOME OF YOUR CRACK? I JUST DROVE ALL THE WAY FROM DC TO FIND OUT THAT MY MOTHER'S ALREADY ASLEEP.
I'M SORRY FOR YOUR LOSS. AND IT'S NOT CRACK. IT'S METH. BUT YOU CAN CERTAINLY HAVE SOME, IF YOU'D LIKE.
YOU LOOK JUST LIKE THE GIRL FROM THE NEWS, YOU KNOW.
PEOPLE ARE ALWAYS TELLING ME THAT.

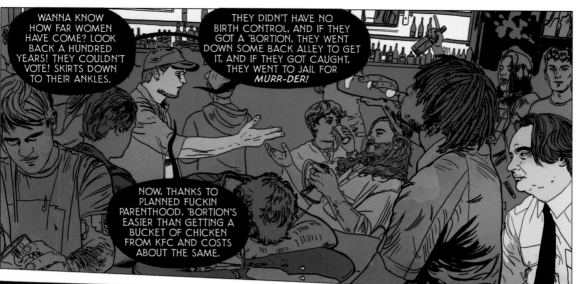

WANNA KNOW HOW FAR WOMEN HAVE COME? LOOK BACK A HUNDRED YEARS! THEY COULDN'T VOTE! SKIRTS DOWN TO THEIR ANKLES.

THEY DIDN'T HAVE NO BIRTH CONTROL, AND IF THEY GOT A 'BORTION, THEY WENT DOWN SOME BACK ALLEY TO GET IT, AND IF THEY GOT CAUGHT, THEY WENT TO JAIL FOR *MURR-DER!*

NOW, THANKS TO PLANNED FUCKIN PARENTHOOD, 'BORTION'S EASIER THAN GETTING A BUCKET OF CHICKEN FROM KFC AND COSTS ABOUT THE SAME.

THEY CAN RUN FOR PRESIDENT! THEY JOIN THE SEALS AND THE RANGERS! THEY CAN MARRY THEIR LESBO BUDDIES!

IF THAT AIN'T *TERRORISTIC,* I DON'T KNOW WHAT IS!

SIT DOWN AND SHUT THE FUCK UP!

BOOO!

PREACH IT, CARSON!

ALL IN JUST ONE HUNDRED YEARS. THEY AIN'T JUST PULLED EVEN, LIKE THEY SAID THEY WANTED--*THEY DONE PULLED AHEAD!*

I'M THROUGH LISTENING TO THIS REDNECK ASSHOLE. YOU WORK UP AT THE PRISON, RIGHT?

YEAH. WELL, I--

LET'S TALK.

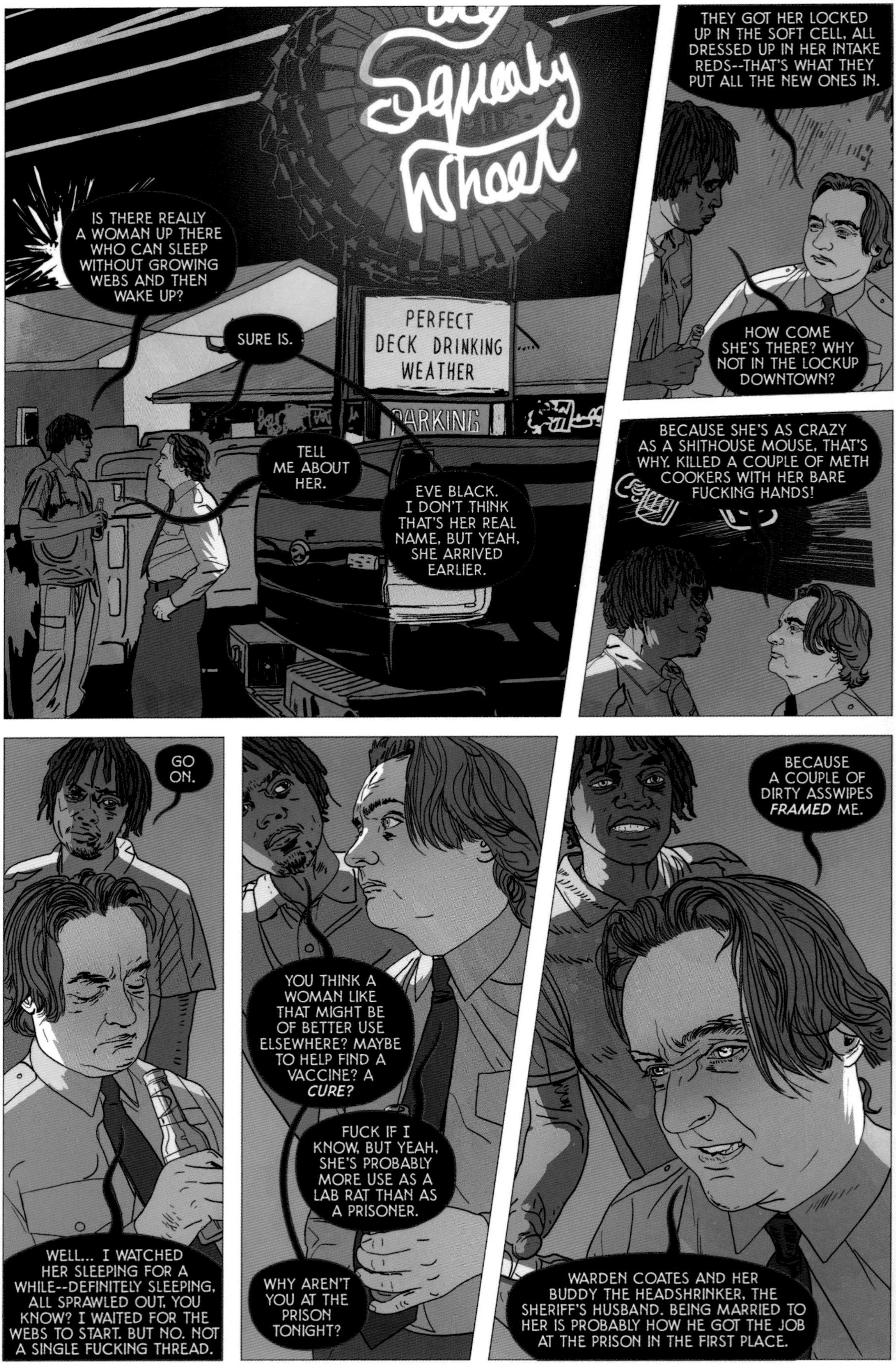
Squeaky Wheel
IS THERE REALLY A WOMAN UP THERE WHO CAN SLEEP WITHOUT GROWING WEBS AND THEN WAKE UP?
SURE IS.
PERFECT DECK DRINKING WEATHER
PARKING
TELL ME ABOUT HER.
EVE BLACK. I DON'T THINK THAT'S HER REAL NAME, BUT YEAH, SHE ARRIVED EARLIER.
THEY GOT HER LOCKED UP IN THE SOFT CELL, ALL DRESSED UP IN HER INTAKE REDS--THAT'S WHAT THEY PUT ALL THE NEW ONES IN.
HOW COME SHE'S THERE? WHY NOT IN THE LOCKUP DOWNTOWN?
BECAUSE SHE'S AS CRAZY AS A SHITHOUSE MOUSE, THAT'S WHY. KILLED A COUPLE OF METH COOKERS WITH HER BARE FUCKING HANDS!
GO ON.
WELL... I WATCHED HER SLEEPING FOR A WHILE--DEFINITELY SLEEPING, ALL SPRAWLED OUT, YOU KNOW? I WAITED FOR THE WEBS TO START. BUT NO. NOT A SINGLE FUCKING THREAD.
YOU THINK A WOMAN LIKE THAT MIGHT BE OF BETTER USE ELSEWHERE? MAYBE TO HELP FIND A VACCINE? A *CURE?*
FUCK IF I KNOW, BUT YEAH, SHE'S PROBABLY MORE USE AS A LAB RAT THAN AS A PRISONER.
WHY AREN'T YOU AT THE PRISON TONIGHT?
BECAUSE A COUPLE OF DIRTY ASSWIPES ***FRAMED*** ME.
WARDEN COATES AND HER BUDDY THE HEADSHRINKER, THE SHERIFF'S HUSBAND. BEING MARRIED TO HER IS PROBABLY HOW HE GOT THE JOB AT THE PRISON IN THE FIRST PLACE.

AND HOW MANY GUARDS THERE NOW?

NOT MANY, WITH EVERYTHING SO SCREWED UP. MAYBE SEVEN. EIGHT IF YOU COUNT HICKS, THE DEPUTY WARDEN. NINE IF YOU ADD IN MR. SHRINKY DINK, BUT THOSE TWO AIN'T WORTH A FART IN A HIGH WIND.

WHY? WHAT ARE YOU THINKING?

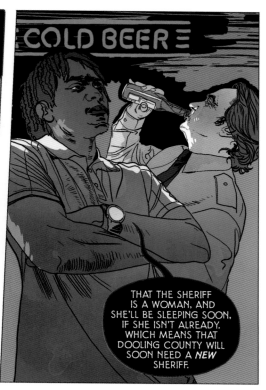

COLD BEER

THAT THE SHERIFF IS A WOMAN, AND SHE'LL BE SLEEPING SOON, IF SHE ISN'T ALREADY. WHICH MEANS THAT DOOLING COUNTY WILL SOON NEED A *NEW* SHERIFF.

AND THAT NEW SHERIFF WOULD BE PERFECTLY WITHIN HIS RIGHTS TO REMOVE A PRISONER FROM CORRECTIONAL.

ESPECIALLY ONE THAT HASN'T BEEN TRIED FOR ANYTHING, LET ALONE CONVICTED.

YOU THINK YOU MIGHT APPLY FOR THE JOB?

I'M PRETTY SURE TERRY COOMBS IS THE SENIOR MAN.

HE'S GOING TO NEED SOME HELP PICKING UP THE SLACK, THOUGH. I'D CERTAINLY PUT MY NAME FORWARD IF HE NEEDED A DEPUTY.

COLD ... RE KITCHEN OPEN

I LIKE THAT IDEA. MIGHT THROW MY NAME IN THE HAT, TOO, SEEING AS I'M IN NEED OF A JOB.

LET'S GET SOME SLEEP AND SOBER UP, THEN WE CAN TALK TO TERRY ABOUT GOING UP THERE AND GETTING THAT WOMAN OUT OF PRISON.

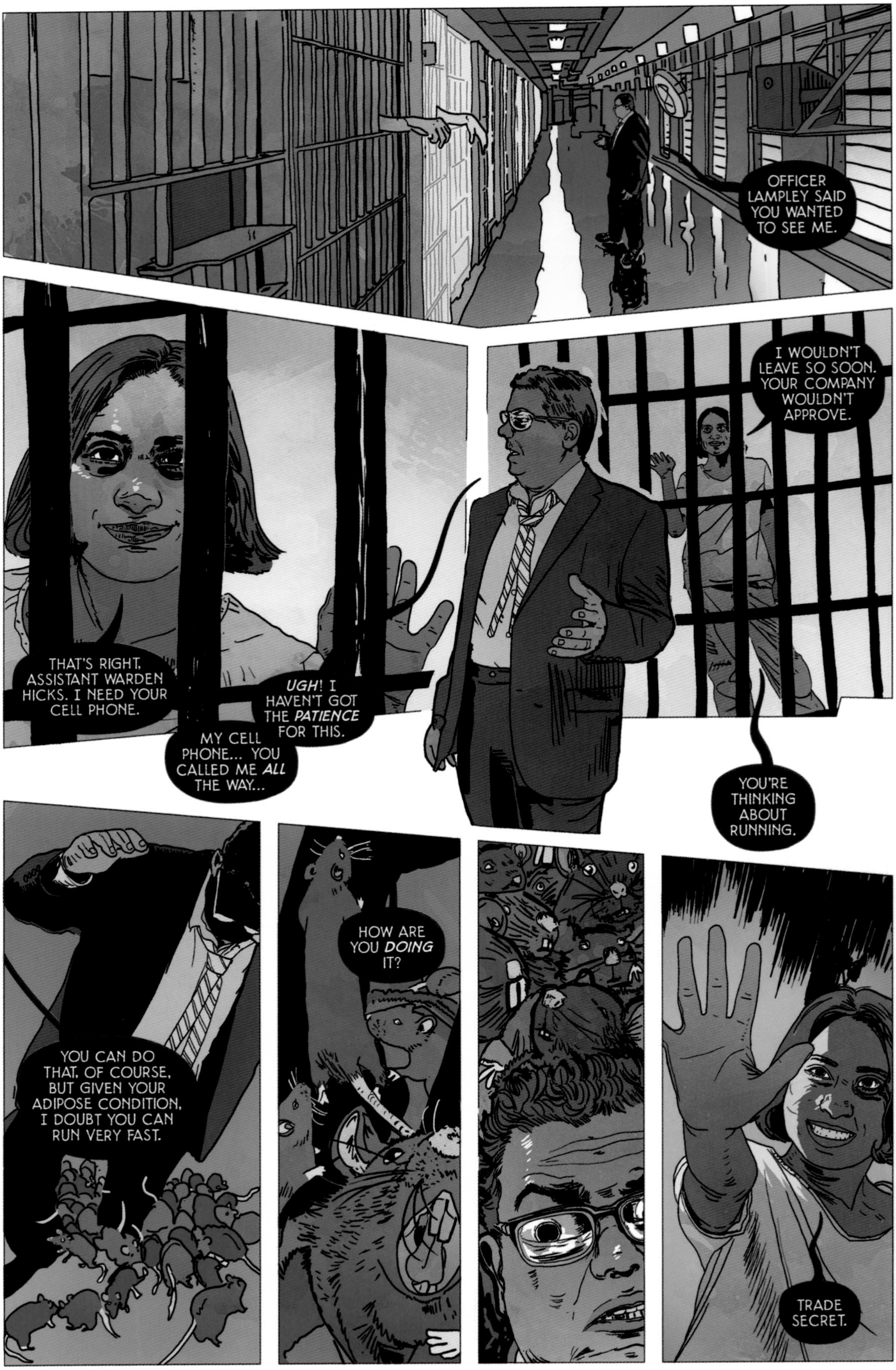
OFFICER LAMPLEY SAID YOU WANTED TO SEE ME.
I WOULDN'T LEAVE SO SOON. YOUR COMPANY WOULDN'T APPROVE.
THAT'S RIGHT, ASSISTANT WARDEN HICKS. I NEED YOUR CELL PHONE.
MY CELL PHONE... YOU CALLED ME *ALL* THE WAY...
UGH! I HAVEN'T GOT THE *PATIENCE* FOR THIS.
YOU'RE THINKING ABOUT RUNNING.
YOU CAN DO THAT, OF COURSE, BUT GIVEN YOUR ADIPOSE CONDITION, I DOUBT YOU CAN RUN VERY FAST.
HOW ARE YOU *DOING* IT?
TRADE SECRET.

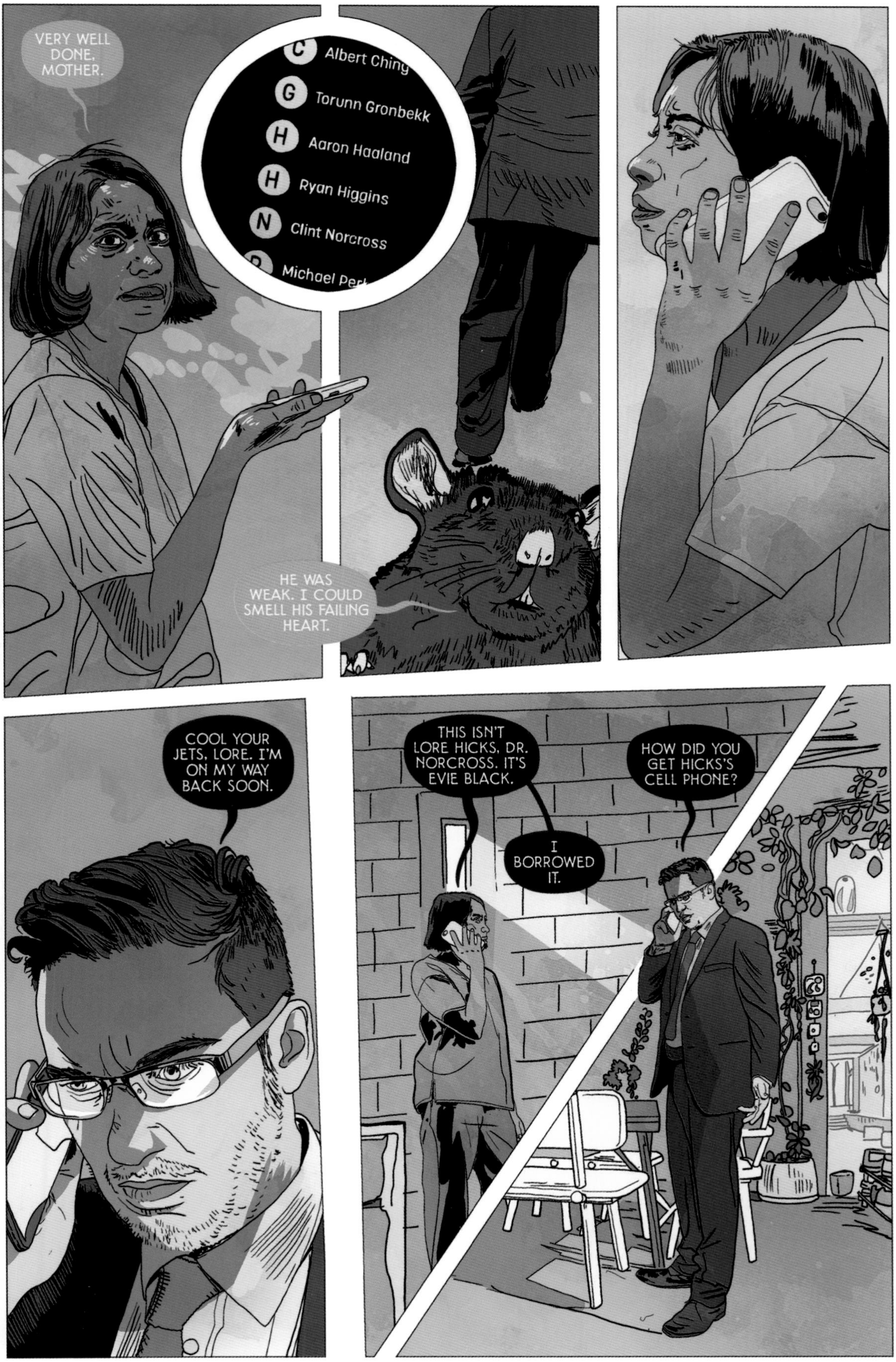
VERY WELL DONE, MOTHER.
Albert Ching
Torunn Gronbekk
Aaron Haaland
Ryan Higgins
Clint Norcross
HE WAS WEAK. I COULD SMELL HIS FAILING HEART.
COOL YOUR JETS, LORE. I'M ON MY WAY BACK SOON.
THIS ISN'T LORE HICKS, DR. NORCROSS. IT'S EVIE BLACK.
I BORROWED IT.
HOW DID YOU GET HICKS'S CELL PHONE?

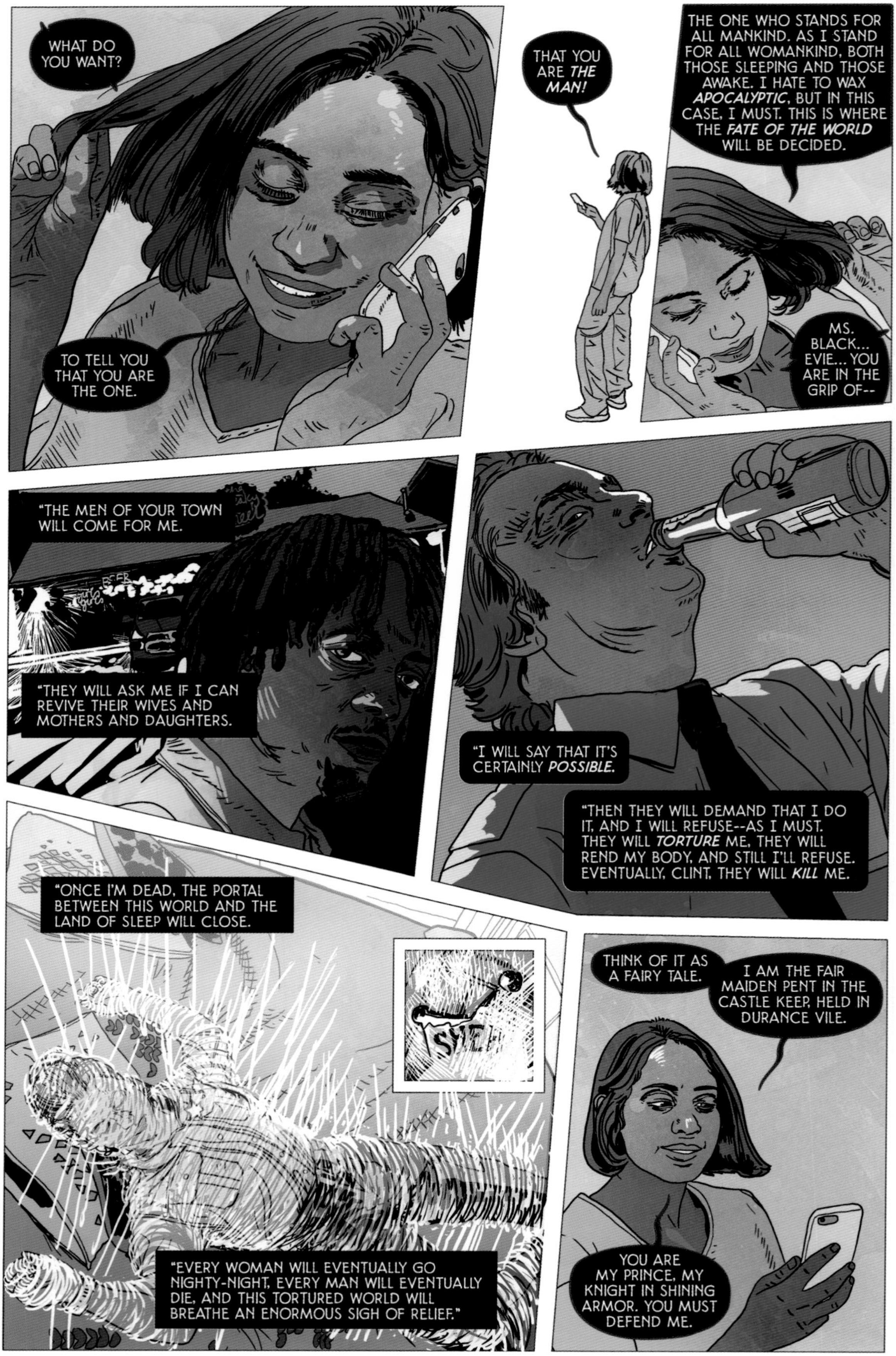
WHAT DO YOU WANT?
TO TELL YOU THAT YOU ARE THE ONE.
THAT YOU ARE *THE MAN!*
THE ONE WHO STANDS FOR ALL MANKIND. AS I STAND FOR ALL WOMANKIND, BOTH THOSE SLEEPING AND THOSE AWAKE. I HATE TO WAX *APOCALYPTIC*, BUT IN THIS CASE, I MUST. THIS IS WHERE THE *FATE OF THE WORLD* WILL BE DECIDED.
MS. BLACK... EVIE... YOU ARE IN THE GRIP OF--
"THE MEN OF YOUR TOWN WILL COME FOR ME.
"THEY WILL ASK ME IF I CAN REVIVE THEIR WIVES AND MOTHERS AND DAUGHTERS.
"I WILL SAY THAT IT'S CERTAINLY *POSSIBLE.*
"THEN THEY WILL DEMAND THAT I DO IT, AND I WILL REFUSE--AS I MUST. THEY WILL *TORTURE* ME, THEY WILL REND MY BODY, AND STILL I'LL REFUSE. EVENTUALLY, CLINT, THEY WILL *KILL* ME.
"ONCE I'M DEAD, THE PORTAL BETWEEN THIS WORLD AND THE LAND OF SLEEP WILL CLOSE.
"EVERY WOMAN WILL EVENTUALLY GO NIGHTY-NIGHT, EVERY MAN WILL EVENTUALLY DIE, AND THIS TORTURED WORLD WILL BREATHE AN ENORMOUS SIGH OF RELIEF."
THINK OF IT AS A FAIRY TALE.
I AM THE FAIR MAIDEN PENT IN THE CASTLE KEEP, HELD IN DURANCE VILE.
YOU ARE MY PRINCE, MY KNIGHT IN SHINING ARMOR. YOU MUST DEFEND ME.

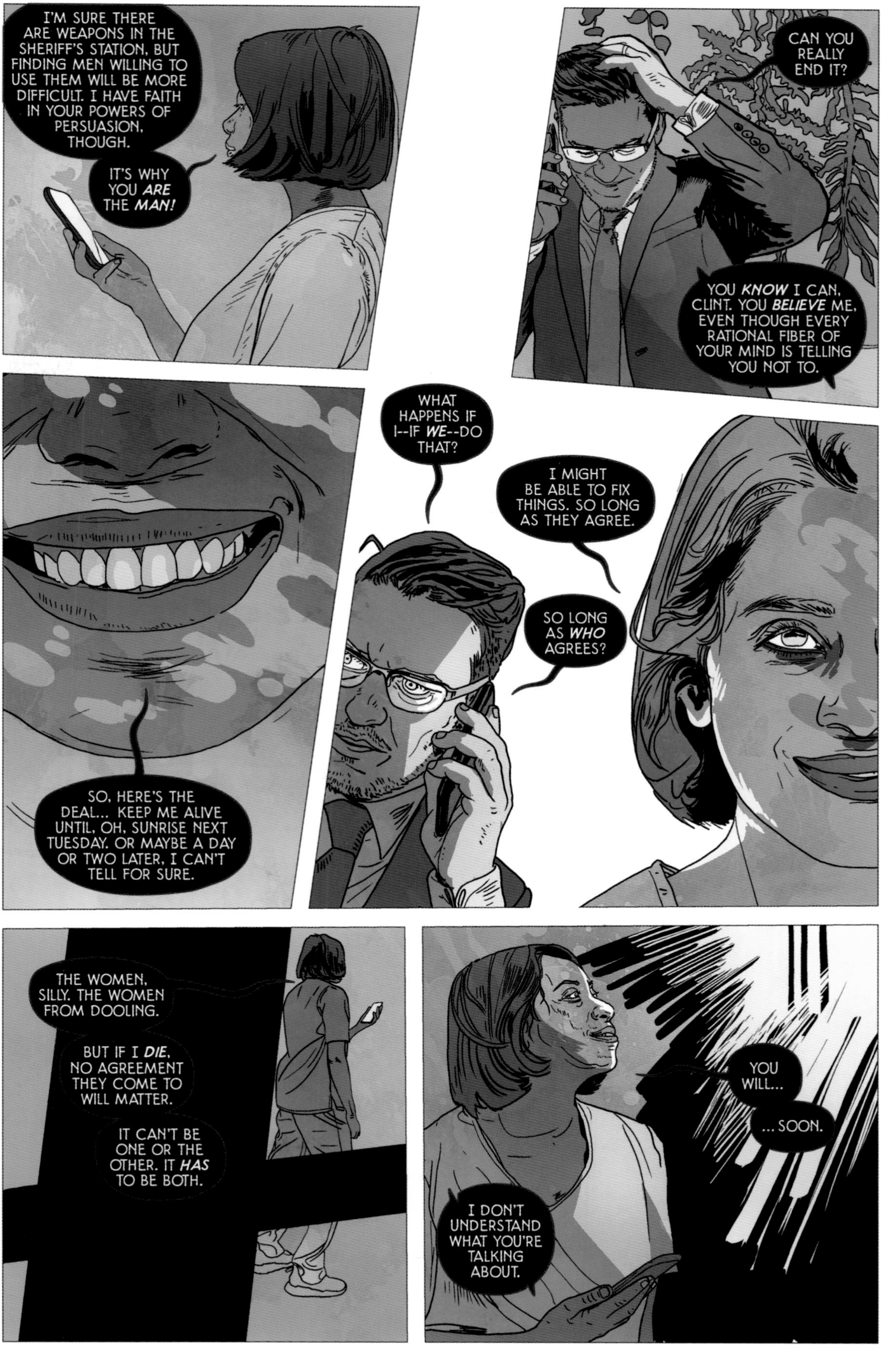
I'M SURE THERE ARE WEAPONS IN THE SHERIFF'S STATION, BUT FINDING MEN WILLING TO USE THEM WILL BE MORE DIFFICULT. I HAVE FAITH IN YOUR POWERS OF PERSUASION, THOUGH.
IT'S WHY YOU *ARE* THE *MAN!*
CAN YOU REALLY END IT?
YOU *KNOW* I CAN, CLINT. YOU *BELIEVE* ME, EVEN THOUGH EVERY RATIONAL FIBER OF YOUR MIND IS TELLING YOU NOT TO.
SO, HERE'S THE DEAL... KEEP ME ALIVE UNTIL, OH, SUNRISE NEXT TUESDAY. OR MAYBE A DAY OR TWO LATER, I CAN'T TELL FOR SURE.
WHAT HAPPENS IF I--IF *WE*--DO THAT?
I MIGHT BE ABLE TO FIX THINGS. SO LONG AS THEY AGREE.
SO LONG AS *WHO* AGREES?
THE WOMEN, SILLY. THE WOMEN FROM DOOLING.
BUT IF I *DIE*, NO AGREEMENT THEY COME TO WILL MATTER.
IT CAN'T BE ONE OR THE OTHER. IT *HAS* TO BE BOTH.
I DON'T UNDERSTAND WHAT YOU'RE TALKING ABOUT.
YOU WILL...
...SOON.

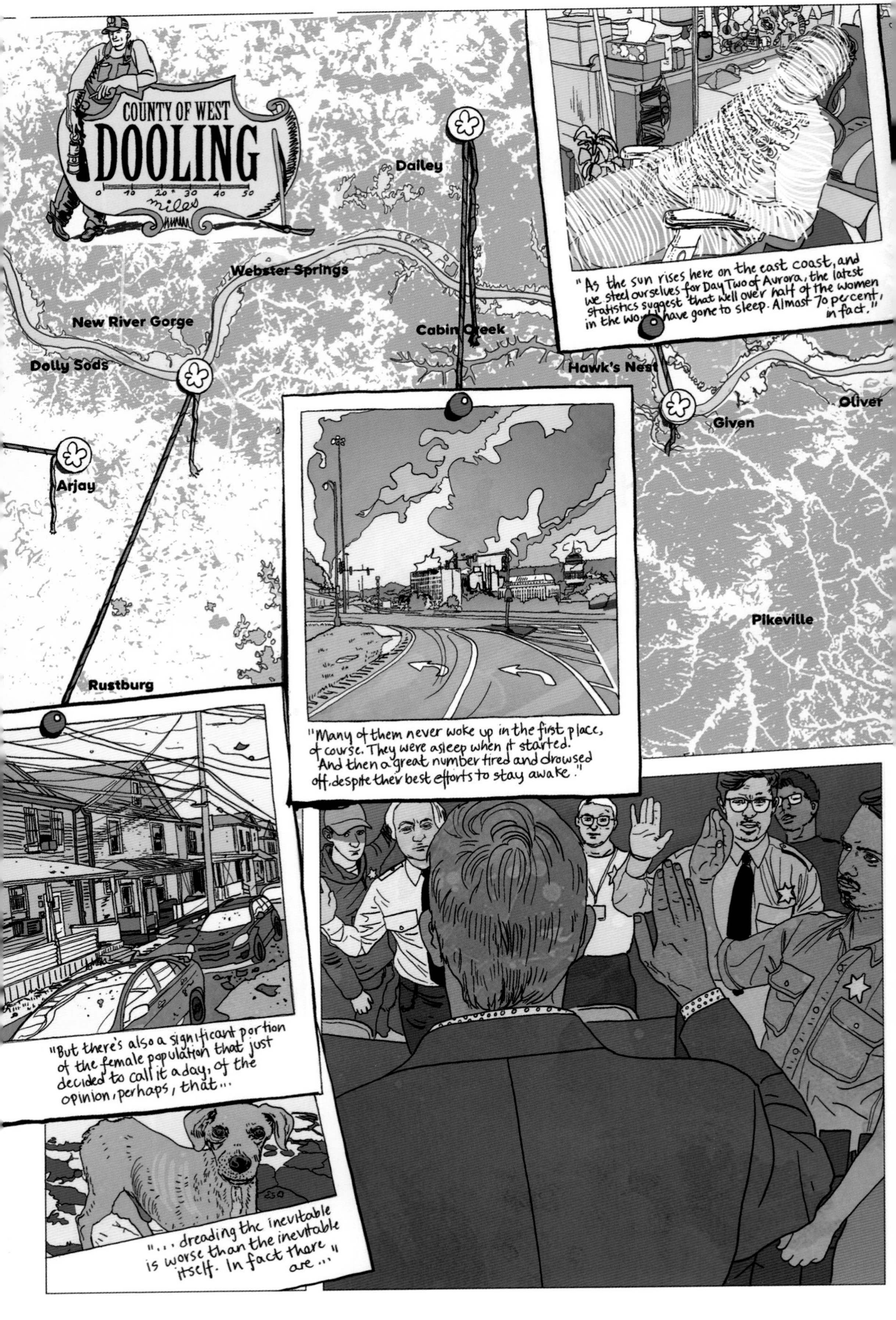
COUNTY OF WEST
DOOLING
0 10 20 30 40 50
miles
Dailey
Webster Springs
New River Gorge
Cabin Creek
Dolly Sods
Hawk's Nest
Oliver
Given
Arjay
Pikeville
Rustburg
"As the sun rises here on the east coast, and we steel ourselves for Day Two of Aurora, the latest statistics suggest that well over half of the women in the world have gone to sleep. Almost 70 percent, in fact."
"Many of them never woke up in the first place, of course. They were asleep when it started. And then a great number tired and drowsed off, despite their best efforts to stay awake."
"But there's also a significant portion of the female population that just decided to call it a day, of the opinion, perhaps, that...
"... dreading the inevitable is worse than the inevitable itself. In fact there are ..."

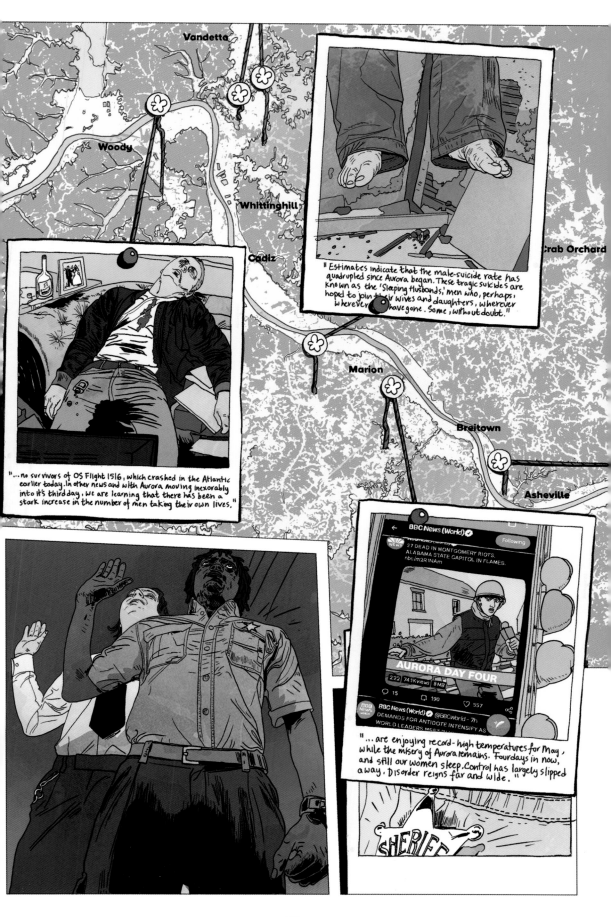

Vandetta

Woody

Whittinghill

Cadiz

Crab Orchard

Marion

Breitown

Asheville

" Estimates indicate that the male-suicide rate has quadrupled since Aurora began. These tragic suicides are known as the 'Sleeping Husbands,' men who, perhaps, hoped to join their wives and daughters, wherever wherever they have gone . Some , without doubt. "

"...no survivors of OS Flight 1516, which crashed in the Atlantic earlier today. In other news and with Aurora moving inexorably into it's third day , we are learning that there has been a stark increase in the number of men taking their own lives. "

BBC News (World)
Following
27 DEAD IN MONTGOMERY RIOTS.
ALABAMA STATE CAPITOL IN FLAMES.
nbc/m2R1NAm

AURORA DAY FOUR
222 74.1Kviews 8 MB
15   190   557

BBC News (World) @BBCworld · 7h
DEMANDS FOR ANTIDOTE INTENSIFY AS
WORLD LEADERS MEET

" ... are enjoying record - high temperatures for May , while the misery of Aurora remains. Four days in now, and still our women sleep. Control has largely slipped away. Disorder reigns far and wide. "

SHERIFF

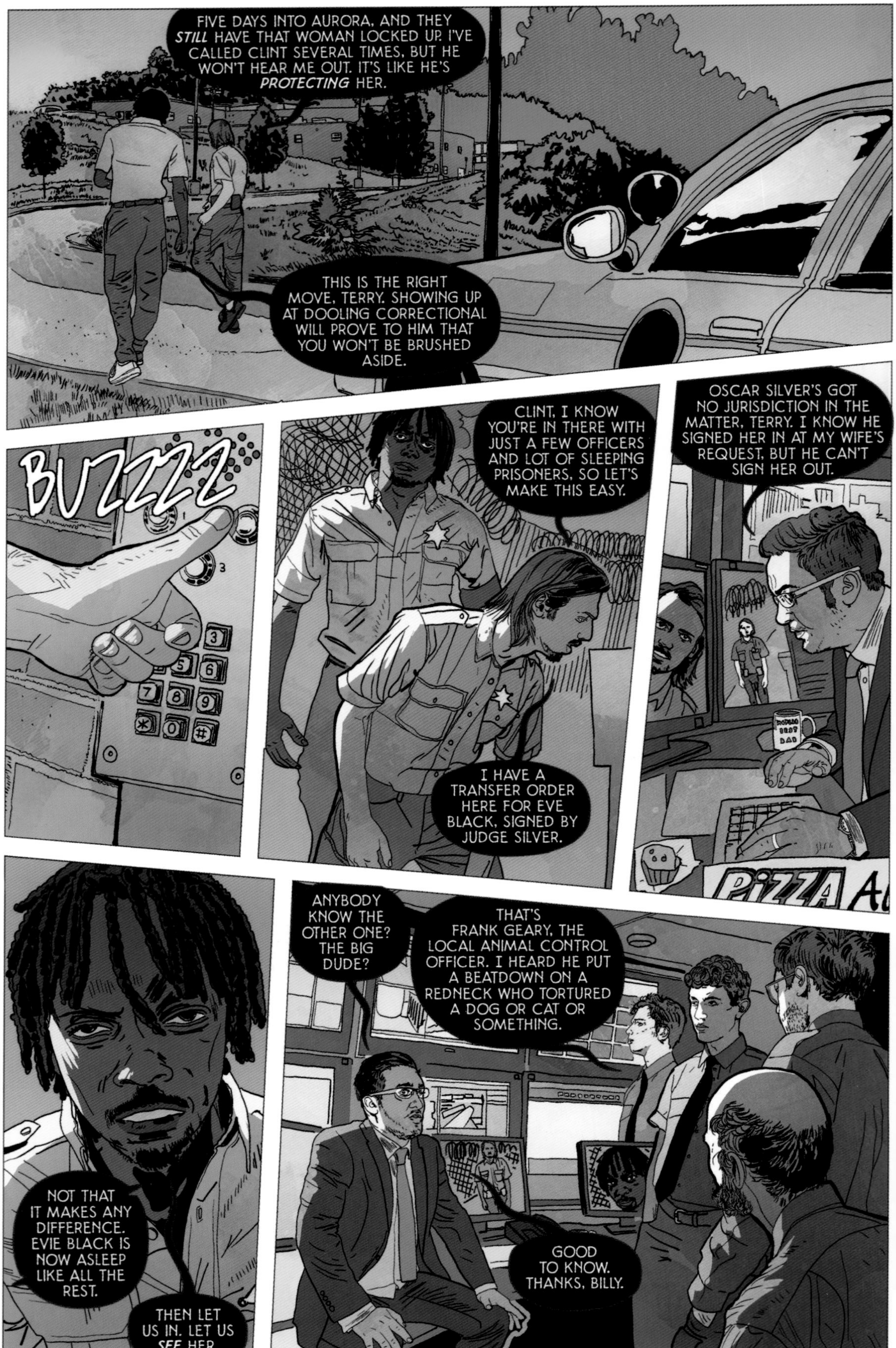

FIVE DAYS INTO AURORA, AND THEY *STILL* HAVE THAT WOMAN LOCKED UP. I'VE CALLED CLINT SEVERAL TIMES, BUT HE WON'T HEAR ME OUT. IT'S LIKE HE'S *PROTECTING* HER.
THIS IS THE RIGHT MOVE, TERRY. SHOWING UP AT DOOLING CORRECTIONAL WILL PROVE TO HIM THAT YOU WON'T BE BRUSHED ASIDE.
BUZZZZ
CLINT, I KNOW YOU'RE IN THERE WITH JUST A FEW OFFICERS AND LOT OF SLEEPING PRISONERS, SO LET'S MAKE THIS EASY.
I HAVE A TRANSFER ORDER HERE FOR EVE BLACK, SIGNED BY JUDGE SILVER.
OSCAR SILVER'S GOT NO JURISDICTION IN THE MATTER, TERRY. I KNOW HE SIGNED HER IN AT MY WIFE'S REQUEST, BUT HE CAN'T SIGN HER OUT.
PIZZA
NOT THAT IT MAKES ANY DIFFERENCE. EVIE BLACK IS NOW ASLEEP LIKE ALL THE REST.
THEN LET US IN. LET US *SEE* HER.
ANYBODY KNOW THE OTHER ONE? THE BIG DUDE?
THAT'S FRANK GEARY, THE LOCAL ANIMAL CONTROL OFFICER. I HEARD HE PUT A BEATDOWN ON A REDNECK WHO TORTURED A DOG OR CAT OR SOMETHING.
GOOD TO KNOW. THANKS, BILLY.

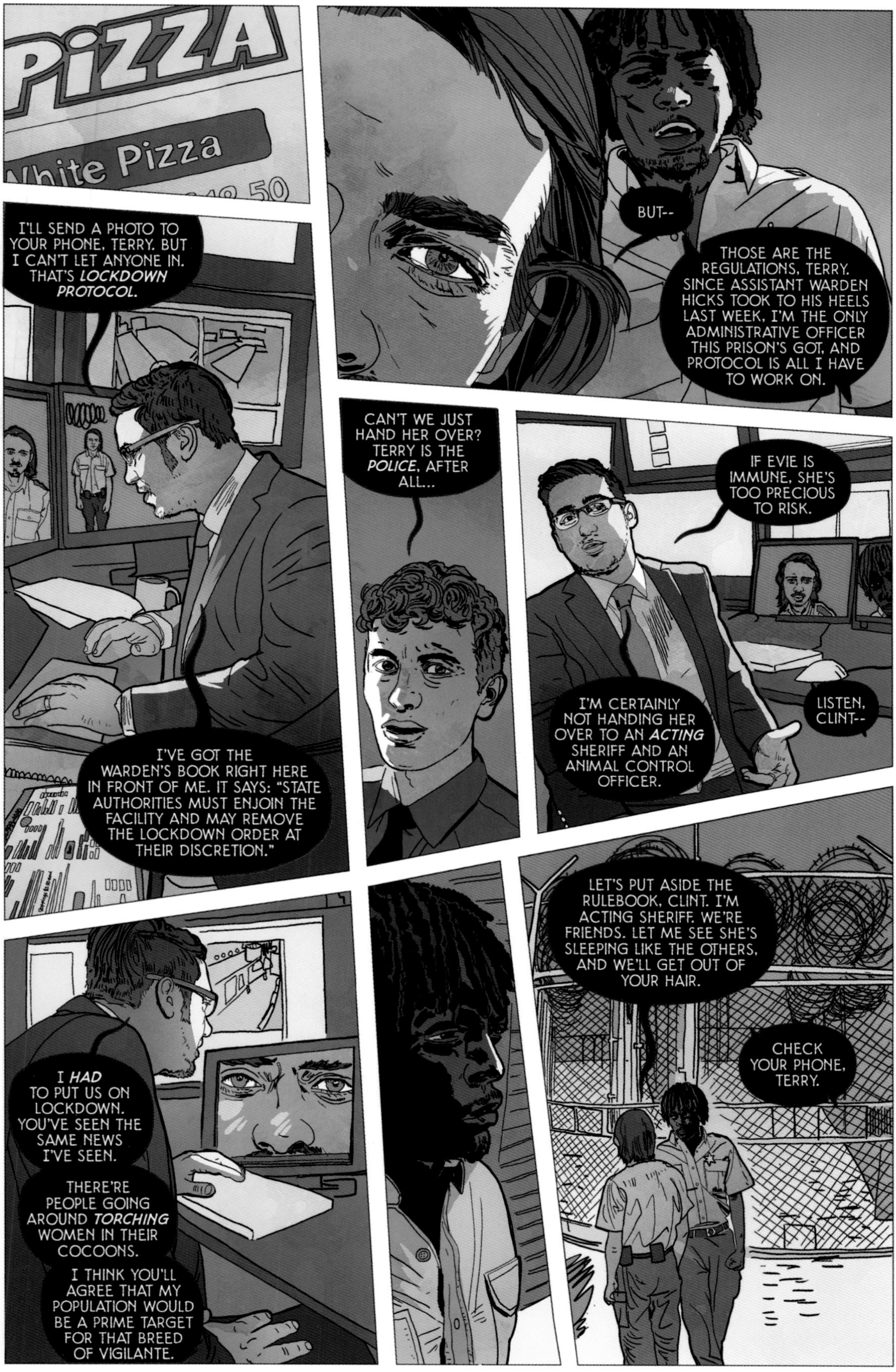
PiZZA
White Pizza
I'LL SEND A PHOTO TO YOUR PHONE, TERRY. BUT I CAN'T LET ANYONE IN. THAT'S *LOCKDOWN PROTOCOL*.
BUT--
THOSE ARE THE REGULATIONS, TERRY. SINCE ASSISTANT WARDEN HICKS TOOK TO HIS HEELS LAST WEEK, I'M THE ONLY ADMINISTRATIVE OFFICER THIS PRISON'S GOT, AND PROTOCOL IS ALL I HAVE TO WORK ON.
CAN'T WE JUST HAND HER OVER? TERRY IS THE *POLICE*, AFTER ALL...
IF EVIE IS IMMUNE, SHE'S TOO PRECIOUS TO RISK.
I'M CERTAINLY NOT HANDING HER OVER TO AN *ACTING* SHERIFF AND AN ANIMAL CONTROL OFFICER.
LISTEN, CLINT--
I'VE GOT THE WARDEN'S BOOK RIGHT HERE IN FRONT OF ME. IT SAYS: "STATE AUTHORITIES MUST ENJOIN THE FACILITY AND MAY REMOVE THE LOCKDOWN ORDER AT THEIR DISCRETION."
I *HAD* TO PUT US ON LOCKDOWN. YOU'VE SEEN THE SAME NEWS I'VE SEEN.
THERE'RE PEOPLE GOING AROUND *TORCHING* WOMEN IN THEIR COCOONS.
I THINK YOU'LL AGREE THAT MY POPULATION WOULD BE A PRIME TARGET FOR THAT BREED OF VIGILANTE.
LET'S PUT ASIDE THE RULEBOOK, CLINT. I'M ACTING SHERIFF. WE'RE FRIENDS. LET ME SEE SHE'S SLEEPING LIKE THE OTHERS, AND WE'LL GET OUT OF YOUR HAIR.
CHECK YOUR PHONE, TERRY.

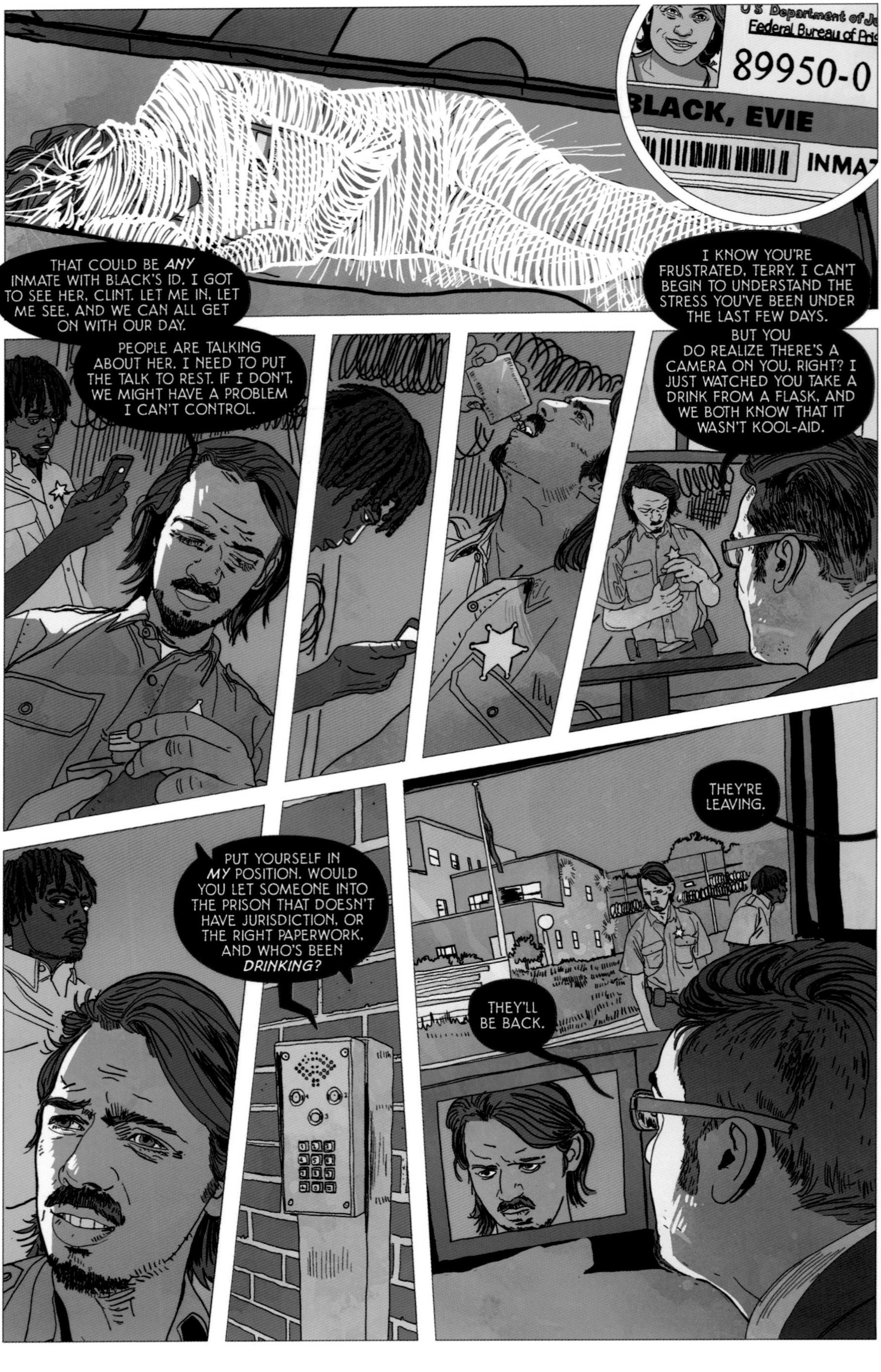
U S Department of Ju
Federal Bureau of Pris
89950-0
BLACK, EVIE
INMA
THAT COULD BE *ANY* INMATE WITH BLACK'S ID. I GOT TO SEE HER, CLINT. LET ME IN, LET ME SEE, AND WE CAN ALL GET ON WITH OUR DAY.
I KNOW YOU'RE FRUSTRATED, TERRY. I CAN'T BEGIN TO UNDERSTAND THE STRESS YOU'VE BEEN UNDER THE LAST FEW DAYS.
PEOPLE ARE TALKING ABOUT HER. I NEED TO PUT THE TALK TO REST. IF I DON'T, WE MIGHT HAVE A PROBLEM I CAN'T CONTROL.
BUT YOU DO REALIZE THERE'S A CAMERA ON YOU, RIGHT? I JUST WATCHED YOU TAKE A DRINK FROM A FLASK, AND WE BOTH KNOW THAT IT WASN'T KOOL-AID.
PUT YOURSELF IN *MY* POSITION. WOULD YOU LET SOMEONE INTO THE PRISON THAT DOESN'T HAVE JURISDICTION, OR THE RIGHT PAPERWORK, AND WHO'S BEEN *DRINKING*?
THEY'RE LEAVING.
THEY'LL BE BACK.

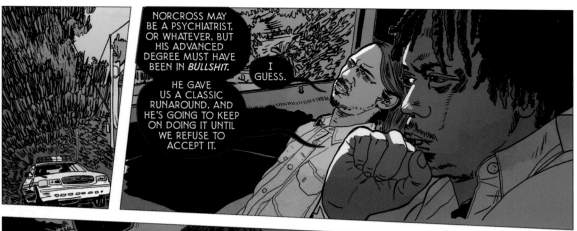

NORCROSS MAY BE A PSYCHIATRIST, OR WHATEVER, BUT HIS ADVANCED DEGREE MUST HAVE BEEN IN *BULLSHIT*.

HE GAVE US A CLASSIC RUNAROUND, AND HE'S GOING TO KEEP ON DOING IT UNTIL WE REFUSE TO ACCEPT IT.

I GUESS.

THAT WOMAN IN THE PHOTO HE SENT IS *NOT* EVE BLACK. JESUS, DOES HE THINK WE'RE STUPID?

WE NEED TO SHOW HIM HOW *SERIOUS* WE ARE.

YES.

WE COULD RAISE A POSSE, MOUNT AN OFFENSIVE, AN *EXTRACTION*. BUT THAT'S A LAST RESORT, DON'T YOU THINK?

WE COULD USE HIS WIFE.

HUH?

OFFER A SWAP. YOU GIVE US EVE BLACK, WE GIVE YOU YOUR WIFE.

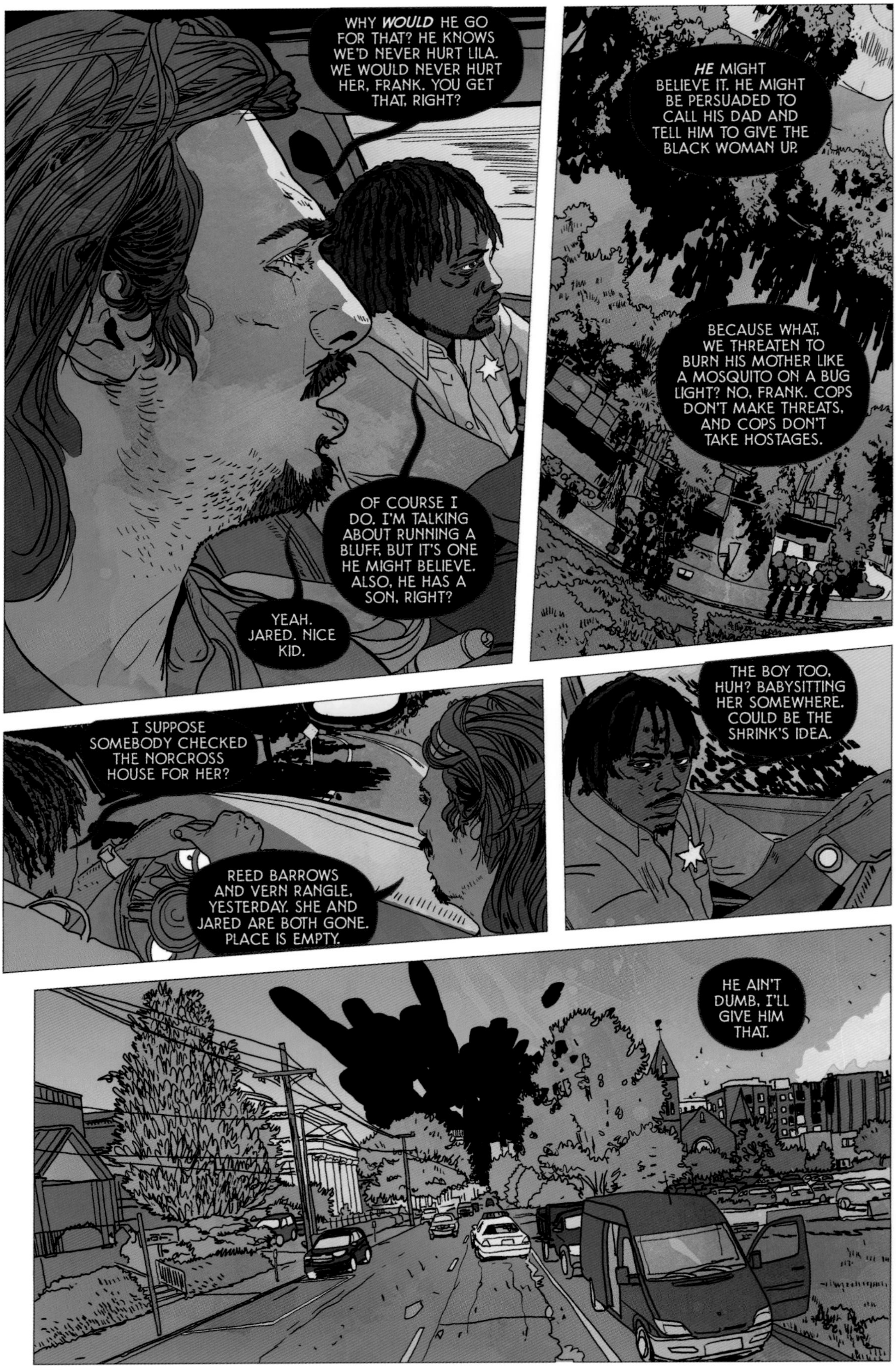
WHY *WOULD* HE GO FOR THAT? HE KNOWS WE'D NEVER HURT LILA. WE WOULD NEVER HURT HER, FRANK. YOU GET THAT, RIGHT?
OF COURSE I DO. I'M TALKING ABOUT RUNNING A BLUFF, BUT IT'S ONE HE MIGHT BELIEVE. ALSO, HE HAS A SON, RIGHT?
YEAH. JARED. NICE KID.
HE MIGHT BELIEVE IT. HE MIGHT BE PERSUADED TO CALL HIS DAD AND TELL HIM TO GIVE THE BLACK WOMAN UP.
BECAUSE WHAT, WE THREATEN TO BURN HIS MOTHER LIKE A MOSQUITO ON A BUG LIGHT? NO, FRANK. COPS DON'T MAKE THREATS, AND COPS DON'T TAKE HOSTAGES.
I SUPPOSE SOMEBODY CHECKED THE NORCROSS HOUSE FOR HER?
REED BARROWS AND VERN RANGLE, YESTERDAY. SHE AND JARED ARE BOTH GONE. PLACE IS EMPTY.
THE BOY TOO, HUH? BABYSITTING HER SOMEWHERE. COULD BE THE SHRINK'S IDEA.
HE AIN'T DUMB, I'LL GIVE HIM THAT.

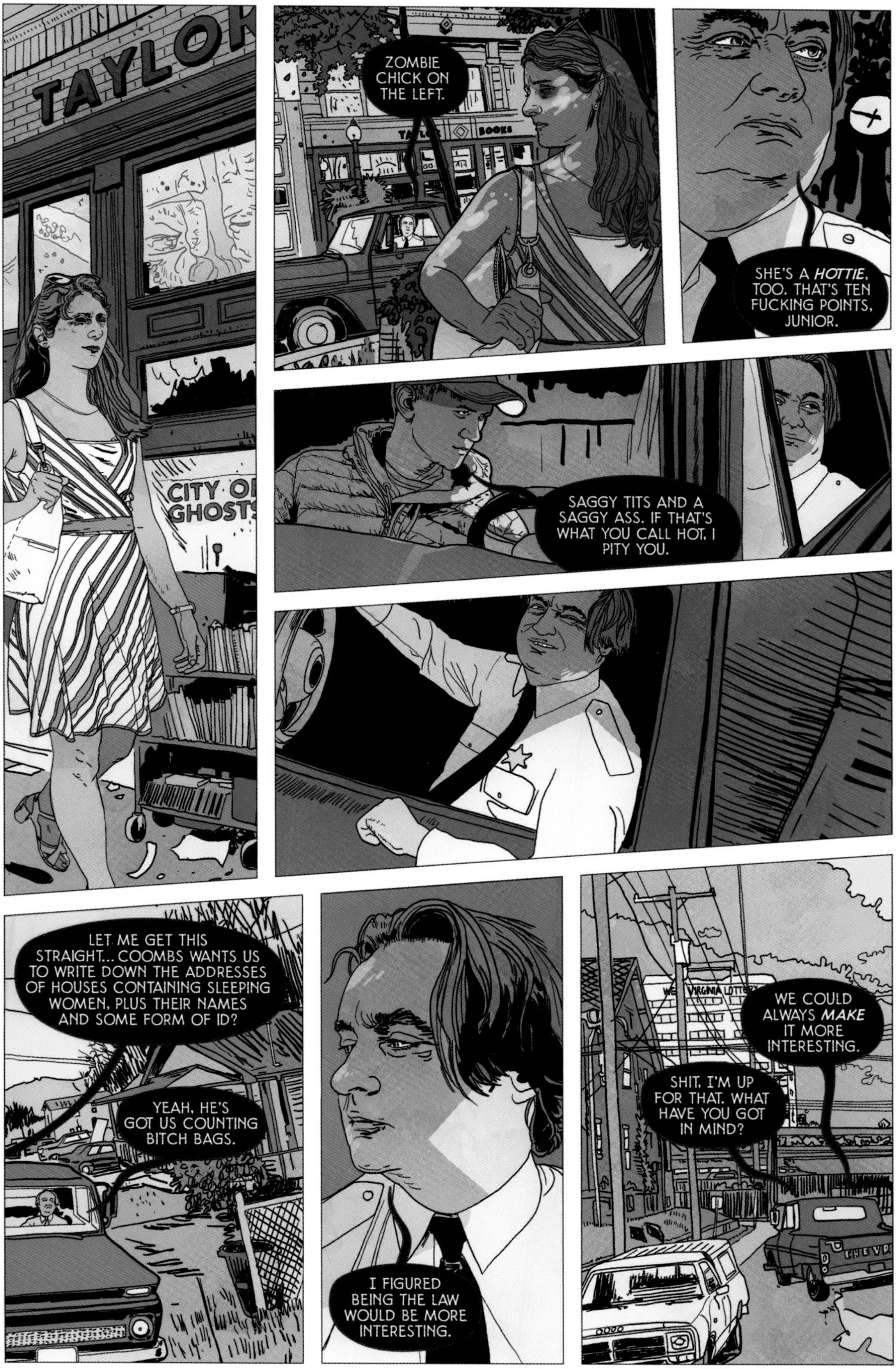
TAYLOR
CITY OF GHOSTS
ZOMBIE CHICK ON THE LEFT.
TAYLOR BOOKS
SHE'S A *HOTTIE*, TOO. THAT'S TEN FUCKING POINTS, JUNIOR.
SAGGY TITS AND A SAGGY ASS. IF THAT'S WHAT YOU CALL HOT, I PITY YOU.
LET ME GET THIS STRAIGHT... COOMBS WANTS US TO WRITE DOWN THE ADDRESSES OF HOUSES CONTAINING SLEEPING WOMEN, PLUS THEIR NAMES AND SOME FORM OF ID?
YEAH, HE'S GOT US COUNTING BITCH BAGS.
I FIGURED BEING THE LAW WOULD BE MORE INTERESTING.
WE COULD ALWAYS *MAKE* IT MORE INTERESTING.
SHIT, I'M UP FOR THAT. WHAT HAVE YOU GOT IN MIND?

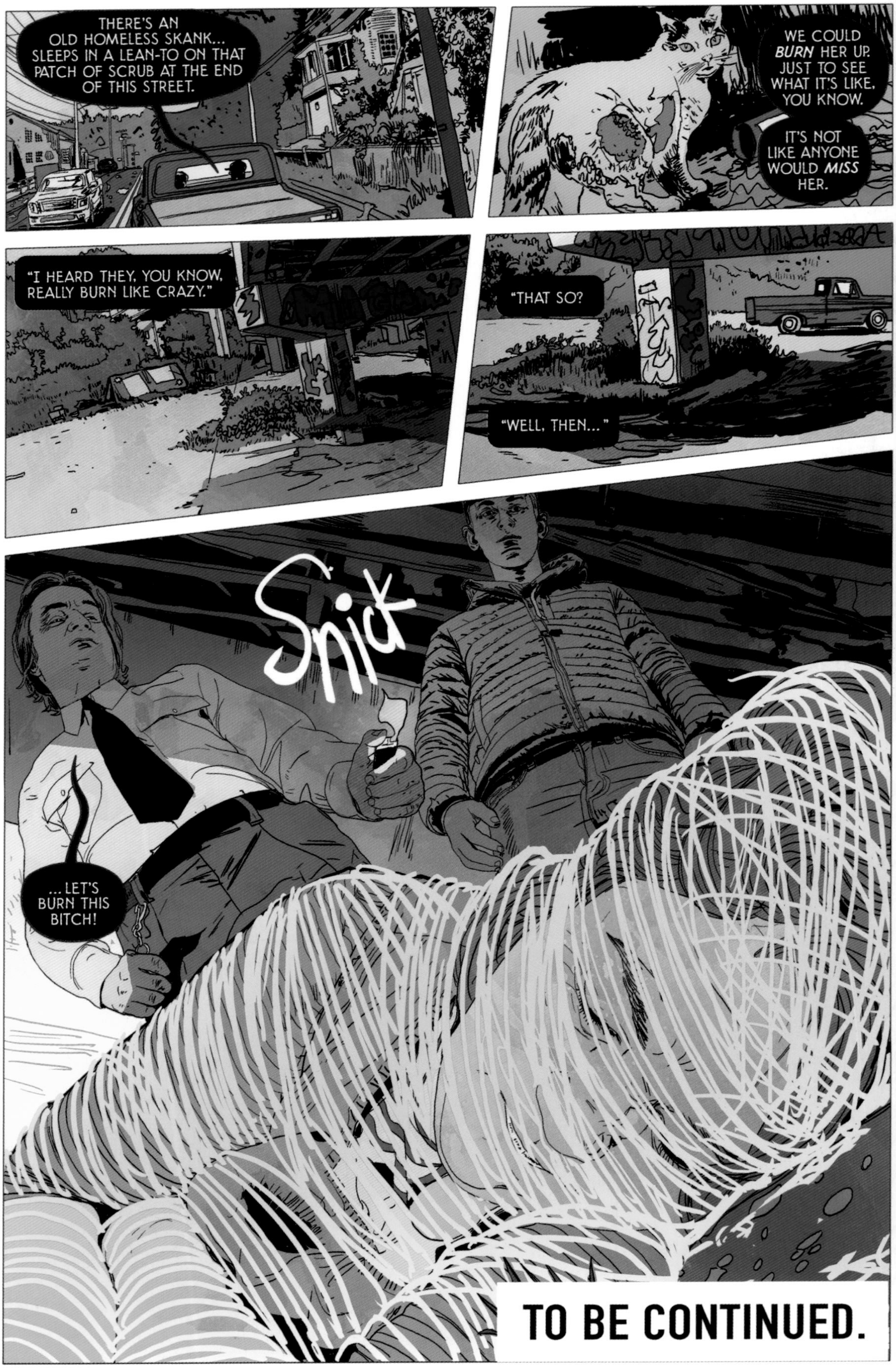
THERE'S AN OLD HOMELESS SKANK... SLEEPS IN A LEAN-TO ON THAT PATCH OF SCRUB AT THE END OF THIS STREET.
WE COULD BURN HER UP. JUST TO SEE WHAT IT'S LIKE, YOU KNOW.
IT'S NOT LIKE ANYONE WOULD MISS HER.
"I HEARD THEY, YOU KNOW, REALLY BURN LIKE CRAZY."
"THAT SO?
"WELL, THEN..."
Snick
...LET'S BURN THIS BITCH!
TO BE CONTINUED.

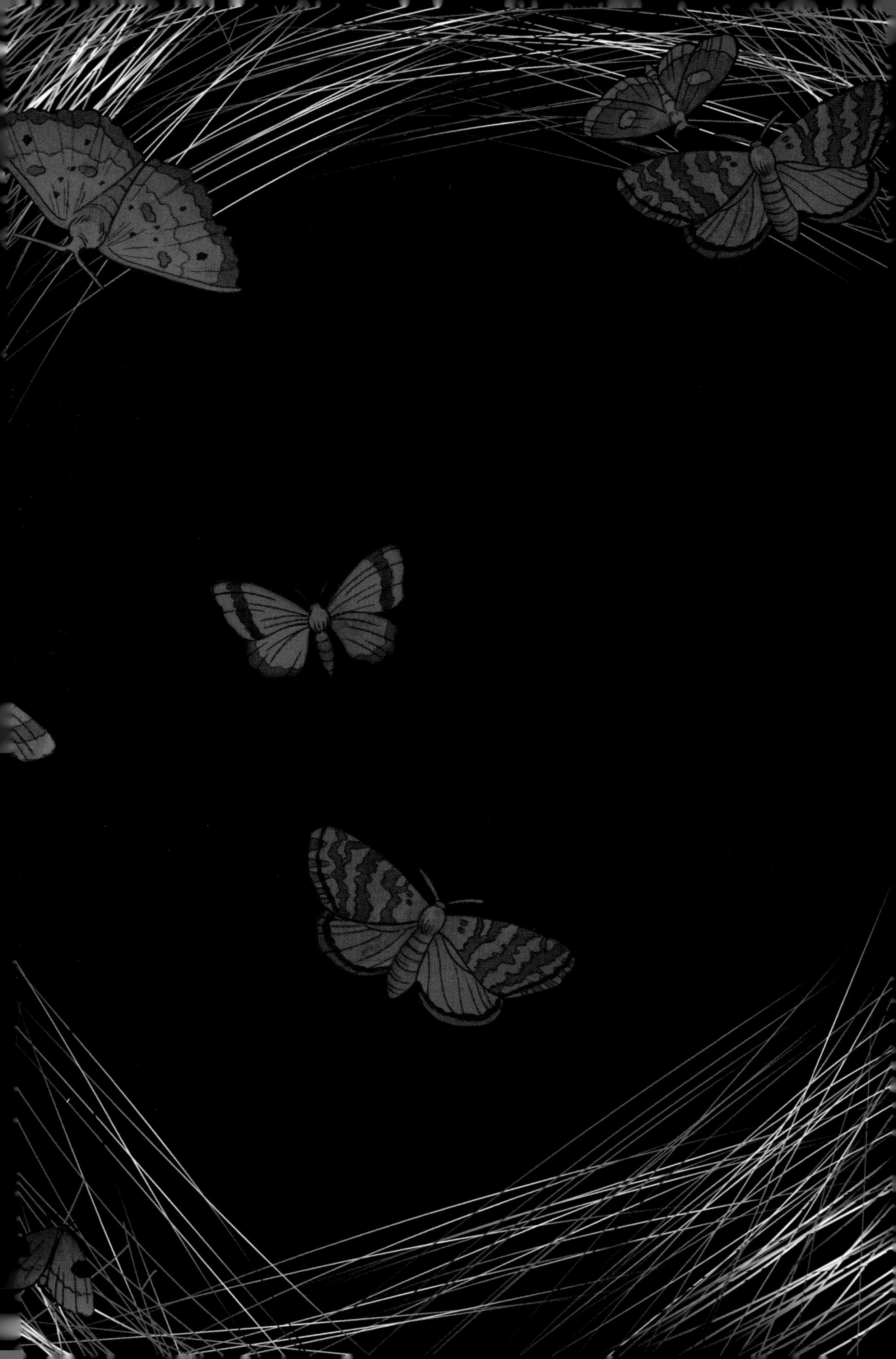

ART BY JENN WOODALL

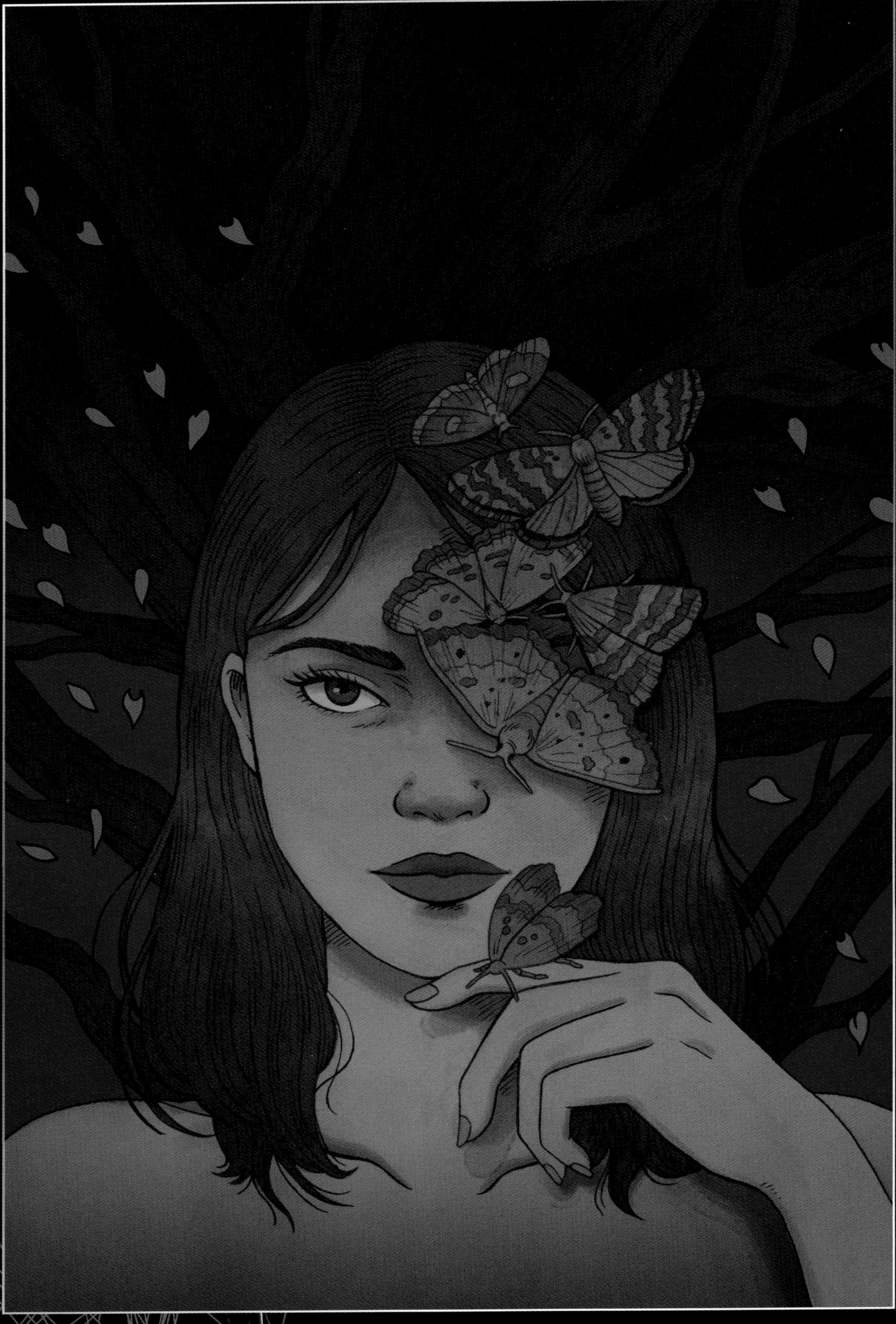

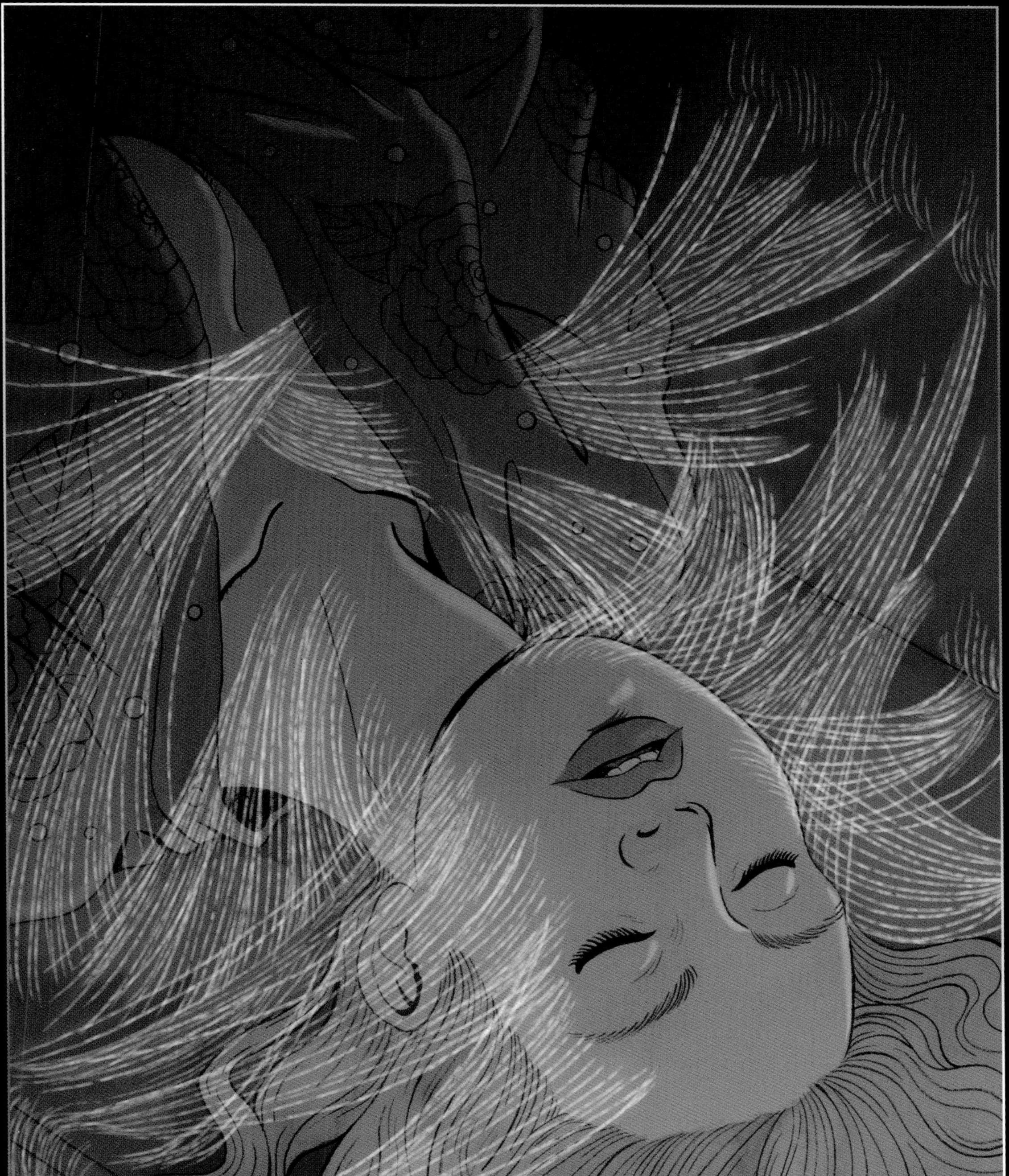

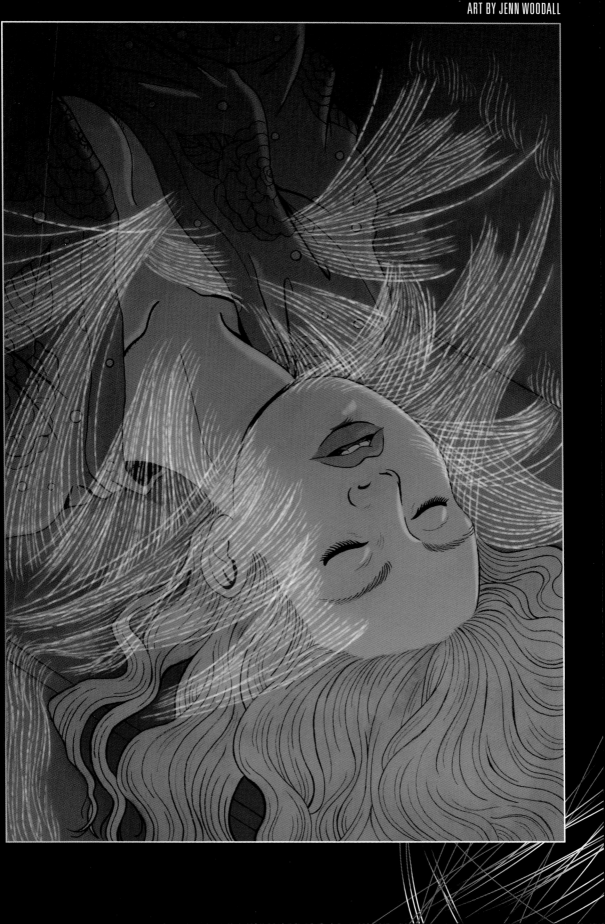

ART BY JENN WOODALL

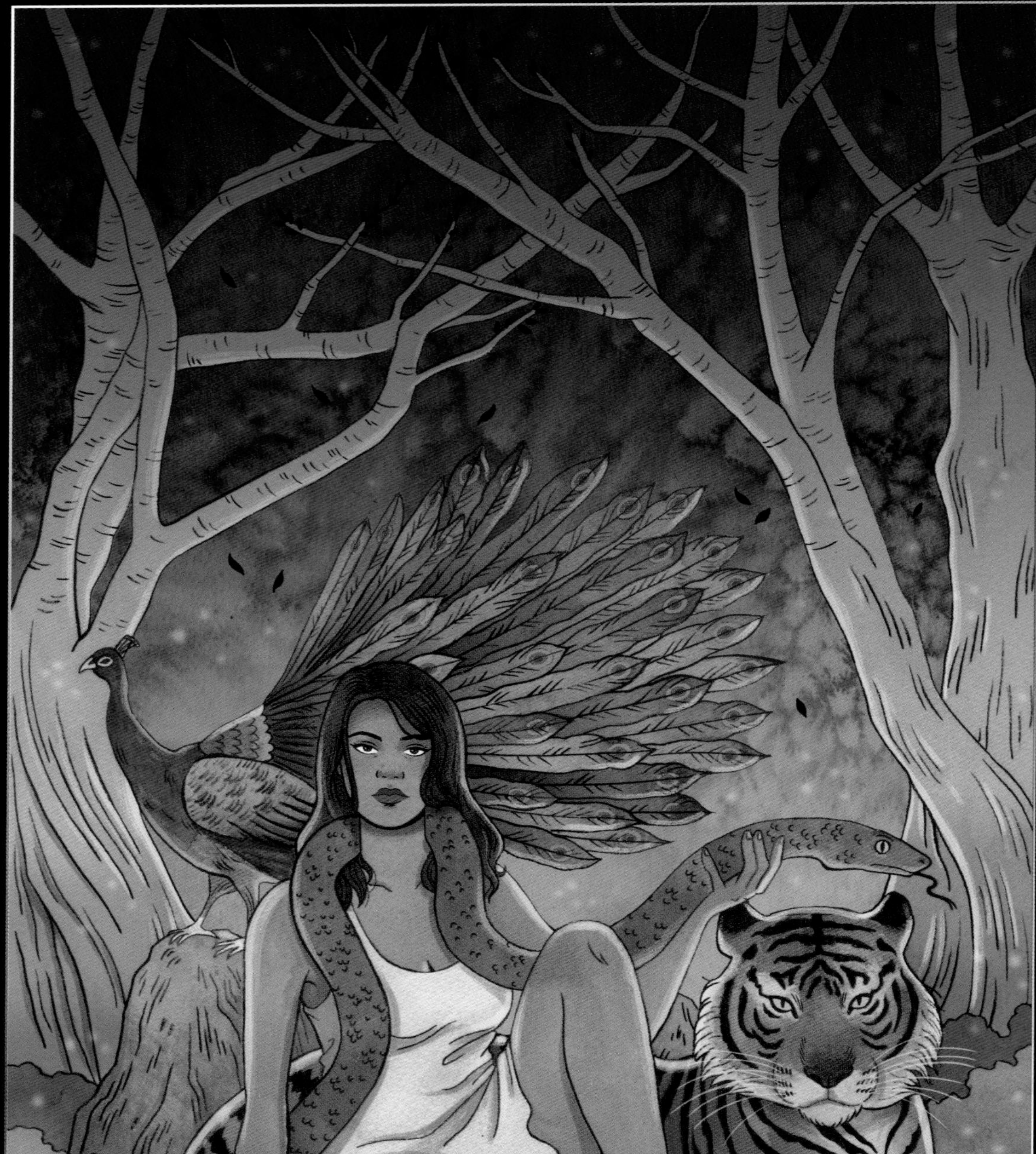

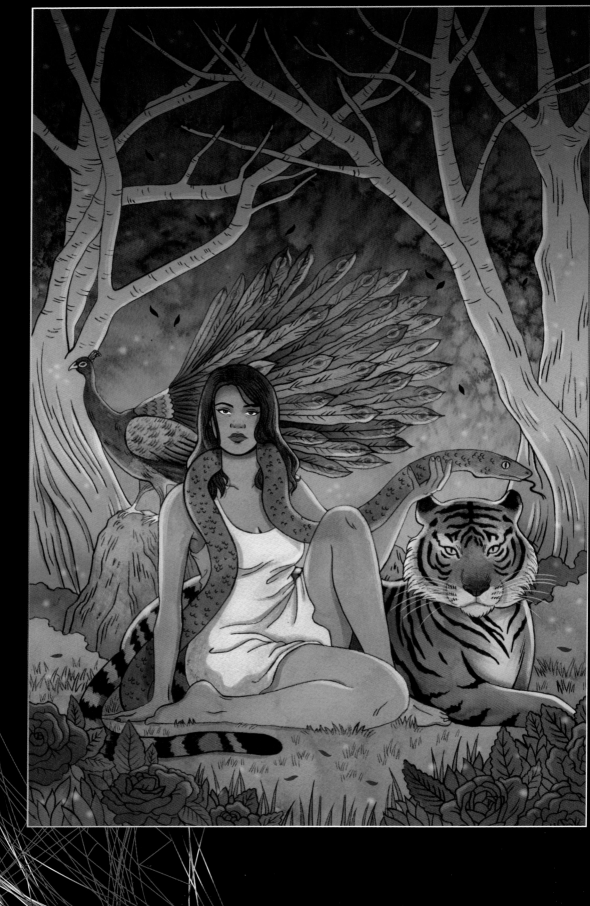

ART BY JENN WOODALL

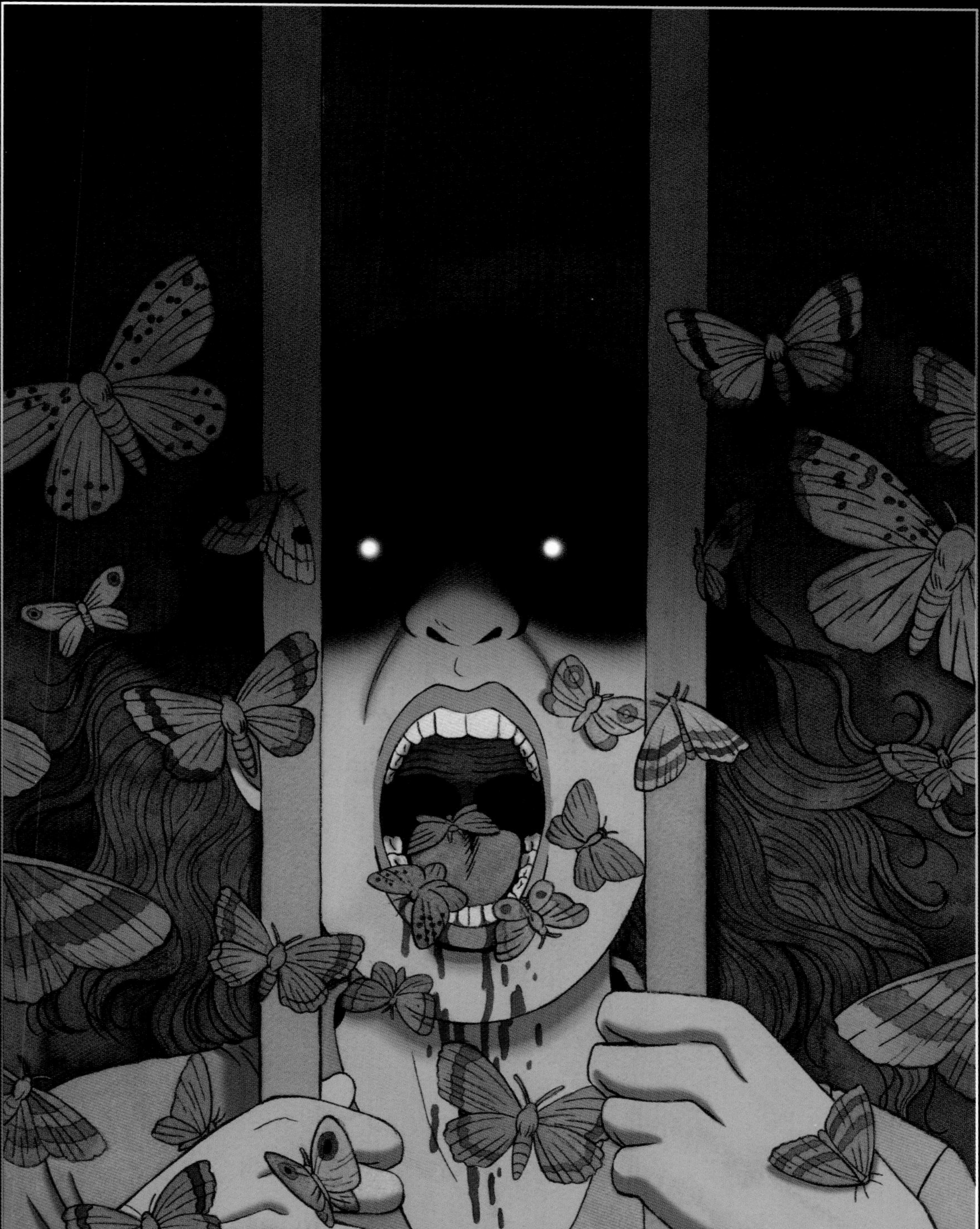

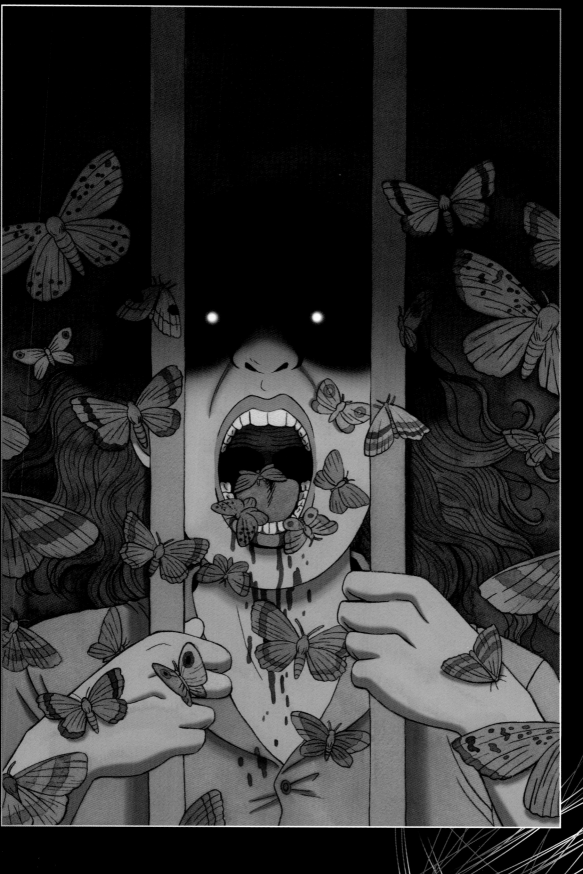

ART BY JENN WOODALL

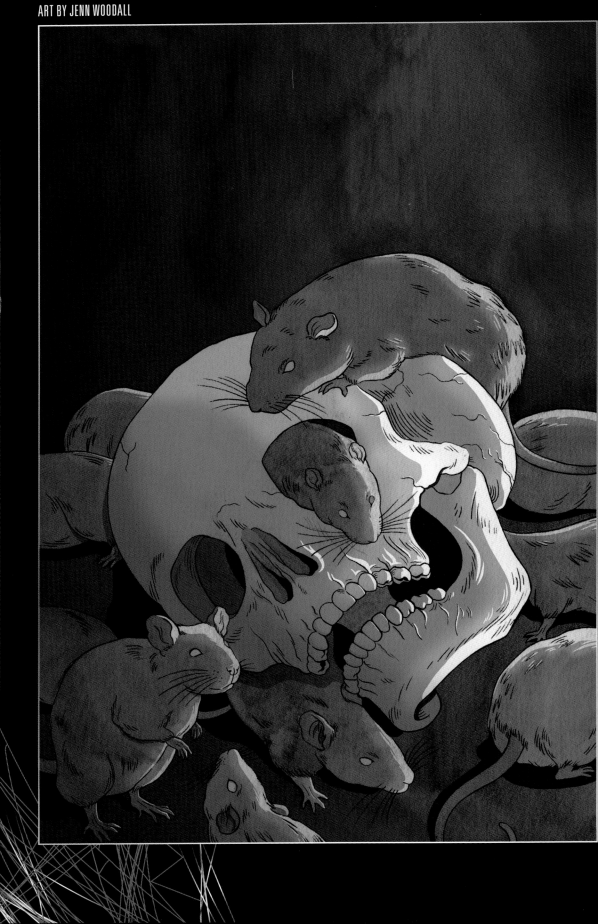

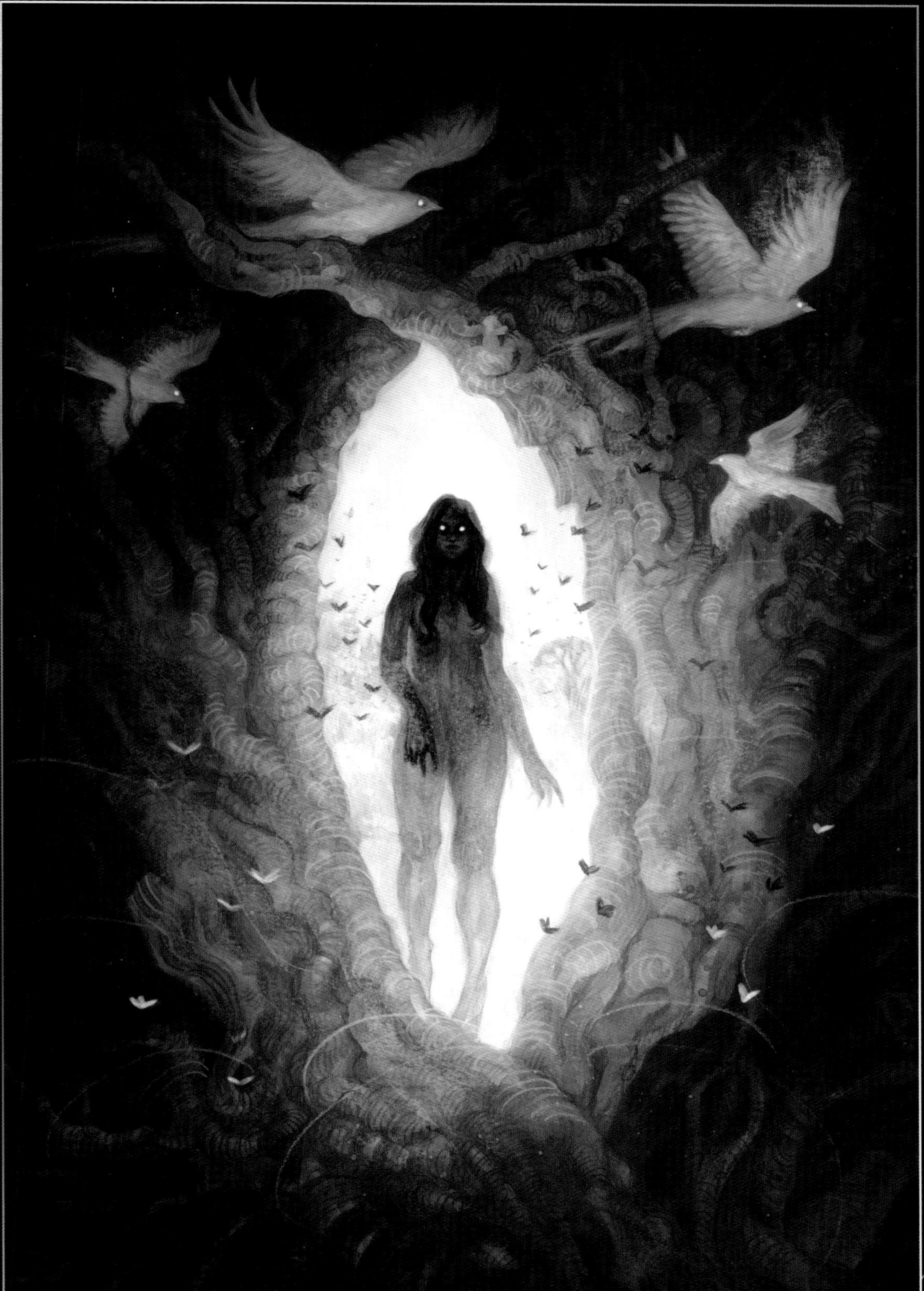

ART BY JANA HEIDERSDORF

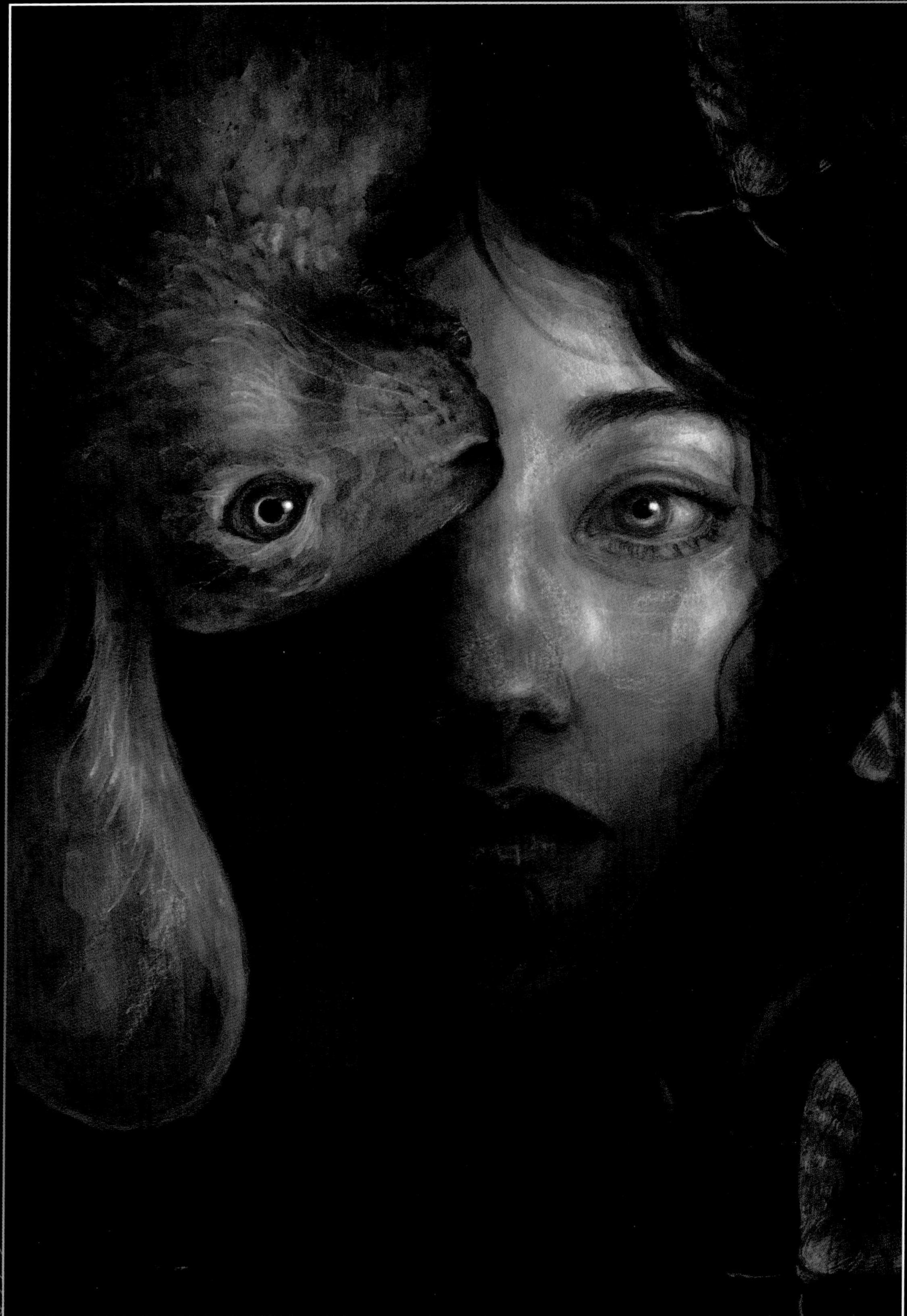

ART BY JANA HEIDERSDORF

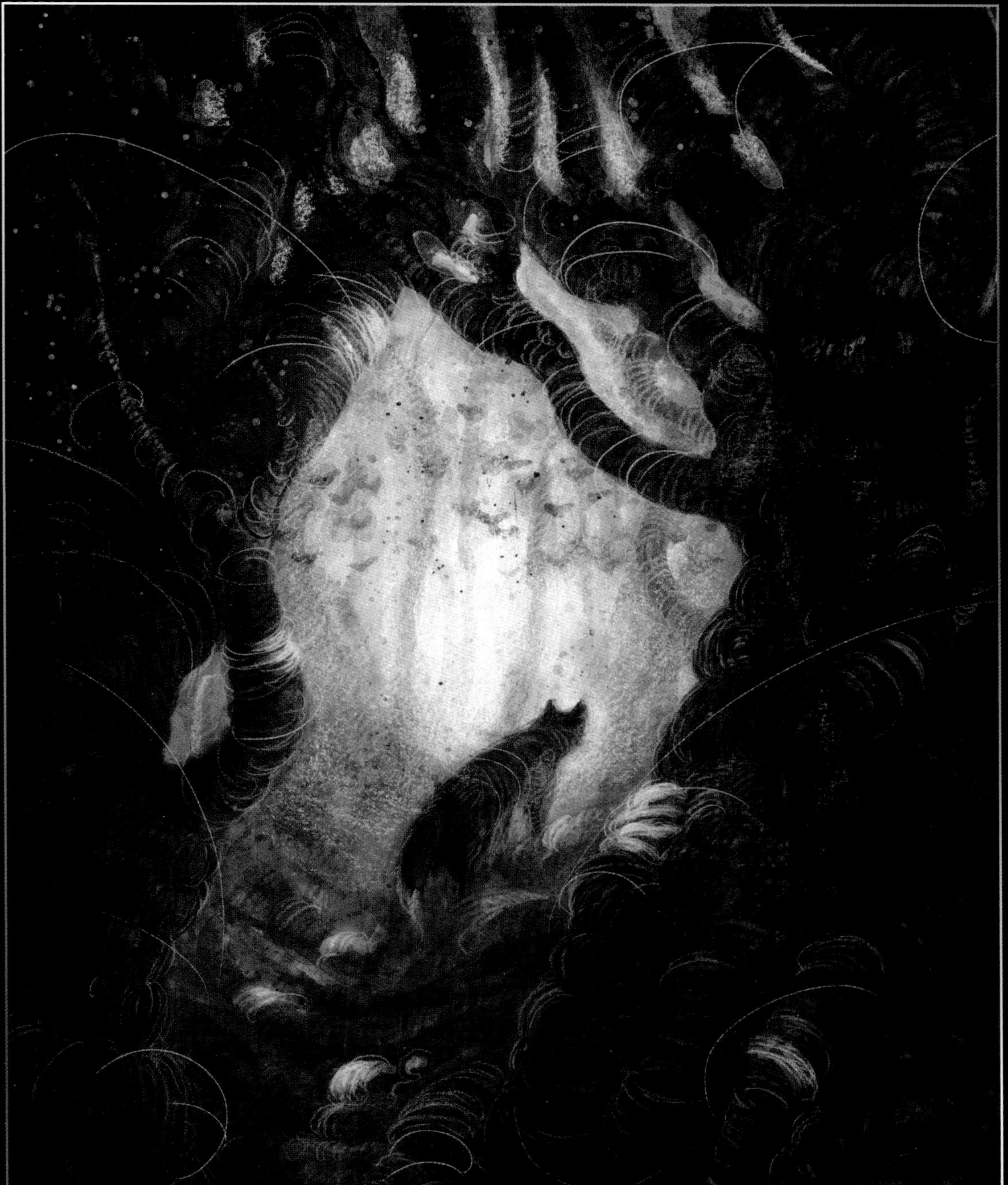

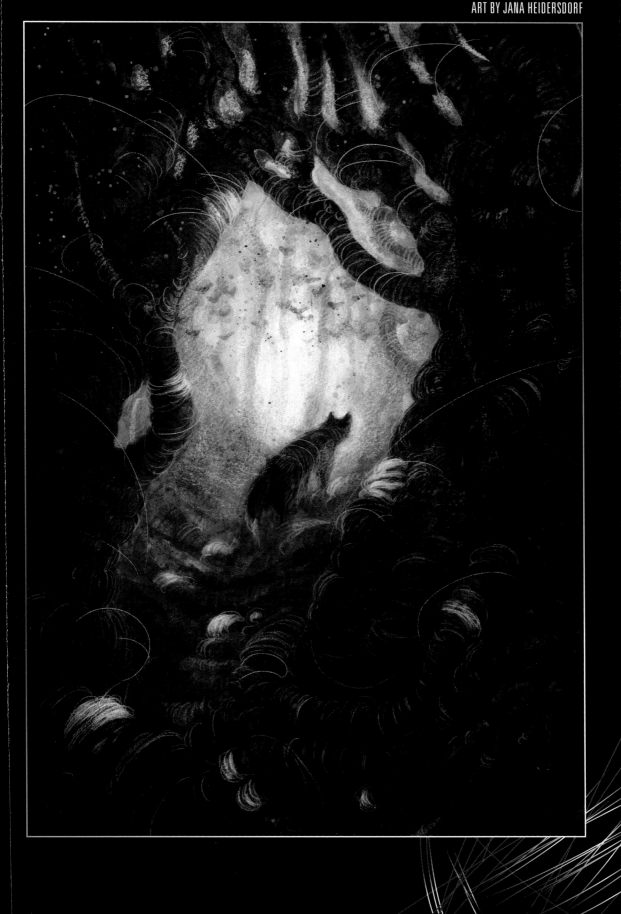

ART BY JANA HEIDERSDORF

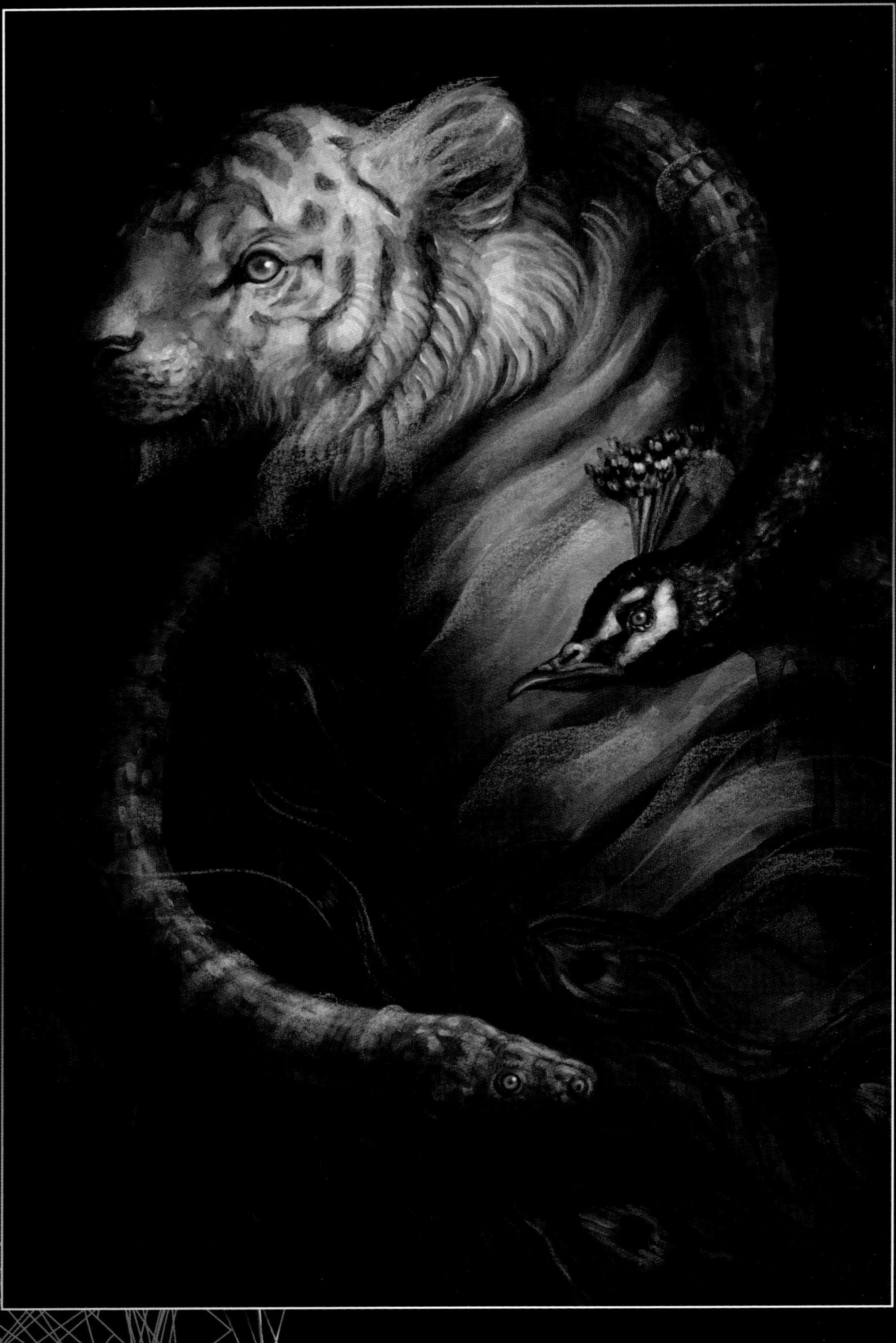

ART BY JANA HEIDERSDORF

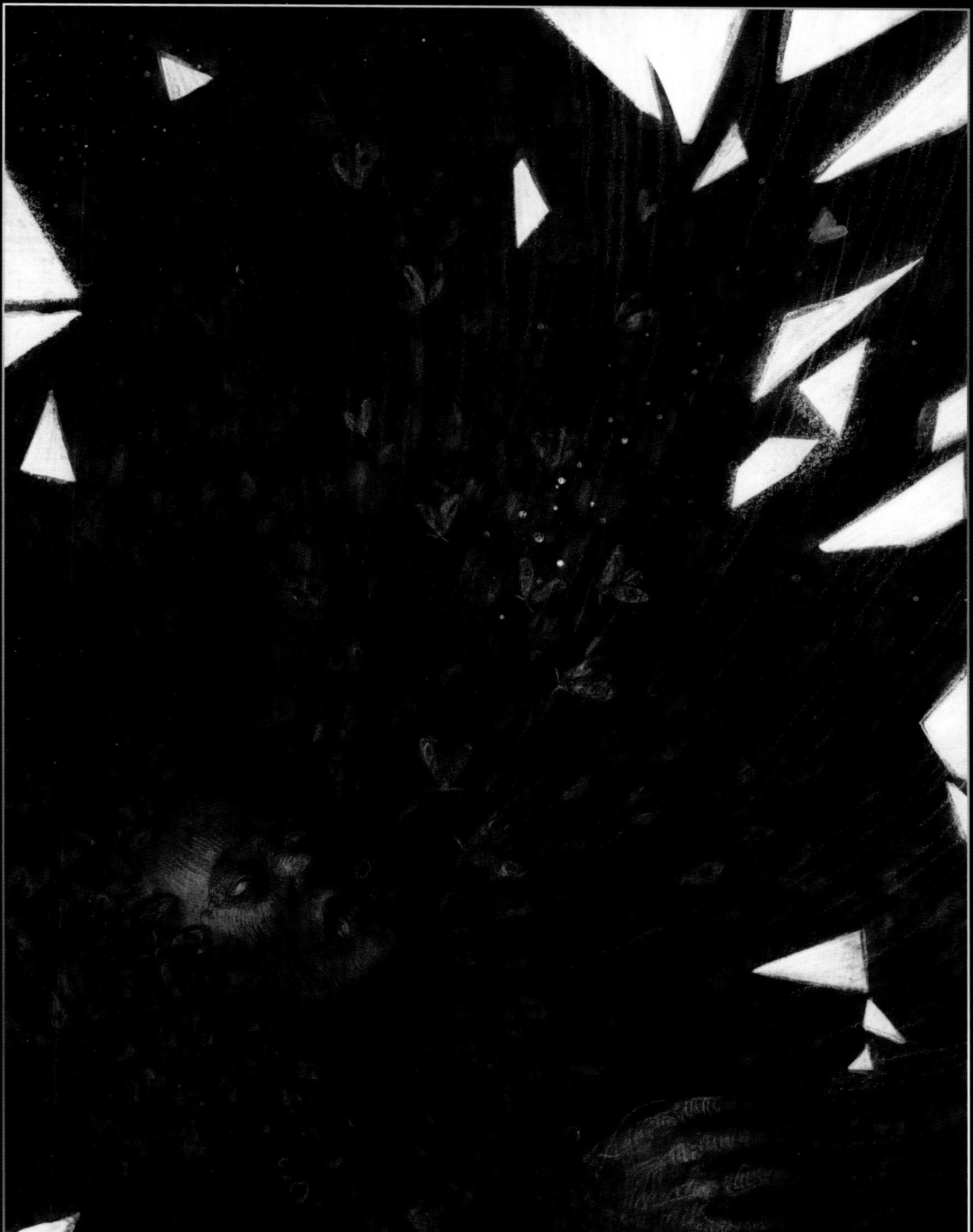

ART BY DIANA NANEVA

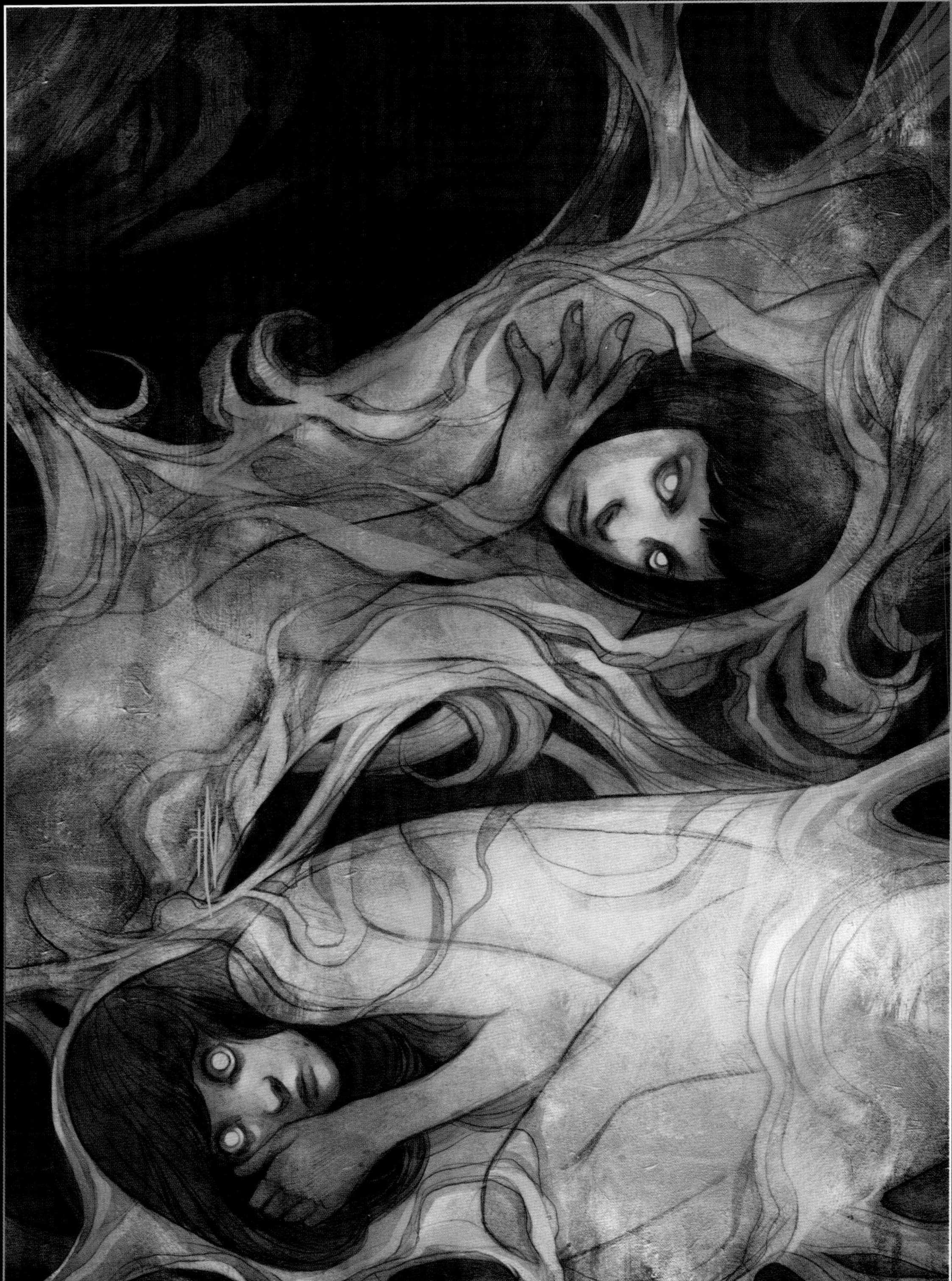

ART BY PEACH MOMOKO

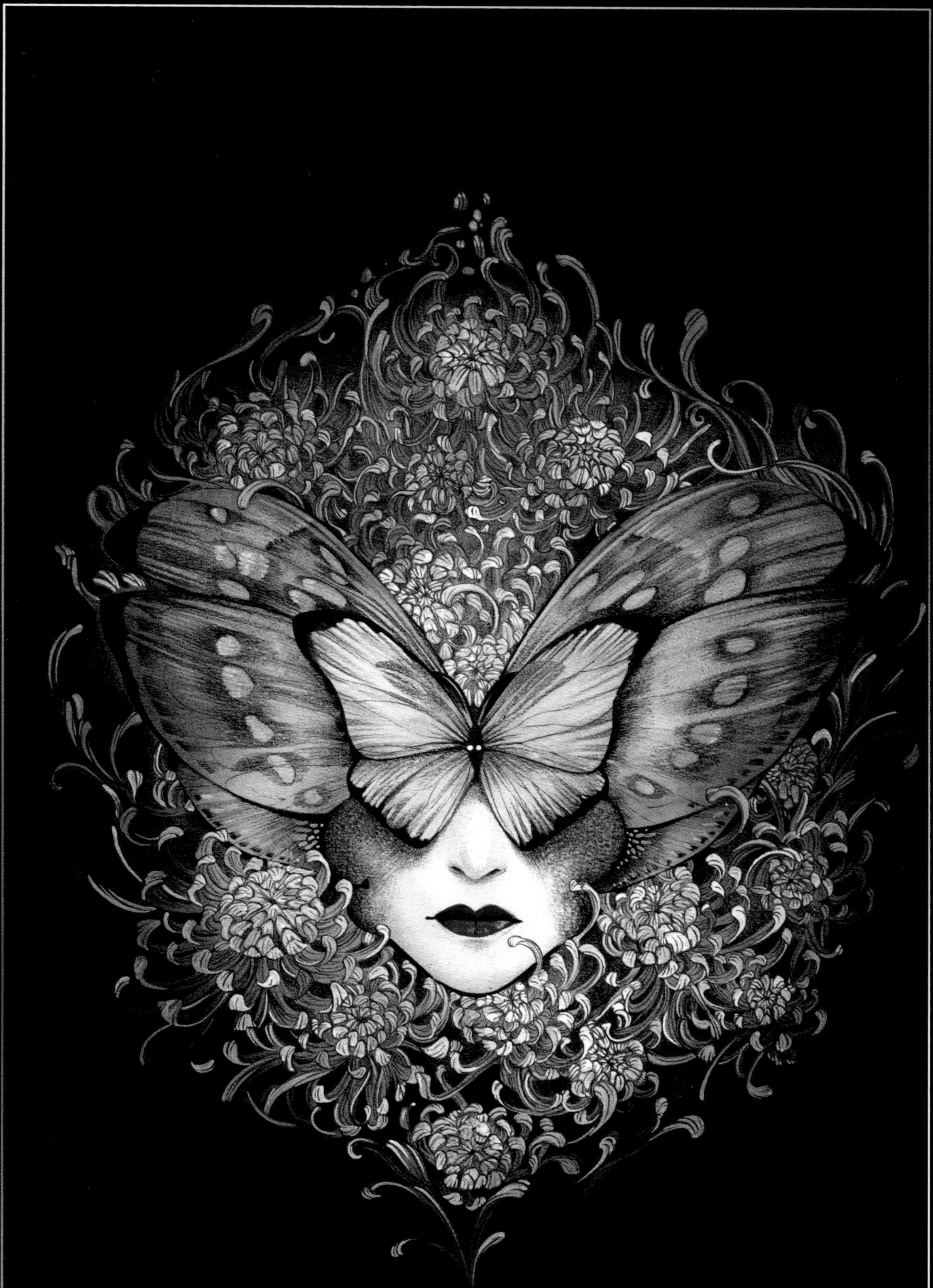

ART BY PEACH MOMOKO

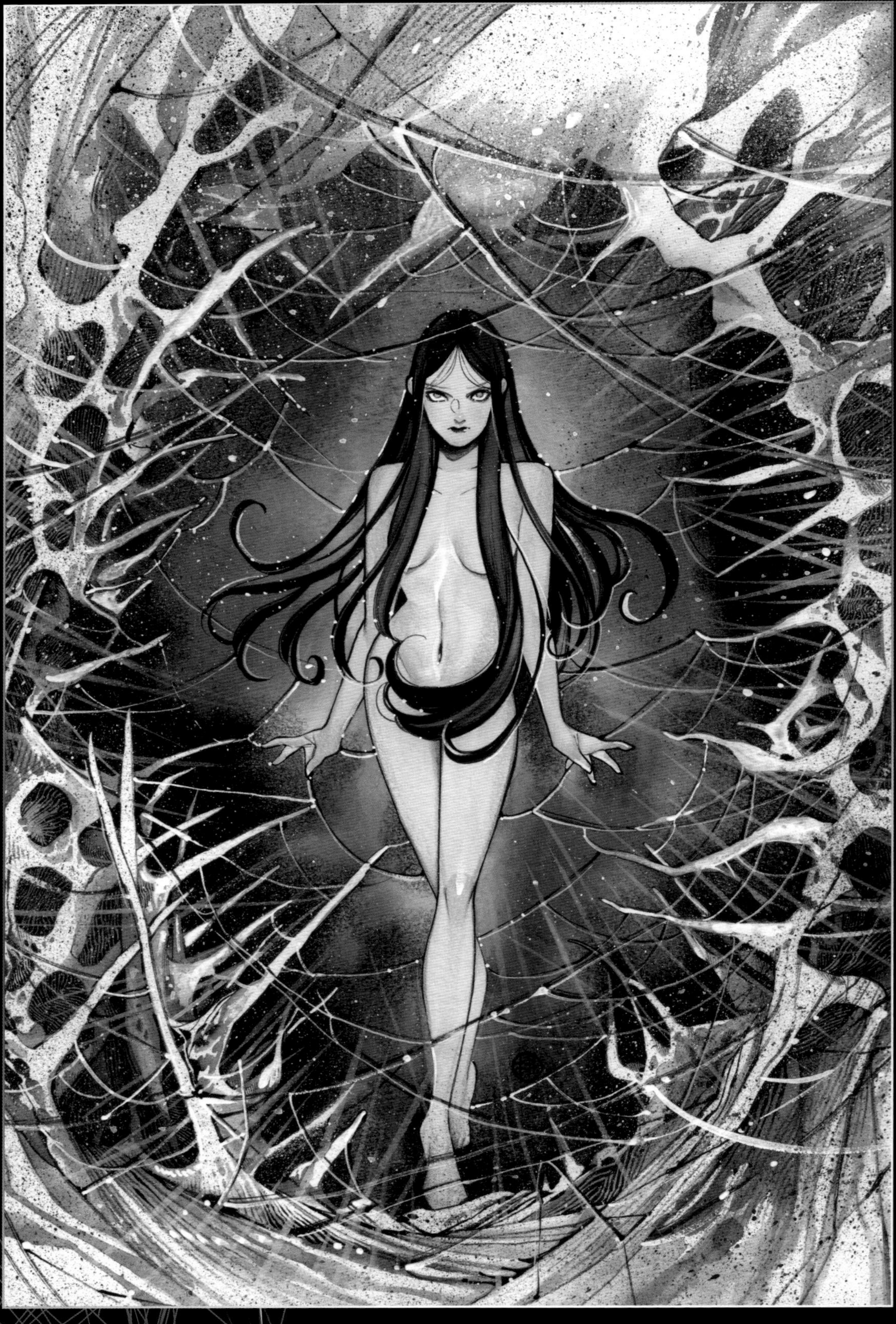

GN
YOU

Youers, Rio
Sleeping beauties

AMHERST PUBLIC LIBRARY
221 SPRING ST.
AMHERST, OH 44001